MAYBE MORE

ASH FITZSIMMONS

MAYBE MORE

THE LOST HALLS, BOOK THREE

Print Edition ISBN: 978-1-949861-73-0

Cover design by MiblArt.

www.ashfitzsimmons.com

CHAPTER 1

Eyeliner is not for the faint of heart…or in my case, the unsteady of hand.

Carefully, *ever* so carefully, I drew the soft, charcoal-colored pencil along my eyelid, bracing the heel of my hand near my chin as I pinched the plastic casing in my fingers. I wasn't even going to attempt a wing—Rose had drawn them on me with ease using liquid liner, but I lacked the expertise to make more than uneven blobs, and my volunteer makeup team hadn't had time to get me up to speed. Basic liner it was, and if I could manage vaguely matched smudges on my upper lids, I'd call it a win.

Cosmetics were novel for me. Back in East Branch, no one had ever used them, and if someone had dark lashes or rosy cheeks, that was a natural boon. Outside the rural mountain compound I'd once called home, however, a range of pigmented powders and sticks and lotions could give anyone a face hardly recognizable as her own—and in the Pactlands, it wasn't unusual for women and men alike to deploy them for formal occasions if they didn't mask. I knew little of such—my elven classmate Keef wore light makeup to school, and our friend Sage, four years younger, had begun to experiment with mascara and lip gloss—but frankly, I'd had too much to worry about that year without adding foundation and blush to the mix.

Now that the spring dance was upon us, however, I had some major catching up to do.

Two weeks prior, I hadn't thought I'd be going. The dance was a formal event, only for students in Year 10 and older. Sage had just surpassed the cutoff, and she was going with a mixed group her age, friends she'd made when she left our tutorials and joined the rest of her year for classes like art and physical education. Most of them, like her, were junior members of North Lake's rowing team, and they'd gone shopping as a pack to look for dresses and robes.

I was happy for her as Sage recounted the details of the shopping trip over lunch. Like me, she was a Georgia girl, but the little she discussed of her childhood in Whitford was horrifying. Half sorcerer, half centaur, Sage was...well, *odd* from the waist down, and the cretin who'd raised her had convinced her she was some sort of demon. Now far from him, and having learned to mask her appearance, she seemed comfortable in her skin—just an average sorcerer, albeit a slightly undersized one with a strange accent.

Keef was going with a guy in our year, another elf from the rowing team. They were just friends, she insisted, as Sage and I teased her. Yes, he came from an appropriate Hall, and no, her mother probably wouldn't have minded had the two of them dated, but their relationship was purely platonic. Keef's older sister, Fellora, had taken her shopping at the sort of boutique I'd never visited, but when one's mother was the lady of Hall ti'Mal, one kept up appearances...at least as much as one could when one's father was locked up at a penal farm for murder and more. Keef didn't talk about her dad if she could avoid the subject, but word had a way of getting around, even to my family's corner of the dorms.

I'd have liked to have been on the rowing team with my friends, but that wasn't an option for me. Heck, I'd had to turn down an invitation to try out for the melee team, and *no one* messed with them, a level of protection I'd have greatly appreciated. But the research healers who poked and prodded at me every other week said sports were out of the question. Whether I'd been born with a weak heart and exacerbated the problem with two rounds of the notoriously harmful bloodline potion or simply done all the damage with the potion itself was up for debate, but in any case, I was confined to limited activity so as not to end up needing a transplant. The expensive healing potions I took daily were helping, but they could only do so much with my body's subpar regenerative capabilities. I might have been almost three-quarters elf, but from the looks of things, I'd inherited my human ancestors' brief lifespan and limited healing ability, and the potions couldn't perform actual miracles. While I didn't mind having an extra study period instead of physical education, I envied my friends for the camaraderie of the rowing team.

But I *was* improving, and the healers had cleared me for the dance, just as long as I took it easy. I hadn't thought much of it when they made the pronouncement, since none of my cousins planned to attend. The older ones had their little kids to look after, and some of the unaccompanied kids were too young, leaving only my cousins Justin, Hannah, Heidi, David, Marshall, Zoe, and me. None of us had ever been to an event like the dance, and as I was the only one of our group to have yet made friends outside our family, they weren't especially keen on the idea. We had Lake Day, the school's big all-ages party, to look forward to the following weekend. Plus, there was a flu going around, and it hadn't spared us. With my luck, I imagined I'd end up kneeling in front of a toilet or shivering in bed instead of dancing.

I'd caught the flu early and recovered, however…and then Eddic had cornered me.

Having grown up in a community barely fifty members strong, I'd long imagined that my best bet for a partner was my cousin David, which hadn't been a thrilling prospect. Now that we had options beyond East Branch—theoretically, at least—I'd let my eyes wander over my fellow students, and they'd landed squarely on Eddic ti'Dir.

To me, and to quite a few other girls at North Lake, Eddic was gorgeous. He had the typical elven build, tall and slender, but he'd worked out enough to gain a pleasing bulk. His hair was long, glossy, and chestnut brown, and he tended to wear it in a loose braid, the sort of style that seemed effortlessly polished on him but made me look like I was between washes. But it was his eyes that sucked me in, large and pale blue like the morning sky. They crinkled when he smiled, which he did easily—even at me.

I knew I was no prize. Shorter than most of the full-blooded elves in my year, with unremarkable brown hair and eyes, I'd have been average at best if not for my ci-fyent, the genetic condition that made the tops of my ears flop over like I was some sort of puppy. It was a condition known in the old southern Halls—and after a dozen or so generations of remixing in East Branch, it had become almost universal among us, the isolated descendants of the southern kingdom's lone survivors. If you had magical talent at East Branch, you almost certainly had "the flop," pointed ears that couldn't support their own weight. I'd hidden mine with a masking pendant during my first se-mester at North Lake, and by March, I'd finally learned to manage a mask without the aid of jewelry, but Eddic surely knew of my condition, even if I'd barely spoken to him. Since he was in the year above me, I'd done most of my admiring from afar.

But the Friday a week before the dance, he stopped by my table at lunch and asked if he could have a word in private. Leaving Keef, Sage, and my half-eaten tray, I hur-ried after him and slipped into an empty classroom. There, he pulled a small bouquet from his bag and asked if I'd go to the dance with him.

I was too stunned to speak at first—the object of my silent pining couldn't have approached *me*, could he?—but I managed to nod and squeak out my response. Eddic flashed his perfect smile as I accepted the flowers, but then I did seemingly everything I could to dissuade him. I told him that I was still on limited activity, and I confessed that I didn't know the dances. He laughed and gently stroked my cheek, sending shivers up my spine even as I babbled my litany of failings. "I don't care if you don't know a single dance," he said, cutting me off. "I'm just excited that I finally get a chance to spend time with you, Maebe. You're…something special. Very special."

I practically floated back to my table, flowers in my arms…and then I realized that I had no clue what I was doing.

That night, I called Jane Fortune in a panic. Sure, Jane only had a few months' more experience in the Pactlands than I did, but unlike me, she'd grown up in Ragged Gap, a real town with wonders like asphalt and electricity. While Jane was a sorcerer, she was dating my cousin Connor, and she'd proven to be a reliable source of information about the goings-on of the wider world. She congratulated me on snagging a date to the dance, but then she admitted that she'd never been to one. "Homeschooled, remember?" she said as I curled up on my bed, knees tucked to my chin and phone pressed to my masked ear. "Who was I going to dance with, my dad?"

But though Jane had no experience with school dances, she quickly roped in the rest of her expat posse. Annie Humphries and Rose ti'Dana had made homes for themselves in the Pactlands, but they were Richmond natives who'd survived traditional high schools and understood the contours of North Lake's dance, if not the fine details. Jane called me back early Saturday morning and told me to get dressed. "We'll be there at nine," she announced—in English, to my relief. While I could understand Pactish, my groggy brain defaulted to my mother tongue.

"We?" I asked through a yawn.

"Your fairy godmothers, Cinderella. Brush your teeth."

When I appeared on the steps at the front of the school, I found the three of them waiting for me in Rose's car, a blue Outback that had seen better days. Rose's great-grandfather, Diriem, owned a garage full of cars that would make an aficionado weep—or so Jane told me—but Rose preferred to get around in her reliable Subaru, dings, chipped windshield, and all. I slid into the back and strapped in, feeling rather grown up to be driving through Beukal with my twenty- and thirty-something companions, but my stomach fluttered as Rose parked near a block of boutiques in District 3. I'd only been shopping there once, mostly for basic supplies, and that time, I'd had a handler on a mission. Now, I was on the hunt for a formal dress, and I had a card in my purse that would give me access to over half a million marks.

(Well, not exactly. My account had grown a bit—I studied my monthly statements to familiarize myself with them—but I couldn't pull more than a few thousand marks at once without approval. As all of my cousins were underage by Pactlands standards and none of us but Connor had any real experience with money, Diriem and Te-olm ti'Cren served as trustees for our funds, investing them conservatively and standing by in case one of us decided to splurge on a yacht.)

Luckily for me, my accomplices didn't leave me to wander off on my own. We spent the next few hours combing through likely shops—or rather, I spent much of the morning in the dressing rooms of those shops while the others pulled dresses from the racks—and by lunchtime, I had a gorgeous purple gown and silver shoes, sparkly but designed for comfort. The only jewelry I owned was my delicate gold masking pendant, and Annie had insisted on finding a new necklace to coordinate with my shoes. There would be no matching earrings; only male fauns went for such in the Pactlands, and in any case, I'd never had my ears pierced.

That afternoon, we drove out to the sprawling ti'Dana mansion in Viratta for the next part of the dance prep. Rose had an apartment within the house, and the four of us clustered in her large bathroom while my elders tried to teach me how to apply mascara without poking myself in the eye. As they debated the best shades for my face and style for my hair, a thought occurred to them: none of them had ever been to a school dance in the Pactlands, so perhaps they were missing something and inadvertently leading me astray. Hair and makeup ceased while Jane called her cousin Canna, a Beukal native who was both twenty-nine years older and considerably wiser in the ways of Pactlands education. Canna told us there was a series of dances that virtually everyone knew, traditional and taught from early childhood, so unless I wanted to be forced to the sidelines for awkward breaks, I needed a primer. As her four children were spending the day with their grandparents, she roused her husband, Pars, from the couch and told Annie to pick them up.

Having a friend who could teleport really did come in handy.

With Pars as her partner, Canna demonstrated the routines I would need to know—or rather, she tried to demonstrate them, but her assistant wasn't quite up to the task. Pars was enormous for a sorcerer, about seven feet tall and built like a bear, but he wasn't exactly *graceful* as a dancer. Fortunately for my tutorial, Rose's fiancé, Yven, came up from the greenhouse and walked in on the festivities, and Canna immediately benched her husband in favor of his buddy. Smaller, slighter, and lighter on his feet, Yven knew the steps and could lead and follow, and Pars seemed only too happy to let him fill in.

After dinner that night, Rose drove me back to school with my new clothes in the rear of the car. "You're going to have a great time," she told me as she parked by the front steps. "Now, remind me, who's your date?"

I beamed at her in the security lights' glow. "Eddie ti'Dir."

"Ti'Dir, huh?" She leaned toward me, smirking. "He does realize that you outrank him, right?"

"Uh…I guess," I mumbled.

"It took me a while to get the major Halls down," she said. "Ti'Dir's, um…well, let's say it's at the high end of the lowest third of the old Halls. Lord ti'Dir's currently on the Forum. Never met him, but Pop doesn't have many complaints—none that he's shared with me, anyway. Not that I'm judging the Hall," she hastily added. "Is Eddic main-line ti'Dir?"

"I, um…I don't know," I admitted. "Never asked him."

"Mm. Not like it matters, but some people might give you a hard time." She leaned back against her seat and softly sighed. "I don't get nearly as much crap for being with Yven as I would if I were of…shall we say *purer* extraction, but I've still heard some comments suggesting that it's not right for me to tie myself to someone from a Hall as low-ranking as ti'Ansha, especially when he's not even main-line. Pop gets more of those comments than I do," Rose continued, "but he says he just wants to see me happy, so he hasn't tried to break us up. Now, once you're old enough to make your debut, you might get the same sort of commentary for dating a ti'Dir. *I'm* telling you it's stupid, but don't be surprised, okay?"

We said our goodnights, and I thanked Rose again while I gathered my things. As I watched her drive off, my thoughts drifted toward Eddic, and I inwardly cringed once more as I mulled over my Hall problems.

All elves belonged to a Hall. Before the Pactlands, in the days of the two kingdoms, the Halls belonged only to the noble families, who had actual fortifications to match. Once the kingdoms disappeared—the north by choice, escaping into the Pactlands, the south by force, mostly obliterated by encroaching humans—the untitled elves had banded together into the new Halls, massive conglomerations of families that managed to obtain political power, if not prestige. Even if all were technically equal in the Pactlands, the old aristocracy managed to keep its hold, and only the lords and ladies who headed their Halls ever served on the Forum.

While Rose was the product of two half-human parents—a blot in the estimation of many—she was the recognized heir to Hall ti'Dana, the top of the heap. Diriem had been the last king of the north, the one who'd facilitated the Pactlands' creation and taken his people there to save them from the fate that awaited their southern peers, and while he hadn't worn a crown in many centuries, he'd never lost his prominence. That his only child had taken the death draught to be with a human woman was a tragedy; that the only living fruit of that union was a uniquely talented farseer, elven in all but her looks, was a...*complication*, but Diriem didn't give a damn. Equally scandalous in some regards was that the ti'Dana heir was planning to marry a rather ordinary guy from a low-ranking Hall—an old Hall, yes, but not one of prominence. Yven wasn't anywhere close to main-line ti'Ansha, and his family couldn't begin to compete with the ti'Dana wealth, but he'd been willing to die for Rose, and that was good enough for Diriem.

Growing up in poverty in the Georgia mountains, I'd had no idea what an elf *was*, let alone that my flopped-over ears and minor magical talent marked me as anything but human. I hadn't known there was an *option*. Nine months later, I'd lost my home, been orphaned in horrific fashion, and wrestled with the fact that half my community was dead, in part due to choices I'd blithely made, but I'd gained a Hall: ti'Ammaas. The final king of the south was Ivari ti'Ammaas, and when times grew desperate for him and his band of seventeen other survivors, they did the unthinkable and joined forces with an equally desperate band of humans...with all that entailed. Generations later, I was legally Ivari's heir, even if he refused to claim me, and thus, when the Forum had reestablished the surviving southern Halls in the Pactlands, I'd been made Lady ti'Ammaas.

Those of us from East Branch who'd received titles back in November had kept the matter quiet. Our biggest concern was school, and none of us was part of a Hall more than two members strong. Our ancestors had been elven nobility, but we were just the remnants of an insular, undereducated community too poor for luxuries like flush toilets. We weren't exactly the type to put on airs.

But word got around, as it always did at North Lake, and for some of our detractors, the news of our change in status was *hilarious*. As usual, I bore the worst of it. The most outspoken of our critics was Ainnet ti'Har, a popular girl in my year with a pack of friends who did her bidding, and she'd zeroed in on me as her number-one target back in the fall. Sure, she'd backed off for a while after I broke her nose in a dining-hall fistfight, and she'd kept her distance for a time after the top sports reporter in the city praised me on television, but the glow had worn off by March, and Ainnet's catty whispers had begun to reemerge like weeds in a freshly plowed field. On paper, I outranked her—she wasn't even main-line, while I was the lady of a royal Hall second only to storied ti'Dana—but in truth, she was pretty and knew how to play the game, while I was a bumpkin who'd only just learned how to disguise my ears without resorting to a masking pendant. So, unable to best Ainnet, I did what I could to ignore her.

At least I had a few people in my corner. I wasn't entirely back in my cousins' good graces, as some still blamed me in part for the destruction of East Branch, but they weren't actively shunning me anymore—a positive development. Sage, who attended remedial tutorials with me, continued to be a reassuring presence, another student who looked a little freaky under her mask, drawled in English natively, and understood the misery of an unairconditioned Georgia summer. Most students were wise enough not to pick on Sage, as her father was one of the three sorcerer representatives to the Forum, and Mirrik Voln wasn't shy about calling the school if he thought his little girl was being slighted. And when I left the safety of our tutorials and joined the rest of my year, I had a solid ally in Keef ti'Mal. Annie had saved Keef's older sister's life some two years prior, and since then, Keef had decided that the human-adjacent weren't all bad. She'd taken me under her wing, and when Ainnet started in on her crap, Keef could spit it right back at her. While ti'Har outranked ti'Mal, Keef was main-line, and she knew how to deploy that to her advantage. When Ainnet tried to retaliate by bringing up the fact that Keef's disgraced father would be on a penal farm for years to come, Keef simply shrugged it off.

"They lose their power if their insults don't bother you," she'd quietly told me more than once. "Let them run their mouths. If they get physical again, I'll jump in with you, but for now, try to remember that insults are only hot air."

Easier said than done, though I reminded myself that I'd survived worse. Ainnet was a thorn in my side, but she'd never killed anyone I loved, pushing her far down the list of my problems that year.

But Ainnet's teasing didn't matter that Saturday. I'd turned nineteen the day before, I was going to the dance with the boy for whom I'd been silently pining for months, I had a beautiful new dress, and my eyeliner looked *just* about even.

By nightfall, I was ready, and I gave myself a final perusal in the mirror on the back of my door. Floor-length purple gown that swished when I walked and made me feel like a princess? Check. Silver shoes peeking out below the hem, the soles already scuffed against slipping on the dance floor? Check. Silver necklace in lieu of my gold pendant? Check—and to my relief, my mask seemed to be firmly in place. My makeup didn't skew into clown territory, my brown hair stayed in the updo I'd built over a painstaking half hour with a pack of bobby pins, and my eyes didn't even look bloodshot, which I'd feared in light of my restless sleep the night before.

I was ready.

I smiled at the mirror and smoothed my skirt, then murmured, "I'm going to the dance, Mama. Wish you and Daddy were here."

If my parents could somehow see me from the beyond, they'd yet to send me a sign, but it gave me comfort to imagine that they might be watching me with pride.

Swallowing hard to clear the sudden tightness in my throat, I opened the door and headed for the large common room, the central space in our end of the dorm. A few of my healthier cousins had gathered around the TV to watch a movie, and Heidi stopped me before I could slip out. "Hold it, let's see," she ordered. "Give us a spin."

I obliged, and once she and Hannah deemed my attire satisfactory, our older cousin Laurel, my uncle Kyle's wife, looked up from her knitting and nodded. "Have fun," she said. "We won't stay up."

I felt like I might pop from excitement as I hurried through the halls and emerged onto the wide front steps of the school, where dozens of other students had already gathered. Scanning the knots of people, I spotted Keef and Sage, then ran halfway down the stairs to join them.

Per tradition, the spring dance was held in a rented ballroom in District 4, a swanky venue. While the school ran shuttles, the more popular alternative was for couples and groups of friends to arrive via their own transportation. One of Sage's friends had organized a party bus, which pulled up just as I was saying my hellos. "That's my ride!" Sage announced, beaming, and waved to us as she hurried off after her group in a swirl of pale blue tulle. "See y'all there!"

Though Keef's English was limited to a bit of profanity, she seemed to understand Sage's departing call. "Bye!" she shouted, and waved back at the bus as it pulled away, the lights inside shifting through a spectrum of neon colors in time with the thudding bass audible through the closed windows. "I rode in one of those my first year," she told me, hugging her bare arms against the chilly evening. "Almost lost my hearing by the time we arrived. The speakers in those things are *superb*."

"Looks like fun," I replied, and glanced around at our waiting peers while the line of vehicles snaked forward. Near the bottom of the steps, I spotted Ainnet and her girls, all wearing short, flirty dresses that seemed a moderate breeze away from impropriety. I'd tried on a few like that at my stylists' insistence, but I lacked the confidence to carry off the look. Briefly, I counted the members of the clique—all present, so perhaps they were going with dates instead of as a group.

"You look great, Maebe," Keef murmured, nudging me in the side. "Eddic's going to be stunned."

I laughed. "Am I that bad normally?"

"No, you know what I mean. He's not going to be able to take his eyes off you tonight. Maybe not his hands, either," she added in a low murmur, and waggled her eyebrows.

"Yeah, yeah," I replied, brushing her off. "Hennda might have to rethink being your friend after tonight."

She smirked back at me. "We're just friends. I mean it."

"*Sure*, you are."

Before she could retort, a sleek black car pulled up, and the rear door opened to reveal Hennda, who'd shed his usual slightly grungy school attire for a brown robe that coordinated nicely with Keef's dark green dress. She waved at him, then gave me a quick hug. "I'll see you in a little while. Have fun with Eddic."

Keef and Hennda were quickly on their way, and I stood alone in the throng, watching as the others left with dates or in groups. Just as I was beginning to chill and reconsidering my decision not to wear a jacket, a long gray car pulled to the front of the line, and out stepped Eddic.

I had to stifle a gasp as my heart hammered against my ribs. He cleaned up *nicely*, having opted for a black robe with silver trim—a fortuitous choice, I thought, imagining my dress pressed up against it. Clinging to what little decorum I could muster when all I wanted to do was fly into his strong arms, I waved in greeting and started down the stairs.

But before I could reach the ground, Ainnet had taken his outstretched hand.

I stopped at the bottom, perplexed, and the two of them shared a look before Ainnet burst into a peal of laughter. "You thought he was serious?" she asked me, her blue eyes practically sparkling in the white glow of the security lights. "Honestly, Maebe, you're such an *idiot*."

"What's going on?" I asked, focusing on Eddic, who had wrapped an arm around Ainnet's waist. "Eddic, I…I thought we were…"

"You really thought I wanted to take *you* to the dance?" he asked, and snorted. "Be serious. That was a joke."

"But…the flowers…"

Ainnet looked at him and smiled. "A nice touch. Almost too much."

"What can I say?" he replied, and then, to my horror, he stooped and kissed her cheek.

I stood there, frozen and praying I'd wake up, as Eddic helped Ainnet into the car, but he closed his door in my face.

And as Ainnet's girls tittered on the stairs and the susurrus of the crowd grew almost as loud as the rushing in my ears, I stiffly turned away and walked off toward the lake, away from my humiliation.

The swing by the lake shore was far from the glare of the security lights, a place of quiet and relative privacy by night. I sat on the wooden bench in my finery, hair still pinned up but shoes off, and slowly swung as I shivered in the darkness.

This was stupid, I chided myself. The temperature was dropping, I was wearing a sleeveless dress, and my arms had erupted in goosebumps. I couldn't stay outside all night...but I couldn't bring myself to go to my room, either. There was no way to sneak in without passing through my family's busiest meeting area, and someone would surely be awake to witness me slink off to bed. I could have taken a shuttle to the dance, but I couldn't bear the embarrassment of showing up alone—not after Ainnet and Eddic made a mockery of me in front of the school. I supposed that Keef and Sage would wonder where I was, but that couldn't be helped. At least by then, the last shuttle had departed, so I didn't have to stew over my choice to skip the dance.

As a bat flew by overhead, swooping after bugs, I heard footsteps approaching across the grass but didn't turn away from the dark water. The lake was serene that night, barely lapping at the small beach and glassy beneath the waxing moon. If I sat still, I mused, perhaps the newcomer would pass me by.

Instead, a weight settled onto the other end of the swing, and I finally looked over to see Diriem sitting beside me, contemplating the water. "Not a good night for a swim, I should think," he murmured. "I'd wait for summer, were I you."

"What are you doing here?" I asked.

"Rosie wanted to see the full effect and make sure you got to the dance without complications, and when you headed this way, she called me. I was taking care of a few matters at the office this afternoon and lost track of time, it seems." With the moonlight, I could tell when he turned my way, though I saw him only in shades of black and gray. "I'm sorry, youngling."

"Did you know?"

"No."

"Would you have told me if you did?"

He hesitated before responding. "Perhaps."

That was the best I could hope for. Farseers were notoriously selective in what they chose to reveal, especially future-oriented ones like Diriem. In fairness, there was no reason why he should have known what Eddic and Ainnet had planned. He headed the Division of Intelligence, after all, and had more important matters to worry about than one teenager's public embarrassment. Still, the knowledge that he hadn't seen it coming and simply declined to warn me put me slightly more at ease.

"I feel like such a fool," I muttered to the lake. "Thought he actually liked me…"

Beside me, Diriem softly sighed. "It happens. You're not the first, and you won't be the last. That doesn't lessen the sting, I suspect," he added, "but you're in good company, Maebe." He pushed back on the swing, and we rocked for a moment in silence before he asked, "Who's the boy?"

"Eddic. He's in the year above me."

"Eddic…"

"Ti'Dir."

Diriem grunted. "Not main-line, no? I think I'm familiar with most of the children in that family…"

"No, I checked. He's a cousin or something. I don't know how close he is."

"Ah. I could have a word with Hemar, if you'd like."

While I certainly didn't share Diriem's deep knowledge of the Halls, I recognized Lord ti'Dir's name, as one of his aides at the Forum had been working on the sly with the group trying to kill my family months before. "No, thank you. I just want this to go away."

"Can I offer you a ride to the dance? It's not too late."

I shook my head, rubbing my arms against the cold. "Not going, but thanks anyway."

"So…the plan is to sit out here all night, then?"

"I don't know," I mumbled. "I'm a laughingstock, and it's going to be worse once my cousins find out."

"Well, in that case," said Diriem, "Rosie asked me to tell you that you're invited over to choose from her selection of questionable films and eat an unhealthy amount of ice cream. She claims this has therapeutic benefits."

"That's nice of her, but—"

"But what? You're going to freeze if you stay where you are, and this will give you a reason to postpone facing your cousins, right? Come along," he said, standing, and turned to offer me his hand. "Put your shoes on, dear."

We spoke little on the ride out to Viratta, though I noticed that Diriem had stealthily turned up the heat and engaged the seat warmer on my side of the car, giving me a chance to thaw out before we arrived at the mansion. Walking in with him from the massive attached garage, I felt ridiculously overdressed, a mussed storybook princess paired with an escort in a simple sweater and khakis, but we'd barely made it to the foyer when Rose appeared in a ratty bathrobe and plaid flannel pajamas to heighten the absurdity.

"Hey, hon," she said, slipping into English from the start, and hurried over to claim me from her great-grandfather. "Are you okay? Frozen?"

The corner of my mouth twitched. "Been spying?"

"Off and on," she confessed. "I was worried you were thinking about taking a dip in that dress."

"Not quite."

"Well, in any case, let's get you into something warmer. I'm glad you came," she said, steering me toward the staircase to the second level, the quickest way to her apartment in the tower of the southern wing. "Yven's out with Pars and the boys, and if I know those two, that'll devolve into late-night karaoke once there's enough booze in play. It's been way too quiet tonight. Hey, didn't you have a birthday this week?"

"Yesterday," I mumbled, bunching my skirt in my fists

as I trailed upstairs after her.

"Ack. I've got to put that in my phone…but did you do anything special?"

"Just class. Jane called, and so did Connor." I held off on providing further detail until I'd reached the second floor and caught my breath. My overtaxed heart had had quite enough already for the night. "He's coming here next week for lessons."

Rose glanced back at me, her gray eyes narrowing—an expression I knew far too well from my dealings with Diriem. "I thought he was on a weekly schedule."

"He's supposed to be, but one of his officers was out this week with a stomach bug. Connor's been picking up the slack."

"All week? Dang," she muttered, "that's one hell of a bug."

"Connor said he had to go to the hospital and everything. Got, um…"

"Dehydrated?"

"Yeah, that." While I spoke English natively, growing up in a community with minimal access to the outside world had left a few holes in my vocabulary. "So, he had to skip his tutorial."

"Ah, yes," said Rose, "because Whitford's such a crime-ridden war zone. He should really consider coming on at Laws—I know he feels beholden to the Whitford PD," she added before I could answer that, "but between us, I think he's wasting his talent."

"He doesn't use his talent back home—"

"Not magic, I mean. Your cousin's a pretty damn good cop…as cops go," she added with a grin.

I followed Rose to the end of the long hallway, then up the spiral tower staircase, chatting about my cousin and his girlfriend—and for a moment, everything seemed fine. But then Rose showed me into her apartment and closed the door. "Let me find some PJs for you, hon," she began, sizing me up, then said, "I want you to know that you look beautiful, okay? That son of a bitch is blind."

Just like that, I remembered why I was far from the dance, hanging out with Rose on the Saturday night that I'd been anticipating, and the dam I'd been holding together through force of will all evening finally cracked.

Rose hugged me as I sobbed on her shoulder. "It's all right," she soothed, rubbing my shuddering back. "Let it go."

After a long moment, I managed to choke out, "I'm never going to be enough. I…I try…I really do—"

"Honey, she's a bitch, and he just wants to get in her pants. This *sucks*, but it's not the end of the world. Come here."

With Rose steering, I plopped onto one of her den's trio of leather couches and sniffled as she took a seat beside me, gripping my hands. "When I was in high school—almost sixteen—we had a Sadie Hawkins dance. Do you know what that is?"

I shook my head.

"The girls invite the boys," she explained. "So, there was this guy, Mark. I thought he was the hottest thing in our grade, and we'd always been friendly—like, we worked on group projects and stuff together—so I screwed up my courage and asked him to be my date. He said yes, and we arranged that we'd meet for dinner beforehand at Applebee's." She chuckled at the memory. "He was old for our grade, so he already had his driver's license, and he could take us to the dance, then drive me home. Well, the night arrived, I squeezed myself into this godawful dress—aqua satin with rhinestone accents, I don't know what I was *thinking*," she said with an exaggerated shudder—"and my mom dropped me off for the classiest of pre-dance dining. I got a table for two and ordered a drink, and I watched the door so I'd catch Mark when he came in…but he never did. So, I sat there nursing my Coke for an hour, and I kept texting him to see if he was okay, but he didn't answer me. By that point, I was thinking he might have had a wreck, so I called my mom, and Mom called Mark's mom, and *she* was confused as heck because Mark had driven off to pick up his date for the dance more than an hour and a half before. Turns out the little weasel got an invitation from Bridget Henderson after he'd accepted my invite, and he didn't have the decency to let me know he was going with the better option."

"That's awful," I said.

Rose shrugged. "Eh, in retrospect, I can't really blame him. Bridget was this modelesque cheerleader, so definitely a step up for Mark. But I was still stuck there at the Applebee's with my Coke and no dinner *or* date, and I started crying, and my waitress felt bad and brought me chocolate cake. She was really sweet. Mom left her a big tip," she said with a sad smile. "After Mom got me into the car, I went home and washed my face, and I made myself sick on ice cream, just like we're going to do tonight. Sound good?"

I nodded. "What did Mark say the next time you saw him? Did he even apologize?"

At that, Rose's smile turned considerably more sinister. "Well…you know, I'm not the most graceful of women, and I certainly wasn't in high school, and I might have accidentally spilled a bottle of V8 all over him the following Monday at lunch."

"What's, uh…"

"V8? Largely tomato juice. Whoops." Leaning toward me, she whispered, "Food for thought, yeah? By the way, nice job on your eyeliner. I'm glad we went with the waterproof option."

"It's still on?" I asked.

"Yup. Your mascara, however…you know, just come with me," she said, and pulled me into the bathroom.

CHAPTER 2

"*There* you are! Where've you been, mitta?"

Busted. I'd hoped that the folks in the common room on Sunday morning would be too engrossed with the television or their kids to notice me slink by, but Monica and Laurel had developed the uncanny maternal ability to spot the slightest sign of mischief and were on me before I could sneak past the open doorway.

"Uh…hi," I said as their husbands, Peter and Uncle Kyle, turned toward me. The babies, Winston and Tobias—toddlers, now, three and almost two and a half, respectively—ignored my arrival in favor of a brightly colored cartoon. With as much local programming as the boys had consumed over the last eight months, both had begun to develop eerily good Pactish accents.

"Maebe Amos," Laurel continued, folding her arms, "are you *just* now getting home? What were you doing all night?"

Uncle Kyle, my mom's little brother, arched an all-too-familiar eyebrow.

"It's not what you're thinking," I hastily told them.

"I don't know," said Uncle Kyle, "but that sure ain't what you were wearing when you left last night—"

"But that's not some boy's clothing, either," said Laurel, who was more perceptive than her husband. "What did you—"

"Loaners from Rose," I explained, sweeping my empty hand up and down over my borrowed sweater and leggings. My dress had been packed into a garment bag, which I'd slung over my shoulder, though I'd worn my silver shoes home.

Peter frowned. "Rose…"

"Ti'Dana."

"*Oh*. Her," he said with a curt nod.

Most of my family seldom saw either of our nominal guardians, Diriem and Teolm. Connor and I had drifted into their orbit through Jane, who'd not only made friends with Rose and Annie but had also been lured into a job at DOI under Diriem's watch.

"What were you doing with Rose?" Peter asked. "I thought you were going to that dance."

With all four of my elders staring me down, I knew I had no chance of dodging the question. "I, uh…I didn't make it to the dance," I muttered.

Monica reached behind her and gestured at the TV until the volume dropped. "Why not?"

I sighed, then entered the common room and draped my bag across the back of an unoccupied chair. "The guy who invited me to be his date didn't mean it. He took Ainnet. They just wanted to embarrass me in front of the school, so…" I shrugged. "Didn't feel like dancing after that."

Laurel's and Monica's expressions softened almost as if they'd been choreographed. "Aw, hon," said Laurel, "I'm sorry. That's—"

"Who's the kid?" Uncle Kyle interrupted, and slammed his fist against his palm for emphasis.

"Eddic ti'Dir," I replied. "He's in the year above David and me."

"*Is* he, now?"

"It's okay," I said before my uncle could truly get his dander up. "Rose saw it happen, and Diriem drove me out to their place, and I stayed up late watching this movie called *Mean Girls*, so I'm going to take a nap."

"Or we could go to the principal," Monica suggested. "You don't have to sit back and let her humiliate you."

"I want to forget last night," I said. "If I don't make a big deal about it, then maybe everyone else will forget in a few weeks—"

"Doubtful," said Peter. "The last time she escalated, the two of you ended up brawling. I don't want a repeat of that, do you?"

"No," I mumbled.

"And she isn't just picking on you, mitta. This is a slap in the face to *all* of us."

The others nodded. Peter might have been the lord of a low-ranking Hall, but he was the eldest of us left, and that carried a certain degree of respect.

"Can we talk about this later?" I pleaded. "Really, I was up late, and—"

"You're worn out," Laurel finished, shooting Peter a warning look before he could protest. "Get some rest," she told me. "We'll regroup this afternoon."

By the time I shuffled groggily from my bedroom, lunchtime had passed, and word of the previous night's events had spread among my cousins. With our dorm parents out of the way—Chennis ti'Van was finishing her weekly reshelving in the library, while Dalm Curshin was overseeing a weekend practice with the rowing team—we had a chance to speak freely, and my cousins wasted no time. The ones old enough to have a voice in the matter were divided as to the best course of action; some wanted to go to the principal first thing in the morning, but others like Heidi, four years my senior, and Laurel, who was older than us both but my heir to Hall ti'Ammaas, suggested restraint. "Look," said David, who spent as much time with Ainnet as I did, "she's a pain, but she's a wealthy pain, and she's got a lot of wealthy friends. Remember the dining hall fight? Ainnet started it, her girls lied to support her, and Maebe still got suspended."

David neglected to mention that none of them had

jumped in to help me, but since they were speaking to me again, I wasn't about to bring up *that* time.

The wait-and-see group won out, and though he clearly didn't agree, Peter backed off. "See how Ainnet acts tomorrow," he told me. "If she's up to her old tricks…"

"I'll handle it," I said, though the thought of facing her left my guts in knots.

I was feeling no better Monday morning—not queasy, just sick with dread—and so I feigned a case of the bug going around and asked Heidi and David to make my excuses to our tutor. Their expressions told me they didn't believe me—fair, as I'd already been through this particular wave of illness—but they let it go and left me to hide away in the twilight of my shaded bedroom.

I tried to sleep that morning, but my rest was fitful, and by eleven, I surrendered and crawled out of bed. I brushed my teeth and hair, washed my face, and finally opened my computer to see what assignments our tutor might have sent me. But before I could click the icon for my mailbox, someone pounded on my door. "Maebe?" came Sage's voice through the wood. "Are you awake?"

"Well, she is *now*," said a muffled voice I recognized as Keef's. "Open up, Maebe."

Sighing, I tightened my bathrobe belt and unlocked the door. "Hey," I said, stepping back to admit them. "What's up?"

"That's exactly what we wanted to ask you," said Keef, folding her arms as she blocked the doorway. "What happened Saturday night?"

"We saw Eddic with *Ainnet*," added Sage, wrinkling her nose. "Why didn't you come with him?"

I beckoned them into the room, then closed the door behind them as Keef plopped into my desk chair and Sage claimed the foot of my unmade bed. "It was a setup," I muttered. "Eddic was never going to take me. They just wanted to make me look like an idiot in front of everyone. Or maybe crazy, I don't know. Either way—"

Keef swore in the sort of colorful Low Elvish that surely would have made her mother gasp.

"It's okay," I hastily continued. "Diriem came to get me, and I spent the night on Rose's couch. But after Ainnet and Eddic made a scene, I didn't want to go to the dance."

"We've been trying to reach you since Saturday night," said Sage. "Did you not get our messages?"

"I…did."

Keef shot the younger girl a look, then focused on me. "It's all right, Maebe. Glad you're back…and you're not actually ill, are you? *Again*?"

"No," I admitted, leaning against the wall. "Just a touch on the yellow-bellied side, that's all."

Keef cocked her head, bemused, but Sage followed me. "I wouldn't want to face her, either," she said. "You know she's going to rub it in."

"She's been asking about you all morning," Keef added, then minced, "'Has anyone heard from Maebe? She didn't come to the dance.' I knew she wasn't really concerned, but that does explain why she's so eager to see you."

"Yeah, well, tell her I'm puking or something, won't you?" I replied.

"*Maebe…*"

"I'm taking a sick day. Back tomorrow, I promise," I forced myself to say, though in truth, I'd have preferred not to show my face again for the rest of the semester. "But not today. I…I *really* don't want to deal with her."

"Tomorrow, then," said Keef. "I'll stay with you in class, yeah?"

"And I'll be with you all through lunch," said Sage, flexing her thin biceps. "Backup."

While I didn't like our odds, and I suspected that Ainnet would find a way to be annoying no matter how many I could recruit to my side, I appreciated the support. "Thanks," I said, and managed to smile. "You two had better get back to the dining hall before you miss lunch altogether."

"Needed to make sure you were alive," said Keef, and patted my shoulder before she unlocked the door to take her leave. "Priorities."

I might have been feeling a little yellow-bellied that week, but I was a woman of my word, and I trudged off to our tutorial with David and Heidi the next morning. Sage met us there and snagged her usual spot to my right, smiling as she settled in and set up her computer. "It's going to be fine," she whispered. "Glad you're back."

I wasn't nearly as confident as my friend was, but I opened my books and did my best to pay attention, willing the morning hours to stretch. When we broke for lunch, Sage quickly packed up and cut her eyes toward the door. "Hungry? They're doing pesto pasta today."

Sage always knew the menu. We'd had our hungry days at East Branch, but she'd been starved as a kid, and mealtimes were almost sacred.

"Sounds good," I replied, "but...you know...I think I'll grab something in my room."

She frowned, perhaps confused by how anyone could turn down the dining hall's admittedly excellent pasta, then nodded. "Okay, I've got this. You grab us a table in your common room or something, and I'll get the food."

"Sage—"

"You're not going hungry because of freaking Ainnet," she insisted, and shooed me on my way.

Though she was undersized, Sage had quite an appetite, and she soon joined me with two generously laden trays. We ate with the TV on in the background, catching snatches of the midday news. Just as the weather reporter was finishing his segment—cool with scattered rain for the next week, a milder version of what central Virginia was experiencing, as usual—Uncle Kyle appeared from down the hall where the family apartments had been set up. "Maebe?" he said, poking his head into the common room, sandwich in hand. "Oh, hey, Sage. What are y'all doing here?" he asked, slipping into English.

"Watching the news," Sage replied, all innocence.

"Uh-huh." Giving me a look, he pressed, "You haven't caught the stomach flu again, *right*, mitta?"

"No," I mumbled.

"Atta girl. Isn't your lunch period about over?"

Unable to delay my fate any longer, I helped Sage return our dishes to the dining hall, then parted from her to join my year in the art room.

The faculty at North Lake who had designed my family's educational track meant well. As we were so far behind our peers in subjects both magical and mundane, we spent our mornings in remedial tutoring, trying to make up for the failings of our informal schooling in East Branch. Much of our afternoons were taken up with tutorial sessions as well—mine in particular, as I had a private tutor to help me manage my aeromancy, a wild talent—but for an hour or two after lunch every day, we joined the other students our age for classes like physical education and the arts. After all, we were farm kids—we could certainly run and throw balls, and perhaps the teachers thought we could be trusted with art supplies without heavy supervision. Though I understood the impulse to give us time to socialize with the rest of our year, in practice, it hadn't worked out smoothly. Sure, some of our classmates were kind and welcoming, quick to step in with a guiding hand when we slipped up, but then there were the ones like Ainnet, who, forced to tolerate our presence, tried to turn us into the butt of a long-running joke.

While I'd been excused from physical education since the fall because of my heart condition, I had no reason to miss art class, and usually, I liked it. The closest we came to painting at East Branch was the odd coat of whitewash, and clay was used only to make dishes. I enjoyed the opportunity to experiment, and aside from our teacher's lessons about art history within and outside the Pactlands, I could hold my own.

That Tuesday, I slipped in just before class began and made a beeline for the seat Keef had saved beside her at one of the front tables. The room was set up with rectangular tables for two aligned in neat pairs on either side of the aisle, and our teacher, Ms. Taregga, sat at the front behind her own long desk, the better for demonstration. We'd been working on a collage project, and while some of my classmates found it tedious, I enjoyed the cutting, arranging, and gluing.

"Hi," Keef whispered as Ms. Taregga passed out our portfolios. "Sage said you were eating in the dorms?"

I grimaced as I nodded, and she patted my arm.

"Look who's back!" Ainnet called from two tables behind me. "Why, Maebe, I'd heard you were *sick*. Must be those human genes, hmm? It's a wonder any of you survive."

I clenched my jaws shut, biting back the retort I wanted to shout at her.

"Maebe? You haven't lost your hearing, have you? Did those freaky ears go deaf?"

Before I could snap, Ms. Taregga intervened by calling the class to order. "You have until Friday to finish," she told us as we got to work. "I want to see progress today, please."

No one made the obvious joke: *How's she going to see over the tables to tell?* Ms. Taregga was a gnome, a woman barely three feet tall who dyed her naturally white hair in vibrant streaks of color—greens and blues that week—and while she was diminutive, she had little patience for smartasses. Even I had heard the story about the kid who'd sassed her during her first year at North Lake, a centaur who'd played melee, and how she'd knocked him to the *floor*.

As Ms. Taregga strolled around the room, pausing occasionally to take a peek on tiptoe, answer questions, or offer feedback, I tried to focus on my project. But even above the normal hum of activity, I could hear Ainnet and her cluster of lackeys whispering to each other and sniggering at their own comedic brilliance, which I suspected was at my expense. Still, I forced myself to concentrate on my work, envisioning the final collage and deciding how best to get there…

Then, out of nowhere, I felt a brief, sharp tug on my hair and heard the unmistakable *snick* of metal blades.

I whipped around to find Ainnet standing between me and the table at my back, smirking. In her right hand, she held a pair of scissors, but in her left was a chunk of brown hair. "Oops," she said, her blue eyes widening in feigned surprise. "There I go being clumsy again. Silly me."

By then, Ainnet's friends were laughing, and Keef had turned around in alarm, but I was seeing red—and my talent seemed to strain against the underside of my skin, a tethered dog begging for release.

I was born with mild magical ability, though like most of my cousins, I barely showed it back in East Branch. "The touch," we called it, and really, that's all it was— maybe objects would twitch at our silent command, or perhaps we might slow a punch with an invisible barrier of force, but that was all. After eight months in the Pactlands, however, and with concentrated remedial work, our abilities had strengthened and grown more controlled. None of us held a candle to the full-blooded elves around us, but at least we'd figured out masking.

But I had an additional gift I'd never understood back home. My touch had been weaker than many—things wouldn't really move for me, but I could call up a little wind that might make napkins flutter around. *That* had been the stirrings of my underdeveloped wild talent, a particular ability to manipulate air, and once it had burst forth, I'd been shocked by its strength. Having been released, it refused to crawl back in its hole, and it waited for my command, always present and quick to engage. If my temper spiked, if my heart raced, my talent was at the ready…and then some. Violet ti'Comros, my aeromancy tutor, knew *exactly* what that felt like and how dangerous our shared wild talent could be, and she'd worked with me to tighten the reins and learn to hold it back when I was stressed.

That said, I had my limits, and Ainnet just kept pushing me over the edge.

A wind began to blow around me, barely ruffling my hair but flinging my classmates' projects off their tables. The funky chandeliers Ms. Taregga had installed began to sway wildly above us, and the windows at the far end of the room blasted open as my anger manifested in quasi-tornadic form. Ainnet's eyes widened in fear as her pretty blonde hair whipped around her face—*good*—but a sudden clamp on my arm drew my focus to the aisle, where our teacher had forced her way through the wind to grab me. With me sitting, we were much closer to the same height, so I got the full brunt of her best *oh, no, you don't* glare.

"Maebe," she snapped. "Outside, *now*."

Cringing, I withdrew my power, and the wind—and all of our portfolios—dropped immediately. "Sorry, *sorry*," I mumbled, my cheeks heating as I saw the extent of the damage, "I—"

"Out," Ms. Taregga ordered. "Wash your face, calm down. Get a drink. Come back when you're in control."

I hurried out as my grumbling, windblown classmates started searching for their projects, then ran down the hall, locked myself in the nearest bathroom, and braced myself against the sink. The cold porcelain gave me something to focus on beyond my anger at Ainnet and my shame for having lost control—again—and I wiped a wet paper towel over my flaming skin as the adrenaline rush began to ebb.

A knock at the door interrupted me. "Maebe?" called Keef. "Are you in there?"

I flipped the latch, and she joined me. "Sorry," I said,

"I didn't mean to—"

"Are you hurt? Let me see."

"She didn't hurt me," I replied, turning my back to Keef. "Just cut a chunk of hair. No blood. I'm sorry about—"

"It's all right. Frankly, I'd have hauled off and punched her, so she should be glad that all she needs is a hairbrush." Keef spun me around and gave my damp, flushed face a quick inspection. "Feeling better?"

"I guess."

"Calmer?"

"Yeah." I sighed and dried myself off. "Shit."

"Maebe, there's a reason that we have tutors for wild talents," said Keef. "You're not the first person in this school to flare—and hey, that was just wind. Think about someone like Fell when she was our age."

Keef's older sister, Fellora, was a pyromancer like Jane. She'd had her talent well under control by the time Keef came around—Fell was more than forty years Keef's senior, not uncommon in elven families—but Fell had told her sister about the intense training she'd endured to keep her abilities under wraps. Uncontrolled pyromancy was a real concern—no one wanted to deal with spontaneous fires from angry children—and trained pyromancers were handled with healthy respect. Back in Georgia, Jane had made a side career of "arson for the greater good," and though Keef had never mentioned it, I knew from Annie that Fell had killed one of Wylan's brothers in self-defense by slamming him into a stone wall with a jet of fire.

By comparison, a stiff breeze wasn't the worst thing to happen at North Lake, but still, I kicked myself for losing control.

"Come on," said Fell as I adjusted my mask to hide my shortened hair. "We've still got time to work, yeah?"

"Hope so, since I just screwed up everyone's projects…"

She snorted. "Half of this collage thing is glue. And

who knows? Perhaps the, uh…sudden, unexpected shake-up will lead to artistic breakthroughs."

I grinned at her. "You're full of it."

"I'm *trying*," Keef protested, and steered me back to our classroom.

By the time we returned, order had mostly been restored, though drifts of scrap paper still lay against the baseboards. I nodded to Ms. Taregga and slunk to my table, then opened my portfolio—Keef, I assumed, had retrieved it for me—and stared at the half-finished mess inside, wishing I'd been gluing more down as I went…

Suddenly, as I stared at the label on my glue bottle, Rose's "accidental" tomato juice spill popped into my thoughts.

I glanced over my shoulder toward Ainnet's table. She wasn't even pretending to work, instead having turned around to talk to some of her friends at the table behind her.

My talent itched for freedom as I thought about how smug she had to be, having not only gotten a rise out of me but also sending me out of the room in disgrace, my inadequacies on display once again. She was so proud of herself…

Well, two could play at *that*.

With Ms. Taregga focused on a project far from either of our tables, I called up a little spiraling wind in my cupped palm and carefully squeezed a fat glob of glue into the center. The glue hovered above my skin, carried on the wind I controlled, and I cut my eyes to the back of the room again, waiting for my moment. There—Ainnet was still talking, ignoring me.

Perfect.

A precise blast sent the glue ball flying, arcing over the heads of the students behind me and landing at the back of Ainnet's skull. Another quick gust twisted her long hair around, driving as much as I could into the glue. She yelped, then reached back, felt the goop, and screeched.

The other students' heads shot up from their work to see what was causing the fuss. As Ainnet wailed and pulled at her hair, her friends joined the chorus…but I noticed a few of my classmates snickering at her predicament. Ainnet was popular, yes, but she wasn't exactly *liked*, and from what Keef had told me, plenty of them had endured a turn or two as the focal point of her bullying.

But my moment of triumph was brief. Ms. Taregga took one look at Ainnet, then wheeled on me, scowling. "*Maebe*."

"As Ainnet said, oops," I replied.

"Both of you, principal. *Now*," she ordered, jabbing her tiny finger at the door. Though Ms. Taregga was no larger than a kindergartener, I knew better than to provoke an angry gnome, and so I raised my hands in surrender, grabbed my bag, and set off, speedwalking in an effort to beat Ainnet and her hysterical sobbing to the front office.

The principal of North Lake was Keddi Mafatta, a dark-haired centaur of considerable stature who appeared imposing even when she was in a good mood—and that afternoon, she absolutely wasn't.

I'd made it to her first, but Ainnet was louder and pushier, and as she was a snotty, red-faced mess, Ms. Mafatta silenced me and let her snivel out her story. "She *attacked* me!" Ainnet wailed, keeping a few feet between us as if she anticipated a retaliatory blow. "And my ha…my *hair*…I'm going to have to…to shave my head!"

Though Ms. Mafatta's eyeroll was brief, I caught it as Ainnet buried her face in her hands and bawled.

After a moment, the principal said, "Pull yourself together, Ms. ti'Har. You're not bleeding."

Ainnet looked up at her, lip quivering. "I…I…"

"Breathe, girl." Turning to me, she folded her arms over her green robe as her mouth moved into a tight line of distaste. "Well? What do you have to say to that,

Ms. Amos?"

That she didn't address me by my title was, I figured, a calculated move, but I didn't argue with her. "I did it," I confessed with a little shrug, "but only because Ainnet cut off a chunk of my hair first."

Ainnet started to protest, but Ms. Mafatta silenced her with an upraised hand and a barked, "*Wait.*" Her brown eyes narrowed as she looked me over. "Show me."

I turned around and dropped my mask, then flipped my hair past my flopped-over ears to give her the full effect. "See?"

"I do."

"It was an accident!" Ainnet blurted. "I didn't mean to—"

"How did you *accidentally* cut her hair?" Ms. Mafatta interrupted.

Ainnet paused—I supposed she hadn't worked out her story that far—then said, "I was walking behind her, and I tripped—"

The principal gave her a withering look. "I wasn't born yesterday, Ms. ti'Har. So, Ms. Amos, you decided to retaliate for your haircut? Is that all?"

"Not entirely, ma'am," I murmured, keeping my eyes on her as Ainnet huffed beside me. "I might have let it go if Ainnet weren't such a goddamn *bitch*."

I'd used the English term, but Ms. Mafatta didn't require a translation. "Might this have something to do with the dance last weekend?"

"Yes, ma'am."

"Mm."

"She's crazy," Ainnet interjected. "She tried to steal my date—"

"You might want to stop there," said Ms. Mafatta, turning her glare on Ainnet. "See, this school has a network of security cameras, and there's one on the front staircase."

Ainnet froze, calculating, but Ms. Mafatta continued. "I

received a call from Representative Voln, of all people, last night. He had troubling information for me, something he'd heard about you, Ms. Amos, and Mr. ti'Dir from his daughter."

Sage, I mused, was a true friend, even if I wasn't sure that blabbing to her dad was the soundest approach to the problem.

"She wasn't even there! She left before we did!" said Ainnet.

"True," the principal replied, "and Representative Voln freely admitted that everything he had was secondhand at best. But I pulled the footage last night, and the audio was...something. That, and I spoke with a few students this morning who were standing nearby when your little prank was played," she added. "Your stunt was childish and cruel, end of discussion, and you should be ashamed of yourself."

"It's not my fault that the human was stupid enough to fall for it," Ainnet retorted.

I glanced her way and snorted. "You say 'human' like it's a bad thing."

"You—"

"*Enough*, girls," Ms. Mafatta cut in, and we both wisely paused our sniping. "I'm very disappointed in you both."

"I want her suspended," said Ainnet, pointing at me as if the principal needed a hint. "She attacked the whole class with a damn whirlwind, and then she ruined my...my..."

Ainnet's ability to cry on cue was scarily good, but judging by Ms. Mafatta's expression, she wasn't buying it. "Calm yourself, Ms. ti'Dir."

"All I want is for her to leave me alone, ma'am," I said as Ainnet sniffed. "I try to avoid her. I don't even speak to her unless I have to. But she constantly picks at me. Saturday night was...well, awful. I mean, I bought a dress and makeup and shoes for nothing. And then she sneaked up behind me and cut my hair! If anyone needs a suspension, it's Ainnet!"

Ms. Mafatta cocked her head toward my red-faced adversary. "What do you say to that?"

The tears dried in an instant, and Ainnet's expression hardened. "If you suspend me over that stupid half-breed, my parents will have you fired. Is that clear?"

To her credit, the principal held her ground. "Do you think threatening me is your best option?"

"I'm just telling you how this will end," said Ainnet. "All of my parents' friends on the board, the ones who know how much money my family has given this school..." She smirked. "Think about it, *ma'am*."

"No need for that," she snapped, then sighed and stared at us each in turn. "Ainnet, there's an excellent glue solvent in the potions lab. Go ask the teacher on duty to give you a bottle. You're excused from class until you've washed your hair...*ah*, wait," she said, stopping Ainnet before she could run off. "I don't want to hear of you messing with Ms. Amos or any of the East Branch group again, understood? No pranks, no insults, no snide comments. If you can't be civil, ignore them. Is that clear?"

The triumphant edge in Ainnet's smile made my heart sink. "Of course."

"Good. Go on."

"What about Maebe's suspension?"

"I'll deal with that," the principal ground out, and Ainnet practically went skipping on her way. She waited until the door had closed and the sound of footsteps had faded, then gestured toward a chair. "Sit, Maebe."

I eased myself down, warily watching her as she settled in on the long mat behind her desk. With her legs tucked and her lower body hidden behind the wooden furniture, Ms. Mafatta could have passed for a sorcerer.

"So," she said, folding her hands on her leather blotter, "what are we to do with you?"

"Ainnet started this," I said, holding her gaze. "You know that. I only went after her because she went after me first."

"True, but you also exacerbated the problem."

"I'm not allowed to defend myself?" I asked, bristling.

"In kind, perhaps, but you escalated the attack. She snipped your hair. You endangered your entire classroom by creating an indoor windstorm, and then you threw glue at Ainnet—and do correct me if I'm mistaken, but you weren't aware of the solvent when you chose that weapon, were you?"

"No, ma'am."

"So, you thought it would be appropriate to leave Ainnet with little more than a buzz cut for the bit she took off of your hair?"

I dug my fingernails into my palms to stop my talent from erupting into a gale. "Why don't we skip the part where you pretend to be fair and you just tell me how many days I need to stay at Diriem's house?"

"Maebe, that's—"

"Please don't lie to my face. I've had a long week already."

"You need to ignore her," said Ms. Mafatta. "Pretend she isn't there."

"That must be really easy for you to say," I replied. "No one's picking on you, right?"

"Aside from the board. I…appreciate that this is a difficult situation for you to navigate, but I'm not losing my job over you girls' stupid squabbles. Here's what's going to happen," she said, giving me a look that forbade argument. "I'm pulling you out of regular classes for the rest of the year."

My eyebrows rose. "Ma'am?"

"You're already excused from physical education—I'm sure you could use the study periods. This should limit your potential interactions with Ainnet to lunch, and I trust you two can sit at different tables. Understood?"

"I…understand that I'm being punished because she's a bitch."

"Be glad I'm not suspending you for a week after your stunts today."

I sat there, quietly seething but trying to keep my face still. "Is that all, ma'am?"

"Not quite," said Ms. Mafatta. "You're banned from Lake Day."

At that, I couldn't hide my dismay. Lake Day would begin at lunchtime Saturday and go long into the night. There would be fun foods, dancing, boating, games, movies, a faculty–student melee match... Our dorm parents had been talking it up all semester, and now *this*?

"May I at least sit in the dorm and watch from a window, or am I not allowed to look at the party?" I asked.

"Maebe, I'm trying—"

"No, you're not." With as much dignity as I could muster, I stood, tugged down my sweater, and grabbed my bag. "You're just trying to make Ainnet happy. Now, if you'll excuse me, I should probably go to my study period so that the sight of me doesn't offend the princess."

"There's no need for that tone—"

I shot her a look of deep incredulity, and to my surprise, she fell silent. "Excuse me," I muttered, and headed for the door.

Before I could turn the knob, Ms. Mafatta asked, "Should I expect another visit from Lord ti'Dana?"

"What difference would that make?" I shot back, and stormed out.

CHAPTER 3

My cousins were angry on my behalf, Keef was *pissed* when I told her Wednesday at lunch that we wouldn't be in class together for the rest of the year, and Sage offered the services of her father, who knew at least as many board members as Ainnet's parents did. But I was tired of fighting. Since June, I'd discovered my community's hidden heritage, kicked off the chain of events that led to Ivari murdering half of East Branch, and confronted him at his trial, at which he'd thrown a knife at my face. My talent was strengthening, but my control was still woefully behind that of my peers, and I had a long way to go on the magic front. Plus, since I'd only learned in the last months that I'd grown up in a state called Georgia, my mundane education was also grossly lacking. In other words, I had enough on my plate without wasting more of my energy on Ainnet.

She could have the victory, I decided. Someday, she'd get her comeuppance, but for the time being, I'd keep my head down and focus on my studies.

When my phone rang Thursday night and I saw Jane's name on the screen, I wasn't surprised. I hadn't told Jane about my school situation, but word spread—and since she was in a relationship with my cousin, she was almost one of us.

"Hey, Jane," I said after tapping the button, sliding into English. "How's it going?"

"Eh, not bad. You doing okay, Maebe?"

"Fine," I fibbed.

Jane hesitated, and something told me she didn't buy it.

"Listen, I've got a proposition for you," she said. "Con and I are driving home tomorrow afternoon, and I was thinking this might be a good time for you and me to have a little…girls' weekend, shall we say?"

I frowned at the dark window. "That's, uh…that's nice of you to offer, but what's going on?"

Jane chuckled weakly. "Not as smooth as I'd hoped, huh?"

"Nope."

"Then I'll be straight with you. I heard about the mess with Ainnet."

Sighing, I asked, "How much did you hear?"

"Oh, a fair bit. Let me see…Keef told her sister, asking for suggestions. Then Fell talked to Annie, and Annie looped me in, and I spilled the beans to Con. He's working this weekend, but you know I've got a spare bedroom, and I'd love to have you over."

My guts clenched at the thought. I hadn't been back to Georgia since September—not since East Branch was burned to ashes. "Um…"

"Please," Jane pressed. "A little time away would do you good, kiddo. Come with us, take a few days to clear your head."

Yes, the notion of going home made my anxiety spike…but what was the alternative? Sitting alone in the dorm all day Saturday while everyone else had fun without me? Hell, the toddlers were invited to Lake Day, and they didn't even go to school yet.

"Okay," I heard myself tell Jane. "Thanks."

"Sweet. We'll get you around four tomorrow, all right? Have us some girl time while Con's writing speeding tickets or whatever."

"What're those?"

"Citations for driving too fast, mostly. You have to pay a fine."

"Huh. Has Connor ever given you one?"

Jane snorted on the other end. "He knows better than that. Plus, I ensorcelled my truck against police radar, so good luck *proving* that I speed."

There were definite perks to being a sorcerer in a town full of humans, even if one's use of magic had to be sneaky.

"But I'm a good driver," she assured me, "and we'll have fun this weekend. Promise."

And as I hung up and put the phone back on the desk, I began to smile for the first time in days.

My last tutorial on Friday ended at three-thirty, which gave me just enough time to pack. With my extra study periods, I'd finished most of my weekend homework, and I figured that I could cram in the little bit left after lunch on Monday. I threw a few shirts and pairs of jeans into my suitcase, tossed in pajamas, then remembered to glance at my phone for the forecast outside.

As Jane had explained to me, the Pactlands sat alongside the outside world like a lace placemat atop a tablecloth. The artificial world had been anchored in North America when it was built in the sixteenth century, as its architects had been a group of mostly European sorcerers who'd decided there would be less risk if the Pactlands fell apart if it were built over a more sparsely inhabited area. Thus, the foundations had been laid near present-day Richmond—never mind the Native Americans—and Beukal sat slightly west of the city. The architects hadn't stopped there, however, creating territory for settlement and expansion far beyond Virginia, though they'd left gaps in the map that had never been filled. While the weather in the Pactlands tended to reflect whatever was going on outside, it was generally milder—cooler summers, warmer winters, gentler rainstorms, and so on. Early March in Richmond was comparable to that in north Georgia, which meant I needed to be sensible and throw in something heavier than the zip-up sweatshirt I'd favored of late.

I had closed my bedroom door and was on my way out when I ran into Dalm in the big common room, doing a crossword puzzle. "Hi, Maebe," he began, then spotted my bag. "What's that for?"

"I'm going home for the weekend," I told him. "Be back Sunday evening."

"Whoa, now." He put his puzzle book aside and rose from the little table he'd commandeered. "You're going *where?*"

"Home," I repeated. "Well, close. Ragged Gap."

"So...*outside?*" he asked, arching a brow.

I nodded. "My ride's on the way..."

"Not so fast. Did you get permission to leave?"

Though that briefly took me aback, I recovered and planted my hands on my hips. "*Permission?* I didn't realize this was a prison."

"It's not," said Dalm, "but generally, we need parental permission to let students leave. The school's responsible for—"

"I'm sorry, but how the hell would you like me to get parental permission?" I snapped.

To his credit, Dalm winced. "Yeah, that came out wrong. Parent or guardian—"

"I don't have either, but if you feel like bothering Lord ti'Dana on a Friday afternoon, be my guest."

I grabbed my bag and started off, but Dalm followed me. "What about Lake Day? You don't want to miss that, do you?"

Laughing incredulously, I looked back at him and said, "I've been banned from Lake Day, or haven't you heard?"

"Uh...no..."

"Ms. Mafatta doesn't want Ainnet ti'Har's precious little feelings to be hurt, so she's punishing me. I'm going home. Goodbye."

He gave up after that, but I only released my breath once I was safely in the elevator, heading down. As dorm parents went, Dalm was kind and great with the little kids, but he was also easily distracted. Chennis might have given me greater pushback, but she was on library duty until dinnertime, and so I'd dodged *that* blow.

A few minutes after I'd escaped to the front steps, which were mercifully empty that day, Jane's blue pickup truck came down the driveway and slowed to a stop. By East Branch standards, her ride was top of the line: it had a working engine, a functional muffler, and doors and panels all of the same color. By anyone else's standards, her truck had seen better days. It was a 2011 F-150, well-loved and well-used on the mountain roads around Ragged Gap, and Jane joked that she didn't have to lock it because no one would bother stealing it. Since she'd taken a job at DOI, her truck had undergone some magical modifications, and now, like all Pactlands vehicles, it didn't need gasoline—which, since trucks weren't known for their great gas mileage, was a real perk.

The passenger-side window rolled down as the truck idled by the stairs, and my cousin waved. "Come on, mitta!" Connor called. "Let's hit the portal before the traffic gets worse."

I climbed into the back seat and shoved my bag atop Jane's and Connor's luggage beside me. "Hey," I said, buckling up as the truck started off. "Thanks for the ride."

"Not going to make you hitchhike, hon," said Jane, glancing at me over her shoulder long enough to flash a grin. "All set?"

"Ready to go." I could almost feel my stress drain as the school shrank behind us out the rear window. "How was training?"

Connor groaned. "Gonna be living on Advil all weekend…"

"Which is why you were sent home with pain potions, you big baby," said Jane.

He turned around to me and rolled his eyes. "'This'll be fun,' they said. 'Nothing to worry about,' they said. 'It'll be good for you—'"

"It *is* good for you," Jane interrupted.

"I never needed pain potions when I was working with your dad," he protested.

"Because Dad was going easy on you."

"Yeah, well, DOI don't play," he muttered, turning to face the front, and grunted as he adjusted his position in the seat. "Does Diriem try to hire sadists, or was this an incidental perk?"

Jane shook her head and merged into traffic. "Once you get the hang of shielding, you won't hurt nearly as badly after lessons."

I felt for my cousin. Defensive magic was one of the subjects we covered in our tutorials, but from the sound of things, DOI took a much less gentle approach than our tutors did.

"So, Maebe," said Jane, "while Con goes home and licks his wounds tonight, I thought that you and I could go out to dinner."

I perked at the offer, as I could count on one hand the number of times I'd been to a restaurant in my life. "That'd be great. I don't have any money for Georgia, but I can repay you from my account in—"

"Keep your money. You're my guest, yeah? Besides, it's not like we're going out for lobster and fillet mignon. I was thinking more like Mama Hen's."

"What's that?"

"It's in downtown Ragged Gap," said Connor. "Do you like chicken?"

"Sure…"

"Then you'll be fine."

"They also do good burgers," Jane told me. "My friend Tabitha is going to meet us there."

"She's the pharmacist, right?" I asked.

Jane nodded. "Uh-huh. She hasn't been to the Pact-lands, but she knows a lot about it and us. Kind of got roped in a year and a half ago when we had a rogue sorcerer on the loose. She's cool."

"And…Diriem knows about all this?"

"They've met, and he's promised not to wipe her memory, so we can work with that."

Satisfied, I made myself comfortable in the back seat and watched out the window as Jane navigated through Beukal. District 6, where North Lake was located, was on the far northern side of the city, while the external portal building was on the southern end, past all the skyscrapers and government buildings of the inner districts. Most of the outbound traffic would be heading for the internal portals, which would take commuters home to towns that, if mapped onto the outside world, would be halfway across the country or more. Use of the external portals was restricted for security reasons, as anyone who went outside needed to know how to mask and get around without arousing suspicion. There were exceptions, of course, folks who'd bought access to the portals with large bribes, but the average citizen couldn't just drive up and go for a scenic ride in the real world.

Jane's credentials were secured through DOI, as she was an agency employee, but my cousins and I also had permissions in the system…or so I'd heard. On paper, DOI managed them, but I'd never discussed the issue of my ability to come and go with anyone at the agency. Still, as Connor sometimes came in and out with Jane, I trusted that mine would work.

The backup plan was to call Annie, who didn't *need* the portals to get around and seldom objected to giving folks a lift. I hoped it wouldn't come to that, but Jane seemed confident as we entered the portal building and pulled up to the security booth. "Afternoon," she said to the attendant, and flashed her badge. "Three for Central."

The portal attendant, a naga wearing a dark green shirt and nothing else, slithered out of the booth and rose on his snakelike tail until he was on eye level with Jane. "May I?" he asked, reaching for her badge.

She handed it over, and before he could ask, she said, "Connor Willow and Maebe Amos. They should be in there under DOI as well, if you could manually check."

He nodded and retreated to the booth, his muscular tail curling into a tight coil of brown scales while he checked the computer, then nodded and returned to the truck with her badge. "Agent Fortune," he said with a nod, then looked at my cousin and me. "Lord ti'Catama, Lady ti'Ammaas. Everything's clear. We've got two inbound, but you'll be on your way once they've passed."

Jane thanked him and rolled up the window, then patted Connor's knee. "Easy, babe."

"It's still *so* weird," he muttered.

"I know, but on the bright side, they don't give you much grief with a title in front of your name."

"Maybe not here," I grumbled. "The only people who use my title at school are the ones making fun of me."

"Yeah, and we're going to have a *talk* about that. Not this weekend," she assured me, "but soon. Diriem and Teolm need to know what's going on."

"I don't want to drag them into another one of my messes."

"Honey, you're being bullied. When that happens, sometimes, you have to break out the big guns. If I know Diriem, he won't mind reading your damn principal the riot act."

While I wasn't quite sure what Jane meant by that, her tone was enough to give me the gist. "Except Ainnet's parents have a bunch of friends on the board of directors."

"So? They've got money and a bit of clout, so what? I guarantee you, hon, you put a ti'Har cousin up against Diriem freaking ti'Dana, and every elf on the board is going to see things his way."

"You think?" asked Connor.

"I…might have done a bit of recreational snooping," she replied, "and I took a look at the North Lake board and donors. Hall ti'Dana has been a major donor since the school's founding. They don't really show up to meetings or make demands, so I guess they're not the principal's first concern, but let's just say that if Diriem threatened to pull the funds, I bet little Ainnet would be out on her ass."

Feeling slightly lighter of heart, I waited until the bright pinprick of the opening portal widened into a rainbow-bordered hole in the fabric of the world, and then the barrier arm lifted to give us passage. "Here we go," said Jane, and drove us into South Carolina.

The Central portal was only about an hour's drive from home, so I wasn't starving by the time we pulled up to Connor's house in Whitford. He kissed Jane and thanked her for the ride, then limped around the truck to open the back door and retrieve his bag. "Y'all have fun," he began, then stiffened, his eyes widening. "Uh, mitta, your mask."

"Shoot," I hissed, and made the quick adjustment to round off my ears. "Better?"

He nodded. "Nice work. I'll see y'all for dinner tomorrow, okay?"

"Don't violate anyone's civil rights," said Jane, leaning out the window to kiss him again.

"Yeah, yeah. Behave yourself, Firebug."

Jane waited while I climbed up into the front seat, then set off toward the southwest. Home—East Branch—lay at the far northern end of a little valley. The nearest settlement was Whitford, but the biggest town of note anywhere in the vicinity was Ragged Gap, which occupied the valley to the southwest of ours. Getting there required a bit of a winding drive over and around the mountain between them, but Jane was familiar with the route and sped along through the late afternoon light. Sunset came early in the mountains, and though the sky would continue to glow for about another hour, the shadows were already growing long.

While Ragged Gap was a hamlet beside Beukal, it was a

metropolis compared to the compound where I'd grown up. The downtown area, which I'd barely seen, nestled in the center of the valley, while the mountainsides around it were pocked with cabins and larger homes. I'd stayed at Jane's cabin before, a cozy two-bedroom house with an impossibly large bathroom, the result of her magical renovations, but that and a visit to a strip-mall restaurant was the extent of my exploration of the town.

Instead of turning toward home, Jane drove us into the valley and toward the heart of Ragged Gap. "It's not exactly bustling," she said apologetically as we wound our way past stands of trees and little subdivisions of tourist cabins. "Especially not in March. If we can't get a parking spot, I'll be stunned."

I withheld judgment until we reached what passed for Ragged Gap's commercial district, a few blocks of shops and restaurants extending from the grassy town square. A public parking lot sat on one side of the square, directly opposite a relatively tall brick building whose sign marked it as Ragged Gap Baptist. Most of the shops seemed closed, their windows either darkened or left with just enough lamps on to spotlight the displays, but the door of the store directly across from the square was still propped open, and warm light spilled out onto the sidewalk. I slowed as we drew near, noticing the sparkling rocks on the front stands, but Jane nudged me onward up the street without slowing.

Our destination was one of the few places still open that Friday night, Mama Hen's Café. As Jane and Connor had warned me, the decoration leaned heavily toward chickens, from the sun-faded wallpaper border of marching poultry to the cement hen by the hostess stand. I'd counted three taxidermied roosters perched around the booths by the time a waitress showed us to a table, and as I took a seat, I noticed that the salt and pepper shakers were a pair of eggs.

"The owner is Henrietta Grange," Jane whispered after

we put in our drink orders. "She kind of leaned in on her nickname when it came to fixing up this place…ah. Over here!" she called, looking past me at the front door and waving.

I turned and saw a dark-skinned woman in a thin purple sweater and black dress pants quicky maneuvering around the tables to join us. She flashed Jane the kind of straight, white smile I'd only achieved through magical dentistry, and as she drew near, I saw that her thick ponytail was comprised of tiny braids, her hair mostly black but threaded with glints of silver.

"Hey, y'all," she said, pulling out the chair beside me. "Sorry, hit every light on the way. Have you ordered yet?"

"Just drinks," Jane replied. "Tabitha Bradley, Maebe Amos."

"I *figured*." She grinned at me and patted my shoulder. "Nice to finally put a face with the name."

"Good to meet you," I said, smiling back at her. "Have you been here before?"

"Oh, my, yes. The options around town are kind of limited," said Tabitha. "But the chicken sandwich here is good…the chicken-fried chicken is nice if you don't have to worry about your cholesterol…and the meatloaf is surprisingly decent," she added, pointing to each item on the laminated menu. "So, what's speaking to you tonight?"

"I…don't really know." Leaning toward her and lowering my voice, I explained, "This is only my second restaurant in Georgia. The food's a little different, uh…"

"Over there," she finished. "Got it. Well, if I were you, I'd start with the chicken sandwich and tater tots, and if Jane's paying, I'd throw in a milkshake."

"Knock yourself out," said Jane, waving to me in a gesture of largesse.

I'd been afraid that dinner would be awkward, the number of people I knew without a connection to East Branch or the Pactlands being approximately zero, but Tabitha was friendly and quickly put me at ease. She and

Jane chatted about her business—Tabitha was a compounding pharmacist, which she explained as sort of like a potion brewer without the magic part—and then the conversation switched to Connor's misadventures in Beukal. My cousin could shoot straight and work wonders in an interview room, but he had a lot to learn when it came to his talent. "*My* tutors are great," Jane told Tabitha. "Con's feel like it would be insulting if they went easy on him, so he's suffering right now."

She frowned. "Why can't they just teach y'all together?"

"Couple reasons. One, I've got a *much* better foundation, and he's still a beginner. Two, there are some differences between what he and I can do and how we do it, so he's working with elves, and I'm working with sorcerers."

"Bet he regrets having that blood test, huh?"

"*So* much."

The two of them chatted and laughed throughout dinner, making efforts to include me, and by the end of the meal, I was stuffed on fried food and ice cream, just on the cusp of feeling ill. When Tabitha suggested a walk for digestive purposes, I eagerly agreed.

We set off up the street first, heading away from the square, and I paused every few yards to peer into the darkened shop windows. Ragged Gap couldn't hold a candle to the designer boutiques of District 4, or even the funkier shops of District 3, but since I was new to shopping, period, the offerings grabbed my attention all the same. The biggest store on that end of the downtown district was Ragged Gap Mercantile, which seemed to have a little of everything crammed onto the displays: a starburst quilt in shades of peach and green, a small pyramid of glass jars of apple butter, wooden honey dippers, a metal tub of colorful bath bombs, candles in scents like "Fresh Laundry" and "Mountain Stream," and even a ceramic serving tray with Ragged Gap painted across the middle, sandwiched between two stylized mountains. "Y'all should stop in tomorrow," Tabitha said. "You know Bitsy wouldn't mind."

Jane sighed. "Yeah, I know, but I don't want to try to explain Maebe to *Bitsy.*"

I glanced at her face in the streetlight's glow, trying to figure out what I was missing. "Who's Bitsy?"

Patting my shoulder and steering me on, Tabitha said, "There's water under that bridge. Jane used to sell her stuff at the Mercantile until Bitsy got her hands on a potion that she thought was going to give her power. Instead, she had a seizure. Annie gave her something to neutralize that crap, but Bitsy blamed Jane and kicked her out."

"It's always so nice to find your products left out back in boxes," Jane muttered. "She wrote 'Bitch' on them so I'd know they were mine."

"Bitsy got over herself eventually," Tabitha continued, "and she knows now that she was suckered with that potion."

Jane nodded. "We're back on decent terms. But she wants me to start selling at the Mercantile again, and frankly, I haven't had the time to make new stock. Fortune's Fancies has pretty much shut down. I just don't want to have to explain to her why I suddenly killed off my own business—it's not like I can tell her I got a job offer I couldn't refuse."

"You could have refused it," said Tabitha, nudging her in the shoulder. "Good thing you *didn't,* but you could have said no."

"I mean, Diriem wasn't holding me at gunpoint or anything, but…" She shrugged. "He was right. *Dad* was right. I didn't know how much I didn't know, and the tutoring has been fantastic."

"I'm sure," Tabitha replied, and steered me onward. "Still, I guess it's probably best if we shop somewhere else, Maebe. I mean, if it came out that you're from East Branch, there'd be no end of questions."

Questions I most assuredly didn't want to answer: how closely related our families were, why we kept to ourselves, whether we could read and write, what the hell had *hap-*

pened to the place, where the survivors had gone. I hadn't seen East Branch since the night it burned, and I had no desire to concoct a story to satisfy our nosy neighbors' curiosity.

We walked around a bit longer, peeking down side streets and alleys, and then we turned and headed back toward the square and the parking lot. As we drew near, I saw that the store with the pretty rocks was still open, and I stopped by the windows to better examine the display.

"Mystic Mountains," Tabitha quietly told me, then smirked at Jane. "How about it? Think the truce is strong enough to let the kid browse?"

Jane rolled her eyes. "Just don't get too attached to anything in there, Maebe. The prices are ridiculous."

Duly warned, I slipped through the open door and into the warmth of the shop. Frankly, I didn't know where to look first—everything seemed to sparkle, and though I barely had any jewelry to my name, even I could recognize the beauty in the display clusters twinkling around us. As I stepped deeper into the store to goggle at a hollowed-out rock half as tall as I was and filled with translucent purple crystals, I noticed a woman sitting on a stool behind the check-out desk, watching us. She was older than Jane, maybe closer to Tabitha's age, and though her hair was mostly blonde, her face was framed with pink streaks. Her brown eyes were rimmed with thick, smoky eyeliner, a look I'd only managed upon smudging my makeup. A lilac sweater in a chunky knit fell off one shoulder, exposing the black tank top beneath. Over it all she wore a silver necklace from which a clear crystal point as long as my index finger hung, bobbing as she straightened up to take us in. She glanced past me and arched a brow.

"Hi, Stephanie," Jane murmured, coming up behind me. "She's visiting and wanted to look at the rocks. Okay?"

Stephanie nodded. "Yeah, sure. Looking for anything in particular?" she asked me. "Are you a practitioner?"

Befuddled, I turned to Jane, who answered for me. "Not exactly, but you can't fault her for liking the geodes, right?"

"Not at all. Well," said Stephanie, glancing my way again, "if you have any questions, let me know."

"What's that?" I blurted, pointing to the purple crystals that had caught my eye.

She chuckled. "Good taste. That's an amethyst cathedral—it's a special kind of geode," she explained. "Comes from Brazil. Amethyst inside, bit of cement on the outside to keep everything nice and stable. You're drawn to it?"

"Uh…I think so," I said.

"Amethyst is a powerful stone. It's associated with your third eye and crown chakras," said Stephanie, pointing to the spot between her eyebrows and the top of her head. "Good for protection, warding off stress, enhancing psychic intuition, understanding dreams, healing and cleansing…a whole host of good things."

"And the ancients thought it'd help prevent you from getting drunk," said Tabitha, throwing her arm around my shoulders. "I can tell you from experience that it leaves something to be desired as a sobriety aid."

Stephanie snorted. "Had a little too much fun, did we?"

"You've got to let your hair down every so often when you're suffering through orgo," she replied, then plucked a smaller chunk of the spiky purple stone out of a basket and handed it to me. "Many Wiccans use crystals for ritual purposes. If it speaks to you, maybe we could get one without a four-figure price tag, hmm?"

"Oh, absolutely," said Stephanie, who seemed to be warming to us. "I mean, the cathedral is *gorgeous*, if I do say so, but for the practitioner on a budget…pick your favorite," she continued, sweeping one hand toward a display unit packed with stones sectioned off by color. "The nice thing about amethyst is that it grows in relatively large crystals, and it's not all that expensive. Go ahead, take a look."

Tabitha escorted me over to check out the merchandise. As we crossed the store, I glanced toward the back half. The side closer to the desk was a café—closed for the night, obviously—but the other side was lit and lined with thin black mats. Moving as a group, half a dozen women bent themselves into odd poses to the sounds of gentle music and falling rain.

"Yoga," Tabitha whispered, catching me staring. "Some like it for the health benefits, others for the meditative aspects. Stephanie's been hosting yoga classes for a while."

"That looks…painful," I told her, watching the participants contort their bodies into a new position.

"Nah. Not my cup of tea, but plenty of folks enjoy it. Okay, here, let's see how overpriced these things are," she said, plucking a fat piece of amethyst from the shelf.

I slowly walked around the display, examining the crystals, but a sudden blur in my peripheral vision made me straighten up and follow it. The shape was a dark-haired man in a long black garment—not a robe like the ones I'd come to know in the Pactlands, but rather a coat, which he wore open. It flapped behind him as he strode straight for the yoga class, which was just wrapping up.

"What the…" Stephanie muttered, then called after him, "Hey! I banned you! Get out of here if you don't want a trespassing charge!"

He ignored her, but by then, the women at the back of the store had noticed his approach, and a brunette in a purple sports bra and matching leggings jumped to her feet and held her hands out as if she could make him stop in his tracks. "You can't be here," she said, her voice loud but wavering. "Restraining order's still valid."

The man in the black coat chuckled low in his throat. "What's a little piece of paper going to do against *me*, huh? You *know* what I'm capable of, Nikki."

She seemed to shrink and retreated a step as he drew nearer. "No closer, I'm warning you."

"If you don't get out of here *right now*," Stephanie snapped, phone in hand, "I'm going to call the cops!"

The man reached into his coat, and when he withdrew his hand, he raised it above his head, revealing the dull sheen of a pistol. "Wouldn't do that if I were you. Now, y'all just be calm," he continued as the women in front of him froze in place. "No one needs to be hurt tonight. Stephanie, be a good girl and put down the phone, or I might just get angry."

I was conscious that Tabitha had gripped my arm and was trying to pull me out of the man's line of sight, but my attention was fixed on Jane, who glared at him with murderous intensity. "Hey, Warner!" she bellowed.

Instantly, his shoulders stiffened, and the room seemed to hold its breath.

"I thought I told you to stay the fuck out of my town," said Jane.

"Who is he?" I whispered to Tabitha.

"Warner Cavanaugh," she whispered back. "You've seen Sage's scars?"

Though Sage didn't particularly like discussing her childhood in Whitford, we were close enough friends that I had some inkling of what she'd endured. The man who'd found and raised her—who'd told her she was a demon and made her call him "Master"—had kept her chained up by the neck in his barn. He'd lied to Sage, claiming he was a powerful warlock, but once she'd shown actual talent, he'd sold her to Jane before she could grow strong enough to fight him.

The man with the gun, the one who'd turned around and was staring at Jane with wide blue eyes, was the asshole who'd tortured my friend. Sage still went to weekly therapy sessions to work through the trauma.

"You stay back," he ordered Jane, pointing the gun at one of the terrified women. "Stay right there, you hear? So help me, I'll shoot these bitches, and then I'll shoot you…"

His voice faded as white flames began to flicker over Jane's arms and hands. "I warned you."

"Fortune—"

"Drop the gun. *Now*."

The woman with the gun in her face whimpered, and Warner yanked the pistol away from her to point it at Jane. "You ain't bulletproof, are you?" he said, though the tremor in his cracking voice and the matching one in his hand weakened his attempt at bravado. "Well, you fucking freak? Are you?"

That did it. My talent needed an outlet, and I had just the target in mind.

A blast of wind shot across the store, whipped around the big amethyst cathedral, and lifted it off the floor as easily as if it were a dry leaf on an autumn breeze. Warner didn't have time to duck before the geode went hurtling past Jane and plowed into him, slamming his body against the back wall. The gun fell from his hand as he wheezed for air, and the yoga instructor snatched it and ran toward Stephanie with her prize.

Jane looked from Warner, still pinned by a floating chunk of rock, to me, then nodded. "Nice work, kid. Your control's coming along, isn't it?"

"Getting better," I mumbled, focusing on keeping Warner stuck.

"You can drop the amethyst now," she said. "I'll take it from here, hon."

"Uh…maybe let's not *drop* the amethyst," Stephanie interjected. "Could you, um, put it down gently? Please?"

I flew it over to the café and set it on a table, and Stephanie mouthed *Thanks* before she hurried after Jane, who was strolling toward gasping Warner like a cat stalking an injured mouse. He'd fallen to his knees, and considering the way he clutched his chest, I figured I'd broken a rib or two.

"So…you never did tell me why you ran Warner off," said Stephanie to Jane.

"Short version," she replied, "he kept a child chained up at his place."

"*What?*"

"Yeah, and I'm pretty fond of her. Her dad would rip Warner's little balls off if he were here, but instead, I guess I'll have to handle him. *Again.*" Glancing at Nikki, she asked, "What'd he do to you?"

"We went out *once*," Nikki mumbled. "Pity date. I wasn't interested in a second one, and he couldn't take a hint. Hid by my car and grabbed me when I left work one night. I…I didn't want to go through with a rape trial, but the cops got me that restraining order."

"I'm so sorry," she said, her voice momentarily softening, but it hardened again as she neared Warner. "You know, he should really take that as a hint, but some people are just stupid."

Warner looked up, his face pale with fright, as a fireball the size of my head appeared in Jane's hand. "Please…please don't…"

"I'm not going to kill you," said Jane. "You're not worth it. However…"

The fire winked out, and as Jane whispered, Warner *screamed*.

To be fair, both of his arms had suddenly developed new joints below the elbow, and it surely didn't feel any better when Jane threw another concentrated blast of power at his knee.

As Warner wailed and toppled over, Jane turned to Stephanie and deadpanned, "Wow, it looks like he had a really bad fall. You might want to call an ambulance."

"On it," said Stephanie, stepping away with her phone.

Jane looked at the stressed-out yoga class and said, "He *fell*, right?"

The women were no fools, and they nodded emphatically.

"And that's what you're going to tell the paramedics once they show up, yes?"

More nods answered her.

"Great. May I?" she asked, extending her hand toward the yoga instructor, who passed her Warner's pistol. "Thanks. This nasty little thing is coming with me. And as for you," she said, nudging Warner in the side with her toe, "if I catch you in this county again, it'll be worse. You want to keep your manhood? Don't try me."

We waited around while Stephanie finished her call, and then she and Jane shared a long look. "Thank you," she murmured.

"Sure."

Glancing at me, Stephanie asked, "*Where* did you say you were from?"

"Out of town," I replied.

"Uh-*huh*," she said slowly. "Look, um…I don't think you actually need it, but why don't you take one of those amethyst points, hmm? On the house."

I grabbed a polished purple stone the size of an apple and thanked Stephanie as Tabitha and Jane hustled me out into the night, the sound of the nearing ambulance siren crescendoing on the breeze.

CHAPTER 4

Though Tabitha had arrived separately, she climbed into the back of Jane's truck while I was buckling in. "Figured we should work out the game plan and any necessary cover story before we take off," she explained.

Jane turned on the ignition, and the overhead lights went out. "I don't think we need to work up a cover story. Um...shit," she muttered, "Maebe, this was supposed to be an easy night out—"

"It's fine," I assured her. "Are you okay?"

"Who, me? Peachy." She cracked her knuckles. "Though if I see that son of a bitch again, I might just have to break my 'no killing' streak."

"Something tells me he wouldn't be widely mourned," Tabitha replied, "but good job at not setting him on fire tonight. Stephanie's insurance probably appreciates that."

She snorted. "Unless Warner tries to make a claim for being injured on her property."

"I sincerely doubt he's got the balls for that."

"Are you going to get in trouble, Jane?" I blurted.

"For that business back there? Nah," she said. "Folks who hang around Mystic Mountains know that I'm not normal. Remember when we went to Jay-Jay's and it got robbed?"

My laughter was brief and incredulous. "Uh...*yeah.*"

"Figured. So, Zach, the guy who comped our dinner that night? He's one of Stephanie's woo-woo brigade. They don't know exactly *what* I am or the extent of what I can do, but they know not to ask too many questions, especially since I've saved quite a few of their asses. And since I used my bag of tricks tonight to defend them, they have no reason to start telling the cops that I'm an honest-to-God witch or whatever."

"In fairness," said Tabitha, "a good number of them consider themselves witches, too."

"Right. Anyway, Stephanie and I have a sort of truce," Jane continued, "and since Ernie Flores, the Mouth of the South, wasn't there tonight, I think we'll be just fine. But, uh…I think it'd be best if no one mentioned this in Beukal, yeah?"

Tabitha chuckled behind us. "No worries here."

"Forget Beukal," I told Jane. "Isn't the bigger problem Connor?"

"*Yeah*," she drawled. "Tell you what, I'll take you to Dairy Queen and get you the biggest Blizzard on the menu if you don't tell Con about our little fun tonight. Deal?"

I grinned in the darkness. "Deal."

"Make it three?" asked Tabitha.

"Absolutely. Come on, we'll carpool," Jane replied, and drove off through the parking lot as the paramedics arrived.

By the time Jane and I made it back to her house, I was pleasantly stuffed and coming down off a mild sugar high. I followed her inside with my suitcase, grateful for the wave of warm air that greeted us at the threshold—having grown up in a poorly insulated log cabin, I still regarded central heating and air conditioning as nearly magical—and she led me back to the spare room, where the big sleigh bed with the thick mattress was already turned down in invitation. "Sleep well, hon," she said as I lifted my bag onto the luggage rack. "If you want to shower tonight, be my guest, but I'm hitting the hay. Help yourself to the kitchen," she added, then drew the door almost closed behind her, giving me a moment's privacy.

As nice as a hot shower sounded, I figured it could wait until morning. I sloughed off my clothes, slipped on my pajamas, and filled a glass at the kitchen tap in case of midnight dry mouth—another luxury for a kid raised on well water. My teeth, I decided, wouldn't rot before morning, and I flopped into bed with a sigh. Our accommodations at North Lake were nice, but Jane's put them to shame, and I wondered how long I'd need to study before I'd be able to create a mattress that'd make me want to melt.

Snuggling beneath the blankets, tired and toasty, I called to mind the Maebe of almost ten months prior, the runaway camping in the mountains without a tent, food, or the ghost of a plan. The girl who'd never been twenty miles from home, who hadn't understood how restaurants worked, who'd stepped into an elevator for the first time and screamed in terror. Now I was sleeping in an outsider's home, unfazed by the wonders of electric lights and flush toilets but somewhat weary from having magically thrown a rock into a man to disarm him. And not just any man, but my good friend's tormentor. I almost wished I'd taken pictures of Warner crumpled on the floor to give to Sage. This version of me...well, she'd come a long way in a brief time, still naïve in some aspects, fractured by loss, but growing into something stronger than she'd been.

Sure, the thought of dealing with Ainnet for the rest of the year still made me a little queasy, but I could get through this. That weekend with Jane might be just the thing to get me to summer, I mused, as I rolled over and fell asleep.

Brunch was not a word that had ever entered my vocabulary at East Branch, but I decided that I could get used to it.

Jane, Tabitha, and I met up at Waffle House, which, Jane explained with a bit of embarrassment, had become their brunch spot of choice. "It ain't fancy," she said after the waitress left us with laminated menus, "and there's no mimosa option—"

"There is if you BYOB and spike the orange juice," Tabitha whispered.

"Which is neither legal nor encouraged."

"Oh, come on, since when are *you* the responsible one?" she retorted.

Jane grunted, and Tabitha grinned back at her across the booth.

"Anyway," Jane continued, "it's cheap, it's filling, the people-watching can be *superb*, and no one asks too many questions about Canna's accent."

"No frills, but it's safe," Tabitha concurred. "Now, on to the important question, Maebe: how do you like your hash browns?"

We had no firm post-brunch plans that Saturday, and as Jane began running through the options, Tabitha made her own suggestion: "Y'all want to go bowling?"

I'd never been, and Jane was only marginally better than I was, but Tabitha was a pro, and she wiped the floor with us. Tempting though it was, I didn't remotely nudge the pins over when my ball fell into the gutter once again—yes, cheating was wrong, but there was also a birthday party two lanes over, a rowdy group of kids who didn't need to witness magic in action. Silently grumbling that the kids got to use bumpers, I lost handily, even though Tabitha took pains to help me with my form. Still, I enjoyed myself, and Tabitha seemed to have a blast. "You're getting the hang of it," she told me as we returned our shoes. "Come back some weekend, and I'll make a bowler out of you."

We parted company after that, Tabitha having promised herself that she'd try a new cake recipe that day, and Jane took me back to her place. "Connor should be off by three," she said as we headed up the mountain. "Y'all can hang out while I make dinner."

"I could help…"

"You're my guest," she said firmly. "And surely I can make fajitas from a box without burning down the kitchen."

My cousin arrived about an hour after we did, having stopped by his house first to change out of his uniform. "No more shifts this weekend," he told Jane once he'd dropped his duffel bag by the door and kissed her. "Barring Armageddon, of course."

"Naturally. You know, I think the guy handling your scheduling is going easy on you," she teased.

"He knows I'm still sore from Friday," Connor replied.

"Are you taking the pain potions this time?"

"Yes, ma'am."

She kissed him again. "Good boy. Want a beer?"

"Rain check. I was thinking that Maebe and I might go for a drive," he said.

I paused the program I'd been watching and glanced up inquisitively.

"You should at least *see* Whitford," he explained. "Not that there's much to it, and I know Jane's taken you around a bit, but—"

"Sounds good," I interrupted, but paused as I started to slip on my shoes. "Uh, unless Jane needs—"

"Go on, y'all," she insisted, pointing to the door. "Dinner's at sixish. Don't hit any deer."

Connor chuckled and pecked her cheek before ushering me outside. "You're so bossy, Firebug."

He was still smiling to himself as he buckled in, which pleased me. Whatever else might be said for my cousin, he had it *bad* for Jane.

He'd driven his personal SUV that afternoon instead of the Whitford PD Explorer, which suited me nicely, as his vehicle wasn't nearly as cluttered up front. I made myself comfortable and waited while Connor started down the road toward Ragged Gap, then asked, "So, what's on the driving tour of Whitford?"

"Not a heck of a lot," he replied, "so I thought we'd go for a spin around Ragged Gap first. Got plenty of light left," he added, glancing up at the sky through the tinted glass. "Daylight Saving shift tonight, so at least we won't have to rush to get you back before dark tomorrow."

"Huh?"

"Daylight Saving Time?" He looked my way, caught my bemusement, and muttered, "*Right.* Uh…around here, the clocks go forward an hour in the spring, then go back in the fall. Wartime feature that just hung around. I don't know if they switch in the Pactlands, but in any case, the sun won't go down tomorrow until seven forty-five or so."

I nodded, taking that in. Life at East Branch was never regulated by clocks—there were precious few in the community and even fewer that kept good time—so the notion of arbitrarily adjusting my schedule seemed odd. But my school *was* on a timetable, and I made a mental note to check with our dorm parents on Sunday night to be sure I wouldn't miss tutorials on Monday.

Connor made a decent tour guide, first covering some of the areas that I'd already visited with Jane, then taking me back through the pass between the valleys to Whitford. We drove around the tiny downtown and into Connor's neighborhood, and once I'd seen the highlights of that sleepy community, he took us by the county schools he'd attended, the church where he'd had Cub Scout meetings, the cracked parking lot where he and his friends had practiced bike tricks on summer evenings until the sun set. He drove me up into the mountains to a spot where he swore he'd heard a sasquatch call one night when he was a teenager, and though I wasn't altogether sure of what a sasquatch *was*, I took his word for it.

As we stretched our legs beside his SUV and I gratefully shoved my hands into the pockets of my jacket against the chill, I asked, "Could we go out to East Branch?"

Connor hesitated, then gave me a slow nod in reply. "Sure. If you want to see it, I'll take you, but, uh…it's not what you remember, mitta."

"That's okay. I…I'd like to know. All I've seen are those pictures from Ivari's trial, and…"

He waited until my voice faded, then said, "Better to know than to keep imagining, yeah? Come on, hop in. We've got time before sundown."

The ride back to Whitford was quiet, and as Connor drove toward the far northern end of the valley where the ruins of our family's community lay, my stomach knotted itself until I thought I might be carsick. I didn't *want* to see what was left of my home—I *needed* to know, to have that finality, but the heavens knew I didn't want to see what our murderous ancestor had done to the place. Somehow, I kept my lunch down, though I white-knuckled the door handle for the last mile or so.

Finally, Connor drove up to the place where East Branch had been and pulled onto the shoulder of the lonely road. "That's really fucking something, ain't it?" he murmured, letting the engine idle while I took in the destruction.

I recognized the shapes of the mountains that cupped around East Branch like a protective hand, and I knew the split rail fence that surrounded the property, but nothing else was familiar. We'd left the woods close to the fence largely untouched, giving the community a measure of privacy and encouraging the deer to wander in for easy hunting. Now, the only trace of the thick woods was a smattering of blackened stumps and skeletonized trees. The usual carpet of dead leaves, brown and decaying with the winter's punishing cold, had been replaced by ash and mud. Looking past the trees, tracing the narrow, rutted road with my eyes, I could see clearings where buildings had once stood—my cousins' homes, *my* home, the barns…

"I'll take you in if you want," said Connor, "but that's up to you. It's…sobering."

"I want to see it," I heard myself tell him, and blinked back tears.

He drove us up to the break in the fence, where someone had erected a new steel gate across the road. No Trespassing signs were posted every few feet along the fence, and the posts on either side of the gate had been topped with security cameras. As if sensing my questions before I could give voice to them, Connor explained, "We were getting way too many lookie-loos, even before the crime scene tape came down. I put up the cameras, and the sheriff's slapped a few explorers with trespassing charges, so that's died down somewhat, but East Branch is still a draw."

"What do they want?"

"Satisfy their curiosity. This place has been off-limits for so long, and now folks have a chance to poke around. I don't mind much if they just want to hike in and see, but it's vandals I worry about."

"Why?" I muttered. "What's even left to vandalize?"

"The cemetery," he replied immediately. "I don't want some asshole teenagers tagging tombstones or knocking them over. Don't want anyone taking *souvenirs*," he said with distaste. "Hang tight, I'll be right back."

The gate was held closed with a thick chain and a heavy-duty padlock, which opened with a key on Connor's ring. He pushed the gate back and drove us through, then locked up behind us before taking me on to see what remained of our community.

The lone road through East Branch had been a bumpy drive when I last traversed it, and the months of winter weather and outsiders' vehicles had done it no favors. Connor took it slowly, cursing under his breath as his SUV rocked over the uneven ground, then finally pulled to a stop near the place where the meeting house had been.

I recalled our trip out there the previous summer, sitting beside Connor with Jane and Diriem behind us and my frightened, armed kinfolk gathering around. My parents, my grandparents, the elders…

The meeting house was barely rubble. Someone had

pushed what remained of it into a pile at the edge of the clearing, but the much smaller piles of debris scattered around showed me where our homemade picnic tables had been. Behind us, back up the road, was the little clearing where my childhood cabin had stood, but without the trees and buildings to act as landmarks, everything seemed alien. Yes, I could orient myself with the mountains and try to superimpose my mental map of home on the wasteland, but that map was fuzzy around the edges. The only pictures in existence showing East Branch how it had once been were the set I'd taken on my phone's camera and given to DOL.

I climbed out of the vehicle and pulled my phone from my pocket.

"What're you doing?" Connor asked, joining me.

"Documenting." Slowly, carefully, I turned in a circle, taking pictures to capture as much as I could of the place that our community had considered its heart. The others had a right to know what had become of it.

Once I finished, Connor said, "Let's go for a walk."

I kept pace beside him in the fading afternoon light, picking my way down the ghost of the path that had once led through the fields to the cemetery. The fields themselves were fallow swaths of dirt marked with the treads of the outsiders' invading vehicles—perhaps a fire engine or the sheriff's SUVs—and though the first shoots of green were breaking through, I suspected they'd be nothing but weeds. East Branch had planted its final crops and brought in its last harvest.

The founders of East Branch—well, the quasi-human ones, the inhabitants who'd needed a cemetery on a regular basis—had built a low stone wall around ours, a plot pocked with hand-carved tombstones and brown with winter-dormant grass and weeds. Connor and I stepped over the wall and took a seat upon it, the better to survey the one part of East Branch that hadn't been wiped away by fire.

After a silent moment, I murmured, "What's going to happen to this place?"

Connor sighed. "Well...nothing today. I've got friends in the county government, and they know this is a weird case." He paused, gnawing on a hangnail. "I'm paying the property tax for now. The problem is that there's no clear owner of this land."

"What about our deed?" I asked, then groaned. The deed, like all other important documents, had been kept in the meeting house...and like the meeting house, it was surely no more than ashes.

But Connor surprised me. "The deed's on file, but no one's really paid attention to it in ages because the county's kind of avoided thinking about East Branch. Since there's no clear indicator of who would have inherited the property down the centuries, no one is quite sure who's inherited East Branch now."

"Why not you?"

He shrugged. "That's what they're going with temporarily. But the problem with keeping a community isolated from the rest of the county is that no one knows how many people were living out here. Twenty-five corpses and me, and I'm sure as hell not telling anyone that the rest of y'all have taken up residence in a freaking pocket world. I believe the plan right now is to wait and see if any claimants come forward saying they should own East Branch, and if no one appears, then they might let me keep it. Might not, though."

"Huh?"

Smirking as he glanced my way, my cousin said, "It's a big, undeveloped tract of land in tourist country, mitta. You could build a whole neighborhood out here. Property ain't cheap, and I know for a fact that a couple developers from out Blue Ridge way have been by, sniffing around." With a softer sigh, he said, "The taxes are massive now, and if the county rezones...I mean, I could probably take a chunk of the money I got from Ivari and keep it paid for a while, but—"

"No," I interrupted, gripping his wrist. "That's for your future, Connor. This…" I hesitated, gazing out at the graves, then murmured, "This is our past. If no one's going to live here, then it makes sense for someone else to put it to good use. I…I really can't imagine that we'd ever rebuild. What's here for us?"

"Not much. Still, feels like I'm letting everyone down to give it up—"

"You're not. You and your folks kept us together," I insisted. "We don't have a right to ask anything more of you there."

Silence descended between us again, and I listened as a hawk cried somewhere in the mountains.

"The good news," said Connor, "is that whatever happens to East Branch, the cemetery's going to be preserved."

"Yeah?"

He nodded. "Yep. There are little family cemeteries all over the region, and the county believes that ours should be protected, especially considering the age of some of the graves in here. That's in motion now, so at least that's one matter off my mind."

"Speaking of graves," I said quietly, "could you show me where my parents' are?"

"Sort of," he replied, and stood. "This way."

The cemetery had been used judiciously, filling from left to right over the generations. Just to the right of the last graves I remembered was a line of fresher graves, each marked with a small stone. To my surprise, the headstones were blank…but then Connor pointed to a larger monument at the end of the line, a piece clearly purchased outside the community and carried in. "Aside from little Joseph, there was no way to make a firm ID on any of the bodies," he explained. "Sheriff took up a collection to see that they were buried properly out here, caskets and all. Folks donated money for that," he added, nodding toward the monument.

I stepped closer to examine it and saw that it was carved over with the names of the dead and the date of the fire.

"Best I could do," said Connor.

"It's lovely," I said, picking out my parents', grandparents', and uncle's names in the stone. Unable to do more, I kissed my fingertips and pressed them to the letters, trying to ignore the echo of my mother's terrified scream in my memory.

As we stepped over the cemetery wall again, Connor pointed to a little metal plaque affixed at hip height:

EAST BRANCH

1749–2022

STRANGERS IN A STRANGE LAND

"I thought there should be some record that East Branch was here," he said. "Didn't quite know how to sum it all up…"

"You did good," I told him, and cocked my head toward his waiting SUV. "Want to get out of here before sunset?"

"If you're ready."

I stepped back and took a few more photos of the cemetery, then put my phone away and turned to go.

Connor didn't complain when I held his hand all the way back to his vehicle.

Having only had fajitas once before—and then in the Pactlands—I didn't have a solid idea of what they were meant to taste like, but the dinner Jane made was pretty good, if messy until I got the hang of rolling tortillas. The conversation was pleasant at first—Connor and I didn't discuss our trip to East Branch, and I kept my lips sealed about Mystic Mountains the night before—but then Jane and Connor shared a look I knew all too well, one I'd seen pass between my parents before they broached a difficult topic with me, and I braced myself.

"Mitta, I don't mean to put a damper on the weekend," Connor began, "but what're we going to do about Ainnet?"

My shoulders tightened, and I took a big bite of my fajita to stall for time.

"There's no shame in asking for help," Jane murmured. "Really."

"I'm okay," I mumbled around my food.

"Oh?" she countered. "She obviously has no problem with putting hands on you, hon, and right now, she's got your damn principal wrapped around her finger. Why are you being punished and not her?"

I glowered at my plate to avoid her gaze and swallowed.

"You're being bullied," said Connor. "Happened to me, too, and it didn't stop until I got big enough to beat the crap out of the ringleaders. We all got a week's detention, but they shut up after that because they knew I wouldn't sit there and take it."

"Yeah, well," I muttered, "when I fight back, I get in trouble, and Ainnet goes skipping off."

"Which is why it might be time to call in the bigger guns. Bullies don't stop because they see the error of their ways—they stop when they face actual consequences for their actions. So, why don't we give Teolm and Diriem a call, fill them in, and see if something can be done?"

With an exasperated huff, I said, "I'm a grown woman, and I can deal with this. I don't need to be running off to tattle at every little thing."

"Yes, you're grown," said Jane, "but you're not *that* grown, Maebe, and even adults call for backup on occasion. Hell, I can't tell you the number of times I've gone to my dad in a pinch."

"You're trying to be mature about this, and I'm proud

of you," Connor added, "but if you want help, just ask. I'm *pretty* sure the guys wouldn't mind having a word with your principal or the board of directors."

"I don't want to cause more problems—"

"Honey, you're not," said Jane. "But look, there's no need to harp on this tonight. Why don't you and Con go out back and have a drink while I clean up?"

Connor's brow furrowed. "No, you made dinner—I'll handle the mess."

She patted his hand. "Trust me, babe, you don't want to see the state of my skillet. Y'all scoot, out of my kitchen. Might want to grab a couple of blankets, eh?"

My cousin glanced at me and made a face. "Think we've been told."

A moment later, as I wrapped an afghan around my shoulders and settled into one of the chairs on Jane's back porch, Connor joined me with two bottles of beer. "Cheers," he said, passing me one.

I eyed him suspiciously as he pulled up the chair beside mine. "I'm not still underage?"

"Oh, you're *absolutely* underage, but considering the circumstances, I'm just going to look the other way tonight."

Having not had a beer in months—I was, unfortunately, also underage in Beukal—I sipped slowly, enjoying myself. We had brewed and distilled at East Branch, much to Connor's chagrin, and while the beer in my hand didn't taste quite like the homemade brew I'd been drinking on occasion since I was eleven, it was close enough to hit the spot. Connor and I sat quietly side by side, listening to the evening wind in the awakening trees and the quiet burbling of the creek at the foot of Jane's property...and then, through the thin glass door separating us from the house, I heard Jane singing to herself as she cleaned up the kitchen. I didn't know the song, and I suspected it'd have been unfamiliar even if it were in tune, but what Jane lacked in skill, she more than made up for it in enthusiasm.

My mother used to sing like that when she did

chores—not well, but happily enough—and I drank to loosen the sudden tightness in my throat.

Connor quietly laughed to himself. "She has no idea how loud she is out here."

"You've never told her?" I murmured.

"What, and make her self-conscious in her own home?" He waved the notion away with his bottle. "Janie only does that when she's in a good mood. I like it."

Nursing my beer, watching my cousin smile as he eavesdropped on his girlfriend's solo, I knew without question that he was well and truly smitten. "Hey," I said, poking him in the arm, "when are you going to marry Jane?"

That sobered him, and he grimaced slightly before taking a pull of his drink. "It's complicated."

"What's complicated about it? You love her, she loves you, and there's nothing illegal about your relationship."

"Finally," Connor muttered.

"Make up for lost time, then. I'm sure she'd marry you."

He didn't answer me right away, instead stalling with his beer, but then he put it aside and looked back at me. "Remember what I told you about sorcerers' lifespans? Janie could live to be three hundred."

"Yeah, so?"

"So," he continued in a low voice, "in fifty years, I'll be old and gray at best—maybe bald, maybe *dead*—and she won't even be middle-aged. The decent thing to do would be to break up with her."

"Connor," I replied, holding his stare, "you've heard her say she wants to be with you, right? I know I haven't been imagining that."

"Janie can say whatever she likes, but I love her too much to do that to her. She's got a long, hopefully healthy, happy life ahead of her. Might even make it onto the Forum someday, though she'd probably have to bite the bullet and use the Aniap name if she went that route. She's got the Aniap fortune, at any rate."

"You've got money, too."

"Half a million's nothing to sneeze at, but it doesn't touch Jane's inheritance. She's got an eight-figure bank account—and I didn't tell you that." Catching my surprise, Connor chuckled. "Don't let the old truck fool you. Janie lives fairly frugally, but she doesn't have to work another day in her life. The one nice thing her grandfather ever did for her," he added, and drank again. "But she's going to make something of herself, just watch. Descended from a Pact signatory, *talented* pyromancer, got a foot in the door at DOI...and hell, if it came down to it, I suspect Diriem would put in a good word for her, whatever she wanted to do. She doesn't need me dragging her down."

I finished the rest of my beer, listening as Jane continued her muffled one-woman concert, then stood and pulled my blanket around me.

"Going somewhere?" Connor asked.

"Getting a glass of tea or something," I replied, glancing down at him. "And just so you know, you're being an idiot. *Talk* to her," I said, and let myself back into the house before he could argue with me.

I awoke around dawn Sunday morning with a chill in my room, a rumbling in my stomach, and a stale taste in my mouth. The first was no problem, as I'd practically swaddled myself in the guest bed's linens, which smelled faintly of lavender. The other two were annoying, though, and when I pulled my phone toward me to turn on the flashlight, I was momentarily surprised to see how late it was before I recalled the weird time shift. Seven forty-five— later than my usual breakfast time, even if my body didn't quite believe the numbers on the screen.

A good first step would be to make coffee, I decided. I'd acquired something of a taste for it at North Lake, though I still went heavy on the sugar, and I'd learned to work the coffeemaker in our main common room. I thought I'd seen a similar one on Jane's kitchen counter, which suggested she had to be hiding coffee *somewhere*.

Lighting my way by phone, I flipped on the lamp over the sink and inspected Jane's machine, then started rummaging in the pantry. She did have coffee, a blue tub of grounds that smelled about right, and I found a filter for the basket and began measuring out grounds for a pot. Surely Jane wouldn't begrudge me a morning wake-up mug if I made enough for everyone.

As I started the brew cycle, I noticed sudden motion from the corner of my eye and turned, expecting to find Jane or Connor coming to investigate. Instead, to my surprise, I saw another couple in the glow of the lone yellow bulb: Annie and Wylan, neither of whom appeared to have slept or, more worryingly, masked. In the semidarkness, Annie could almost pass for human, a pretty woman about Jane's size with a dark brown ponytail, wearing a black fleece jacket over gray leggings. On closer inspection, however, her ears rose to points like a shorter, perkier version of my own, and her odd amber eyes glowed like a cat's when they caught the light. There was no need to look twice at her husband to knew he wasn't a local: Wylan was about six and a half feet of toned muscle, with shoulder-length brown hair, a scruffy beard, and eyes and ears like his wife's, but atop it all was a rack of antlers bigger than any of those once mounted in the East Branch meeting house. The points were sharp, and I had no doubt that Wylan could put them to good use if provoked. He sported a white lace-up shirt and close-cut leather pants—an odd look, certainly, but from what I'd seen of the Wild Hunt, his attire was fairly standard.

"Hey, y'all," I whispered, not bothering with Pactish. Annie was Virginian by birth, and Wylan had taken a language potion. "Want coffee? I just put it on—"

"*There* you are," said Annie with a relieved huff. "We checked Connor's house first, but no one was home."

"I came over for the weekend," I explained, frowning at them. "It's okay, I'm just hanging out here. Uh…are you looking for Connor?"

As if I'd summoned him, the other bedroom door opened, and my cousin, shirtless and groggy, poked his bed-mussed head around the corner. "Mitta…oh, hey," he said, his voice rumbly with sleep. "Sorry, are there brunch plans today? No one said anything…and, um, you've got a little something there," he said, pointing to the space above his head as he shot Wylan a look.

"We're not staying long," Wylan replied in his accented English. "And this isn't about brunch. There's been an incident at North Lake, and you two may not be safe," he said, cutting his eyes from Connor to me. "We need to get you back to the Pactlands *now*."

Connor squinted at him, apparently trying to process Wylan's announcement, then squeezed his eyes closed and muttered, "Goddamn it, not again. Is anyone dead?"

"Not that we know of yet," said Annie.

"What the hell happened?"

"Tell you once we're out of here. Get Jane up…and you might want a shirt while you're at it." Turning to me, she said, "Pack your stuff, kiddo. I'll handle the coffee."

CHAPTER 5

We were ready to go within ten minutes. While I shoved my clothes, toiletry bag, and new amethyst chunk into my suitcase, Jane hastily dressed, threw together a bag for herself, and filled Connor's duffel with pieces of clothing he'd left at her place. When the two of us emerged to find Annie waiting with travel mugs of coffee, Connor was in the den, still shirtless, running one hand through his hair in agitation while he lied to his second in command about a fake emergency. "Might be her appendix," I heard him say. "She's down in Atlanta, and she doesn't have anyone to help out, so I'm on my way."

Once he hung up, Jane asked, "What was that about?"

"My cousin Darlene," said Connor, already heading to the bedroom, presumably to find his clothes. "Who's been hospitalized and has a deployed husband."

I frowned. "Who the heck is *Darlene*?"

"A convenient fiction," Jane explained, and took a mug from Annie with murmured thanks. "Let me lock up," she told the newcomers. "Do I need to get my dad out of town?"

"Not that we've heard," said Wylan, as Annie shook her head. "You're not a target, but Connor and Maebe might be, and—"

"I'm going with them," Jane finished. "Is this coming from Diriem? Has he seen something?"

Annie grimaced. "He's involved, but this isn't farsight talking. Look, we'll explain everything once we're out of here. Hurry it up, Chief!" she called toward the bedrooms.

"Socks and shoes, let's go!"

Jane locked the doors, checked the stove, and flipped off all the lights. "Are we taking a vehicle?"

"We'll get you an agency ride if you need one," said Annie. "Don't worry about those...and here you go," she added, handing Connor the third travel mug as he appeared.

He wasn't exactly *dressed*, but he'd thrown on sneakers and added a T-shirt to his sweatpants, and he took his duffel bag from Jane. "Gun's packed in here," he said, then nodded curtly. "All right, let's move."

To my knowledge, there was no faster method of travel than going with the Hunt. For their more-or-less annual rides, they used flying horses, but their much more effective alternative was teleportation—blinking out of existence in one location and almost immediately appearing in another. Sure, it felt freaky, and it could leave one nauseated, but it beat a long car ride. More importantly, the only way to get to the Hunt's hidden enclave within the Pactlands was by teleportation, making the lodge a fantastic place to hide out.

While Annie hadn't been born a Huntsman, Wylan had made sure she had the same abilities as his many brothers, and she wasn't shy about employing her favorite trick. "Circle up," she instructed, and waited until the five of us were holding hands before she closed her eyes. "Everybody hang on..."

The world went dark around me as the floor fell away, but before I had time to yelp, gravity and daylight returned. I released Connor and Wylan and glanced around, expecting to see the Hunt's timber and stone lodge in the middle of the forest, but to my surprise, Annie had had a different destination in mind. Behind me, rising from an immaculate and prematurely verdant lawn, was the ti'Dana mansion.

"What are we doing here?" I asked, confused.

Connor scowled at the massive stone house. "And why

are we outside?"

"Because he turned the wards on," said Annie, heading for the front door.

"What wards?" my cousin pressed.

"Maybe they're not wards. I don't know all the nomenclature," she replied with a shrug. "But Diriem's got a set of protections on this place that can stop even us, and he warned us that it probably wouldn't feel great if we tried to teleport past them, so the polite route it is." With that, she bounded up to the door and rang the bell, then stepped back a couple paces and waited.

In short order, the door opened, and Scel, Diriem's house manager, nodded to Annie and slid aside. "Agent Humphries, nice to see you. You're expected."

"Good morning, Scel," she said. "You're overdressed for the hour, I think."

The sorcerer, a middle-aged man with short gray hair and a taste for simple but fastidiously neat robes, chuckled softly. "Begin as you intend to go on, dear girl. And good morning, sir," he said, nodding deeply as Wylan followed Annie into the foyer. "All's well?"

"At least nothing's on fire this time," Wylan replied. "*Yet.*"

Jane, following on Wylan's heels, slipped through the door. "Hi, Scel."

"Agent Fortune," he said with another nod, then beckoned for Connor and me to join them. "Lady ti'Ammaas, Lord ti'Catama—"

Connor wearily lifted a hand to stop him. "Way too early for that, Scel. Morning. Now," he said, turning to Annie and Wylan as Scel locked up, "would someone like to tell us what the hell is going on?"

"This way," a voice called from down a corridor, and Diriem, who'd opted for a cashmere sweater and khakis, the closest I ever saw him come to casual dress, motioned us closer.

We followed him deeper into the house, then into his

home office, and situated ourselves on the couch and chairs as he closed the door. I sized him up as he leaned against his desk: auburn ponytail slightly cockeyed, gray eyes deeply shadowed. It didn't take a farseer to deduce that DOI's director had passed a sleepless night.

"So, what's up?" said Connor, folding his arms and staring Diriem down. "Who's after us, and has anyone warned the school?"

"I wish it were that simple," he said. "And I'll be straight with you: your cousins are missing."

"*What*? Who?"

"All of them, even the young children. They're not the only ones to come up absent—"

"Whoa, hold it," Connor interrupted. "Back up. How the fuck did twenty people go missing?"

"We're working on that," said Diriem, which did little to calm my suddenly sick stomach. "But here's what we know right now. There was some sort of party yesterday at the school—"

"Lake Day," I mumbled.

"Precisely. You weren't interested?" he asked me.

"Ms. Mafatta said I couldn't go. Not important," I added before Diriem could pry. "What happened at the party?"

"Apparently, it devolved into chaos. The...*festivities* went on long into the night, especially for the older students, and quite a few of the day students ended up sleeping on campus. Couches, the floor, down by the lake...basically, no one was counting heads in beds. So, the two dorm parents assigned to your group reported that they checked around three this morning and realized no one had come in. They alerted security, the principal was called, and the cameras are being reviewed."

"And there's no sign of them?" asked Jane.

Diriem shook his head. "Not yet. Ganti's working on it, but this is a mess."

"You said other people are missing," I interjected.

"Who?"

"We're still trying to determine that, and part of it is waiting for North Lake to locate all of the students sleeping off last night in odd places, but the initial thought is that all of the missing are elves. Again, it's possible that they're not actually missing," he cautioned, "but as of this moment, there are some yet unaccounted for."

Connor propped his head in his hands and massaged his face. "Tell me no one's dead," he muttered.

"So far, so good," said Diriem. "Rose is working on it upstairs right now."

My spirits lifted at that, as Rose, uniquely among farseers, could see present events. "Has she found anyone?" I asked.

Diriem's expression sent my hopes crashing back down. "No. At first, she thought they were dead—she couldn't get a lock on them—but she says that what she sees when she tries to find them is subtly different. They're not dead, just blocked, and she doesn't think this is blinding potion at work."

"Wouldn't that block her, though?" asked Jane.

"Certainly, but she says the potion feels different— everything's white like she's in the middle of a blizzard. She sees only darkness now, but it's...*grayer*, she said. Frankly, I don't know what she's seeing, and now's not the time to worry about the nuances, but Rose is convinced that they're still alive."

As Diriem spoke, the answer hit me. "Those rings," I said. "Ivari's ring. You thought he and the others were dead, too."

"That's my fear. And since no one here knows how Ivari's rings are made..."

The conclusion was obvious: somehow, our New York kin had to be involved.

Before I could begin to mull over the possibilities, Connor said, "There's *one* person here who's familiar with them."

"Perhaps, but does he know how they're fabricated?" asked Diriem.

"Only one way to find out, right? Get Culta's ass in here. And, uh…" He paused, glancing down at himself, then asked, "Firebug, by any chance, did you pick up my clothes from yesterday when—"

"There's plenty in your bag, hon," Jane replied, patting his shoulder.

"Want us to grab him?" Wylan asked Diriem. "Do you have a location?"

"Not offhand," he said, "but thank you. I'll make a few calls. You know," he added, a glint in his tired eyes, "sometimes, a long ride works *wonders* before an interrogation."

About an hour later, after Connor had made himself slightly more presentable and the coffee had kicked in, the three of us sat at Diriem's dining room table, picking at the breakfast spread Ranarma had thrown together. Unlike his employer, Diriem's cook had caught a few hours of sleep, and he'd quickly whipped up a meal that put Jane's beloved Waffle House to shame. None of us was hungry, however, which was a pity—I'd never had a bad meal from Ranarma's kitchen—but he kept the coffee coming, strong and hot.

As I tore a piece of toast into strips, the doorbell rang. Jane stiffened, and Connor started to rise, but Diriem, who'd taken up a spot against the wall with his third espresso of the morning, motioned him back down. "He'll be brought to you," he murmured, and pulled out a chair halfway down the table. "Do you want backup?"

Connor pushed his plate aside. "You don't trust me with this?"

"On the contrary, but if you *want* support, I've conducted my share of interrogations."

He nodded. "Appreciated. Standby?"

"Your show, Chief."

Jane and I had offered to leave, but Connor wanted us to stick around. "He's probably going to be disoriented, maybe anxious or pissed off, and having y'all here will make it seem more like a friendly chat and less like the precursor to lockup," he'd explained. So, there we sat, breakfast forgotten, as the sound of heavy footsteps grew in volume.

When the door opened, I saw three figures in the hallway. On the left was a sorcerer in all black, an unsmiling man who looked like he spent every free moment in the gym. On the right was a troll, also in black, who stood a good eight feet tall and looked like he—or she, I couldn't be sure—could bench-press the sorcerer. Between them, sporting plaid flannel pajama pants and a white T-shirt with a logo in the middle of the chest, was a thin elf with mussed blond hair and nervous green eyes that fixed on Connor as he was shepherded into the room: Culta ti'Pul.

"Thank you, gentlemen," Diriem said to the troll and sorcerer. "Scel, if you could please show them to a more comfortable waiting area—"

"What the fuck is going on?" Culta demanded in rapid English, staring at Connor. Though he had an accent to my ear, Connor had said it was normal for New York. "What's with the G-men?"

"Sit down," Connor replied in kind, pointing to the chair across from him. "You want coffee?"

He groaned. "Shit. Yeah, man. I kind of overdid it last night…"

"We've all been there," said Connor, and slid him the silver coffeepot and a clean mug. "Sorry for the early wakeup."

Culta glared at him as he poured. "*Sure*, you are. What gives? I've done nothing. And where the hell are we? Benson and Stabler wouldn't tell me where we were going," he said, tilting his head backward toward the door through which the other men had disappeared.

"His place," Connor replied, thumbing one hand toward Diriem.

"Seriously? *Shit*," said Culta, impressed.

Diriem smirked over his espresso cup. "It's home."

"Beats the hell out of a studio apartment. And you two," he said, pointing to Jane and me as his eyes narrowed. "*You*, you're the one Father tried to stab in court, right?"

"I'm Maebe," I said, briefly lifting my mug.

"Mitha," he replied, slipping briefly into High Elvish, then turned to Jane. "You are…"

"Jane Fortune, DOI."

Culta eyed her uneasily but returned his attention to Connor. "What do you want? I suspect the Sunday-morning kidnapping wasn't just to get me out here for breakfast."

Connor sipped his coffee, giving Culta a moment to stew, then said, "We've got a situation. All of the East Branchers except Maebe and me are *missing*."

"Missing?" Culta echoed, raising a pale eyebrow.

"Yeah, and blocked from farsight. I know Ivari has a way of making that happen, so I'm going to need details, bub."

"Hold it," he said, raising his hands as if to stop Connor from lunging at him across the dishes. "You think Father's involved? How the hell would he manage that? He's still locked up, right?"

The eyes of the table turned to Diriem, who nodded. "Laws has already checked."

"And there's got to be someone else here who knows how to stop farseers," Culta continued. "Surely some of them like their privacy."

"Yeah, they've got a way," said Connor, "but it's not the same…uh…"

My cousin's gaze flicked toward Diriem, who recognized the request. "There's a potion we use," he explained, "but it's expensive to brew and infrequently used by those without official need—representatives, top agency staff, and so on. Part of the problem is that there's a spell that goes with it, and even if you do everything correctly, it's only good for about three months. The odds of someone bringing twenty doses of the blinding potion to North Lake with the appropriate personnel seem long."

"Fair," muttered Culta.

"And there's another wrinkle," Diriem continued. "People protected by blinding potion look different with farsight than those protected by your father's rings. To me, at least, his group appeared to be dead."

Culta winced. "Not to be a downer, then, but what makes you think the missing are still alive? Wouldn't that be the more logical option than trying to pin this on Father?"

"Perhaps, but there's a slight difference between dead and hidden. Almost a color variation. My great-granddaughter noticed it, but then she's an artist, so…" He shrugged. "More sensitive to such things, I suppose. For now, we assume they're alive."

"Which brings us back to your old man," said Connor, staring at Culta. "Now, I'm not saying Ivari necessarily did it—"

"I mean, aside from that pesky incarceration detail, it's not a bad guess," Culta muttered.

Connor snorted. "But even with him sidelined, don't you think it could be one of your crew? Ivari's not the only one of y'all we pissed off."

"You're right about that," he allowed, "but if you're looking for recent intel, I've got nada. The ones back in the City don't talk to me. Persona non grata, right here," he said, and sipped his coffee. "Ooh, this is smooth."

"I get that you're out of the loop, man," said Connor, "but what do you know about the rings? How do they work?"

He sighed and drank again. "Look, I've told you I'm a fuckup. I can work locks, right, but other than that, complicated magic isn't my forte. Now, I can build a PC from scratch and design a website, but if you want someone to teach you how to, like…forge magical rings, then I am *not* the elf you're looking for."

One corner of Connor's mouth twitched. "You mean to tell me that doesn't come with the territory?"

"Surprisingly, no," he replied, and rolled his eyes. "So, do I know the details of the rings? Absolutely not. All I know is that there's a spell on them that does the work— and it's a complex thing. Takes multiple people to pull off."

"Multiple elves, you mean, or is this the sort of thing that could be done by sorcerers?"

"Fuck if I know," said Culta, "but I've only ever seen it done by elves, so do with that what you will."

"How do you make them work?" asked Connor.

"Just put them on. Father insisted that we wear ours at all times," he added, then raised his naked hands and turned them back and forth. "Mine was taken from me when I was arrested, and I never got it back."

"Laws may still have it, then," Diriem murmured. "Ivari's as well."

"If you find it, let me know," said Culta. "More to the point, I don't recall us ever having a big stash of them around. Newborns would get them, and we had a spare or two in case someone's broke, but we weren't, like, mass producing rings."

Jane's brow knit. "How the heck do you keep a ring on a *newborn*?"

"Strung on a necklace, with a spell to keep it from choking the kid. Eventually, it'd be moved to a finger with another spell to make it stay on—and before you ask, they're adjustable. They grew with us."

Connor lifted his mug. "Convenient."

"Right? But also annoying as hell. I used to get in so much trouble if my parents caught me without mine, so, no lie, this still feels weird," Culta said, wiggling his fingers.

"But back to your problem. Unless folks have been busy, I don't think they'd have enough rings to force them onto all of your people."

"They *could* keep them on, though," said Connor.

"Mm-hmm. I mean, the spell's only effective until you're old enough to break it, but…"

Culta didn't need to finish that thought. Those of us from East Branch who weren't kids still lagged far behind in magic.

"Question," said Jane as Culta sipped again. "This spell that powers the rings, does it have to be attached to a ring to work?"

He frowned. "Come again?"

"Is the jewelry key to the spell's effectiveness, or, like, can it run on its own?"

"Uh…" He scowled to himself, contemplating as he drank his coffee. "I don't think it has to be attached to a *ring*, per se, but it's got to be connected to something. It's a sort of barrier spell, yeah? Ring goes around a finger, and okay, the barrier hides everything connected to that finger. You need an object of some sort to set the parameters, I think."

"What about a summoning circle?"

The look Culta shot her spoke of deep incredulity. "I don't know what kind of magic *you* were taught, but in my experience, drawing a pentagram and putting some candles around seldom helps."

"Not like *that*," she snapped. "What I'm asking is whether you could anchor that spell on a drawn circle. Put a bunch of people in the middle, cast the spell—"

"And hide them," he finished, then whistled softly. "I…don't know why that wouldn't work. If you could keep them in there. Shit," he muttered, clutching his mug.

"Assuming for the sake of argument that your dad arranged this," said Connor, "where would they be? If you had to hide twenty people."

"At least," Jane reminded him. "There might be more."

"Okay, twenty-plus," he amended. "Where would y'all put them?"

"Well…" Culta mused, "I mean, physically, they could all fit in our building in Manhattan. In light of recent events, however…"

"It's been burned?" asked Connor.

"I'd think so, yeah. That and the place in Minnesota. Since you guys know about them, I doubt we'd hide anything important in either location. But Father has other properties."

"Where?"

"And *that's* the question," said Culta, pointing finger guns at him across the table. "I know about Minnesota, but the rest? He didn't tell me *shit.*"

Connor looked back at him, his mouth tight. "Uh-huh. Got a bridge to sell me, too?"

"Honest. I'll swear by whatever you like," Culta insisted. "Get that sorcerer in here from Father's trial, the one who cast the truthfulness spell. *I don't know.*"

My cousin cut his eyes to Jane, then to me. I shrugged.

"So…what," Connor said to Culta, "your dad's got bug-out hideaways or something?"

"Close enough," he replied. "I'm no shrink, but it's pretty obvious that all of the old folks are messed up. You lose your home and your family, you're forced to go wandering…"

"You hook up with humans," Connor muttered.

"Yeah, all that jazz. It's left scars. I think the rationale for the additional properties was that we'd have safe places to run in case of emergency. Father may have told my siblings about more of them, but he's never had much use for me. Probably thinks I'd make a list and put it online or something," he added, and finished his coffee.

When no one rushed to fill the silence, Diriem slipped in. "If we retrieved your ring from Laws' custody, would you loan it to us?"

"Sure," said Culta. "I've got nothing to hide. And…"

He paused, then said, "I think we can agree that my father's a son of a bitch. If he's behind this and I can help you, I will."

"Appreciated." Diriem and Connor shared a long look, and when Connor asked no further questions, Diriem rose. "Would you accompany us back to Beukal? You'll need to sign for your property."

"Could do. Since I don't have my car and you people don't seem to have discovered Uber yet..."

"We'll give you a ride. Excuse me for a moment."

As Diriem stepped into the kitchen, I quickly followed him, and he turned and regarded me expectantly as I caught up, my decoy coffee mug in hand. "Something on your mind, Maebe?" he asked quietly.

I nodded and stepped closer so as to keep my voice down. "Did you see this coming?"

"Not enough. I've seen flashes," he said, "but nothing that made sense. A brawl in the dark, blood...a few glimpses of faces that I associate with your school. Hints, certainly, but I didn't get a sense of *this*." With a long exhalation, he leaned against the counter and folded his arms. "I've had a growing feeling of foreboding for a while. Perhaps this is the cause."

"What else could it be?"

His smile was grim. "Ah, youngling, you didn't think that we've kept the Pactlands intact for this long without threats, did you?"

"What kind of threats?" I asked. "Have folks outside—"

"No. Internal threats. But that's not a matter to concern you today," he said. "That's what DOI is for."

I hesitated before asking, "Have you seen anything about finding my family?"

"Not yet, and it's possible that I won't," said Diriem. "My sort of farsight can be difficult to work with when you're in the middle of unfolding events."

"Why?"

"Why?" he echoed. "Because what I see are probabilities, Maebe—possible outcomes. But those outcomes are influenced by the decisions being presently made, and…things get murky. I'll try," he assured me, "but in all honesty, I'll be of more use now getting us into the DOL property locker, so…" He reached into his pocket and extracted a cell phone. "Finish your breakfast, and let me make the arrangements."

Culta was less than pleased to learn that his ride back to the capital was the back seat of the black DOI vehicle that had brought him to Viratta, especially as the taciturn agents seemed no warmer toward him as they escorted him from the mansion.

"I suppose I could have taken a larger car," remarked Diriem as he pulled out of his massive garage, "but I thought we might want a moment to compare notes. Also, the Benz just handles nicely."

"You don't trust him, eh?" asked Jane from the front passenger seat. She'd brought her work computer back from Georgia with her and was charging it off a port in the console while she had the chance.

"Not wholly, but I don't get the sense at the moment that Culta is trying to deceive us. Connor, what does your gut say?"

"If we're going on vibes alone," replied my cousin, who'd taken the seat behind Jane for the added legroom, "then I think he's sincere. Rattled, conflicted, and hungover, but I don't get the feeling that he's lying…"

His voice faded as a phone rang, and Diriem tapped a button to take the call. "Rosie?"

"Hey," croaked Rose, her tone low and gravelly. Virginian like Annie, she'd slipped into her mother tongue. "Scel said you left?"

"Heading for Laws," he replied, following her linguistic choice—though, judging by the sound of Rose's voice, I wondered whether she could even process Pactish that morning. "Are you all right?"

"Taking a break, and…ooh, thanks, babe."

Diriem chuckled as we heard a slight slurp from the other end. "Yven's looking after you?"

"He is."

"Good. Have you seen anything?"

Rose sighed. "Zip. I went through every picture again, and they're all coming back the same: blocked but not dead."

"You're *sure* they're not dead?" Connor asked, leaning toward the front of the car.

"Oh, hey," she said. "When did you get here?"

"Annie and Wylan picked us up around eight," said Jane, answering for Connor. "And Maebe's here with us."

"Well, that's two of you safe," Rose muttered. "At least my farsight didn't lie about that. Y'all weren't attacked, were you?"

"No, no sign of trouble," Connor told her. "Didn't know what was wrong until we got here. But you're positive that they're not dead?" he pressed.

"Absolutely. I've seen what it's like to try to locate a dead person, and this ain't it. Bet you a million bucks. Unfortunately, they're all still blocked."

Connor nodded to himself. "Thanks for trying."

"Of course. I'm going to keep at it—"

"Take a break," Diriem interrupted. "Eat. You've been searching for hours, Rosie."

"I'm fine," she protested.

Diriem's hands tightened on the leather-wrapped steering wheel. "Please listen to experience, hmm? There's plenty of food left downstairs. Have a plate sent up, hydrate, take a nap. A *real* nap. Half an hour, minimum."

"Pop—"

"Please?"

"I don't see you babying Ganti," she retorted.

"Ganti has been working for me since 1850. He knows

his limits. You're still learning, girl."

"And you're not actually the boss of me, remember?"

"Rose Lea."

She groaned. "Fine, sheesh. I want updates," she said, and ended the call.

Jane smirked as we drove past Viratta proper. "Deploying the middle name?"

"When one must," said Diriem, reaching for his travel cup of coffee. "Perhaps her grandfather would have listened better had I given him one of those."

The Division of Laws wasn't a popular hangout that Sunday morning, and we had the lobby to ourselves—well, us and the green-skinned troll behind the reception desk, who answered to Little Fox and said something incomprehensible to Culta's troll escort when the DOI agents departed.

I didn't speak a word of Trollish, which wasn't unusual. Even those non-trolls who could understand the language seldom attempted to speak it, as the vocal cords of most other species simply weren't capable of mimicking the sounds required. Thus, the fact that the captain of North Lake's melee team and his clear successor were both trolls was a real boon to our team, as many of the opposing players had no clue what the two of them were shouting across the field.

The five of us had barely settled in on a bench when the door from the agency garage opened, and in strode the director. A gnome, Kabno Erenani stood barely more than three feet tall, but she moved with surprising speed, her footsteps striking the marble floor in a rapid staccato. Up close, she seemed better rested than Diriem was, but she'd skipped out on formal attire in favor of jeans and a lilac twinset, and she'd pulled her white hair back into a simple braid.

"Any change?" she called to us by way of greeting.

"Nothing from Rose," Diriem replied, "and I've yet to

hear an update from Ganti. You?"

"We finally secured the camera footage from the school. My people are delivering it to your shop for review, unless you'd rather us take the first look."

"Thank you, but that's unnecessary. We've got analysts standing by."

"Good." Sizing up the rest of us, she said, "No word from any of your kinfolk, I trust."

"None," said Connor, and I shook my head. "We're here about—"

"Mr. ti'Pul's ring," Kabno finished, and looked up at Culta. "I do apologize. All legal property is meant to be returned once detention ends. Let's go get it, eh?"

We followed her into an elevator, and after scanning her badge, she pushed the button for the third floor. "Truly, I'm sorry about this," she said to Culta. "I wish you'd mentioned it sooner. Oversights happen, but that doesn't mean they shouldn't be corrected in a timely fashion."

"It's no big deal," he replied in his oddly accented Pactish. "With all the string-pulling and such last fall, I didn't want to cause a fuss."

"Really, we wouldn't have kicked you out for requesting your jewelry back."

"Better safe than sorry," he said. "Anyway, I haven't been hurting for it. If you people have been spying," he added, glancing at Diriem, "I've been pretty boring of late."

"I know of no reason why anyone should be looking in on you," Diriem told him as the elevator stopped and chimed.

"Really? You aren't concerned?"

Following Kabno out, Diriem said, "There's not much damage you can do in a vocational program, is there?"

"You know about—"

"I know you're being trained to work with our computers, and I'm aware that the calls you've made and received from outside the Pactlands are harmless." Looking over his shoulder at Culta, he said, "But we're not *spying* on you."

"By whose definition?" Culta muttered under his breath.

Kabno led us onward at a brisk pace, then scanned us through two sets of locked doors and into a white-walled conference room. "Have a seat," she offered, gesturing toward the wooden table and the variety of chairs and mats arrayed around it. "I'll be back momentarily."

She scanned open a door at the rear of the room, revealing a glimpse of long metal storage racks beyond it before she slipped through and firmly shut it behind her.

"Question," Culta murmured. "What if my ring's on the top shelf?"

"That's a very dangerous question to ask a gnome, particularly *that* gnome," said Diriem, taking a chair. "A word of advice: don't offer help unless they request it."

Jane's mouth quirked. "Speaking from experience?"

He grunted, which was as good an admission as anything.

About ten minutes later, Kabno returned, but instead of the ring, she carried a printed piece of paper. "Problem," she said, standing on a chair, and slapped the paper onto the table. "It's missing."

"Are you sure?" Culta asked. "If you want another set of eyes—"

"Thank you, but we don't allow civilians into the property locker. It was logged with the rest of your belongings," she told him, "and I checked the drawer and all of its neighbors. No sign of it, and no mention of it on the return receipt." Spreading her hands, she said, "I'm afraid I don't have answers for you today. I can have the security footage reviewed to see who took your belongings from the holding cells up to the locker, but the only camera on the locker itself is right there," she said, pointing to the one mounted on the wall near the door.

"Who has access?" Connor asked.

"Quite a few agents. I'd need to borrow a farseer to do a proper search."

"That can be arranged," said Diriem, "but—"

"Not today, of course," Kabno finished.

"What about Ivari's ring?" he asked. "Surely he wasn't allowed to take that to the farm with him."

"No, no, that was logged as well," she replied, her thin lips tight, "but guess what's missing from his drawer?"

"Sounds like someone here has sticky fingers," Connor remarked.

The director frowned. "Sticky...*oh*. I see. It wouldn't be the first time. Items occasionally go missing in any agency of sufficient size, but we haven't had an active thief in quite some time. Unless there's something I should be aware of?" she said, turning to Diriem.

His expression remained neutral. "I don't know the identity of the person or persons who currently have custody of the rings. However, I also don't believe that Laws has identified all of the agents on Silver's payroll."

"Oh?"

"Most, but not all. Perhaps someone recognized the potential in those rings and had them removed."

With a little huff, she took a seat on the table and crossed her arms like the world's most dangerous petulant toddler. "All right, let's assume Inade's behind this. How would he know the value of the rings?"

"I'm not sure," said Diriem. "Culta, when did your father first make those rings?"

The best Culta could offer in reply was a shrug. "Way before my time, but we've never discussed it."

"I see. Then it's possible that he developed the spell long enough before the Pact that someone like Inade could have learned of it. I don't *know* that," he stressed, holding Kabno's stare, "but it's a possibility worth considering."

"I'll have Inade's communications checked," she replied, "but he's smart enough not to use direct channels.

Old boy's a criminal, not an idiot. In the meantime, any hints as to who my moles might be?"

"Not offhand. Sorry," he said, and rose. "Well, I'm afraid this trip was for nought. Kabno, how's your afternoon looking?"

"Unscheduled as of yet. Are we meeting?"

Diriem glanced at his watch. "Let's say four at DOI. Give my people time to look at the footage from North Lake."

"I'll be there," she said, and slid off the table. "Let me escort you out."

We were halfway to the elevators when Culta said, "Hey, just wondering, but is someone going to take me home?"

The directors traded glances, and Kabno said, "Sure, I can give you a lift."

Down in the garage, as the four of us walked toward Diriem's sedan, Kabno led Culta toward a large SUV. "This is me," she said, then pushed a button on her key fob. The driver's door opened, and a little stepladder folded down to give her access to the seat. "Climb in, boy, don't be shy."

I hadn't quite buckled in before Kabno's vehicle went zooming toward the exit, and Diriem shook his head. "A tip," he said, starting the engine. "Don't ride with Kabno if you can avoid it. She's a good driver, just...*aggressive*."

Feeling almost sorry for my distant cousin, I leaned back and looked out the window, willing the knot of sick fear in my stomach to loosen.

CHAPTER 6

Despite the fact that the DOI building had no windows, the conference room on the tenth floor boasted excellent views of downtown Beukal and District 2. Glass apparently being a security risk, the agency opted to procure their daylight through magical means…which I supposed had to stop seeming bizarre at some point. Diriem certainly gave the nonexistent windows no thought other than to comment on a wreck in an intersection down below, and Jane, who worked and slept in the building, joined him only long enough to make a face at the scene on the ground. "*Someone's* getting a new car," she muttered, then took a seat at the long table.

Kabno arrived a few minutes before four, completing our group: Diriem, Jane, Connor, and me, Rose and Yven, Ganti, and a pair of analysts I'd never met. The analysts, a male faun and a gray-skinned metal nymph whose gender I couldn't begin to guess, sat beside Ganti with their computers open. Unlike the rest of us, they'd thrown on formal robes for the occasion.

Ganti, to be charitable, looked like shit. The lead past-oriented farseer's blond hair hung loose over his shoulders, and he'd probably gone a bit too long without a shower. He wore ratty jeans and a wash-faded DOI T-shirt that might once have been black, and he stared blearily at the room through bloodshot hazel eyes.

Rose, who'd also been pushing herself for hours, appeared to be in only slightly better shape, and I suspected much of that was due to Yven, who'd been feeding her and making her tea all day long. Though both Yven and Rose worked for the Division of Plants and Potions, Diriem had already called their director and made their excuses for Monday…but on that count, it probably didn't hurt that DPP's head was Rose's great-great-uncle and cognizant of the many reasons the agency's lone farseer might need to be loaned out.

As for Jane, Connor, and me, we'd been fairly useless, bored but restless in the mansion. Jane had convinced Annie to come over and take her home to pick up her truck, but she and Diriem both insisted that Connor and I stay put. "You're safe here," said Annie, who'd emphatically concurred when she came to get Jane. "This place is a fortress right now. Even if someone out there is running a blood trace on y'all, they won't be able to get past the door without approval."

Annie's mention of a trace only fueled my desire to take the bloodline potion again. That would be the simplest way to find our family: I could down it and endure a few hellish minutes while the team running the spell zeroed in on any bright dots on the map projection, and then a retrieval group could go outside and snatch them. Easy enough when described like that. I'd survived two rounds of the potion, and I knew what I was signing up for if I swigged it a third time. But there was a wrinkle now, my healing heart. The bloodline potion didn't just put the drinker through incredible pain—it also caused internal damage, often targeting the heart, or so the healers in my life had told me. As I had yet to be cleared to play school sports, I suspected that the healers would jump up and down if I tried to take the potion once more.

In the meantime, I hoped that Ganti would bring us good news.

Diriem locked the door behind Kabno and pulled out the chair at the head of the table. "Thank you for coming," he said, reaching for his travel mug. I didn't want to think about how much coffee he'd consumed that day. "Ganti, what do you have?"

The agent straightened in his seat but clutched his own mug like a teddy bear. "The East Branch group are currently shielded...yes? That's unchanged?"

Rose nodded wearily and rubbed her forehead.

"But they were unshielded last night," he continued, "so I've spent the last hours tracking their movements on Saturday. Here's what happened...uh, Dienk?"

The faun made a few clicks, and a projection appeared, hovering in the middle of the table. The image was one I recognized, a picture of our main common room in the dorm.

"Here are the East Branch missing," said Ganti. Another click from Dienk produced a list of my cousins' names rendered phonetically into Pactish characters. "Yesterday, the school threw a campus-wide party. Everyone from the East Branch group attended except Maebe," he said, pointing across the table at me. "Age-wise, we're talking mid-thirties down to toddlers. So, here's how they split up."

Dienk switched the view to an aerial map of campus. Groups of green and orange dots broke off from the main building to various locations around the grounds, moving in and out as the time at the bottom of the projection advanced. "Nothing unusual happened until after sundown," Ganti said. "From what I saw, they were having a fine time. Some of the parents brought the younglings back inside for an afternoon nap, but everyone was out of the dorm by dinner."

When Dienk clicked again, a selection of photographs appeared—pictures of my cousins in little groups, many taken outside. "These are from the school security footage," he explained. "We tried to find pictures that matched what Ganti was seeing."

Ganti waited until the full set had appeared, then said, "Dinner was announced at six, very close to sunset. Everyone moved to this pavilion structure by the lake shore."

I knew what he was talking about even before Dienk popped up a new group of photos. The pavilion was a wooden-framed picnic area large enough to accommodate the entire school. On the nights it was used, it was illuminated by strands of colorful lightbulbs that crisscrossed the rafters like a glowing spiderweb. A prep kitchen occupied the end farthest from the main building, complete with deep sinks, a trio of ovens, and a grill wide enough to hold a wild boar. Judging by the pictures, the grill was mostly serving vegetables, bean patties, and soy skewers that night, but that was pretty common for school fare.

"The problem really started at dinner," said Ganti. "There was alcohol provided for the older students during the afternoon, but most didn't begin drinking in earnest until nightfall."

"So…you're telling us that they got wasted?" Connor interjected.

Ganti frowned. "Wasted…"

"Drunk," Diriem murmured in Low Elvish.

"*Oh.* Not really. Lubricated, sure, but they weren't staggering. No, the issue came from *this* group."

As Dienk switched the pictures, I groaned.

"Friends of yours?" Ganti asked.

"Ha," I muttered. "That's Ainnet ti'Har in the middle, the blonde. The girls around her are her clique."

"And him?"

My shoulders tensed as another picture appeared. "Eddic ti'Dir. I don't know if he's in a relationship with Ainnet or just her friend, but they're close."

"Whatever they are to each other, they don't hold their drink well," the other analyst said quietly, and Dienk snickered.

Ganti nodded and paused for coffee. "Near the end of the meal, when most of the students had wandered off, the East Branch group remained at one table, and those seven were at another. Ainnet and Eddic began making loud enquiries as to where you might be," he said, looking at me.

"Laughing about it, being obnoxious. Eventually, one of your kinfolk had enough and confronted them."

"Who?" Connor asked.

He consulted his notes. "Kyle?"

"That's my uncle," I told Ganti. "My mom's brother."

"Ah. Well, he got up in their faces. Asked them what their problem was, why they picked on you, what the East Branch group had done to them."

I couldn't help but be touched that Uncle Kyle had stuck up for me.

"Ainnet started arguing back at him," Ganti continued, "and then some other East Branchers joined in. Then Ainnet's group piled on, plus some of Eddic's friends. I didn't catch all of their names," he said, "but the group was heavy on elves, and I could pick them out of school photos if someone could show me."

"We'll get a set from North Lake," Diriem told him.

"Great. So, uh…" He paused, frowning, and sipped his coffee again as he focused. "Right, the fight. Started as yelling and turned physical. Both groups left the pavilion and went down to the lake. There was a movie being shown on a big portable screen on the main part of the lawn, but they moved off to a quiet corner, and that's when the brawl began."

"Oh, no," Connor muttered.

"It wasn't as bad as you might think. Remember, Ainnet, Eddic, and their friends had been drinking *quite* a bit, and so they weren't nearly as proficient with magical attacks as they should have been. It started with Eddic—he tried to punch Kyle and missed, and Kyle…" He grimaced. "One thing I can say for East Branchers is that your self-defense skills are excellent. If I had to choose a winning side, it would be yours."

"You don't know who won?" I asked.

"The simple answer to that is 'neither,' but let me explain. Dienk?"

The analyst changed the view to an overhead picture of

an isolated part of the school grounds. I recognized the place, a spot where students could and did get up to all sorts of mischief. It was on the edge of the property, tucked back where the lake shore curved, and the boundary line was demarcated with a stone wall about five feet high. Other than a security light on a pole about twenty feet from the wall, the area was dark—perfect for folks who needed a smoke, a nip, or a little private time with a partner.

"The fighters were there," said Ganti as a cluster of dots appeared near the wall, "and the noncombatants stood back—some of Ainnet's friends, a few of the East Branch women, the little children." Another set of dots appeared to mark the spectators. "Considering the number of people I've observed today, I have a fairly good idea of how the fight went, but our photos aren't great. There was a fog drifting in from the lake, and since there's only one light, things were dark and chaotic. And then the knock-out potion hit."

"Huh?" said Connor.

Ganti looked to the nymph. "Nim?"

Before the analyst could speak, Kabno pointed down the table. "Detective Gemellu, yes? I remember you. It's been an age."

The nymph smiled. "Indeed, Director, and I've not been a detective in some time. Had my centennial here last month."

"*Truly*? Has it been that long? You've settled in, I take in."

Nim—who was male, judging by his surname, a quirk of nymphic naming that was often one's only clue as to a nymph's gender—nodded. "My spouse is much happier since I left DOL. I haven't been stabbed in…gosh, decades."

"There is that," she allowed. "I'm sorry, please continue."

He nodded and turned to Connor. "Knock-out potion.

Here, it's generally used for riot control."

My cousin's eyebrows rose. "Are those...common?"

"No, fortunately, but it's nice to have a weapon in the arsenal. The last time I recall having to deploy it was after a melee championship—the victors' fans became drunk and destructive."

"We take it outside as well," Yven offered, and Connor looked his way. "In case of emergency, if humans see something they're not meant to...hit with the knock-out first, then go in with a memory potion if needed."

"You've used it, huh?" said Connor.

"Only once, and that was on Annie and her friends."

"It was necessary," Rose insisted, rubbing her temples. "They had wings and antlers and corpses."

"We carry it in vials that are designed to be thrown and break on impact," said Nim. "It's an orange-colored potion, and when it hits the air, it quickly vaporizes into a mist of the same color. Ordinarily, this isn't a problem..."

"But add in fog, a single light, and some subpar cameras," said Dienk, "and you've got a mess."

"Make that *camera*, singular," Nim muttered. "Only one angle on the fight. But when we slowed the footage and enhanced it, we could see bottles fly, and then the fog definitely turned orange. Students started collapsing."

"And that's the point at which I lost my view," Ganti cut in. "Almost all of them went down—fighters, bystanders, the little ones. A very few who'd been watching from the far edge were able to flee before the potion reached them, but they just went back to the pavilion and hid until they sobered up and realized they should have alerted the faculty. But I didn't see anyone die," he stressed. "That feels very different. They're hidden now, but unless they've been killed in the time since I was blocked..."

"I'm still not getting any coming up as dead," said Rose. "Just..."

"Frustrating, isn't it?"

She grunted in agreement, and her fiancé nudged a

glass of water closer to her.

"With Ganti out, all that's left is the camera," said Nim, picking up the thread. "Dienk and I did what we could, but the footage would be of low quality on a clear day at noon. However, we're fairly confident that the potions were thrown from the far side of the rocks. Dienk, would you…"

He changed the projection, and a video began to play—grainy and silent, the scene half obscured by mist. Suddenly, a plume of orange began to rise from the ground, and the people closest to it tumbled to the grass. "Let's slow it down," he said, and reversed the footage. "All right, they're fighting, and then here, from the left— see it?" A red circle appeared around a small shape I'd overlooked, then followed it as it arced down toward the brawl. "We surmise that whoever threw that and the other bottles was hiding behind the wall. Unfortunately, the picture gets worse from here. They used a *lot* of knock-out."

Dienk pulled up another video, one showing the scene after all of the potion had been thrown. The view was of little more than an orange cloud, but if I squinted, I could see shapes moving within it. He froze the video, and then red circles appeared around the ambulatory bodies. "These are our culprits, or at least some of them. We don't have a solid count. They moved in once the potions were working, then extracted most of the fighters. Gone long before the potion dispersed."

"Interesting," said Kabno. "They'd taken the antidote, clearly. Any guesses as to species?"

The analysts shared a quick glance. "Nothing firm," said Nim. "Bipedal, almost certainly not trolls or gnomes, probably not fauns, but that's not much to work with, especially if they were masked."

"But if I were to wager, I'd say elves," his partner added.

"And why is that?" asked Diriem.

"Two reasons, sir. One," said Dienk, holding up a

stubby finger, "if you watch the kidnapping closely, the students float out of the area. That suggests an elf or a sorcerer at work."

"Or an air nymph," I said.

He shook his head, then tucked a wayward curl back behind one horn. "Not a bad guess, youngling, but for an air nymph, we'd expect to see the potion cloud or the fog moving with the wind generated. There's none of that. Now, once the potion *does* move away, you'll see my second reason…"

The video sped forward, and when the worst of the obscuring orange blanket had disappeared, I could make out a few shapes lying by the wall, unconscious.

"The kidnappers were fairly thorough, but they didn't take everyone," said Dienk. "Male, female, almost adults, practically babies, but all the victims had one thing in common: they were elves."

"Or partly elven," Nim added.

"Right. We cross-checked the video with Ganti to see whether we could figure out who was missing. All of the East Branch group is gone, but so are a good number of their opponents—that Eddic boy and some of his friends, Ainnet and some of hers. The ones left behind…well, it's difficult to make out, but if we advance the video to morning…"

When dawn broke, the people on the ground still hadn't budged, but I could recognize them in the strengthening light. Half of Ainnet's friend group was there, the sorcerer and two nymphs who laughed at her jokes and egged her on. I didn't know Eddic's friends, but the closest guy to the camera was clearly a faun.

"So," said Connor, studying the image, "what's the plan?"

"Plan?" Nim echoed.

"My family and some of their asshole classmates have been abducted. How do we get them back?"

The table fell uncomfortably quiet for a moment, and

then Ganti sighed. "Farsight's useless while they're blocked, or at least Rose and I are of no help. I can't speak for the boss…"

"It's muddled at best," Diriem murmured.

"Which means we'll need alternative methods," he continued. "Go out to the school, see what can be found. Interview people. Look for forensic evidence."

"The good news is that they're not dead," said Kabno as Connor scowled at Ganti. "If the kidnappers wanted them dead, they'd have killed them at North Lake once they were incapacitated. Because they took them instead, that tells me they want something."

"Ransom," said Connor.

"Exactly. I'll send a team to the school, but our best bet may be to wait for a ransom note. Those tend to come quickly, in my experience—"

"Give me the bloodline potion."

The others turned to me, and Jane vehemently shook her head. "Absolutely not," she snapped. "That shit would kill you."

"She's right," said Diriem. "You're not strong enough for a third round, Maebe."

"Which is why it's my turn," Connor announced. Before Jane could object, he said, "I've got the same bloodline Maebe does. We can find them that way."

Kabno's brow furrowed as she considered his proposal. "Are you healthy?"

"Far as I know," he replied. "No problems at my last physical."

"Which was when? More importantly, *where*? I mean no insult," she quickly added, "but how thorough of an examination were you given?"

My cousin shrugged. "The usual. Blood pressure, cholesterol, diabetes screening, urinalysis…I was getting over a twisted knee, but that's all."

"You've never been examined here?"

"Uh…no, ma'am. Her cousin did my genetic workup,"

he said, thumbing one hand toward Jane, "but no more than that."

Kabno looked at Diriem, who hesitated before speaking. "Considering what's been learned about the East Branch population—"

"I'm *fine*," Connor insisted. "Unless cifyent's worse than a cosmetic issue."

"Not that. The research healers working with your cousins have found problems in nearly all of them, some minor, some concerning. Before you take the bloodline potion, you need to be checked out."

"I—"

"Please?" Jane murmured, gripping his arm. "Just to be safe?"

Though he seemed poised to argue, Connor folded under Jane's stare. "Fine," he muttered. "But let's make it quick. The sooner I'm cleared, the sooner we find them."

She turned to Kabno. "Canna?"

"Works for me," the director replied. "Shall I call her in?"

"Nah," said Jane, pulling out her phone. "She likes me. I'll be the bad guy."

"It's not that I don't enjoy coming to the office on Sunday evenings," said Canna, stepping off the elevator onto the twentieth-floor medical unit of the DOL tower. "Weird cases can be fun. But now Pars is home alone with the kids, trying to simultaneously finish dinner and keep the twins from killing themselves, and he's less than enthusiastic about this change in plans."

"What's his poison?" Connor asked.

She glanced back and grinned. "He's not picky, but if you could get your hands on a bottle of Yacovi's better hooch, I think we'd all be back on his good side."

Jane chuckled. "Consider it done. And tell you what, if you get home after this and Pars has burned dinner, I'll spring for pizza."

That, at least, was one dish that had crossed the border into the Pactlands and taken root. Personally, I preferred the pizza back in Georgia, but I was amenable to just about anything topped with tomato sauce and cheese, and the local offerings did the trick.

Canna smirked at her. "Ah, yes, that healthiest of meals."

"Put some veggies on a slice and call it a night. Come on, they're kids."

"Pushing for 'favorite cousin' status, are we?"

"Making up for lost time," Jane replied, and followed Canna into an examination room.

Once the four of us were inside, Canna reached into a drawer and produced a green paper gown, which she passed to Connor. "Take everything off and put that on. Let me get this heating for you," she said, reaching around him to tap a button by the patient table, "so that'll be a bit more comfortable."

Clutching the gown to his chest, Connor frowned as Canna made her preparations. "So, uh…just how invasive is this going to be, anyway?"

"*Men*," she replied with huffed laughter. "Not particularly, at least not in terms of my putting hands on you. The gown is so that nothing interferes with the spell."

"Come again?"

"I can do a physical the old-fashioned way in many situations, but since we need to check your organs and do so quickly, I'm going to use a visualization spell. It won't hurt," she assured him. "You change clothes and lie on the bed, and I'll start the spell, which will give me an internal look…right *here*," she said, pulling a white screen down from its holder on the wall. "With any luck, we'll have you out of here in half an hour. Of course, if your plan is to then take the bloodline potion, I wouldn't call that good luck," she added with a shudder.

The three of us stepped into the hall for a moment,

giving Connor privacy to change, then returned to find him awkwardly stretched out on the table, clutching his gown closed where it wrapped in the front. I snickered, and he used his free hand to flip me off before Canna approached with a thin blanket. "Here, this should help," she said, spreading it over him. "Now, just try to be still, all right?"

She muttered under her breath, and a bright light flashed over Connor, first spreading to encompass his entire body, then narrowing to a white spot the size of a dinner plate. "We're up," she said, and whispered toward the screen.

"*Ew*," I said, retreating from the sudden picture of churning viscera.

"Probably should have warned you," said Canna. "This is the live view. Let's see, that's a little deep, let's get it higher...okay, abdominal wall. Keep breathing normally, Connor," she said, glancing toward the patient. "No need to hold your breath."

Not five minutes into her exam, Canna found a problem. "You've never been to a cardiologist, have you?" she asked my cousin.

"Uh...no. Never had any issues."

"That's good, but you should know that you have two malformed valves."

"Seriously?" he asked, starting to sit up.

"*Hey*, freeze, back on the table," Canna ordered. "Be still while I'm working."

He mumbled an apology and flattened. "What does this mean?"

"One minute." She stepped closer to the screen and peered at the image—Connor's heart, I imagined, though the picture meant little to me. "If they're not causing you trouble right now, that's fine. They're functional, just imperfect, and you're fit. But the bloodline potion is notorious for causing heart damage, and I'm concerned that if you take it, you're going to be looking at a real issue. With everything else going on, I suspect you don't want to deal with heart surgery as well."

"Can't I do what Maebe's doing? Lots of potions and rest?"

"I...suppose," Canna reluctantly allowed, "*if* the damage isn't too severe. There's no way of knowing ahead of time how badly you'll be injured. But put that aside for now," she said, and slowly moved the image toward his head. "Let's finish this, and then we'll go over your options and my recommendations."

I leaned against the cabinets, watching the weird view of my cousin's organs change while Canna inspected them, then cut my eyes to Jane and whispered, "Didn't think you'd ever see this side of him, huh?"

"Definitely not what I was expecting," she whispered back.

We hadn't been quiet enough, however, as Connor muttered, "I think it's only fair that I get to come to your next physical, Firebug."

"Trust me, hon, this is nothing you want to see—"

"Hold it," Canna interrupted, her voice tense. "Connor, don't move. Stop talking."

He did as she asked, and Canna zoomed in on a part of his brain. "Something wrong?" Jane asked.

"Don't move," Canna repeated, tapping Connor's covered foot. "I'll be right back."

Once she'd hurried out of the room, Connor slipped into English. "Think she'll get mad at me if I breathe?"

"Behave, you," said Jane.

"What's on the screen? My evil parasitic twin?"

She stepped closer and briefly studied the image. "It's your brain, but I can't give you more than that."

"So, you're saying I do have a brain, then."

"I know! Wonders never cease."

Staring up at the ceiling, he grinned, and Jane carefully bent to kiss his forehead. "In all seriousness," she said, "if you've got two bad heart valves, you don't need to be taking that potion."

"What better option do we have?" he retorted. "Maebe can't."

"What about Culta? Surely all of y'all have a connection to ti'Ammaas or ti'Pul."

"That…might work," Connor allowed, "*if* he were willing. He watched Ivari take it—he might not be game, especially once he gets the full warning spiel."

Before Jane could answer that, Canna returned at a jog, a gray-skinned troll in a purple healer's coat right behind her. "Everyone, this is Shallow Rapids," she said. "Jane, back up."

Jane did as instructed while the two healers turned to the screen. "Am I seeing things?" Canna murmured.

Shallow Rapids, who had to stoop slightly to get a good view, spotted the problem Canna had seen and muttered, "*Heavens.* No, your eyes are fine. That thing's ready to blow."

Connor started to sit up again. "What thing—"

"*No!*" the healers shouted in unison, and he froze.

"What's going on?" asked Jane as Connor lay down again.

Her cousin pointed to a spot on the screen. "That's a cerebral aneurysm. A *massive* one."

"What?" Connor demanded.

"It's operable," said Shallow Rapids, "but if it ruptures on its own…"

"Likely fatal," Canna finished. "So, don't you move a muscle, Willow," she ordered. "I'm going to call the hospital and get you in for emergency surgery."

"I'll organize the transport," her colleague offered, and left the room.

"Why do I need surgery?" Connor protested. "I feel fine! I don't have a headache or anything—"

"The scan doesn't lie," Canna interrupted, "and we need to fix this immediately."

"What if we wait until after I take the bloodline potion

and do that and my heart at once?"

She looked at him like he was speaking gibberish. "Do you understand what's going on?" she said slowly. "There is a blood vessel in your brain showing a large ballooning pocket. If it ruptures—*when* it ruptures—you'll have an instant brain bleed, and given the size of this thing, it will probably kill you. There will be no bloodline potion in your immediate future. Understood?"

Connor didn't lift his head, but his eyes sought Jane, and she returned to his side to grip his hand. "It's going to be okay, Con," she murmured. "I'll stay with you."

"That's a good idea," said Canna, who'd begun rummaging through the cabinets. She produced a small bottle and a syringe, then drew up the contents of the potion. "This is a sedative," she told Connor. "Mild, but it'll keep your heart from racing. You may become drowsy, and if so, feel free to sleep."

He held Jane's stare while Canna injected it into his shoulder. "You know, I wasn't expecting brain surgery this weekend."

"Just be glad we caught it," said Canna. "Now, try to relax. Let the potion work."

There were several medical facilities in Beukal, but fortunately for my cousin, the one in District 2 had the best neurological unit in the city. What it *didn't* have, however, was a useful blood supply.

"It's common practice for those of multi-species lineage to get blood-tested early," said Canna as she wiped an antiseptic swab over my fingertip. "Some can take transfusions from one species, some from both. But once you figure out a workable donor species, you then have to deal with antigens and such."

"Meaning?" I asked, and braced myself as she readied a familiar plastic device. The research healers who came to North Lake sometimes drew blood from our arms, but more often, they used a little lancet—less invasive but surprisingly painful, considering the size of the wound.

"Different individuals have different combinations of antigens on the surface of their red blood cells and antibodies in the serum, the fluid that carries them," she replied, then jabbed my finger and grabbed a tube to collect the sample. "If you transfuse blood with the wrong combination, the cells can clump, which can clog blood vessels, and that's never a good thing. So, to avoid problems, I'm typing the three of you." With that, she added my sample to the ones she was processing from Jane and Connor, who had fallen asleep before his results came back.

"Uh, question," said Jane, raising her bandaged finger.

"Yes?"

"Why are you testing *me*? I'm not human…"

Canna's mouth tightened like she'd tasted soap, and she cut her eyes to the closed door before quietly answering Jane. "You've heard the theory that we're genetically…close?"

Jane snorted. "The theory no one wants to talk about?"

"It's more than a theory. It's been an idea for ages, but since the advent of genetic testing, it's almost certainly fact. But *I* didn't say that—"

"Because them's fightin' words," Jane finished in an exaggerated drawl.

"Precisely. In here, however, I can tell you that, barring antigenic incompatibility, you could donate blood to a human."

Jane frowned in thought. "So…we're the same species?"

"No," said Canna. "Not the same, but…a subspecies, perhaps. There's debate about how we should actually be classified. The working hypothesis is that we're the result of a cluster of mutations, and a stable population developed out of that. Now, whether these mutations appeared in one place and spread, or whether they arose independently at various points, we can't yet determine. I mean, if every sorcerer had, say, East Asian features, that would suggest a single common ancestor, but seeing as our features are as diverse as those in human populations…" She shook her head. "It's a puzzle, certainly. For our purposes here, there are distinct genetic markers seen only in sorcerers, but one area that hasn't been affected is blood type." She glanced over as the humming machine beeped, then reviewed the report on Connor's sample. "All right…looks like he can accept transfusions from both species. At least some part of this evening is going to be easy," she muttered.

In the end, I couldn't help Connor, but Jane could. By the time the ambulance arrived, Canna had spoken with the surgeon, who was on her way in, and passed along the results. Jane trailed the gurney as the transport team wheeled Connor toward the elevator, leaving me with Canna and Shallow Rapids.

"Go home," Shallow Rapids told Canna, patting her shoulder with a hand bigger than my face. "We've done what we can. He's in good care."

"I know, but that's my little cousin's boyfriend, and…well, they're in a mess beyond this," she replied, avoiding the details. "Maebe, dear, where are you staying?"

"Um…my things are at Diriem's house…"

"Thought so." With that, she pulled out her phone and made a quick call. "Hi, Rose? How are…oh, you sound *exhausted*…" She listened for a moment, then said, "Oof. To be brief, Connor's off for emergency surgery, Jane's gone with him, and the agent who drove them over from DOI didn't stay. I've got Maebe here…cerebral aneurysm, plus two defective heart valves. Suffice it to say he's not a candidate for the bloodline potion. But Maebe's stranded at the moment, and I can drive her out to Viratta, but…oh, great. Thanks. I'll have her waiting."

Ten minutes later, Diriem walked into the DOL lobby, and Canna and I rose from the bench we'd commandeered. "What's this about surgery?" he asked without preamble.

"Connor's got a time bomb in his head. We caught it," Canna replied. "He's not going to be of any use in your investigation, but he should *live*, so—"

"He's very fortunate. Thank you for coming in to-night—and if word has yet to come from your director, you're off the schedule tomorrow," said Diriem, then nodded to me. "Shall we?"

I followed him into the garage and slid into the front seat of his Mercedes. We headed for the portal building, the silence stretching between us, until he said, "There's nothing you can do for him tonight, youngling. He'll be monitored once he's out of surgery, and if Jane's with him, then I strongly doubt he'll come to harm."

"I know," I murmured, "but…" I huffed a sigh and leaned against the cool window. "If I could take the po-tion, we could find them tonight."

"But you can't," he said gently, "so we pursue other options."

"I *could*—"

"No, Maebe. Take your rest, and tomorrow, we'll re-group. I'll drive you back to North Lake after breakfast."

"You're dropping me off?" I asked, thinking of the empty rooms where my cousins were meant to be. Inexpli-cably, my heart began to race, and my mouth dried out.

"Certainly not," said Diriem. "I just thought you might like another change of clothes—you only packed for the weekend, correct?"

"Oh, uh…right. Thanks."

He chuckled low in his throat as he eased into the por-tal traffic. "Too much on your mind, hmm?"

"Glad one of us can keep things straight," I grumbled.

Diriem slowed while a troll-sized SUV merged in ahead of us, then steered us onward. "You're doing well. And before you make unwise comparisons, recall that this isn't my first emergency. A certain degree of chaos is to be ex-pected."

CHAPTER 7

I slept fitfully, too anxious and frustrated to do more than stare at the ceiling between bouts of flipping over like a landed fish, looking for the cool spots in the sheets. Shortly before dawn, I gave up and shuffled to the shower, then headed downstairs to see about breakfast.

Ranarma, an early riser by necessity, was already at work when I peeked into the kitchen, and he made me a cup of strong coffee to tide me over until the meal was ready. "No offense intended, but you look like you could use this," he said as he plonked it on the counter in front of the barstool I'd selected, then slid the sugar cannister within my reach. "Cream?"

Growing up, sweetness had been limited to fruit, honey, and the odd bit of candy brought back from Whitford, and my palate had yet to adjust to the sugar available in abundance outside of East Branch. Even the bread seemed sweeter. But I'd also never grown up with coffee, and having become accustomed to it at school, I knew darn well that I needed to use a heavy hand with the sugar to make it an enjoyable experience.

The combination of sugar and caffeine was just beginning to take effect when my phone rang. Seeing Jane's name on the screen, my heart rate spiked, but I took the call and tried to sound calm. "Hey, there."

"Hi, hon," she replied, her voice lower than usual and froggy. By the sound of it, Jane had slept even less than I had. "You okay?"

"I'm fine. How's—"

"Connor came through it beautifully," she assured me. "They had to open his skull, but I've seen the new scans— the aneurysm is much smaller, and they strengthened the vessel walls. The surgeon's pretty confident that it'll hold, but Con's going to be back in for fresh scans every three months for a while. And they found a couple other spots while they were in there."

"Aneurysms?" I asked, feeling my way through the unfamiliar word.

"Uh-huh. Smaller ones. Canna might have caught them on her scan eventually, but she stopped when she hit the big one, so…"

"Can they be fixed, too?"

"Already taken care of."

"What caused them?"

"See, that's the question," Jane replied through a yawn. "Mm, sorry. He doesn't have any real risk factors, so the folks here think it might be something genetic. Y'all will *all* be getting checked for this, and the research team has been informed."

"If we find the others," I mumbled.

"No change on that front, huh?"

"Nothing that I've heard about. Is Connor feeling okay? I don't have any update for him…"

"He's still sleeping it off," she said. "They're keeping him unconscious for now."

"So that he doesn't hurt?'

"That's part of it. Sleep is best for healing, and he's being pumped full of potions to help that along. The team here wants to keep an eye on him, monitor him for swelling and bleeding, look for infection…"

I heard a long exhalation on the other end of the phone, testament to Jane's relief and exhaustion.

"The problem," she continued, "is that y'all's physiology skews human, and that makes you relatively slow to heal. Elves, no problem. Sorcerers can be back on their feet in pretty short order. But he's going to take some time to recover, and since we're talking about brain surgery, I'm going to keep him in bed until the healers clear him, even if that means chaining him to the mattress."

"Will you let me know when he wakes?"

"Sure, Maebe. And you keep me posted, too, okay? I, uh…I'm going to crash on the couch in here for a little while, I think, but if something arises—"

"I'll text unless it's an emergency," I replied.

Too weary to worry about my poor spelling, Jane thanked me and hung up, and I found Ranarma watching as he chopped fruit. "Connor's alive," I told him. "The healers are making him sleep."

"*Good*," he said, slicing an apple in two. "I'm sure the poor boy needs it." He paused, regarding me as I drank my coffee, then asked, "Breathing a little easier, are we?"

"A little. One down," I said, thinking of the pictures I'd seen the previous afternoon. Uncle Kyle had tried to stick up for me. If he hadn't…if he'd just let it go, and our family had stayed closer to the other students, where there was light and safety…

Why did everything I touch fall to pieces?

North Lake looked dead as Diriem pulled up to the front a little after nine that morning. No one sat out on the front steps between classes, enjoying the sun, and though I could see the remnants of the decorations from Lake Day beside the building, they hung drooping and abandoned over the silent lawn.

I took a deep breath as I slid out of the car, willing myself to maintain my composure, then tugged my shirt straight and followed Diriem inside.

The way up to my dorm was through the office, and we hadn't made it ten feet inside the door before Ms. Mafatta came running toward us, her eyes bloodshot and her hooves striking the stone so hard, I was almost surprised not to see sparks. "*Maebe!*" she cried as she barreled toward us. "Where did you come from?"

I froze, unaccustomed to being charged by a centaur, and Diriem quickly slipped between us to intercept the principal. "She was with me last night," he said as Ms. Mafatta put on the brakes. "All things considered, I thought it safest."

"Where are the others?" she demanded.

He stepped to the side once the danger of being bowled over had passed. "We're working on that."

"But…" She looked back and forth between us, perplexed. "If you found Maebe, then—"

"I wasn't with my cousins," I said. "You banned me from Lake Day, remember?"

"I…yes," she said slowly, taken aback, "I recall, but—"

"Went home to Georgia. I came back yesterday when we heard about what happened here."

Ms. Mafatta planted her hands on her waist. "I had no idea you were off campus this weekend. Why didn't you check out?"

"I told Dalm where I was going," I replied. "He didn't stop me."

Though she still seemed irked and frazzled, she let it go. "Well, then, I suppose that's a matter we can take up later. You're unharmed?"

"Yes, ma'am."

"Good." Turning back to Diriem, she said, "Surely you know something. What's become of the other students?"

He spread his hands. "I'm sorry, but we have nothing yet for public knowledge—"

"Come on," she snapped, "give me *anything*. I've got angry, terrified parents beating down my door, and I don't know what to tell them. You have to find these children."

"I assure you, we're doing our best—"

"Because this isn't just about the East Branch bunch," she interrupted. "We've got seven other students missing, and their families are demanding answers, and I just don't…um…"

Diriem stared up at her until she fell silent. "DOI is aware," he said. "So is Laws. We're doing everything in our power to find the missing, but these matters can take time. For now...tell the parents our best intelligence suggests that the students are still alive."

That didn't placate Ms. Mafatta, however. "You don't understand, I've already been fielding calls from Lady ti'Har about—"

"I'll deal with Nadull if it comes to that, but I'm afraid there's nothing else I can provide at this moment." With that, Diriem gently gripped my shoulder and steered me toward the elevator.

"Where are you going?" she asked.

Standing as close as we were, I heard him huff a faint sigh. "With Maebe. She needs to visit her room."

"Just visit? Because I don't think it would be a good idea for her to stay here right now."

Diriem turned back to her. "Oh?"

There was, I reasoned, quite a bit going on in that single word, and Diriem's tone suggested that it would be a great idea for Ms. Mafatta to shut up while she was ahead. But my principal was obviously not in the sharpest mental state, so she plowed on.

"The other parents wouldn't like it if she stayed," she said, pointing to me. "Since the East Branch children are such a risk. Having her here—"

"We've merely come to collect her things," Diriem replied, his voice frosty. "The child had clothing only for a weekend, after all. I take it you won't begrudge her a few minutes in the dormitory."

"Oh, uh...no, I suppose that's all right," Ms. Mafatta allowed.

"Good. And so that we're perfectly clear, I would not risk Maebe's safety by leaving her in such an unprotected place," he added. "You might think of allotting some of your *considerable* budget for security guards and cameras made in the last decade. Having seen the state of your security footage, I will be bringing this matter to the board's attention at a more opportune date."

And with that, leaving Ms. Mafatta sputtering, Diriem marched me on.

My shoulders sagged as we rode the elevator up to the fourth floor.

"All right, there?" Diriem asked.

"She makes me tense up," I quietly replied, staring at my warped reflection in the steel door.

"Mafatta? I'm not surprised. Your interactions with her haven't exactly been positive." As we stopped, he asked, "What's this about being banned?"

"Got into it with Ainnet again," I muttered, leading the way toward our quiet end of the dorm. "Ms. Mafatta decided to punish me."

"Retribution for the dance?"

"She was being bitchy, and then she cut a chunk of my hair off"—I made a quick gesture, dropping my mask to show him the damage—"so I lost control for a minute and made a mess in the art room, and then I threw a ball of glue into *her* hair."

He snickered behind me.

"She wailed like I'd cut off her arm," I said. "Anyway, we ended up in the office, and Ms. Mafatta told me I couldn't go to Lake Day, so Jane and Connor took me home with them." Pausing before I pushed open the door, I glanced back and said, "Guess I got the better end of the deal after all. If I'd been here…"

"True," Diriem replied, "but the fact that the ti'Har girl was kidnapped doesn't negate your principal's failure to punish her."

"Not going to matter if she turns up dead," I pointed out, then waited, hoping Diriem would let something slip.

If he had the answers I sought, however, he kept them close. "As far as Rosie knows, they're not dead yet. Let's pack your belongings, hmm?"

Diriem took a seat in the big common room to check his messages, giving me a moment's privacy to sort through my clothes. My suitcase was at the mansion, so I grabbed an assortment of bags out of the closet—my backpack, a tote bag from the school library, a pair of re-useable bags from a dorm outing to the grocery store—and started loading up what I could, rolling my clothing into tight ropes to save room. I packed my pair of nice boots—pretty but practical—and I'd just gotten around to my computer when I heard footsteps running down the hall toward my open door.

A few seconds later, Chennis burst into my room, her blue eyes wide. "*Maebe!* When did you return? Where have you been? And the others, where—"

"I don't know where they are," I replied, cutting her short. "The farseers are trying to find them."

"But…how did you…"

"I wasn't at Lake Day. I went home for the weekend."

Her face screwed up. "Home?"

"Yeah, back to Georgia."

"You left without telling us?" she demanded, her hands migrating to her hips, much as the principal's had.

"I told Dalm," I protested. "Did he not mention it?"

"No, he certainly did not." I didn't have to see her expression to know our dorm mom was peeved—the tone of her voice was enough to warn me against foolishness. "Honestly, Maebe, you know better than that. Dalm's been distracted all week. There's that rowing competition on Saturday, he's nervous, and if he remembers to put on pants, it's a good day. Why didn't you bother to tell me? These sorts of trips require prior approval, you know."

Bristling, I said, "You're not going to stand there and tell me I can't come and go."

"You—"

"I've got portal credentials, and if that fails, I can ask the Hunt for a lift. Now, I'm *tired*," I continued, as Chennis, who surely hadn't been expecting pushback, retreated a pace toward the hall. "I'm worried sick, and the only cousin I have who's accounted for had surgery last night. So, I'm *really* not in the mood for one more person at this school to yell at me, okay?"

She floundered briefly, then scowled and started to advance again. "You do *not* talk to me like that—"

"Is there a problem?" asked Diriem from the doorway.

Startled, Chennis spun around, then emitted a frightened sort of squeak.

He looked past her and met my eyes. "Everything under control, Maebe?"

"Fine," I fibbed.

"And who might this be?"

"This is Chennis ti'Van," I told him, needlessly gesturing toward her. "She's a librarian here and one of our dorm parents. Chennis, uh, this is—"

"Lord ti'Dana," she blurted. Her demeanor had shifted from angry posturing to almost cringing deference. "I…I apologize, I didn't know—"

"That's quite all right," he murmured. "You must have had a difficult weekend."

She nodded emphatically.

"I see. Well, Maebe and I will be out of your way in just a moment. If you don't mind, I'll keep an eye on the youngling to speed this along."

"Oh, uh…um…" she stuttered.

"I'm sure you have important things to do, Ms. ti'Van."

"Uh…yes, sir. I'll just, uh…"

We watched as she scurried off, and when the door slammed behind her, Diriem glanced my way, faintly smirking. "There are certain perks, I'll admit it."

After we'd loaded my bags into the trunk of the Mercedes, Diriem stared out at the lake, absently cracking his spine. "Let's take a walk," he finally said, and nodded in the direction of the path toward the edge of the property, where my cousins had disappeared.

I glanced back at the front door of the school. Ms. Mafatta hadn't seen us off, but I was sure someone in the office was watching us. "You don't think we'll get in trouble?"

"No. Come along."

I followed him across the lawn toward the lake, then veered to the left, heading toward the rock wall and the lone camera. To my surprise, the air shimmered as if it were a sweltering summer day, and the answer occurred to me a beat later.

"Who put up the barrier ward?" I asked.

"Laws, presumably," Diriem replied, "but that seldom presents an impediment." He paused outside the ward, then made a series of rapid, complex gestures. Soundlessly, the ward parted in front of us, a hole about seven feet tall and half as wide through the otherwise almost impenetrable dome. "Watch your step," he cautioned me, then carefully made his way inside.

While I'd been hoping for a clue to leap out at me once I was within the ward, the area seemed remarkably mundane. The grass might have been a little trampled, I mused—and yes, those scuffs down to the dirt suggested a rough fight—but there was nothing to draw my attention, no helpful sign pointing to an overlooked piece of evidence that would lead us straight to my kinfolk. I took a moment, trying to make out the contours of the lake through the obstruction of the ward, then glanced down and froze as something glinted in the grass.

Crouching, I found that the object was a jagged piece of glass, clear and unmarked. I turned it over in my hand, hoping to derive *some* meaning from it, but the glass had refused to reveal its secrets by the time Diriem's shadow fell over me. "What did you find?" he enquired.

I stood and showed him the glass. "Just some trash."

"Mm. May I?" He took the fragment from my palm,

held it appraisingly to the light, and grunted. "Probably from one of the potion bottles. The evidence technicians sweep well, but they don't catch every scrap. Nasty surprise if you'd sat on it."

He passed it back to me, and I shoved it into my pocket. "Who'd have access to all that knock-out potion, anyway?"

"Well," said Diriem, "it's common in the agencies. Part of the standard field kit for those who go outside, particularly in Laws. If you're cornered and need to make a hasty escape, that potion can be invaluable."

"So…the people who kidnapped my cousins were agents, then."

"Not necessary. There's plenty on the black market, too."

"Black market?"

"Unofficial channels," he explained. "It's a restricted potion, but if you know the right people and are willing to part with enough money, you can find sellers. Laws arrests them every so often, but it's too lucrative an enterprise to eradicate." As he began slowly pacing along the edge of the dome, studying the grass, he said, "You recall Teolm's father, yes? Inade?"

Hard to forget your first time visiting a prison. "Yes, sir," I replied, following him.

"He kept himself blocked to farsight for *years*. Him, his top lieutenants, his producers—anyone who might send suspicion his way. I haven't bothered trying to tally how much he must have spent on the blinding potion, but it's surely a small fortune. Restricted, but also expensive to make and difficult to brew."

"How so?"

"Without going into the technicalities, if you aren't careful, you end up with a fireball instead of a potion. Anyway, it's out there for the right price. Laws ignores it for the most part—it's not a harmful potion, just annoying to my group. But all of that is to say that even regulated potions can find their way into the wrong hands."

I thought about Inade ti'Cren, the sullen man with the limp brown ponytail, farmer's tan, and hairy birthmark he'd tried and failed to hide. There wasn't much of him in Teolm, as far as I could tell, and I wondered what he must have been like before his incarceration, when he had money, power, and employees willing to make inconvenient people disappear. If he'd combined forces with Ivari back then…

"Do you think Inade and Ivari could be working together?" I blurted.

"No proof of such yet," Diriem replied, continuing his methodical circuit. "Inade's at Cavimet, and Ivari was placed at Eonu. Laws has already pulled their phone records, but there's no unusual activity to suggest cooperation between the two."

"What if someone else is making the calls for them? A friend?"

"In my experience, men like those two don't have friends—they have associates who are more or less useful to them. Associates require payment, however, which presents a problem." He paused and crouched, then stood with another piece of glass in his fingers. "Laws has been keeping an eye on the two of them, especially while Ivari settles in, and so far, they haven't found an obvious pattern of calls to suggest messages being passed along through intermediaries. That's not to say it's impossible, merely that there's no evidence."

"You agree?"

Diriem considered the question as he walked on. After a moment, he replied, "I…have no reason to believe Inade is responsible for your cousins' abduction. He's a crook, certainly, but he's far from stupid, and he knows he's under observation, especially after Jomin and Dania's murder-for-hire stunt."

My shoulders tensed at their names. Dania, Inade's daughter-in-law, could go jump in a fire for what she'd tried to do to us five months prior, and if she took her husband with her, so much the better. "Unless Jomin and Dania are still plotting," I muttered.

"Unlikely. Jomin's sentence was lengthened, and Dania's out at Bebala now. Of the ti'Cren siblings who *haven't* been incarcerated…let's see, there's a healer in the bunch, and she keeps her head down. Two of them work in film, and then there's the baby, the idiot child who led Inade right to Rose," he added with a grunt. "Long story," he said, seeing my bemusement. "The girl married someone Inade didn't approve of, Rose tried to hide the happy couple, and the bride decided she liked Daddy's money more than her husband. And then there's Liliol, of course, but she has nothing to do with her father. She helped raise Rosie," he explained before I could ask. "Floramancer like her brother, with an impeccable record. I can't envision her helping Inade with *anything*. So, no," he continued, "I don't think Inade has ready assistance from his family, and he's not likely to conspire with Ivari."

"But they know each other, right? From before the Pact?"

"More like Inade knew of Ivari. Ivari would have dealt with Inade's mother as the lady of the Hall. He might have been aware of Inade, but it wouldn't have been a deep relationship. Age-wise, Inade's far closer to my peer than he is to Ivari's, anyway." Giving the ground one last glance, Diriem straightened and turned back to face me. "Inade wants his freedom, and Ivari can't give that to him. There's no reason for Inade to call in whatever favors he has left to have your family kidnapped as a gift to Ivari. My gut says he's not our man, but…"

My fingers played with the little glass fragment in my pocket, turning it over and over as if I could tumble away the sharp edges. "But?" I prompted.

"But it should be noted that Inade was only the head of his enterprise," said Diriem. "Laws got him and many of his top people, but not all. Quite a few smaller fish slipped through the nets when Inade was hauled in." He glanced out through the distortion of the ward. "I don't know of his people's involvement with certainty yet, but it's something to bear in mind."

CHAPTER 8

Jane didn't call me again until dinnertime Monday night. "Connor's still asleep," she reported, "but his scans look great...or so the healers say, I mean. I couldn't read those things on my own to save my life," she added with a little chuckle. "Anyway, assuming no problems overnight, they're planning to bring him up in the morning."

"And y'all will come out to Viratta?" I asked, leaning toward my phone. Seeing that Jane was calling, I'd put it on speaker mode and placed it on the table so that the others could hear.

"Eventually. Con's going to be on bedrest for the next few days while they monitor him, but his team's expecting a full recovery. He'll have a little scar under his hair, but he shouldn't have a problem hiding it. Guess we'll see how much he's learned about masking while he waits for his hair to grow back, huh?"

"Did they shave his *head?*"

"A small patch—they had to get in there. If he doesn't know how to cover it, I'll do the honors for him."

"Do you need anything tonight?" Diriem asked, raising his voice slightly to compensate for the distance. "Food? Institutional cuisine is notoriously bland..."

Rose slid closer to me and angled herself toward the phone. "And I can take a turn. Bring you dinner, let you get a decent night's sleep."

"*You're* busy," said Jane.

"I'm useless from an intel standpoint," she retorted. "So, if you'd like a hand with babysitting the patient, I'm more than willing."

"Much appreciated, but I'm being looked after. Canna's been feeding me," she said, "and the couch in here isn't too shabby."

Rose nodded. "Canna *is* a pretty good cook."

"Right? And I've got this bag of gummi things," Jane added over the sound of crinkling cellophane. "Can't tell what flavor they're supposed to be, but I'm going with 'fruit' and saying that's good enough."

"Bluish-purple blobs?" asked Yven, coming around the table to join Rose and me by the phone.

"Yup. Covered with sugar and sour powder."

"Supposedly, they're sour grape, but I think they were designed by someone who'd never had a grape in his life. Pars and I used to make ourselves sick on those things as kids," he said, grinning. "I can't believe Canna brought you candy."

"Oh, she didn't," said Jane. "Lots of veggies from her. These came from Xila."

Rose's brow knit. "*She* visited?"

"Well, she texted to check in, and I told her where we were, so she stopped by after school today with these."

"Huh. Does that make her the fun aunt, then?"

"Oh, my God," Jane muttered. "*Stop.*"

I'd learned enough about Jane's family by then to understand her annoyance. Xila Aniap, Jane's biological father's youngest half sibling, was my age, a decade Jane's junior. Since the two of them were Gerem Aniap's only living descendants—and since Jane had quite probably saved Xila's life by exposing his crimes—they'd slowly been getting acquainted. While they had a long way to go before reaching even the level of familial bonding that Jane and Canna had achieved, I took it as a good sign that Xila was making hospital visits with exotic snacks.

But I couldn't join in Rose's teasing. Jane's mention of Xila only served to remind me yet again of my missing cousins, and I excused myself and went to bed as soon as manners allowed that night, too distracted to make good company.

My dreams were long and disjointed, and filled with broken glass.

Right on schedule, Connor was slowly brought up from unconsciousness early Tuesday morning, and by eight, he was sufficiently reoriented to talk to me.

"I'm fine, mitta," he insisted once Jane put her phone on speaker mode. "Not quite sure what planet I'm currently on, and they've made me this lovely gauze hat, but I'm not hurting, and I'm not dead yet, so...winning?"

"Drink, hon," Jane coaxed.

I heard a long slurp on the other end of the line. "She's so bossy," Connor told me.

"That's probably a good thing," I replied.

"Oh, no question about that. Love ya, Firebug."

"Uh-huh. Sure," said Jane, and though she put on a veneer of skepticism, the tenderness peeked through. "Keep drinking, bub. You're dehydrated."

"Yessum."

Once he'd downed a sufficient quantity of water to appease his girlfriend, Connor asked, "How's the investigation going?"

I groaned. "It's not. Diriem and I walked around the scene, and all we found was some glass. There's no ransom note, no *nothing*, and if Laws has any suspects, they haven't told me."

"Disappointing but not surprising. Has Rose seen anything?"

"She keeps checking, and she thinks they're still alive, but she's blocked."

"What about the future-oriented folks?" he asked. "I'm guessing they can't tell us how to get our people back, but if we could have some reassurance that we *will* find them alive, that'd make me feel a whole lot better."

"Already asked Diriem," I replied. "He said there are too many possibilities right now to make firm predictions."

"Fantastic," Connor muttered. "Well, give me a little while to get my bearings, put on some actual pants, and Jane and I will be out there to join you. We'll try to push the investigation along—"

Jane cleared her throat, cutting him short. "Con, sweetie, you aren't going *anywhere* right now."

"I feel fine," he protested.

"Because you're doped up on potions. That IV isn't just delivering saline."

My cousin huffed. "I can manage—"

"No, you cannot," Jane replied in a tone that firmly discouraged argument. "*Brain surgery.* They had to open up your skull. You don't just slap a bandage on that and go about your day!"

"Janie—"

"If I have to tie you to the bed, I will. Try me."

"Janie," he insisted, "that's my family—"

"And you can't help them right now," she said, her tone softening a degree. "Okay? I know it's tough, babe, but you've got to listen to the healers and behave yourself. The better you follow instructions, the sooner you're out of here."

Before Connor could object again, I heard a female voice interrupt in Pactish. "Good morning! How are we feeling?"

"We'll talk to you later, Maebe," said Jane, and cut the call.

Connor could be stubborn, but he wasn't stupid, and so I'd assumed that would be the last I'd hear from him that day while he minded his manners under Jane's watchful eye. With nothing else to do but wander the mansion and wait for news, I opened my computer to find that my tutors had sent me assignments. *I realize this is a trying time for you,* wrote one, *and the principal has explained that you're unlikely to return to school before the others are found. But if you have the opportunity, you should try to keep up with your lessons. Let me know if you have questions.*

A follow-up message from Sage, my only classmate who hadn't been abducted: *Miss you. I got notes. Want to come over? Dad says it's okay.*

Looking backward through my inbox, I saw a message from Violet—sent Monday morning, perhaps an hour after my quick return trip to school: *I'm so sorry, dear. If you feel like your control is slipping, please call me. I'll meet you wherever you're staying.*

While several of my teachers had seen my wild talent unleashed, Violet knew better than anyone just how destructive it could be when my emotions fueled the winds. I'd held myself in check to that point, but I appreciated the offer all the same and let her know. Her response came minutes later: *Go work out, Maebe. Don't let it build up.*

Unfortunately, there wasn't a great place for me to let loose inside the mansion. My emergency training in Diriem's gymnasium months before had led to a slew of broken windows, and though my control had certainly improved since then, I didn't want to take the risk. Instead, I slipped down to the kitchen, borrowed a dozen cans from the pantry, and headed out back to the wide lawn. As weights went, the cans didn't offer a real challenge, but they were useful for practicing precision.

And that's how I spent the morning: standing at the center of a whirlwind of my own making, forcing cans of beans and tuna and peaches to fly in complicated patterns around me. Occasionally, one would drop, and I'd hoist it skyward again with a frustrated grunt and a short blast of air. By noon, when Ranarma came out to check on me and discovered what I was doing with the groceries, I had shed my jacket and was drenched in sweat, a red-faced mess with jelly arms and hair as snarled as if it hadn't seen a comb in years. He coaxed me in with the promise of lunch, sent me to my room to freshen up, and had hidden the cans by the time I stumbled back into the kitchen. "Is that healthy?" he asked from the stove as I inhaled my food at the counter. "I don't have a wild talent, but when I was your age, when we worked on physical magic, it was never for more than an hour at a time."

"Stress release," I mumbled around a mouthful of ham sandwich.

"Mm." He sounded unconvinced. "Well, why don't you take a rest after you eat? Let everything digest, eh?"

As much as the part of me that knew I was a grown woman wanted to protest that I didn't need parenting, Ranarma wasn't wrong. The cook was still young for a sorcerer, barely into his fifties, but he was still a few years older than my mom and dad had been. Though he never treated me as anything less than an adult, I suspected he harbored doubts about leaving me to my own devices—and since Diriem had holed up in his home office that day, I wasn't altogether surprised that Ranarma was looking after me.

Humoring him, I stretched out in my room for a while after lunch, then turned to the slog of my school reading, though it was difficult to focus without the structure of lessons. When my phone rang around two, I jumped out of my chair to grab it from the bedside charger, and I smiled to see Connor's name. *Someone* had to be bored.

"Hey," I said, sitting on my rumpled bed as I took the call. "Still feeling all right?"

"Fine," he replied, his tone curt and strained. "Is Diriem around? I've got Culta on hold, and we need to talk *now*."

I jumped up again, phone in hand, and ran through the halls of the mansion until I came to a skidding, panting stop outside the office door and knocked. It opened from within, and as I hurried across the threshold, I found Diriem still sitting behind his desk, watching me inquisitively. "Maebe? What's wrong?"

Out of breath, I thrust my phone at him, and he turned on the speaker. "Hello?"

"It's Connor," came my cousin's tinny voice. "Culta wants to talk to you."

Diriem frowned at the screen. "Don't you have my number?"

"Nah. Jane does, but Canna stole her for a late lunch, so I made do. Not important. Hang on, let me patch him into the call…"

"Aren't you meant to be resting, boy?"

"I'm *literally* sitting in bed. Here we go…Culta, you there?" Connor asked, switching back to English.

"Yup," he replied. "We good?"

"We good," Connor confirmed. "He's listening."

"All right," said Culta, "here's the deal. I just got off the phone with my kid brother, Theo. Well, *one* of my kid brothers—"

Connor cut him short. "Wait—*Theo*?"

"Yeah. He's been Theo most of his life. You might be, too, had your parents called you Tugga."

I winced, but Diriem said, "It's an old name…"

"And not a great one, but I digress. He said he's seen the East Branch kids."

Diriem's eyes widened. "He's certain?"

"If not, he's pretty damn close. Sounded shaken. They're alive, but they're not in great shape."

"Would he be willing to speak with us directly? Now?"

Culta hesitated, then said, "I can ask. What number should he call?"

Diriem gave Culta his number, then told Connor to call him instead of my phone. Once he'd hung up, Diriem slid the phone to me and said, "Mine records securely. We might need this."

I'd barely had time to shove my phone into my pocket when Diriem's began ringing. Connor was quickly put on hold, and Diriem sat back and folded his hands. "Now we wait. Make yourself comfortable," he offered. "This could take a while."

"You think so, or you know so?"

He flashed a brief half-smile. "Experience. It's one thing talking to your sibling, even an ostracized sibling, but quite another to parley with the enemy. Let's see how persuasive Culta can be."

A long, painful five minutes later, Diriem's phone beeped with an incoming call. Answering it, he said, "Culta?"

"Yeah, I'm back," Culta replied. "And I've got Theo on the other line."

After a bit of fumbling, the calls were successfully merged, and Culta took the lead. "So, uh...this is Theo. He's willing to talk."

"Mr. Rush," said Diriem, sticking with English. "Thank you. I don't know how much Culta has told you..."

Another male voice, one slightly higher than Culta's but with an accent much like his, responded. "Enough. Look, man, I don't want to betray my family."

"That's understandable."

"But..." He huffed an agitated sigh. "I've seen some fucked-up shit, and I can't just sit on it."

"Hey," Connor interjected, "it's Theo, right?"

"Yeah."

"Connor. Hi. Could you wait two seconds and let me grab a pencil?"

"I can take notes," Diriem told him. "*You* are supposed to be resting."

"I'm resting! My feet aren't even on the floor—"

"Wait a sec," Theo cut in, "did you testify at our father's trial?"

"Yeah," said Culta, "the kid's the cop from Georgia."

"*Thought* I'd heard that drawl before. Well, guess it's no wonder you're wrapped up in this, huh?"

"Almost all of my family is missing," said Connor. "Twenty of them. If I weren't currently stuck in a hospital, I'd offer to come to you, but..."

"No, this is fine," Theo replied. "Uh…this is a private call?"

"Private enough," said Diriem. "The four of us and Maebe."

I stood and leaned toward the phone. "Hey, there. Uh…nice to meet you."

"Oh, hi," said Theo, who sounded startled. "Um…you…"

"Also testified," Culta offered. "She's the kid he tried to kill—"

"*Right*, right, the mastermind arsonist blackmailer."

My face began to flush. "I swear, I never—"

"I know," said Theo, cutting me short. "I was there. So, uh…shit," he muttered. "I'm not sure…"

"Why don't you start at the beginning?" Diriem murmured. "What did you see?"

It took Theo a moment to collect his thoughts. "I'm an accountant," he began. "For the family business, right? Based in the City. But you stay in Manhattan too long, especially in the apartments, and you go a little stir-crazy."

"These are the family apartments?" Connor asked.

"Yeah. Father prefers that we live together for safety. A few have been able to strike out on their own—hell, Culta had a halfway decent place."

"Because Father doesn't give two shits about me," his brother retorted. "Artists aren't useful."

"I thought you did web design," said Connor.

"Sure, but that came *much* later. I wanted to be a professional violinist when I was your age, and he wouldn't have it. But then you've got folks like Theo here who managed to acquire vacation homes."

"It's just a cabin," Theo protested.

"It's three thousand square feet."

"Okay, a big cabin, but it's nothing like Father's places."

"Please, keep complaining about your free cabin. You have my sincere pity, little brother."

"Asshole," he muttered, though I thought I heard a note of fondness in his tone. "So, yeah, no big secret that our parents play favorites. Around the time that I got married, they gave me this place in northern Michigan. Middle of nowhere in the U.P., close-ish to Wisconsin."

I looked blankly at Diriem, who pointed up and mouthed *North*.

"It's a good hunting property," said Theo. "I'm not a die-hard hunter, but I like spending the odd weekend in the woods, and it gives the fam a chance to get out of town, breathe some fresh air. My wife sits and reads, our daughter—well, she's in her thirties now, but she used to like to go hiking, and our little boy's only two, so everything's still new and exciting for him. I was planning to go out next weekend and do some repairs, you know, clean up after the worst of the winter. Not the best time to be out there, but I want it in good shape before vacation season starts."

"Tell them about the cameras," Culta urged.

"Right. I'm not out there all that often, and the property's posted, but we get trespassers every now and then, so I installed a set of cameras around the place. That way, if someone breaks in, I can give their info to the sheriff."

"You didn't ward the house?" Diriem asked.

Theo chuckled incredulously. "Uh, *no*. We keep the magic to a minimum where there's a decent chance of human interaction. No, just good, old-fashioned signs, locks, and cameras. And there's a security system on the cabin, too," he added. "Anyway, I like to check the cameras sometimes when I'm at work. Watch the birds and shit, you know? We get pigeons and the occasional hawk around our building, but there's all kinds of wildlife out in the woods, and it's...a little break from the monitor and the books."

"Deer?" asked Connor.

"Oh, totally. Herds of them. We can't plant much in the way of shrubbery around the cabin because the damn things eat *everything*, but they're cute enough. There was this one year that we had fawns all over the place—"

"*Theo*," Culta snapped.

"Right, sorry, sorry. I, uh…"

"Take a deep breath," Diriem suggested.

"Sorry, I just…" He released a long exhalation, then quietly said, "Fucking hell, man. I don't even know what I saw…"

"It's okay," said Connor. "We're in no rush."

"Yeah, but I'm hiding in my bathroom, and if I don't get back upstairs soon, there's going to be questions. Uh…okay. So, I was putting in a few hours on Sunday afternoon, getting ahead, and I needed a break, so I checked in on the cabin. Someone had put up cages in the back. Big ones, the kind of pens you might see with a dog run? I don't know, I've never had a dog, but—"

"I get you," Connor replied. "How many cages?"

"Four, I think. Could have been one out of view, but I counted four. And they were occupied. Big group of people."

My guts twisted. "How many people? Like, ten? Twenty?"

"At least a couple dozen. I didn't get a good head-count," said Theo. "But they were young and definitely underdressed. The highs have been in the twenties and thirties for the last few days," he said, "maybe going into the forties tomorrow, but you need a coat at the *very* least. I didn't see more than a windbreaker on any of them, and quite a few were in short sleeves."

March wasn't *warm* in Beukal, but it was a heck of a lot warmer than what Theo was describing.

"Any heaters around them?" Connor pressed. "Fires?"

"No, and no. Just exposed cages."

"The prisoners, what condition were they in?" Diriem asked.

"I can't give you much," he replied. "They were huddled, presumably for warmth, so it wasn't easy to make out individual features, but many of the ones I could see looked to be in rough shape. Some black eyes, a busted lip, torn clothes. But I caught the ears on a few of them—definitely elves in the mix, and they're unmasked."

"Not all elves?"

"Can't be a hundred percent sure. Some of the faces didn't exactly look elven, but that's me from a distance with a basic security camera, so make of that what you will." He paused for the space of a breath, then said, "I watched for a while, trying to figure out what was going on, and then I saw my brother come out to the cages. Uh, Danirri," he clarified. "He's the eldest of us."

Danirri. I remembered his voice all too well from the previous fall, when Connor and I had hidden in Jane's dad's brew room while Danirri, Culta, and the rest of their recovery team had tried to find us and drag us back to Ivari. Culta swore he'd had no idea that his father was about to slaughter my community, but I suspected the same couldn't be said for his brother.

"What did he do?" asked Connor when Theo fell silent again.

"Nothing. Just walked past them—he was heading for the woodshed, since he came back with his arms full. The folks in the cages tried to talk to him, but he ignored them."

"In what language?"

"A mix, actually. I heard English—southern accents."

My cousin quietly swore on the other line.

"There was some High Elvish, too, which I thought was curious," Theo continued. "But really oddly pronounced."

"That's what happens when you take a bunch of Georgians and give them language potions," Connor replied. "All the vocabulary, none of the accent. Your Pactish is probably just as weird—you got it from a potion for Ivari's trial, right?"

"True," Theo allowed. "But it didn't make a difference

to Danirri."

"Could have been Low Elvish, too," said Diriem. "It's distinct enough from the older version to make communication difficult if you're unfamiliar with both."

Theo grunted. "Well, having seen Danirri and all of those people out back, I called our mother to tell her what he was doing. Danirri doesn't have a key to my cabin or the alarm code, but Mother does, and I thought he might have given her some story to gain access. I told her what I'd seen and about the cage situation, and she…" He hesitated, then muttered, "She told me to mind my own business and keep my mouth shut. But those are all the East Branch people, aren't they?"

"All but Connor and me," I said.

"And there's more missing than our kinfolk," Connor added. "Some of them are just kids who happen to go to school with my cousins. They got caught in the dragnet, looks like."

Theo was quiet when he spoke next. "And you guys are related to us, yeah? All of you?"

"Maebe and I can trace ourselves back to both of your parents," said Connor. "We're, like, ten-plus generations descended from your half siblings, but yeah, the bloodlines are there. Same goes for the rest of us. But if you and Culta want to argue over which of you is your parents' least favorite, let me put in a plug for everyone in the previous batch."

"Fuck," he whispered.

Connor snorted. "Sorry to mess up the family tree—"

"No, that wasn't aimed at you," Theo quickly clarified. "I just…" He struggled for a moment, then said, "I get that our parents are fucked up, right? They went through hell and lost everything, and…well, they did what they had to do to survive. But those kids ahead of us didn't ask to be born, and to have been abandoned in, like, *Deliverance* country—"

"North Georgia is *really* not that bad. We've got paved

roads and everything," said Connor, and I could almost hear him roll his eyes. "Not at East Branch, but the rest of the county's civilized. We're a tourist destination if you don't want to deal with Gatlinburg."

"I didn't mean any offense," he replied, "just—"

"I get it. So, your mother's in on this?"

Theo groaned. "That's the only logical conclusion. And since Danirri is the undisputed favorite—"

"Seconded," said Culta.

"—I'm not surprised that they're working in cahoots. But...I've got a toddler, man," he said softly. "Cute little guy, I'd do anything for him. And I...I saw kids his age in those cages. People were trying to huddle around them— their parents, I guess—but that...that's no condition for kids. They're cold, they're exposed, I don't know if they're being fed or how much, and I *think* I saw a bucket in the corner of one of the cages, but you know the sanitation situation's got to be dire. If it were me and my son in there, I...I don't know what I'd do. But I can't sit back and let them freeze to death in my yard."

"That's why you called Culta?" Connor asked.

"No. Actually, I called Madla ti'Un first."

"Who?"

"She goes by Matilda Ravensworth, correct?" Diriem cut in.

I recalled her from our visit to the Rush and Sons building, the brunette in the gray suit who'd taken us to see Ivari.

"Yeah," said Theo, "that's her alias. She's our Admin chief. I would say she's the head of HR, but...well."

Connor barely chuckled. "What's she got to do with this?"

"She's one of the old folks," he replied, "and I don't work closely with her, but I know her well enough. Always been deferential to my father, never caused trouble...until his trial. Madla attended with our group, and she was *horrified*. He'd lied to us about the blackmail situation, and that was bad, but when the details about the East Branch murders came out…she's been *pissed*. Mother's peeved that Madla's not toeing the line, but frankly, I think Madla's done with them both."

"Really? That's surprising," I said. The little I'd seen of Madla had left me cold, and I couldn't imagine her sticking up for my community.

"Not exactly," said Theo. "See, Madla's the only one of the survivors who's never remarried since leaving Georgia."

"And Deriap ti'Catama," said Connor.

"Okay, the only *living* survivor who's never remarried. Folks don't talk about it openly, but the truth is that Madla loved the human she married. I don't know anything about their kids, but she did have some she left behind. Apparently, she regrets it."

"You've spoken with her about this?" asked Diriem.

"No—I'd heard rumors, but not until after the trial did she say it openly. We came back and had a community meeting, and Mother was raging, and Madla stood up and shouted her down. She couldn't believe their descendants still lived where they'd left them, and then for Father to have killed half of them…oh, she was *furious*. Yelled that they should have killed Father after he murdered Deriap. Mother didn't like that one bit, and the two of them had to be separated, but…suffice it to say I figured I could trust Madla. So, I called her yesterday afternoon and asked if we could meet, and she gave me the address for this café over by Columbia—not somewhere that anyone would be likely to run into us, yeah? We sneaked out last night, and I told her everything, and she said I needed to reach out to Culta, get you people involved."

That Theo had waited more than a day and a half to alert his brother didn't sit right with me, but a late-blooming conscience was better than none at all.

"We appreciate it," said Diriem, "and I do realize this is difficult for you. No mention of your name need be made—"

"Hell, I don't care about that," Theo muttered. "If they're willing to hurt kids…I don't want anything to do with that mess. Not like Father's around to berate me, anyway."

"Can you give us the address?"

"Oh, sure. Just out of curiosity, you *do* know where Michigan is, right?"

Diriem smirked at the phone. "Quite well. If you could perhaps send me a message with the address and some photographs of the location, that would be most helpful."

"Photos?" Theo asked. "Uh…yeah, I can do that. Do you want family photos or stills from the security cameras, or what?"

"Anything depicting the property and its surroundings. Your security footage would probably suffice."

"Okay. I can get that to you. If I may ask, what's the plan?"

"Extraction, and I'll leave it at that."

"Fair," he said, and sighed. "I won't tell Mother or Danirri what's coming, but if you could keep from killing my brother on sight…"

"I'll see that team is instructed to take him alive."

"Good. Good," he repeated, a note of relief in his voice. "The guy's a prick, and I don't know what he's doing on my land, but—"

"He's your brother," Diriem finished. "No more need be said. Send the photos and the address, and if I were you, I'd avoid your mother for a time."

"Can do, but, uh…I heard there was farsight in ti'Dana."

"There is."

"So…was that a warning, or what?"

"Not farsight," said Diriem. "Common sense. Your mother's angry, your brother's in the middle of a massive kidnapping, and they know you're not in synch with them. If Danirri calls home to alert your mother that your house is being raided…"

"*Yeah*," Theo said slowly. "You know, I might take the kids uptown for a couple of days."

"That's probably wise. Will you be reachable at this number?"

"Should be. I'll get you what you need. Got to go," said Theo, and dropped from the call.

After a moment of silence, Culta asked, "Do you need me, or…"

"We'll take it from here," Diriem told him. "Thank you for your assistance."

He waited until Culta had hung up, then said, "Connor?"

"I'm here."

"Good. Put the phone down and rest. It's under control."

As Diriem hung up, I asked, "What now?"

"Now," he said, eyeing me across his desk, "we strike before they suspect they have an informant in their midst."

CHAPTER 9

From what I'd observed of him, Diriem could sit back and be patient, but when he moved, he *moved*.

His first call that afternoon was to Kabno. "We've got a location on the East Branch abductees," he told her without bothering with the niceties of a greeting. "Possibly eyes on them."

"Possibly?" she replied.

I hadn't left my seat in his office, and since Diriem had made his call with the speaker engaged, I suspected that he didn't object to my eavesdropping.

"Security camera. Our source is sending me additional data," he continued, "and once that's in hand, we need to strike. Tonight, I should think."

"Where are they?"

"Northern Michigan."

Kabno hissed on the other end. "Long way from home. Who's got them?"

"From the sound of it, one of the ti'Ammaas sons, and his mother's probably involved. What can you give me?"

"Tonight? *Outside*? Are they anywhere in the vicinity of a portal?"

"Doubtful, but there's always the Hunt."

"And I fear I'll never adjust to the notion of calling the Hunter for a lift. To answer your question, I should be able to put together a strike team, but it won't be large," she warned him. "This will need to be a covert operation. I could give you more, were Special Forces to be activated, but without Forum approval—"

"You know your people," said Diriem. "I trust that you can select a few willing to be quiet about this matter."

"Of course," Kabno replied. "Just don't get your hopes up for an army, old boy."

When Diriem ended that call, I asked, "Are you going to get DPP involved, too? You know Canna's husband, Pars? He's huge, and he's in Interdiction over there…"

He shook his head. "We've met, and I don't doubt his willingness to engage in a slightly less than sanctioned operation, but speed is important today. Plus," he added, lifting his phone to dial another number, "Canna would be *irked* if I took him away with no notice. It's one thing if Pateme sends him into the field, but she has concerns about my decision-making," he added with the ghost of a smile. "Can't say I blame her."

His next call was answered on the second ring, a baritone I recognized even with the speaker's distortion. "Diriem?"

"Do we have privacy?"

"A moment." After a few seconds of muttering and shuffling on the other end, a door clicked closed, and Wylan returned to the call. "All right, that's us, the four walls, and whatever bugs my colleagues have slipped into my office."

Diriem chuckled. "I don't know of any."

"Oh, I'm not worried about *you*—I suspect you know better than to listen in on my dealings. It's my charming fellow representatives whose wisdom I doubt." He paused, then asked, "You know of anyone up to that sort of nonsense?"

"Not that I can confirm, but if I had to wager…Elm Carinar."

"*Her*? She's an idiot!" Wylan protested.

"True, but we wooed one of her aides. Clever young woman, savvy with tech."

Wylan grunted. "Good to know. Now, what can I do for you?"

"Do you have plans tonight? You and the boys?"

"I take it this isn't an invitation to dinner."

"Not exactly. Would you mind rescuing the East Branchers from Michigan?"

"You *found* them? I'd heard they were blocked from farsight…"

"Oh, that hasn't changed, but we've got a source. If I can get you pictures and an address, do you think—"

"Sure. Anyone else going?"

"A handful from Laws," Diriem replied. "I'd prefer a larger strike force, but without Forum authorization—"

"No need to explain. And this isn't the sort of matter we can push to the side while the Forum makes up its mind," he said with a snort. "What are we walking into?"

"Large cabin in the woods, presumably no close neighbors. One of Ivari ti'Ammaas's sons is on the property, but he may not be alone. The children are behind the cabin in cages."

Wylan fell silent for a moment, taking that in, then said, "Yeah, we're absolutely striking tonight. Give me whatever locational data you have and let me know when and where to pick up the Laws group."

"You'll have that information as soon I do," he promised.

And for the first time in days, the knot in my gut began to loosen.

As much as I wanted to go with Wylan that night, I knew this was out of the question. The Hunt had a skillset that I couldn't match, I lacked even the rudiments of agency training, and what I brought to the table was a teenager with questionable control over the winds that were liable to break loose at inopportune moments. While I might have had the will, I admitted to myself that I was a liability.

But that didn't mean I had to go to bed while the operation was underway.

"You know, Maebe," said Diriem upon finding me atop a kitchen barstool shortly after midnight, "you're welcome to sit somewhere more comfortable."

"Close to a plug," I replied, pointing to the outlet in the wall. My computer was a useful thing when I remembered to charge it, which happened with a less than ideal frequency.

"Mm. Coffee?"

"Please."

Diriem didn't have Ranarma's talent with the espresso machine, but he could competently put on a pot, and he grabbed a pair of mugs from a cabinet while the brew cycle commenced. "What are you reading?"

"Homework. I still haven't finished Monday's assignments," I confessed.

"And not to be a downer, but I sincerely doubt that you'll retain anything you're trying to read tonight."

"Yeah, I know," I said with a sigh, "but what's the alternative? At least this is kind of productive…"

Leaning against the counter, he thought briefly, then replied, "I have a few colleagues who swear by knitting for dealing with nervous energy in times like these. Or is it crochet? Eh," he muttered, waving it off, "something with yarn. Fiber arts has never been my domain. Can you knit?"

I had to suppress my laughter; he might as well have asked me if I knew how to boil water. "Made my first pair of socks when I was six."

"Dumb question?"

"It *is* pretty late…" I said with a little smile.

"That's magnanimous of you." He turned to check the rising level of coffee in the pot. "I realize this isn't the healthiest of drinks, but it truly was a game-changer when we first imported it. Some of the sorcerers from the southern and eastern ends of the Mediterranean knew of it at the time of the Pact, but it didn't gain popularity here for another two hundred years. It was a novelty, you see? People who had reason to go outside brought back samples, but no one tried growing the plant here for some time."

I'd learned that coffee came from beans, but I knew nothing of their cultivation. "Tough to grow?"

"Not especially, but consider the work that goes into creating plots of land capable of sustaining agriculture. No one was eager to waste cropland on a weird shrub. Once enough of us realized the utility of the thing, however, it took off. We already had tea," he explained, "but the next step up from that was an early version of the potion colloquially known as 'Happy Juice,' and that stuff is awful if you mess up the dosing."

"What is it?"

Diriem grimaced. "Great if you need a sudden burst of energy, but the crash that follows is no fun, and if you take too much…" Chuckling to himself, he checked the coffee again. "Have you ever wanted to taste colors? Take too much Happy Juice and enjoy the ride."

"*Yikes*," I muttered.

"Indeed, so coffee is the far better option. Speaking of which, how do you take yours—sugar, cream, something else?"

Before I could answer that, the doorbell rang, and Diriem straightened. "Bet I know who *that* is. Let's see how the raid went."

I hurried after him through the darkened corridors toward the foyer. As we reached the front door, Rose came running down the second-floor hallway and swung around the railing to descend the wide staircase, with Yven a few paces behind her. "I'm here," she panted, as if their thundering footsteps hadn't given them away. "Is that Annie?"

Instead of answering her, Diriem unlocked the door, revealing Annie and Wylan standing beneath the decorative lantern. "If you'd told me you were coming, I'd have turned off the wards."

"No big deal," Annie replied wearily. "Bust."

"Complete?"

As she nodded, Diriem stepped back to admit them.

The couple slid past him, and Annie raised a hand in greeting to the rest of us as Diriem locked up again. "Hey," she called. "Did you all stay up to wait on us?"

"Couldn't exactly sleep," I said. "So…you didn't find my cousins?"

"Come with me," Diriem offered before they could get into it. "The coffee should be about ready."

"Wouldn't say no," Wylan rumbled, and we returned to the kitchen. As Diriem located more mugs and I packed my computer away, Wylan settled onto a stool and said, "They *were* there. We could smell them. But the setup you described was gone."

"Deserted," said Annie, taking the stool beside him, and murmured her thanks as Diriem slid their drinks in front of them. "Locked up, dark. No cages."

Diriem frowned. "Our source said he saw them only this afternoon…"

"I'm sure he did, since Laws took one look at the security camera in the back and saw that it's been tampered with. It's not recording—it's transmitting footage on a loop. They recognized the spell pretty quickly."

"And there are marks in the dirt behind the cabin that support the story of people being kept out there," said Wylan. "A grid pattern indicative of the bottom of a cage in four locations. This ti'Ammaas guy didn't bother to cover his tracks."

"Not to mention the stink," Annie added.

Wylan grimaced and sipped. "Sometimes, our sense of smell is a curse."

"What did you smell?" I asked.

"Bodily waste was most prevalent. Elves, I'd wager—I've spent enough time in public facilities in Beukal to learn," he explained, tapping the side of his nose.

Annie nodded. "Blood."

"Definitely blood, though not in large amounts—minor injuries, perhaps, but not pools of the stuff. And a general body-odor funk. You know, if you don't bathe for a couple of days, your odor strengthens."

"Don't forget booze."

"*Right*." After pausing for another sip, he said, "Metabolizing alcohol has its own particular smell—it's easy to pick out of sweat and urine. We caught hints of that. I'd say that at least some of them were intoxicated in the last few days."

That tracked what I'd been told.

"Here's the fun bit," said Annie, cradling her warm mug in her palms. "One of the agents noticed paint in the dirt, and they all got down to map it. *That's* the big piece of evidence that ti'Ammaas tried to erase—he got a lot of it but not everything."

"Let me guess," said Diriem, "spell rings?"

"Bingo. Not enough to show us the contours of the spell or spells, but—"

"That's how they're hiding the abductees," Rose finished.

Annie nodded. "Looks that way."

I felt sick to my stomach. We'd had them—we'd *had* them, right there on camera!—and they'd gone missing again before the rescue team could catch up. If Culta and Theo's brother was so heartless as to lock up my family outside in the cold, was he even feeding them? Giving them water? Had he taken them somewhere worse, some place with snow still on the ground? Frankly, I didn't care what he did with Ainnet, Eddic, and their ilk, but the thought of my baby cousins being held in captivity, hungry and freezing, left me nauseated.

Diriem regarded Wylan over the counter. "The fact that you're here tells me you can't track them."

Wylan grunted and drank. "Not with what we currently have," he admitted, pushing his mug aside. "The scent trail, such as it is, goes cold before the edge of the property. It's very limited. But we picked up on the smells of gasoline and motor oil, and the troll from Laws concurred. *That* we could follow, but only back to the road. Once it hit the pavement…" He shook his head. "One vehicle smells much like another in that regard. Discerning among the scent trails of the traffic would be nearly impossible."

"No blood or anything?"

"Not that could be tracked. Anyway, what we *can* tell you is that the abductees were removed from that cabin in some sort of vehicle or vehicles. I left a pair of agents there to study the tire tracks," said Wylan. "Certainly not my area of expertise. But if there's evidence of multiple vehicles—"

"Then ti'Ammaas isn't working alone," Yven finished, tightening his bathrobe belt. "Perhaps his dear mother decided to take a vacation, too," he suggested, and cocked an eyebrow in query at Rose.

But she could only shrug. "All of them have those rings, remember? I can't track a damn one of that crew!"

He hit himself in the forehead, and Rose kissed his cheek. "It's late, babe," she murmured.

"You can say that again," Annie muttered. "Now, next question: where the hell have they gone? Do we have any hints?"

"None yet," Diriem replied. "And they may have a considerable lead time. Our source noticed activity on the security camera on Sunday afternoon and began asking questions. Assume that ti'Ammaas played with the camera at that point and began his evacuation."

"We could be looking at two days' head start," said Annie. "Since we don't know how many conspirators there are, we can't say whether they're able to drive in shifts, but assuming the worst, say forty-eight hours on the road…"

"Southern Texas," said Rose. "LA. If he's got the right tires, he might be almost to Alaska by now, or maybe deep into Mexico."

She and Annie regarded each other wearily, and then Annie finished her coffee and stood with a groan. "We should probably go get those agents before they freeze. Keep us posted, eh?"

We saw them out, and as Diriem locked the door, he said, "Rosie, Yven, you'll be of no use to anyone without a few hours of sleep."

"Do you want some help?" Rose asked. "Whatever you're up to, Pop—"

"I've got the matter in hand. Rest," he said, and shooed them toward the staircase.

Reluctantly, they plodded upstairs. Diriem and I waited in the foyer until they'd disappeared down the hallway, and then he looked at me and barely smiled. "There's no point in telling you to go to bed, is there?"

"No, sir."

"In that case, follow me."

We retreated to his office, and as I pulled up a chair beside his desk, he took a seat and hunted through his papers only briefly before finding what he was looking for. "This may not be pretty," he murmured as he dialed a phone number, "but he can sleep later."

After five long rings, a groggy voice answered, "Wha'?"

"Your brother has fled," Diriem replied in English, perhaps suspecting as I did that Culta wasn't up for anything more challenging at that time of night.

"Huh?"

"Danirri. He messed with Theo's cameras to make it seem like he was still at the cabin, but he's taken the abductees and fled."

He paused for a moment, letting Culta catch up, and then I heard a low, almost growled, "*Fuck*," on the other end.

"Precisely. Now, I'm calling you instead of Theo because I don't know what company he's keeping, so…sorry to rouse you," he said with less than full sincerity. "I need numbers."

"For Theo?"

"No. For Danirri, for your mother, for anyone else you can think of who might be working with them."

"Uh…"

"I'm going to hang up," said Diriem. "Text me the numbers, yes?"

"Yeah, uh…okay," Culta managed. "Can this wait until mor—"

Diriem tapped the screen, ending the call before Culta could finish his complaint. "You know," he said to me, "I think I'm beginning to understand why Culta isn't his father's lieutenant."

It took Culta nearly twenty minutes to send the awaited text, giving me a chance to return to the kitchen and fetch my computer and coffee, but once the message arrived, Diriem wasted no time. "Good morning," he said into his phone—that conversation, at least, was one in which I couldn't hear both ends. "You're on duty, yes?" He paused, then nodded. "Good. I'm about to send you a series of phone numbers. Outside lines. How quickly can you set up traces?"

The agents working the overnight shift at DOI did their best, but the process wasn't immediate. Shortly before noon, they called with the preliminary results, and as Diriem had been poised to sit down for lunch with Rose, Yven, and me, he allowed us to listen in as we huddled around the dining room table.

"All of the numbers we've investigated are New York numbers, considering the area codes," reported the agent on the other end. "Most are presently pinging in New York."

"City? State?" Rose interjected.

"Uh…City," the agent replied, momentarily thrown by the unexpected voice. "Those phones are located in a shared area. I can provide a map…"

He didn't need to. Common sense suggested they were all still in Manhattan.

"What of the others?" asked Diriem.

"Can't be located. They're active, but the phones are either shut off or blocked."

"How do you block a phone?" I whispered to Rose.

"There's a couple ways to do it with magic," she replied, speaking softly while Diriem made notes of the numbers that his team couldn't track. "The easiest way to disappear is to turn off your phone, and that'll make it stop pinging on cell towers and sending GPS data."

"But there *are* workarounds," Yven added. "Our Interdiction team says it's like an arms race—as soon as we find a way to get through a block, someone comes up with a new spell. It's not just criminals who use them," he explained. "Law-abiding people like their privacy, too, but few are willing to use expensive means to get it."

"And since we're dealing with the New York group, there's no telling what they've worked up," said Rose. "I mean, look at what they can do to farseers."

When Diriem finished with the analyst, he cross-checked the hidden numbers and grunted to himself. "Well?" asked Rose.

"We have our suspects."

"Who are…"

He glanced up and smirked. "Who do you suppose?"

"Danirri," she began, counting off on her fingers, "and his mom…"

"Farral ti'Pul, and yes," he replied. "Who else?"

"Um…who are Ivari's other kids?"

"Not Theo," I said.

"No, not him," Diriem confirmed. "To answer your question, Rosie, per Culta, Ivari has a daughter, Beani, between Danirri and Culta, and another daughter, Dolia, between Culta and Theo. There's a fourth son, Idobo, and a toddler daughter, Luru, who obviously has no number yet. The other hidden numbers belong to Wewel ti'Tola, Danirri's wife, their two eldest children, Pacul and Kentha, and the two eldest of Beani and Votanna ti'Tola, Mirin and Jeviel."

"Keeping things in the family?" said Yven.

"Given the size of that group, they don't have much choice," Diriem replied dryly, "but yes, Ivari and Farral's two married ti'Tola siblings, who are also ti'Eltas, and…" He looked my way. "From what I've seen of their lines, they aren't quite as convoluted as the East Branch lines were, but they're also only on the fourth generation. In any case, the fact that the individuals likely involved are Ivari's kin doesn't surprise me."

While we ate, he sent a message to Theo, asking him to try to make contact with his siblings and their children. Theo was game, but he soon replied that he'd been unsuccessful. *They all go right to voicemail,* he wrote. *Want me to try email?*

Diriem declined, then rose from the table as Ranarma poked in his head into the room to check on us. "I'll be in my office," he said, and took his leave.

Yven waited until his footsteps had faded and Ranarma had returned to the kitchen with Diriem's plate before muttering to Rose, "He really should nap."

"Good luck convincing *him* of that," Rose replied, and nudged him in the shoulder. "If you don't have reports due immediately, you might want to sleep. I'm just going to get some tea and trance for a bit."

"Do you need—"

"I'll be fine," she said firmly. "You worry too much, ti'Ansha."

He kissed her. "Never. You keep getting into trouble."

"I'll be *fine*. Scoot," she ordered, and shook her head as he carried their dishes to the kitchen. I heard Ranarma protest—not for the first time—that cleanup was unnecessary, then the sounds of the dishwasher opening and the clink of porcelain as the cook worked on Rose's tea. When I started to get up, she stayed me with a hand on my arm. "Stick around for a second, would you, hon? We should talk."

I settled back into my chair and regarded her expectantly.

"Here's the thing," she said quietly. "I haven't known Pop all that long in the grand scheme of things—less than three years, I think—but I've got a pretty good sense of when he's up to something he doesn't want to talk about."

My stomach twisted. "Oh?"

"Yeah. And I'd bet a million bucks that he's seen something about you." She paused to glance behind us, but finding no one lurking, she resumed. "He's been trancing, probably more than is healthy. *I'm* not going to point that out to him, but I'll tell you that he wouldn't be going as hard as he is if he were totally blocked."

I frowned. "But the rings, and that spell—"

"Oh, I can't see a damn thing, but I've been trying to find the missing. Pop might not be able to see them, either...which doesn't mean they're doomed," she hastily added as my face fell. "It just means there are too many variables to get a clear picture right now. What I'm getting at is that Pop might have been looking at you and Connor as well, kind of as a backdoor route. All else being equal, Connor's pretty darn effective—"

"But I can't do anything," I protested. "I'm not a cop, I'm still not good with computers, my talent's...*messy*..." Sighing, I said, "The one thing I'm good for is anchoring a bloodline trace. The *one thing*. And they won't give me the damn potion."

"Honey," said Rose, taking my hands, "you're worth more than that."

"I'm not worth twenty lives," I said, shaking my head. "Or however many they actually took. There's twenty I care about, and if they freeze to death in cages—"

"We're going to find them."

"You don't know that."

She squeezed my hands before releasing them. "The ti'Ammaas crew took them for a reason. They're going to have to deliver their terms eventually, and they know as well as we do that there's no value in a dead hostage. No one's despairing yet, okay?"

"Okay," I muttered.

"Atta girl. But back to what I was saying about Pop," Rose continued. "He's keeping you awfully close, Maebe."

"I mean," I said, shrugging, "I don't have anywhere else to go. They don't want me at North Lake—"

"Close as in keeping you in the loop," she clarified. "He's letting you in on phone calls, making you part of this mess. By rights, you and Connor should both be sidelined because you're *way* too attached to the victims to be objective. I think Pop sees Connor's potential—Director Erenani sure does. But as for you, I think he sees something more."

"What could he *possibly* see? I ruin everything I touch," I said, resting my head on the tablecloth.

"He hasn't told me anything, but if I had to guess…it's probably not clear."

I groaned.

"Yeah, welcome to dealing with the future bunch," she replied, softly chuckling. "They're frustrating on their best day. My hunch is that Pop knows you've got a part to play in this, but he doesn't know *what*. That's why he's bringing you in—he wants to make sure you have what you need to do…whatever…when the time comes."

When the kitchen door opened, I raised my head to find Ranarma bringing a pair of teacups to the table. "Thought you might want one, youngling," he told me, then looked between the two of us. "Mm. Plotting?"

"Man, I wish," said Rose, and took a sip. "This is perfect, thank you."

"Of course." He studied me again, then said, "Maebe, I'll be starting dinner prep if you want some background noise while you do your lessons. Or you can help me make bread."

In truth, I studied better in the quiet of my room, but with the way my under-slept mind was racing, sitting alone with the screen and my thoughts was a terrible idea—and judging by Ranarma's expression, he knew it. "Thanks," I told him, forcing a smile, and trudged upstairs to retrieve my computer.

By sorcerer metrics, Ranarma wasn't old—fifty-two was considered barely more than a kid, able to function as an adult but not entirely trusted to do so competently—but he was wise enough to know how to distract me. I'd been kneading dough and baking it in my family's ancient iron stove since I was a little girl, and the familiar rhythms— mix, knead, rest, punch, knead again, shape—soothed the part of me that felt like it was covered in spines. Ranarma's process was easier than the one my mother had taught me, as he had the benefit of an electric mixer with a dough hook, but there was nothing magical about it unless one counted the wonders of yeast, and his quiet praise for my technique served as a balm.

My computer sat on the far end of the counter, utterly neglected, as I spent hours moving among the mixer, the counter, and the ovens. Ranarma hadn't said how much bread he needed, so I threw together a few round loaves, a braid, and two dozen dinner rolls. Having found a selection of dried fruit in the pantry, I even made a pan of raisin buns before Ranarma decreed that the next week's needs were surely covered…but he could use a hand with the vegetables. So, I transitioned to the sink, scrubbing and peeling and chopping as he worked on a roast. "Your knife skills are coming along nicely," he told me at one point. "I needn't worry about you like I do about Miss Rose."

"She still has all her fingers."

"By some miracle. Yven, now, that's another matter. The man can competently cook. But, uh…well, I don't paint, and she does, so we all have our skills," he said, which was as polite a put-down as I'd heard in a long while.

Ranarma told Diriem about my contribution as he served dinner, and after sampling my rolls, Diriem looked down the table at me with pleased surprise. "Very nice texture, Maebe. Should I put you on the payroll, then?"

"It's nothing, but thank you," I replied. "I'm happy to help…"

"And I do appreciate that, but it's unnecessary unless you're enjoying yourself and Ranarma doesn't mind." He tried another bite and grunted appreciatively. "Really, this is quite good."

"Stick around," Yven told me in a stage whisper. "The real baking fun is when Ranarma's not looking."

"I heard that," said the cook as he returned to the dining room with the covered roast platter. "You use all my bread flour again, and we're going to have a *talk*."

Yven grinned sheepishly and started to apologize, but Diriem's ringing phone cut him off. "Excuse me," said Diriem, "it's Kabno," and took the call on speaker. "You're working late," he said by way of greeting.

"Because I just received a package at home," came the director's childlike voice. "There's no return address, but there *is* a note to accompany the severed ear."

I dropped my fork, and even Diriem grimaced at the news. "Dare I ask?"

"It's pointed, it's floppy, and I suspect it's a child's," said Kabno. "Meet me at our tower?"

"On my way," he said, and cut the call as he pushed back his chair. "Rosie, Yven, excuse me. Maebe, I'm afraid this meal may need to be reheated at a later hour."

I didn't object. Much as I appreciated Ranarma's work, I'd lost all semblance of an appetite.

CHAPTER 10

The drive into Beukal was quiet that night. Sick with worry, I had little to say, and Diriem kept his eyes on the road, pushing us along at what I suspected was an improper speed. The only time he spoke before pulling into the DOL deck was when he called ahead to the Viratta portal and curtly requested to jump the line.

By the time we arrived, Kabno was waiting in the lobby, still dressed in a formal robe, which told me she probably hadn't changed before returning to the office. "You made good time, Diriem," she said as we approached. "I'm not going to ask."

"Probably wise. You have the package?"

She patted the gnome-sized canvas tote bag she'd slung over her shoulder, which bore the logo of one of the capital's nicer grocery stores. "Upstairs. They're with me," she called to the sorcerer on the security desk, who nodded and minded her own business as we passed.

We rode the elevator to the top floor, and Kabno marched us through the executive suite of the agency, which was largely deserted by that time of the evening. Her corner office, which smelled of citrus cleaners, was more spacious than Diriem's and featured actual floor-to-ceiling windows instead of the simulated ones in the DOI tower, and to my relief, the guest furniture was proportioned for visitors of greater height than her own. She waited until we'd situated ourselves on the couch, then slipped on a pair of disposable gloves and produced a small cardboard box from her bag. The box was unremarkable, only a little longer and wider than my hand, and the top bore an address in Pactish characters, written out in black marker. In one corner was an unfamiliar stamp. Kabno put the box on the coffee table, then dropped a piece of knotted brown twine beside it. "Came tied and taped," she said. "I cut through both, but just in case…"

"May I?" Diriem asked.

"Be my guest."

He didn't bother asking for gloves. A quick gesture pried open the lid of the box, and we leaned closer to see the promised ear sitting on top, swaddled in plastic wrap. With a grimace of distaste, Diriem gestured it out and undid the wrapping, then let the gory delivery come to rest on a tray Kabno offered.

She was right: the ear was pointed and bent in half, a cifyent case—a smaller version of my own. I swallowed my gorge, not wanting to embarrass myself by vomiting all over the evidence.

"Here's the note," said Kabno, reaching into the box, and extracted a tightly folded piece of paper. "I took a look at home, but I couldn't read it."

With a few rapid movements, Diriem had the paper flattened and sitting on the clean tray beside the ear, and he leaned forward to study the writing. "High Elvish," he said, and I sidled closer to see for myself. "The old script is a bit different from the one you've learned."

Having received both versions from Diriem, I had no difficulty reading the note, though that was cold comfort once I scanned its contents.

"What does it say?" asked Kabno.

Diriem cleared his throat. "Paraphrasing slightly, 'Tell the wolf pup that he has one week to release Lord ti'Ammaas and Hemell ti'Vanil and return the eleven million'…they've rendered *dollars* phonetically. Continuing, 'If these conditions are not met, the hostages will die. We send a gift as proof that we hold your missing.'" He looked up at Kabno, his expression grim. "Wonder why they sent it to you and not to me directly."

Her brow knit. "You're the wolf pup?"

"Not a term of affection, I assure you. So, we have a ransom note. And there was no address at all?"

She gestured toward the open box. "Look for yourself. My home address and a stamp, but that's all." Folding her arms, she said, "I don't suppose it would do any good to call DPL, eh?"

"What's DPL?" I asked, looking back and forth between the directors.

"The Division of Parcels and Letters," Diriem replied, "and Kabno, I've seen nothing suggesting that they'd be any more forthcoming than usual."

Noticing my confusion, she explained, "DPL runs the mail system throughout the Pactlands—"

"And outside it," said Diriem.

"Yes," Kabno allowed, "for growers and such. They only hire sorcerers, and the spells that move the mail around are a closely held secret. DPL prides itself on two things: getting mail where it needs to go, and protecting the privacy of its customers."

"I can't count the number of times that one of our agencies has turned to DPL for information regarding an anonymous package, only for that information to mysteriously disappear from their records," said Diriem, and rolled his eyes. "Annoying, to say the least."

"They're pains in the ass," Kabno muttered, "but since they're the only ones who know how the mail runs, we're stuck with them."

Diriem reached for the phone in his pocket. "Still, I suppose it can't hurt to try. Best behavior, now," he said, and Kabno snorted as he dialed.

After three rings, a male voice answered. "Diriem? Working after hours again?"

"Good evening, Bamtada," he said, his voice smooth and almost friendly. "I'm here with Kabno—"

"Hi," she said in a tone that spoke of long friendship.

"So sorry to bother you…"

"No, I'm just preparing for dinner," said Bamtada. "The stew will keep. What's going on?"

Kabno and Diriem shared a look, and she took the lead. "We've got a hostage situation."

"*Ooh.*"

"Yeah. Possibly outside. Anyway, I came home to find a ransom note in my mailbox, and it would *greatly* assist our investigation if you could tell us who sent it."

Bamtada said nothing for a moment, then sighed. "You know our policy, Kabno."

"I do, but surely an exception—"

"If we begin making exceptions, that sets bad precedent."

"I could find a judge to authorize the release."

"You could," he allowed, "but I'm not sure how much you would find."

As her mouth tightened, Diriem tried his luck. "We don't mean to put you in a difficult situation, but this is quite possibly a matter of life and death."

"And I don't mean to be flippant," Bamtada replied, "but I've heard that line from you two before."

"I know, but do me a favor and listen. The people responsible snatched children," he murmured. "Toddlers among them. At their last location, they were being kept in the cold in cages, and I do mean freezing temperatures. We don't know whether they're being fed, given sufficient water, having their injuries treated…"

"That's…unfortunate," he allowed.

"And the letter Kabno received tonight, the one with no address? It came with a severed ear. A child's, clearly."

The phone fell silent, and I held my breath as we waited for Bamtada's reply. After a long moment, he coughed, then said, "I…cannot give you the sender's identity. You know that."

"Of course," said Diriem. "But if we knew where the package originated, we might be able to shut this down before someone dies. The younglings have been moved, but we don't know where."

A quiet sigh was Bamtada's only response, but the other two directors smirked as they waited. I heard footsteps on the other end, then rapid typing, and finally, Bamtada said, "You're not going to like this."

"And why is that?" asked Kabno.

"Because the package was sent from within the Pactlands. That's all I can tell you."

Though her face betrayed her frustration, she remained collected. "Thank you. We'll leave you to your dinner."

Just before Diriem could end the call, Bamtada said, "I hope you find them, I really do. It's…well…"

"Again, thank you," said Diriem, and shook his head as he tapped the button. "Well, that was slightly better than expected."

"Not good enough," Kabno muttered. "Though it does complicate matters…"

"Um, question," I ventured. When Diriem nodded for me to proceed, I said, "How'd they mail it from in *here*? Would DPL know if, like, they sent it from a grower's mailbox outside?"

"Oh, absolutely," said Kabno. "Which tells me that someone sneaked through a portal."

"Truly a monumental feat," Diriem replied sarcastically.

Coming to my rescue once again, Kabno told me, "The external portals are notoriously porous, shall we say? They let out quite a bit more than they should. And while agency cars always have their odometer readings logged, not every vehicle is so carefully recorded."

Diriem added, "No one ever accused the Portal Authority of hiring the best and the brightest. The attendants' salaries tend to be low, and it's not uncommon to catch them accepting bribes."

"Or worse, secondary employment," said Kabno, scowling at Diriem. "I'll put a team on the Portal Authority and have the external records for the last two days pulled. Won't help us if our sender sneaked in, but it's possible there'll be something noteworthy in the traffic."

"What's your thought?"

"The ti'Ammaas group has someone on the inside," she replied without hesitation. "They wouldn't be able to get in on their own—the only time any of them were allowed across was for the trials, and they were carefully monitored and chaperoned. Do you suppose ti'Pul is their man here?"

His eyebrows rose. "Culta? No."

"You're positive?"

"On this, yes."

Kabno tapped two fingers against her chin. "All right, then, who's your pick?"

He propped his head in his hands and began to absently rub his temples. "I don't have anything firm..."

"I'll take whatever you can offer. Impressions, at least?"

A grunt preceded his answer. "I feel like there's a ti'Cren connection, but it's still vague. Could be a member of Inade's family, could be a cousin, perhaps an associate of his."

She didn't look thrilled at the news, but then anything less than a name would have left her wanting. "I'll tell my people to bear that in mind when they review the portal records. Is there anything else you can give me?"

"Unfortunately, not yet." Raising his face, he said, "We have time, though. There's a clock, and perhaps the visions will clarify—"

"Give me the bloodline potion."

The directors twitched at my interruption, and both turned to me. "Absolutely not," said Diriem. "We've been over this, Maebe."

"That was before the ear!" I protested, jabbing my finger toward the lump of flesh on the table. Dried blood had crusted over the side that had once been attached to my cousin's head. "They're going to kill my family!"

"They've sent their terms—"

"And are you all planning to go along with them?"

"Of course not," said Kabno. "Negotiation with terrorists is seldom wise."

"Okay, so what's to stop them from killing their hostages?" I asked, fighting the urge to blow the pictures off the walls.

"I understand that you're upset, dear," she replied, "but think of it this way: those hostages are the only bargaining chips the kidnappers have. If they kill them, they'll never get what they want."

"Yeah, but if they realize you won't bargain and cut their losses..." Turning to Diriem, I asked, "Is there another potion we could try? Something that won't hurt my heart so badly?"

He considered the question for a few seconds, then said, "The only viable alternative that comes to mind is a tracker."

"Which is?"

"It's possible to brew a potion, prime it with the blood of the missing—or a close relation—and make a tracker. Apply it to a compass, and the needle will point in the direction of the person sought. For your group...if we used your blood and kept you and Connor within the Pactlands, then the compass would point to your kin outside."

There it was. "Great!" I said, almost jumping off the couch. "Let's do it—"

"Whoa, girl," said Kabno, pushing me back into my seat. "It's not that precise. Until you're relatively close to your target, the tracker tells you little."

Diriem nodded. "The problem is that they have a considerable head start. If we took a tracker to Theo's cabin, it might give us a general direction, but how far would be another matter."

"And trackers can be blocked," Kabno added. "If these people are able to stymie farseers, then I wouldn't be surprised if they've taken precautions against tracking as well."

My short-lived excitement fizzled back toward despair. "Can't you *try*?"

The directors exchanged glances, and Kabno said, "We have a supply of the base potion in reserve. If you're willing to serve as the donor, I'll send a recon group to the last known location and see what they can discover."

Before she'd finished speaking, I'd thrust out my arm. "Take whatever you need. Just *find* them."

As I learned that evening, DOL's pace slowed overnight but never stopped, and there were always a few healers on duty. While one of them filled a small vial from my arm, Kabno sent for an agent working the late shift who could pull a tracker together. The agent, a sorcerer with a salt-and-pepper bob and purple-stained fingers—I didn't ask—met us in the medical unit with a bottle holding a pale blue potion and a compass marked with Pactish characters. She added my blood to the potion until it turned purple, then gave the bottle a good shake and poured some of the liquid onto the compass, which began to glow blue. Turning away from the sink with the compass in hand, she aimed it at me, and the needle spun to point in my direction. "It's working," she announced. "Now, who are we looking for? Parents? Grandparents?"

"Cousins," I replied. "One's my uncle…"

The sorcerer made a face. "Ooh. Trackers tend to work best with close, immediate relationships—parents and children, usually. Once you get past that—"

"It's not great, I know, but it's the best we can do," Kabno interjected. "Also, we're looking for the East Branch group, so they're, um…more closely related than one might suspect."

"*Ah.*" The agent gave me a more appraising stare. "I'm still not overly optimistic, but we can try. Where do we begin?"

Leaving Kabno to make the arrangements with her people and ask Wylan for a lift, Diriem and I headed back to his car and out of the city. We were nearly to the portal building when he said, "You seem pensive."

I rubbed the fresh bandage over the crook of my elbow and stared out at the passing streetlights. "Just thinking about what Kabno said."

"About the limitations of the tracker?"

"No." As none of the agency personnel had seemed hopeful about the tracker's efficacy, I was trying to temper my expectations. "About the hostage situation."

"What about it?" he asked, pulling up at a red light.

"So…she said that Danirri's not likely to kill them because they're all he has to bargain with, right? No hostages, no Ivari."

Diriem nodded.

"But what's to stop him from getting more?" I continued. "He—or whoever is working with him—got a couple dozen people away from school and out to Michigan, and no one would have known where they went had Theo not been bored enough to check his cameras. If he did it once, he could do it again. Maybe snatch some people worth more than my family."

My companion said nothing until the light turned blue, and as he sped on, he murmured, "I tend to agree. I…don't believe they're as safe as Kabno surmises."

"Is that farsight?" I asked, my chest clenching.

"No. That's just my thought after having seen Kabno's delivery. Someone who would cut off a child's ear to make a point like that isn't likely to be amenable to compromise." Glancing quickly at me, he added, "I don't want to burden Connor with this while he's meant to be convalescing, but I suppose we'd better inform him. He'll be insufferable otherwise."

He wasn't wrong. "Tonight?"

"Yes. Visiting hours should be over, but we can call once we're home. Probably safer for us that way," he said, and having witnessed my cousin with his dander up, I heartily concurred.

"God *damn* it," was Connor's immediate reaction when Diriem broke the news of the gristly package. Rose had filled him and Jane in on the failed rescue earlier that day, and the latest developments did nothing to improve his mood. "Tell me there's a plan."

"We're trying a tracker," Diriem replied. "It's—"

"A tracker?" Jane interjected. "Like the one I used to find my mother?"

"Exactly."

"*Why*? Those things are crap once you get past three degrees of kinship."

Diriem closed his eyes and pinched the bridge of his nose. Had Jane been in the room, I suspected she'd have received a swift kick under the table. "It's the best option we have at the moment," he finally said. "Without a good anchor for a bloodline trace—"

"Put me in," said Connor. "I feel great."

"Absolutely not. You're still healing—"

"Fuck that! I'm *fine*," he insisted. "The aneurysms have been fixed, my head's closing up, and I'm getting good reports from the healers—"

A sharp double knock interrupted him, and then a female voice said in Pactish, "Hi! How are we feeling? Did you eat dinner...oh, I'm sorry, am I interrupting?"

"No, please, come in," Jane insisted. "We're just, uh, chatting."

"If that's all right, then. This won't take long," said the woman. "Let's see about the patient..."

"Pardon me," said Diriem, leaning closer to the phone, "but are you a healer?"

"Oh, hello, there," she replied with a soft chuckle. "Yes, I am. Doing evening rounds, and Connor, if you'll hold still, I'd like to take a look under that dressing."

"Question for you, if I may."

"Uh…well, that depends on the question. I'm afraid I can't release patient information without their consent, but if there's something more general you'd like to know…"

"A hypothetical, then," he said. "Suppose you had a patient with a known heart defect who'd recently been treated for multiple cerebral aneurysms. Would you consider that patient a candidate for the bloodline potion?"

The healer's incredulous laughter was louder that time. "Not on my life. What sort of hypothetical is that? And Connor, dear, if you keep twitching your head, I'm going to give you an inadvertent haircut."

"Okay," said Connor, "let's change up the hypothetical. What if twenty members of your patient's family were abducted and being held for ransom? Would you let him take the potion then?"

Briefly, she fell silent, then asked, "This isn't a hypothetical, is it?"

"What gave it away?" Connor muttered.

"Your face, for one. Heavens," she said, and whistled. "I…I understand the impetus to do a blood trace, but son, you're in no condition. It might kill you."

"It also might not."

"Yeah, but I don't like the odds. There's no healer in this building who'll clear you for that. I'm sorry, I am, but you're not well enough. Maybe in six months, we can reevaluate—"

"They'll be dead in six months," I blurted. "We've got a *week*."

"Who—" the healer began.

"My little cousin," said Connor, "who's taken it twice. She's in worse shape than I am."

"Last I checked, Maebe didn't have a hole in her skull," Jane retorted. "Con—"

"We don't have a better option!" he cried. "I don't see Culta and his brother lining up to volunteer, do you?"

"Honey—"

"Maebe *can't*. I'm stronger. Let me do this, let me find them—"

"You're talking about suicide," the healer cut in, her voice low and firm. "I don't say this lightly, but if I have to sedate you for your own safety, I will."

"Not if I check myself out of here," Connor retorted.

"You can try, but you won't reach the door."

His tone sharpened. "So…you're telling me I'm a prisoner? Is that it?"

"She's trying to save your life, boy," Diriem snapped. "It's what they do best. Don't tell me you've never heard of a psych hold."

"Butt out, Diriem," he growled.

"I'm sorry," said the healer, "*who*—"

"Let me," Jane interjected, and switched to English. "Boss, back off, I've got this in hand. Con, you can't be a martyr. End of discussion."

"But—" Connor began.

"End. Of. *Discussion*," said Jane, enunciating every syllable. "Don't make me sit on you."

"What if I took it here with healers around?"

"Connor Willow, I swear to God—"

Someone yelped in the background, and I heard Jane revert to Pactish with a hasty, "Sorry, pyromancer. It's under control. Uh…look, let me take this call out of here, and you and Connor do what you need to do, all right?"

I heard footsteps and the latch of a closing door, and then Jane, her voice much louder, came on the line. "He *is* doing better, and he's getting restless. The healers want to keep him for a few more days, which makes sense to me, but—"

"Tell him that I don't see him taking the bloodline potion," said Diriem. "Once he's calm again, naturally."

"Who do you see taking it, then?" she asked.

I studied Diriem, trying to pull meaning from his blank expression. The man could shutter his face better than anyone I'd ever met.

"I'm not positive," he replied after a pause, "but it's not Connor. Whatever his part may be in this matter, it's not to kill himself with that potion."

Jane sighed. "You're not going to give me more than that, are you?"

"I'm afraid not. Keep an eye on him, eh? Or a leash?"

They ended the call shortly thereafter, but I remained seated, watching Diriem, who noticed me and slightly cocked his head like an inquisitive bird. "Yes, Maebe?"

"Who takes the potion?"

"I don't know."

"But someone does? Is that how we find them?"

He held my stare in silence, and I groaned as I rose. "That's *really* frustrating, you know?"

I'd nearly reached the door when he called, "Believe me, child, you're not the first to say so."

I couldn't sleep. Plagued by dreams of half-formed monsters hiding in the shadows of my mind, I eventually gave up and checked my phone for the time. Nearly midnight— too late to be awake, too early to start the day, and a miserable time all around if I couldn't force myself to sleep. But as the thought of trying to drift off again was about as appealing as asking Kabno for another peek inside her delightful package, I climbed out of bed, pulled on my bathrobe, and went for a late-night stroll.

As in the past, I'd been shown to a guest room on the second floor of the southern wing of the mansion, two stories below Rose and Yven's spacious apartment. While my room was nicer than anywhere I'd ever stayed—a leather sofa, stained-glass windows, a bed wide enough for three and soft as a cloud—one of the bonus perks was the long balcony, accessible from the hallway. Diriem had outfitted the balcony with a selection of chairs, tables, and chaises, providing places to sit without cluttering the area. During the daylight hours and the odd rainstorm, a roof extended to protect those who needed a breath of fresh air, but at night, the roof retracted, all the better for stargazing.

I settled onto a chaise and tucked my hands behind my head to take in the view. As Pactlands towns went, Viratta was respectable but still provincial beside Beukal—large enough for a portal but small enough to offer a night sky more black than purple. The waning moon hadn't yet risen, and so the only illumination was the glittering spray above me...well, that, plus the balcony railing, which glowed blue to avert tragedy.

Astronomy as such wasn't taught at East Branch. Oh, we knew a little, and the elders spoke of listening to the radio and hearing about men landing on the *moon*, of all places, but for us, the stars were less about physics or poetry and more for navigation. I could track the seasons by the shifting constellations, even if the ones I knew were unfamiliar to anyone not raised in the community. But on quiet nights, when the weather was fine and I couldn't sleep, I used to creep out of my family's cabin to lie atop one of the picnic tables by the meeting house and stare into space, discovering ever fainter pinpricks of light as my eyes adjusted and the impossible vastness opened above me.

Perhaps that was what sowed the seed of discontentment in my core, the urge to run away and find something bigger than East Branch, though it didn't seem fair to blame the distant stars for my community's destruction. *That* remained my doing.

And now, if DOL didn't free Ivari and beggar all of us, would Connor and I be left alone to carry on the memory of East Branch? Would the rest of our cousins die, yet more victims of my push to seek a better life in the Pactlands?

I'd told my parents I would be *safe* here. The elders, those sweet souls who knew enough of the outside to avoid it, had trusted that I knew what I was doing, that I wouldn't lead our kin into danger. And Diriem swore that East Branch would have fallen with or without me, but…

But.

There was no way of seeing a future that would never come to pass, no way to tell whether I'd sent my family down the best of our bad paths—and if I hadn't, there was no way to undo my mistakes.

Worse still, there was no clear future for us on the path we *had* taken, and the stars, beautiful as they were, offered me no answers that night. Still, I lay there and watched the sky as if the solution might present itself if I peered deeply enough into the void.

And that was where Diriem found me: curled up with my feet tucked inside my robe and shivering in the darkness, trying not to imagine my cousins freezing to death in cages. "Maebe?" he whispered, gently nudging my shoulder until he saw I was awake. "What are you doing outside?"

"I'm about as useful here as I am anywhere else, so…" I shrugged and slid my cold hands into my sleeves. "Whole lot of nothing."

"Can't sleep?"

"Yeah. What about you?"

"Paperwork," he replied, sitting on the chaise beside me. "Do you want a sleeping potion? The hangover's not bad if you take a light dose."

"I'm okay," I said.

"No, you're not." Scooting closer to me, he said, "There's nothing we can do tonight, youngling, so we sleep and hope for clearer heads in the morning. I need you functional."

I stared back at him, seeking hidden truths in the darker and lighter shadows of his face. "Why? If I can't take the bloodline potion, then what can I do?"

Diriem softly sighed. "I don't have all the answers. Never pretended that I did. But sometimes, when all you have is a hunch…you trust it. And I have a feeling about you, Maebe." With that, he held out one hand in invitation. "Come inside before you freeze, hmm?"

I gave the stars one last look, but when no portent appeared, I uncurled and let him escort me back into the warmth of the mansion.

I was safe. My kin were not. And even with the promised sleeping potion, my dreams haunted me until long past dawn.

CHAPTER 11

When I came downstairs Thursday morning, I was perplexed to find a white-frosted cake in the middle of the dining table. It was missing about a quarter, and the cutaway section revealed three chocolate layers with a berry filling sandwiched in between. "Since when is cake a breakfast food?" I asked, making a beeline for the coffeepot.

"It's my birthday," Rose mumbled around a mouthful of chocolate, then swallowed hard. "And Ranarma's a mensch."

I wasn't quite sure of the meaning of the term—heck, I didn't know what language it was from—but the cook appeared a moment later with a more reasonable spread of eggs and toast, and I gratefully dug in. "So...thirty?" I guessed.

Rose nodded and sipped her tea. "Yup. The big three-oh. It's all downhill from here."

Beside her, Yven pointedly snorted and shoveled in a forkful of dessert.

"I'm *teasing* you," she said, and leaned over to kiss him. "And hey, I'm more than half your age. We're making *progress.*"

Before Yven could counter that, Diriem stepped in from the kitchen, espresso cup in hand. He took one look at the cake, then at the others' chocolate crumb–strewn plates, and shook his head. "Youth," he muttered, and eyed my breakfast. "At least one of you chose something sensible for the hour."

"More for me," said Rose, undaunted by the critique, and licked the icing off her fork.

In fairness, she deserved the cake. Rose had been intermittently trancing for days, searching for any sign of the abductees or Ivari's family, but all of her work had turned up nothing. She and Yven were bound for the office after breakfast, and I saw them off, dreading the thought of trying to focus on my backlog of lessons. My tutors continued to send me the assignments they were doing with Sage, but I simply couldn't concentrate.

By ten, I'd brought my computer down to the kitchen, where Ranarma could distract me. I was chopping vegetables at the sink, having by then abandoned all pretense of studying, when Diriem marched in, charcoal formal robe fluttering behind him. "Ah, there you are, Maebe," he said, spotting me with my wooden cutting board. "Busy?"

"I can spare her," Ranarma joked.

Diriem nodded. "Good. I want you on a call at noon. Your computer is charged?"

I glanced at the device, which I'd left on the counter by the bar stools, and made a face. "Kind of?"

"Charge it. You'll need it. And…" He gave my pajamas a once-over. "Perhaps something a little more formal, yes? It's a video call."

Having never had a need for such at school, I quickly ran through my computer lessons but came up emptyhanded. "Uh…sure, but I don't know how to do that."

"It shouldn't be difficult," said Diriem, "but for the slight complication that we're using an outside program. You don't know anything about Zoom, do you?"

All I could offer him was a shrug.

"Thought so," he muttered, though he seemed more peeved with the situation than with me. "All right, go dress, then meet me in my office with your computer and the charger. We'll figure this out now so we don't look like idiots."

I did as he asked, running upstairs to throw on a nice

sweater and dark pants, plus a touch of the makeup I was still learning to use, then came down with my equipment and knocked as I let myself in to his office. "Right there," he said, pointing to the chair he'd pulled closer to his desk but not looking up from his screen. "The outlet's in the wall behind that box."

"What's this about, anyway?" I asked as I plugged in.

"Just a moment, let me finish…"

I waited silently as Diriem set up his account, and then he sat back with a satisfied sigh. "There we go. I'll walk you through this—"

"*What* is going on?"

He twitched at the interruption. "Oh—sorry. Theo called. Madla wants to talk."

I frowned. "Madla ti'Un?"

"Precisely. She wants a face-to-face meeting, and frankly, I don't blame her. I offered to arrange for her to be escorted in, but she opted for the electronic route, so we're having a meeting shortly. Madla and me," he said, counting off on his fingers, "Theo, Culta, Kabno, Wylan, and now you."

"Why me?" I asked.

Diriem barely tilted his head and flashed a small, enigmatic smile, and I groaned.

By ten of noon, we'd both set up and tested our new accounts, and I was scrolling through the backgrounds to entertain myself while I awaited the hour. The beach wasn't believable, I decided, but before I could choose among the other options, the meeting I'd been waiting to enter began, and my screen divided into boxes.

Theo, who was running the meeting, popped in first, followed by Culta and Diriem. Kabno appeared next—sitting at her desk at DOL, I thought, considering the view of the capital behind her—and then Wylan joined from his home office, a room of slate, leather, and dark wood. He'd opted for the Hunt's usual uniform, an off-white homespun shirt that laced up the front, in lieu of the robes the directors sported, and he stared into the camera with an unsettling, almost unblinking gaze.

Finally, the last square popped up, and I saw the pretty brunette I remembered from my ill-fated visit to Rush and Sons appear on the screen. She wasn't nearly as put-together that day; her face appeared to be clean-scrubbed, and her hair hung loose and wavy over her shoulder. She wore a lilac cotton sweater, and surprisingly, a pair of slim silver hoops hung from her earlobes. She wasn't otherwise masked, and I wondered whether she'd simply forgotten her earrings. I couldn't see much of her surroundings, but the steel refrigerator behind her suggested she was calling from a kitchen. Culta likewise seemed to be sitting at a dining table, while Theo, masked, hunched over his computer from a plush chair covered in an ugly beige-heavy pattern.

"I think that's everyone," Theo began in English. "Can you hear me?"

Nods and quick affirmations answered that, and Diri-em stepped in. "Lady ti'Un," he said, switching to High Elvish. "We meet again."

Madla inclined her head. "Lord ti'Dana. Thanks for jumping on the call. If the network acts up, forgive me—my quarters have always been slightly problematic in terms of connectivity."

I thought I was mishearing her until I realized that her speech was peppered with English terms. Of course, seeing as High Elvish was an old and dying tongue at best, it made sense that she had to borrow a few words for concepts that hadn't existed when it was in its prime.

"Not a problem," he replied, and switched to English again. "I believe this is the preferred tongue for your younger compatriots, so if you're unopposed…"

"Oh, heavens," said Madla, waving him off as she followed his lead, "this is fine."

Her accent was quite similar to Culta's, I noted, though it had a slight lilt that his lacked.

Diriem nodded. "Thank you. Allow me to introduce the others. This is my colleague from the Division of Laws, Kabno Erenani…hmm…" Briefly, he scowled at the screen, then gave up. "I never know where to point with these things."

"Hi," said Kabno, lifting a hand and coming to his rescue. "He could just say 'the short one.'"

"If I didn't want to live," Diriem retorted. "And the gentleman is—"

"Wylan," he finished, raising a finger. "Afternoon."

Madla's brow furrowed. "You…you're not with the Wild Hunt, are you?"

"I am."

"You people let the *Hunt* in?" she asked, aghast.

"Well," said Diriem as Wylan wiggled one hand in a *kind of* gesture, "technically, the Hunter showed up and signed on, and no one made a fuss. This is the present Hunter," he continued, "a representative to the Forum, and the head of the strike team sent to Michigan, so I asked him to join us on the call."

"O…*kay*," she said slowly, eyeing her camera as if Wylan might leap through the screen at her. In fairness, having seen the room around her, he probably could have managed it.

"And this is Maebe," Diriem concluded, glancing at me over his computer's screen. "One of the two East Branch survivors presently accounted for."

Madla's dark eyes narrowed in thought as she considered me. "I remember you. Ivari's heir, right? You were the one who set his office on fire."

"That was an accident," I mumbled, reddening.

"But not altogether undeserved, I should think."

The comment caught me off guard, and Madla's lips twitched at my expression. "I attended his trial, you know. Saw your testimony. I, um…I'm very sorry for your loss, little one."

"Uh…thanks."

As I swallowed hard, Theo took the lead. "So, I told Madla that my cabin was a bust, and she wants to help, if she can."

"We'll take whatever we can get," said Kabno, smiling grimly. "What do you have for us?"

"It might help to know what you found in Michigan," Madla replied. "The boys were vague on the details."

Wylan cleared his throat. "Short version, the cabin was locked up and dark. No cages left, but there were impressions in the dirt, and around them was paint indicative of a spell ring. The security cameras were transmitting recorded footage, not current views. We could smell evidence of elves and gasoline, so the working theory is that they were packed into a vehicle or vehicles and driven off the property, but the trail's gone cold."

Madla nodded. "Still blocked to farsight?"

"Unfortunately," said Diriem.

She held up her hand, on which she wore a ring like Theo's. "The spell that powers this is complex but not impossible to pull off with one person. I wouldn't be surprised if Danirri can do it, and I *know* Farral can."

"Any tips on breaking through it?" he asked.

Chuckling, she replied, "Since there isn't a farseer among us, we've never had occasion to experiment. I wouldn't know where to begin."

"That's fair." Steepling his fingers, Diriem asked, "Where could they have gone with a couple dozen captives?"

Absently, Madla ran a hand back through her hair. "From Michigan? Any number of places. I've checked our garage, and none of the vehicles are missing. We've got a few SUVs, but transporting...how many, again?

"Twenty from East Branch," I offered, "and seven other students."

"Oof. Nothing we have is large enough to move a group that size. That said, I did check the petty cash expenditures for the last week, and wouldn't you know that we have payments to U-Haul?"

"Sorry, what's that?" Wylan asked.

"They rent moving vans and such," Madla explained. "You pack, you drive, you return it. Now, there's no reason under the heavens that anyone in our building should need a moving van, and yet..."

Kabno frowned. "They paid cash?"

"No, it's a credit card. Been called the petty cash account for ages, but we went to plastic a while back. Anyone working for the firm has access—it's for things like office supplies, postage, drinks, the usual," she said, spreading her hands. "Farral heads Accounting for us—internal matters, I mean, not the brokerage side. Payroll, licensure, taxes, stuff like that. But since *I* head Admin, I've also got access to the accounts, and I did a little snooping before breakfast. The van's not the first weird charge on the account. I can't tell you who used the card," she continued, "but knowing our people fairly well, I'd say all signs point to Farral or one of her and Ivari's brood. He's always been lax with his children...well, most of them."

Theo nodded, and in the next window over, Culta shrugged. "It's no great secret that Father has no use for me," he said.

"Nor that he's unusually generous with the rest of us," added Theo. "That's the only reason I have the place in Michigan. Granted, my parents have keys, but since Father seldom allowed anyone to move out of the building..."

"Considerable freedom," his brother chimed in. "Though I suspect he let me get an apartment because he didn't want to deal with me day to day."

Theo made a face. "You're...*probably* not wrong. Anyway, since Father's incarceration, Mother hasn't tightened the purse strings."

"Nor would she in this," said Madla, "since my gut tells she's wrapped up in it."

"But back to the pressing matter," Kabno interjected,

"*where* could they have gone? What other properties do they have access to?"

At that, Madla grimaced, a pained flash of pointed teeth. "So, Ivari kept us close, but he—or the firm, at least on paper—has remote holdings all over the country, just in case."

"In case of what?"

Her brow knit. "You *are* aware of what happened to us, yes? Around the time that all of you ran off? We lost everything. Our families, our homes, anything fortified...Ivari's paranoid about us being homeless again, and frankly, I don't blame him."

When Diriem chimed in, his voice was soft. "You were young at the collapse, were you not?"

"Yeah." Madla's jaw tightened briefly, but she held her composure. "I remember Father telling us that your envoy had invited all of the Halls to evacuate. He wouldn't go—ti'Un has never been a Hall of great rank, but Father was loyal to Ivari to the end. A few months after that, he and my mother were killed in a skirmish, and I inherited the Hall. I was eighty."

He winced.

"My little brothers died shortly thereafter—I only had the pair of them, twins, seventeen and foolhardy—and in midwinter, the mob attacked. Slaughtered my vassals, my cousins, those who'd run to the Hall for protection. I fled toward the king with a handful of people, but they were picked off along the way, and by the time I arrived, I was all that was left of ti'Un."

Kabno seemed somewhat impatient, but Diriem looked intently at the screen. "And Ivari protected you?"

Madla laughed bitterly. "For a time, but the mob found him in less than a year. I wasn't the only head of a shattered Hall who had come to him for help by then, and he held us back during the fighting. I...saw then what sort of man he was. My father always led from the front, but Ivari barked orders from the rear. Cowardly, perhaps, but that cowardice did save our skins. When the fighting ceased and night fell, the eighteen of us escaped out a secret passage and fled for our lives."

He nodded. "You remained with him?"

"What choice did I have? He was my king, and where else could I have gone? I had *nothing*," she stressed. "The clothing on my back and a small bag of jewelry I'd taken before running from my home. That's all long gone—we sold whatever we could when food was scarce, and my possessions were the first we sold off. Hall seniority does have its perks," she added with a faint smirk. "But yes, I remained with the group all the way to England, and...well."

"The intermarriage."

She sighed. "Yes. He said it was necessary, that it was our best chance of survival, only a temporary measure, and...I mean, he *was* our king..."

"You needn't say more on the subject," Diriem replied. "We're not here to cause you pain."

But her eyes flashed. "That faithless whore-get murdered my babies' babies. I suppose you have his talent contained?"

"Naturally," said Kabno, "but—"

"Give me five minutes with him in his present condition, and I'll remove him from your list of problems."

Kabno seemed taken aback by Madla's quiet fury. "We...do try not to lose people we're keeping in custody, but, um...thanks for the offer."

"You had descendants among the ones killed at East Branch?" Diriem murmured.

"I don't know for sure," said Madla, "but I have to assume. They did intermarry quite a bit, right? I...I never wanted anything to happen to them, not to my children, but to hear what Ivari did to the remnants of our community, to our *families*...he swore he wouldn't touch them..."

I hadn't expected to see tears in her eyes, but they glistened despite her anger.

"You cared for them," Diriem said, fixing her with a strange look.

"I know how it sounds, I know they were partly human, but—"

"Dear girl, you needn't apologize."

She stared at her screen, her expression vacillating—perhaps bemusement mingled with relief. "They destroyed everything we had, they killed our people, but I…" She hesitated, then said softly, as if releasing a long-held secret, "I loved him so much. My David."

"Your son?" he guessed.

"My husband. David Peters. He…" Again, she paused, glancing away as she gathered her thoughts. "We came upon this village—barely that. More of a settlement. They'd been so ravaged by disease that they were struggling to hold on. We were stronger, and they were too desperate to object to a little magic," she said, shaking her head. "Their elders came to Ivari and suggested a formal alliance—marriages to seal the deal, as it were. We wanted protection and a place to rest, and we'd been wandering for more than a century by then, chased half the time. He agreed, and he told us what we needed to do. I was the first to be married off, and their elders gave me to David. Poor boy," she said, briefly smiling at the memory. "Neither of us wanted it or knew what to do with each other. He was twenty-three and had never been married, and neither had I. I…Ivari told me not to fight if he tried to have his way with me, that this was what I had to do, and I was prepared, but David…he was terrified. We just talked that night, you know? Got acquainted. He told me about losing his family to fever, and I told him about losing mine to humans, and he…" She swallowed hard. "He apologized. That poor, sweet boy *apologized* for something he'd had no part of. And he said he'd be a fool to try to force me, so if we never consummated the marriage, that could be our secret."

"But you did," I said quietly.

"Eventually. He was kind. Naïve in some ways, hardened in others, but he was a *kind* soul. He made me laugh. After we'd lived together for a few weeks, we sort of adjusted to each other, and after a while, he lost some of his fear, and I…" Her face began to color. "I found myself with a handsome man in the bed beside me, and I wanted him."

If Theo and Culta were repulsed by her confession, they bit their tongues.

"And you had children with him," Diriem prompted.

Nodding, Madla said, "Four. Two daughters, two sons. I'd have given David more, but he died the year after our last was born. Pneumonia, I believe. We only had fifteen years together."

Diriem switched back to High Elvish, perhaps for a measure of privacy. "You have my sympathy. I, too, have lost a spouse."

Though her tears still threatened to spill, she managed a tight smile. "Not a human wife, I trust."

"No," he allowed, "but our son married one."

Madla sat up a little straighter, then sniffled as a look of understanding crossed her face, and Diriem slowly nodded. "It's all right," he whispered.

"Thank you," she whispered back.

We waited for a moment while she rubbed her eyes with the heels of her hands, and then I said in English, "Excuse me, Madla?"

"Yes?" she replied, wet-faced.

By then, I'd opened my digitized copy of our records, the log of every birth, marriage, and death in East Branch. "You said you had four children, correct? Caroline, Jacob, Matthew—"

"And Catherine," she finished. "How did you know?"

"Because I have the records right here," I replied, pointing to my keyboard. "From East Branch."

Her watery eyes widened. "Can you…I'm sure there are many generations, but is it possible to see if any of their descendants still live? Did any survive Ivari? My Cath never married, but the other three had families…"

"It would take me some time to trace everyone," I told her, "but if you'll hold on just a moment…" Opening a second document, I scanned the list I'd meticulously made of my own descent. "Well," I said, minimizing the document to look back at Madla, "I can't give you a full breakdown right now, but I come from three of your kids. And my Uncle Kyle, I know he's connected, too. He's got a little boy, Eugene…" I paused as Madla's face crumpled. "Oh, jeez, I'm sorry, I didn't mean to upset—"

"You're serious?" she asked, her voice wavering. "You're…"

"That's what the records say," I replied. "I can trace myself back to your sons and Caroline. And she…wait…" Scanning my lists again, I said, "Yup. She married Richard Willow, right?"

"Uh-huh," Madla managed.

"That's the main ti'Catama line. My cousin Connor comes from them, and he's here. In the hospital, I mean…oh, he's recovering, he's not sick," I hastily added as her mouth opened. "Everyone else is missing, but—"

"Ivari tried to kill you. I watched him…"

"No harm done."

She covered her mouth and slowly shook her head. "I'm so…so sorry," she said, and then she fell to pieces.

After a moment, Theo turned off Madla's camera and muted her, giving her a chance to compose herself in private. "Well, uh," he said, rubbing the back of his neck, "*that* was unexpected."

Switching to Pactish, Kabno asked, "This isn't going to be a quick call, is it?"

"No," Diriem replied, "I should think not. Patience."

"I'll delay my one o'clock. Wylan?"

"Nothing pressing here," he said, leaning back in his chair.

After a long, awkward pause of several minutes, Madla

returned to the call, puffy-eyed but once again able to talk. "I apologize," she said stiffly. "This isn't helping you. What can I provide? You want Ivari's properties?"

"That would be useful, yes," said Kabno.

"Okay. It'll take me a little time to search the system, but I know where to find the deeds."

She murmured her thanks and produced a notepad. "In the interim, can you think of any offhand?"

"Addresses? No," said Madla, "but I know he has property in the Everglades, a place in the Outer Banks, one in a remote corner of Arizona…"

"All south of Michigan, correct?"

My spirits rose, but only for a second. "Those three, yes," she replied, "but he's got more northerly retreats, too. There's a hunting property in Montana."

Wylan nodded appreciatively. "Good hunting there."

"Yes, but the weather's lousy this time of year. If you thought Michigan was bad…"

"They'll die of exposure," Kabno finished.

"That's what I fear. I don't know what Danirri and his whore mother have in mind, but considering the cages at Theo's place and the *ear* that I understand you people received—"

The director raised her pen and grimaced.

"Lovely," Madla muttered. "I'll be honest with you, I'm worried. Farral is nothing if not loyal to Ivari, and she…well, let's just say her marriage back in England wasn't a happy one. Henry was a brute, worse when he was drinking. She wanted to kill him, but Ivari talked her out of it, so she suffered for years. Only gave him two children, but not because *he* didn't try. They weren't born from love, if you understand me."

"You're saying she's traumatized," Kabno replied.

"Precisely. If she ended the rest of East Branch, I don't believe she'd wail and beat her breast. With that said, I'll assemble a list of possible destinations as quickly as I can—"

"Hold on." Leaning toward her camera, Kabno said, "A thought. We might not need it."

"Why's that?" asked Madla. "You're using a tracker?"

"We tried one, but it's turned up nothing so far. Are you familiar with the bloodline potion?"

Madla's eyes rounded, and with a groan, she slapped the side of her head. "Of *course*. If Maebe's correct and I have kin among them, then we can find them if I anchor a trace."

Kabno perked. "You'll do it?"

"Absolutely—"

"*Not*," Theo cut in, shaking his head. "No way."

"I can find them!" Madla protested. "We're wasting time—"

"You were *literally* hit by a bus…what, eight days ago?"

Culta arched a brow. "Wait, really?"

"Yeah," said his brother, folding his arms. "The M22, wasn't it? We barely got her out of there before the ambulance arrived," he continued before Madla could speak. "She was a *mess*."

"I'm sure Revenni had her hands full."

"Oh, it was rough," said Theo. "Uh…sorry, Revenni's my wife," he told the rest of us. "She's also our primary healer."

"I feel fine!" said Madla. "Honestly. I can handle—"

"You're still on sick leave," Theo chided.

"And I'm *healing*. I can handle pain."

Before Theo could answer that, I heard a door slam off-camera, then low voices and a child's squeal. "Hang on," he told us, then called, "Darling? Consult?"

When Theo turned his computer around, I saw that he was in a large bedroom, and the camera picked up two blonde women, one of whom held a boy about Winston and Tobias's age in her arms. "Sure," the woman with the child said, and sat on the edge of the bed. Theo joined her, and she peered at us. "Uh…hi. Madla? *Culta*?"

"Hey," he said, and raised a hand. "We don't tell my

mom about this, yeah?"

"Of course not," she replied, her eyes scanning back and forth as she studied the rest of our windows. "Wait, aren't you the kid from Ivari's trial?"

"I'll explain later," said her husband. "Would you please tell Madla that she can't take a bloodline potion right now?"

Revenni leaned away from the screen, aghast. "What the *hell*? No!"

"Really," Madla tried, "I feel better—"

"Do you like your spleen? How about your liver? You need them both," Revenni snapped. "And I suspect your intestinal perforations are still mending."

"I—"

"That potion is pure poison. Your body can't handle it right now."

"Farral and Danirri are going to kill what's left of East Branch," Madla said, glaring at Revenni. "I can find them."

"And you'll kill yourself in the process," the healer retorted.

Madla crossed her arms and scowled. "All right, *fine*. What about one of you?"

"*Us?*"

"Why not? Surely you have distant kin among the abducted, too."

The couple looked at each other, and Revenni spoke first. "I appreciate that," she said, clutching her son more tightly, "but I've got Geven to think about. Besides, if I'm knocked out of commission and the worst comes to pass—"

"And you, Theo?" said Madla, cutting her short. "Or what about Nidda? I saw her come in with you, Revenni."

"You leave our children out of this mess," Revenni barked.

"I'd consider it," Theo said, even as his wife glared at him, "but Nidda and I can't. Faulty heart," he explained, patting his chest, "and she got hers from me, unfortunately."

"Sounds familiar," I mumbled, as Kabno raised her palms, silencing Revenni's argument before it could begin.

"Understood, and we certainly don't want to injure anyone," said the director. "That's why Maebe isn't taking it—she's had it twice, and the healers haven't cleared her for a third round."

"*Yes*," said Revenni, "I recall that from the trial. I can't believe you people let a child—"

"My choice," I said, staring back at her. "My family."

She backed off, and Kabno tapped her pen against her desk. "What about you, Culta? Can you take the potion?"

He looked like she had just asked whether he felt like bunking down with an ill-tempered bear. After a moment of ever-redder-faced stammering, he said, "No, I...I'm sorry. No."

"Heart problems as well?"

"*Him?* He's never been sick a day in his life," Madla interjected. "Just cowardly, that's all."

Revenni's eyes narrowed. "He's not a coward for not wanting to drink poison!"

"I'm sorry," Culta blurted, "I am, but I can't do it. No." Emphatically shaking his head, he said, "I watched Father do it when he was looking for East Branch. He barely lasted a minute, the pain was so bad, and Father's *tough*. I...I'm *not*, okay? I do web design. Enduring excruciating pain isn't really in my wheelhouse."

"Your brother's captured children," said Madla. "They're *your* kin, too."

"I'm aware," he muttered, "but no. Not doing it. Sorry."

Before Madla could yell at him, Kabno stepped in. "It's fine," she said calmly. "We won't force you. Madla, if you could let us know once you've made your list, we'd appreciate it. Theo has our contact information—"

"Could I speak with Maebe?" she interrupted. "Before we part?"

Casting a quick glance at his irate wife, Theo said, "I'm going to shut down the meeting, but if you want to give her your phone number…"

As I'd taken to carrying my phone with me around the mansion, I pulled it out and typed in the number Madla offered. When the meeting ended, I closed my computer and looked up at Diriem. "Do you want me to call her here, on speaker?"

"That's unnecessary," he replied. "Why don't you take it upstairs, give yourself some privacy?"

I gathered my things and hurried to my guest room, then closed the door and took a seat on the leather sofa by the window. Steeling my nerve, I sent out the call and waited.

Madla answered on the second ring. "There you are," she said, her tone colored with relief. "I thought you might have changed your mind."

She kept the conversation in English, which I appreciated.

"No, ma'am. Just needed to go to a different room," I replied. "Uh…what did you want to talk about?"

A deep sigh answered my query. "I just…I wanted to apologize," she murmured. "We should never have left East Branch, and—"

"It was a long time ago," I tried.

"That doesn't matter. I walked away from my babies." Laugher followed that, a sound mostly of incredulity.

I didn't know if she was waiting for absolution, for me to tell her everything was okay and forgiven, but I couldn't go that far. Instead, I asked, "Why'd y'all do it? They thought y'all sneaked off to die so there wouldn't be so many mouths to feed."

"I know. I was the last to leave, so I heard their suppositions." She paused for so long that I thought she might have hung up, but then she said, "I didn't want to. That doesn't excuse what I did, but…please know that I didn't want to leave them."

"Then why did you?"

"Ivari said it was necessary. That we had what we needed from the humans, and it was time for us to be rid of them. He thought about killing them," she said, her voice low and almost in a monotone. "He floated the idea of wiping them out and moving on, but there was enough sentimentality in our ranks that he was dissuaded. When he told us instead that we'd sneak off without them, I argued that we should stay, but he said that wasn't an option. If we all went willingly, then he wouldn't harm the rest of the community."

"And you believed him?" I said.

"He'd been honest with us from the beginning. Besides, Deriap was vocally against wiping out East Branch, and Ivari usually took his counsel."

"Deriap ti'Catama?"

"Yes. You know of him?"

"They, uh…the Forum reestablished the southern Halls here when they gave us citizenship. Connor, my cousin in the hospital? He's the last of the Willows. I mean, we're probably all Willows if you go back far enough," I continued, "but he's the eldest of the eldest back to Deriap."

"Did they give someone ti'Un?"

I hesitated, suddenly realizing that telling the one-time Lady ti'Un that her Hall had been assigned to another might go poorly, then took the risk. "Kyle, my uncle."

After a moment, she said, "Good. I hope he has better fortune with it than I did."

"If we can find him."

"We will," she insisted. "But as I was saying, it was Ivari's decision to leave like we did. I shouldn't have, and I knew it even then, but he was our king, and…" Again, Madla sighed. "Three days' walk from the rendezvous point, some of us were having second thoughts and discussing the matter. It was Deriap who told Ivari that he intended to return for his family. The rest of us hung back, waiting to see how Ivari took the news. He bade Deriap a safe journey, and when Deriap's back was turned, he blasted a hole through his chest. Killed him almost instantly. That…well, that silenced the dissent," she said. "We were the minority, and Ivari had made it clear that no one was to ever tell East Branch where we'd gone."

"And you stayed with him?" I asked. "Even after that?"

"I know how it looks," said Madla. "I could have fought him, could have run off, found my way back to my children, but…have you heard of trauma bonding? I don't mean that as an excuse, but he'd led us across Europe, across the sea, up to New York, and all we had was each other. We found a place large enough for the group and began pairing off—all but me," she said with a soft, sad chuckle. "None of them could compete with my David. But we never should have abandoned them, and…I'm sorry."

"Why the change of heart? If you've been loyal to Ivari all this time, then why—"

"He swore by his Hall that he wouldn't hurt East Branch if we left with him, and he broke that vow in the worst way," she replied, her voice low but strong. "If Farral and their spawn are trying to finish what he began, then I'll do whatever I can to stop them. This, I promise you—and I do so by my Hall, for whatever that's still worth."

"Thank you," I told her, and meant it. "Listen, uh…someday, if things are better…maybe we could get acquainted."

"I'd like that very much. But for now, I'd best find those damn deeds. Be *safe*," she stressed. "I'll call as soon as I have the information."

We'd barely said our goodbyes when someone knocked at my door. "Come in," I said, putting the phone away.

Diriem poked his head into the room, then beckoned to me with a crooked finger. "Kabno just called—we need to go to Laws," he announced. "Her people may have found something in the portal records."

He waited while I grabbed my purse, then led the way toward the staircase. "Did you and Madla speak?" he asked.

"Just for a minute."

"Mm." Glancing back at me over his shoulder, Diriem said, "You have her eyes, you know. Shape and color. The rest of your features differ, but there's no denying those eyes."

I wasn't sure how I felt about that revelation, but when I thought of Ivari's cold green-brown stare, I supposed a touch of Madla wasn't so terrible.

CHAPTER 12

Kabno gave me a long look as a DOL agent escorted Diriem and me into the executive conference room. Once the
agent had closed the door behind us, she asked, "Maebe's
interning with you now, is she?"

"I have my reasons," Diriem replied in a tone that said
no further explanation would be forthcoming.

Some might have taken that as rude, but Kabno merely
rolled her eyes and stepped up to the head of the table—
quite literally, as a stepstool had been positioned for her
instead of a chair. Diriem nudged me forward, and I stuck
close to his side as we joined her and the five agents already sitting behind their computers and oversized mugs.
"I've been at my desk too long today," Kabno told us,
nodding to the chairs. "Be my guests."

It wasn't lost on me that once we were seated, the tiny
director was the tallest person in the room.

Though the agents were a multi-species bunch, they
were united in their fatigue. The gnome sitting farthest
from his boss clutched a translucent tumbler full of coffee,
a cup so big that he needed both hands, while the naga
who'd curled up on a mat two places down the table
yawned so widely, his jaw unhinged, creating an opening
large enough to stuff in a whole chicken. The nymph sitting to Kabno's right seemed to be the most alert of the
bunch, but the tremor in their hands suggested that was
only due to stimulants.

"So," said Diriem as the naga's nightmarish maw
closed, "did we not want to discuss this on the group call?"

Kabno smirked. "Don't tell me you're that trusting, old boy."

"No. Not overly concerned about those three, but...no. Very well, what have you found?"

She gestured toward the nymph. "Agent Gannid, why don't you begin?"

The nymph—*she*, I mentally noted, not *they*—absently tucked a lock of orange hair that had come loose from her braid behind her long ear. While I was no expert in nymphs, and her brown complexion could have signified several elemental alignments, her hair color marked her as fire-aligned—someone I would *not* want to see lose her temper. "We've been reviewing portal records for the past three days since last night," she said, and made a few taps on her computer.

A diagram of brightly colored dots appeared in the air above a projector near Kabno. Some were larger than others, and each was labeled in Pactish. I spotted one marked Central—external portals, then, and I supposed that the size had something to do with the traffic.

"Most of the trips during this period were by agents, all logged and in order," the agent continued, and the diagram changed: some of the dots disappeared, while the remaining batch shrank. "These are the ones that don't appear in agency records, which I can only presume includes the DOI logs we can't access. Now, whittling this to entrances within six hours of the ear arriving at the director's home..." Again, the dots shrank and vanished.

"Any solid contenders in that bunch?" Diriem asked.

Agent Gannid flashed a weary but satisfied smile. "We were informed that you suggested looking at Silver's connections, sir. Only one of these travelers appears to be related."

His eyebrows rose in interest. "Indeed? One of his associates?"

"No—a grandson."

"Do tell."

The diagram changed to an ID picture of a youthful elf, a man with large blue eyes and close-cropped brown curls—odd, as curly hair was apparently rare among elves, and most of the ones I'd met kept their hair at least long enough for a short ponytail. "Reranel ti'Cren," said the agent.

Diriem rubbed his chin. "Don't believe I've met him."

"He's Kilch's son," said Kabno. "That's the, uh…"

"Seventh ti'Cren child," Agent Gannid offered, "sixth living."

"And doing his sentence at Bebala Farm," the director finished.

"Mm. I never knew of Kilch's children being involved in Inade's enterprise," Diriem remarked.

Kabno folded her arms over her robe. "As far as we know, he wasn't. We have *nothing* on this kid—not even a speeding ticket. He's upstanding."

"A brewer," said the agent. "We pulled his licensure records from DPP, and they're pristine."

Diriem frowned. "He works outside?"

"No, sir. He's employed at Bathim."

"What's Bathim?" I whispered to Diriem.

"Bathim School of Advanced Magic," he told me. "They draw upper-level transfers who show particular promise. Best theoretical magic department in the Pactlands. That's where Kelra Epannae teaches," he added.

Thinking of Kelra, the nymph who'd brought the bloodline potion into my life, made my muscles tense at the memory of the pain.

The diagram shifted once more, showing two dates and a destination beside them. "Ti'Cren left last Saturday night," said Agent Gannid, "and he returned Wednesday afternoon. Out and in through Bruce Crossing."

"Saturday was when my cousins were snatched," I interrupted.

The agent nodded. "The travel times are suspicious. Out around the time that the North Lake students were taken, in before the ear reached the director. But what's *particularly* interesting is the portal he used."

"Bruce Crossing is in northern Michigan," said Kabno. "Upper peninsula. Now, what's a school brewer doing in northern Michigan in *March*?"

Diriem made a face but said nothing.

"And here's another interesting bit," said Agent Gannid, then turned to her colleagues. "Uh...do any of you want to talk about—"

"Keep going," said the gnome, and the naga grunted agreement.

"Right. Sure." She paused for a long drink of what I hoped was merely coffee, then changed the projection to another chart. "We did a deep dive on ti'Cren. Tracked his travels over the last year. He's had a pattern since November: goes out, stays for a few days, and returns. These trips don't happen at regular intervals, but he almost always uses the Woodland portal."

"New Jersey," Diriem murmured. "Closest to New York City."

"Yes, sir."

"And when he doesn't use Woodland?"

The nymph pointed to a few entries. "Miami."

Turning to me, Diriem asked, "How's your Floridian geography, youngling?"

"Um...not good," I replied.

"Well, here's a lesson for you. Miami is a coastal city on the southern end of the peninsula, and the Everglades are inland, to the west."

I snapped my fingers as the pieces fell together. "Madla said—"

"Ivari has property in the region," Diriem finished. "It's not absolute proof, but it's concerning." Looking at Kabno, he asked, "Has anyone cross-checked this with Pateme?"

She shook her head. "Not yet. Do you want to do the honors, or shall I?"

Rising, he said, "I'll do it in person. Thank you," he told the exhausted agents. "Nicely done. Maebe, let's go."

Not waiting for an escort, we saw ourselves down to the lobby, then back to the parking garage. I recognized the name of the person we were going to visit—Pateme ti'Tam, the director of DPP and Rose and Yven's boss—but I didn't understand why Diriem couldn't have called him from what had to be a secure conference room at Laws. As I buckled in, I asked, "Why are we going to DPP?"

"Because," he replied, backing out of the visitor space, "this is a family matter. But first, a little research is in order."

Before he pulled out of the deck, he made a call. "Ganti, hello," he began. "How does your afternoon look?"

The man on the other end paused briefly. "Uh...not too busy, why?"

"Meet me in my office in twenty minutes, and I'll tell you. And do me a favor and call Rosie to come over, please."

"Sure, boss. Should I cancel my dinner plans?"

"You have dinner plans?"

"Figure of speech."

Diriem barely smirked. "Probably not. Oh, and while you're at it, please have Nim and Dienk join us. I have a little project for them as well."

"Ooh," said Ganti. "East Branch, got it. Will do."

He'd barely hung up when my phone began to ring, and I pulled it from my bag, frowning. Seeing Connor's name on the screen, I quickly took the call, leaving it on speaker mode. "Hey, there," I said, slipping into English out of habit. "What's up? How're you feeling?"

"Hey, Maebe. They're weaning me off the pain potions, so I've felt *better*, but I'm all right. Janie's on a conference call, so I thought I'd check in. You still at Diriem's?"

"We're downtown." Cutting my eyes to Diriem, I said,

"Heading for DOI, I think," and he nodded.

"Who's 'we'?"

"Diriem and me. I'm tagging along."

"Uh-huh." He sounded dubious. "No shenanigans without me, mitta. So, what's the latest? Any luck with the trace?"

"You're supposed to be resting, boy," Diriem chided.

"I'm bored out of my skull. Which is healing nicely," he added with a touch of reproach. "If y'all want to spring me…"

"Not against medical advice," he replied, "which I assume is what Jane told you as well, yes?"

My cousin muttered under his breath.

"I'll catch you up, at least," I offered. "The tracker was no good, but Madla ti'Un back in New York is *furious* with Ivari, and she wants to help. She's figuring out where our people might be."

"Huh," he said. "And y'all trust her?"

"For the moment," said Diriem. "She was willing to anchor a trace, but she's in the same position you are."

"Hole in her head?"

"No, apparently, she was hit by a bus a few days ago."

Connor hissed. "Is she ambulatory?"

"From the sound of things. We do heal rather rapidly…"

"Yeah, well, *some* of us didn't get that gene," Connor grumbled. "How about Culta and Theo? Could they anchor instead?"

"Theo has a heart problem," I told him, "and Culta's yellow."

"Son of a *bitch*—"

"But we might know who mailed the ear," I hurriedly continued.

His mood brightened a degree. "Good. Who?"

"The evidence suggests it's a ti'Cren," said Diriem. "His pattern of trips outside is suspicious at best."

"A ti'Cren?" Connor echoed. "As in…"

"Yes, *those* ti'Crens. He's Teolm's nephew."

With a groan, he muttered, "Teolm's got to get his freaking house in order. First his sister-in-law, now this kid…or wait, hell, how old is this punk, anyway?"

"Considering his employment, I'd say he's at least in his sixties," Diriem replied. "The school where he works would have need of the sort of complex potions a beginner wouldn't risk brewing."

"Whatever," my cousin said, sighing. "Y'all all look ridiculous for your age, so…"

Diriem snorted, not bothering to hide his amusement from me. "*Ridiculous?*"

"Come on, man, from a distance, you could be my brother."

"Adopted, perhaps."

"Yeah," Connor allowed, "you missed out on the East Branch 'everyone's related to everyone' look. There are some *striking* similarities among my cousins."

He softly chuckled. "Let's just say that the potential partners for certain Halls are limited, and…you know, you're not the only one with fewer unique ancestors than might be ideal. But back to Hall ti'Cren," he said, sobering. "Remember that Teolm hasn't been in charge for long. His father headed that Hall for centuries, and his tendrils are still deeply embedded. The perks of including family in one's criminal endeavors, I suppose," he mused. "Teolm is aware that rotten fruit remains, but he's a much more experienced botanist than he is a lord. He has his work cut out for him if he wants to undo Inade's influence."

"Suppose that's fair," said Connor.

"Mm. And as for you, Lord ti'Catama, might I suggest you hang up and hide the phone before Jane catches you?"

"I'm fine," he protested, "and she's not the boss of me."

"That's the spirit," said Diriem. "Keep telling yourself that."

"What—"

"*Rest*," he interrupted, and motioned for me to cut the call.

As I put my phone back in my purse, I said, "You just like poking the bear, don't you?"

With a small, sly smile, he replied, "It's good for him."

Right on time, Ganti rapped on the frame of Diriem's open office door, and the director motioned him in. "Thank you for coming," Diriem said. "And the others?"

"Dienk and Nim are on their way up," Ganti replied. "Rose is going to be a few minutes behind them. From the sound of it, one of her colleagues brought in a cake."

He frowned. "A cake?"

"It *is* her birthday," I said from my seat at the carved wooden conference table.

"*Oh*," said Ganti, as Diriem's expression shifted to surprise, then guilt. "I suppose she's still young enough to keep track, eh? Which one is this?"

"Thirty," I told him.

"Round number, got it." His gaze flicked toward Diriem, and he whistled low. "Someone forgot, didn't he?"

Glaring back at the agent, Diriem muttered, "Been a bit preoccupied. We don't mention this to Rose, understood?"

"Mention what, boss? And hi," he said, beckoning as the other two agents appeared in the doorway. "We're just getting started."

After a brief and slightly awkward wait, Rose jogged in with rushed apologies. "Sorry, *sorry*, couldn't leave my own party."

Studying her, Ganti tapped his nose. "Uh, Rose?"

"Hmm?" She touched the tip of her nose, then laughed in embarrassment as she licked a finger and began rubbing. "Thanks. Pars's doing."

"He put food on your face?"

"He's a sweetheart," Rose replied. "Been scheming with Yven to surprise me. He did a little research into human birthday traditions, and there's one about buttering the birthday kid's nose, but he settled for frosting."

Ganti's brow knit. "Why butter?"

"It's for luck, and that's all I know. Anyway," she said, giving her face a final swipe, "what's up?"

Diriem waited until she'd pulled out a chair, then tapped a button on his computer to start a projection in the middle of the table. I recognized the ID picture as it slowly rotated. "This is Reranel ti'Cren," he explained, pausing while Nim and Dienk scribbled on their notepads. "He brews for Bathim. See what you can find on him, please, all of you. Past, present, anything of note."

Rose pointed to the picture. "Is that…"

"Kilch's son. Your, uh…what, first cousin once removed?"

She groaned.

"Fortitude, my dear. You didn't think bringing down Inade would be the end of his business, did you?"

"A girl can hope," she muttered, and drummed her fingers on the table. "Okay, I'll see what I can do. Got a quiet room I can borrow?"

"We've got a suite," said Ganti, pushing back from the table. "You'd know this if you ever joined DOI…"

"Save it."

"And I wouldn't smear food on your face," he added as they took their leave.

They weren't gone long. About ten minutes later, Rose returned, thin-lipped with frustration. "The bastard's protected," she announced as Diriem looked up from his work. "I can't see anything."

"Protected *how*?"

"Blinding potion," she said without hesitation. "Not Ivari's rings. I'm sure about that."

"Interesting," Diriem murmured. "Not altogether surprising, but…interesting."

It was another twenty minutes before Ganti staggered into the office. "Protected, yeah?" he said to Rose, gripping the back of a chair to steady himself.

"Yeah. Sit down before you fall..."

He let her help him, then murmured his thanks and looked at Diriem. "I can see his childhood as clearly as you'd like, but once he hits his thirties, he's a blank. How old is he?"

Diriem glanced at his screen. "Per his license, he's a hundred twenty-five this year."

"He's been protected for a while, then. Any word from the guys?"

That would be a further fifteen minutes in coming. Nim and Dienk were thorough, and they managed to pull together a decent dossier on Reranel: school records, driver's license, medical history, DPP documentation, taxes, and even a list of charitable contributions. "On paper, he's clean," said Dienk, tapping one cloven hoof as Diriem reviewed their file. "Nothing suspicious in his library history, no citations, no fines, *excellent* grades—small wonder he's at Bathim."

"He's a graduate, actually," Nim offered. "Third in his year. Did a few internships after graduation, and then he came back in his sixties as a brewer. He's been at Bathim ever since, so I suppose they compensate their staff well."

"I doubt he needs to worry about his finances," said Diriem, looking up from the folder they'd presented. "Recall that his father is main-line ti'Cren."

"Right," the nymph muttered. "But with his father incarcerated..."

"Good old Uncle Teolm is probably available to assist the lad. So," he said, meeting the agents' and Rose's eyes in turn, "why is a school brewer taking blinding potion?"

"Maybe he suspects that we're spying on him because of Inade," Rose suggested.

"Could be," said Ganti, "but what does he have to hide? He's *pristine*."

She shrugged. "What if he's a little kinky? You don't want word of *that* getting out if you're from the most image-conscious Hall in the freaking Pactlands…"

Nim made a face. "A possibility, sure, but that doesn't strike me as likely. What's the simplest explanation?"

"He's dirty as hell," said Rose.

"My thoughts precisely. Dienk?"

The faun chuckled low in his throat. "*Yeah.* I could be wrong, but…"

He let that thought die unspoken, but then there was no need for him to finish.

Diriem nodded to them and stood. "My thanks, all of you. Keep this quiet for now, yes?"

"Sure, boss," said Ganti. "What's the plan?"

"The plan," he replied, closing his laptop with a firm *click*, "is to see what might be learned at DPP."

Nim frowned. "You think they've locked down files we can't access?"

"Not this time. I want to see who's currently handling Reranel." As he packed his things into a messenger bag, he asked, "Rosie, do you want a ride back to the office?"

"Thanks, no, I'll drive," she replied, and smirked at Diriem when he looked her way. "You be nice to Pateme, now, Pop."

Like DOL, its sister agency, the Division of Plants and Potions was housed in a tower in District 2, but it seemed to be the less favored of the pair. DPP's tower was only twenty stories tall, compared to DOL's thirty, and had been constructed with less glass. Next to the opulent marble-covered DOL lobby, DPP's seemed almost plain, a high-ceilinged room with limestone walls and a slate floor. However, DPP also had a café off the lobby, which appeared to be doing a brisk business even hours past the lunch rush.

Noticing the direction of my gaze, Diriem said, "That's Mangia Due. Annie and her friend started it, and now Kabno's niece helps run it. Best espresso in the city, should you be so inclined."

"Not a bad perk for DPP," I replied.

He grinned. "And a source of consternation for Kabno, but she really should learn to share. This way, now."

Diriem led us to the desk where the lobby attendant sat and nodded as she straightened in her chair. "Good afternoon," he said. "I need to see your director, please. As soon as his schedule permits."

"Uh...yes, sir," she mumbled, and grabbed the desk phone.

Ten minutes later, equipped with a mocha from the café, I followed Diriem and a sorcerer in a black robe into the elevator. "He's just finishing a meeting, sir," the sorcerer told Diriem as the elevator headed for the top floor. "If you wouldn't mind waiting in his office, he'll be along momentarily."

Diriem nodded. "Thank you, Dup."

"I see that you're set for coffee," said the sorcerer, and Diriem lifted his paper cup in brief salute. "Anything else I can get you while you wait?"

"No, but thank you. We'll stay out of trouble."

Dup's expression suggested that he found that unlikely, but he escorted us to the director's massive corner office without a fuss and departed.

I did a slow turn as I drank my mocha and studied Pateme's space. His heavy wooden desk was practical but well made, not overly ostentatious and polished to a warm shine. Four blue chairs with thick cushions awaited in a semicircle in front of the desk—visitor seating, I supposed, seeing Diriem select one for himself. The cluttered bookcase reminded me of Diriem's office at DOI, as did the framed landscapes, and I wondered if Rose had painted them as well.

I'd barely settled in by Diriem when Pateme arrived. "Not a social call?" he asked, bypassing the pleasantries.

"Not in the slightest," said Diriem.

Pateme grunted, then gestured until a red light flashed

in the ceiling and swept down the walls, a rectangle that grew and contracted again once it reached the thick rug.

"Privacy spell," Diriem quietly told me.

His DPP counterpart was another elf, a slender man with brown hair and dark eyes who gave me a searching look as he retreated to the far side of his desk and sat. "So," he said in Low Elvish, turning his attention to Diriem, "dare I ask?"

"Tell me about Reranel."

Frowning, Pateme leaned forward in his chair, the better to peer at Diriem. "My sister's grandson? That Reranel?"

"The same," Diriem replied. "He's licensed?"

"Yes," said Pateme, visibly taken aback, "he's a brewer. Perfectly clean. If you want to see his reports—well, I mean, if you want to see them *legitimately* and not through interagency subterfuge—"

Diriem smiled.

"Uh-huh. Thought so. You're incorrigible, you know that?" Shaking his head, he said, "By now, I should think we have a fairly decent relationship. If you have questions, you could always *ask* me."

"Isn't that what I'm doing now?" he countered.

Pateme rolled his eyes.

Returning to business, Diriem said, "You believe Reranel is honest. Who's doing his inspections?"

"I am."

It was Diriem's turn to show surprise. "*You?* You don't trust Regulatory to manage him?"

"Look, the boy's law-abiding. Unlike his father," Pateme muttered. "But with Kilch incarcerated, suspicion fell on Reranel—unfairly—and I stepped in to put the rumors to rest. I obviously never worked for Inade, so I can be trusted to do his grandson's inspections."

Diriem grunted. "And you've had no trouble?"

"None. His setup at Bathim is well within parameters, and the administration has no complaints. Honestly, I don't think he even has a home still."

"Uh…not to be rude, sir," I interjected, "but are you sure about that?"

Pateme glanced toward me. "Your meaning, young-ling?"

"Well…Jane's dad says that all brewers have home equipment. It's in their nature."

Briefly, he chuckled. "Yacovi's not wrong. I mean, look at my niece Liliol—she grows and brews for importation, but her beer is *dangerous*."

Diriem's mouth twitched. "Did Rosie ever tell you—"

"Oh, I got it from Syvin. When ti'Ansha called to tell her that Liliol was missing, he was *plastered*. Rosie explained that they'd gotten into the wrong stuff, trying to keep him out of trouble, but frankly, I think the idea of ti'Ansha drunk was funny enough to Syvin to prevent a write-up. But back to Reranel," he continued, sobering. "I've never known him to engage in hobby brewing. He was always a quiet, studious child, much more interested in theoretical potions than in setting up a basement still. That's why he took the position at Bathim, see? He brews up much of what the school requires, but he also has time to research and experiment."

Cocking his head, Diriem asked, "Should we fear an-other Roulette situation?"

"Not every novel potion is Roulette, and you know that damn well," Pateme retorted. "Reranel's experimentation is above board."

"All right," he replied, "but then why has he been tak-ing the blinding potion for most of his life?"

Pateme sat very still, regarding Diriem like one might watch a perturbed rattler. "I…" he managed after a mo-ment, "I'm sorry…*what*?"

"He's protected. Ganti says he began taking protective measures in his thirties, and Rosie says he's currently blocked. Does Bathim protect its faculty?"

"No," Pateme murmured, frowning into space. "No,

they'd have no reason to do such." Focusing on Diriem again, he said, "You came here with suspicions. What do you know?"

"I came with questions, too," said Diriem. "For example, why would Reranel need to go outside?"

"Uh…" Shrugging, Pateme replied, "I've never asked him about such. Some of the brewers like to visit the growers, you know, see the product in person, especially if they have odd requests. But Reranel isn't the type to go out. He's not been trained for such, to my knowledge. And here." Quickly, he turned to his computer and began typing and clicking, then flipped the laptop around and showed Diriem the screen. "That's his portal use for the last six months," he said with a note of triumph in his voice. "No trips through the external portals."

"That's because he's been using a second set of credentials not tied to DPP."

Pateme's face fell, and he sighed as his eyes closed. "You're certain?"

"Nearly. I need your assistance."

"Of course," he mumbled, putting his computer back in its place. "What can I do for you?"

"I'd like a list of growers within…oh, say a five-hour drive of the Woodland and Miami portals," said Diriem.

"I…can get you that today, sure," he replied wearily. "If I may ask, what do you suspect that Reranel has been doing?"

Diriem hesitated before answering him. "Are you aware of the situation at North Lake?"

"No," said Pateme, cutting his eyes to me, "but that might explain what Maebe is doing here. What's happened?"

"In brief, someone—most likely one of the ti'Ammaas sons and their mother—kidnapped all of the East Branch children, plus a handful of other students, last Saturday night."

His eyes flew open wide. "*All* of them?"

"All but Maebe and Connor, who were outside at the time."

"How?" Pateme demanded.

"Knock-out potions, snatch and grab, but the details are murky. The fun part is that yesterday, Kabno received an ear in the mail—probably a child's, definitely affected by cifyent."

He grimaced, then propped an elbow on his desk and began to rub his forehead. "And you have reason to believe Reranel is caught up in this mess?"

"Circumstantial as of yet, but his portal logs are suspicious. He usually goes through Woodland or Miami, but he made a trip to Bruce Crossing on Saturday, returning Wednesday."

"What's in Bruce Crossing at this time of year?"

"Not much of interest to us, but another of the ti'Ammaas sons has a cabin in the area, and we know the victims were kept there temporarily."

Pateme swore quietly but *colorfully*.

"Looking at his other trips, Woodland is the portal closest—"

"To New York City, yes," Pateme finished. "What's in Miami?"

"Apparently, Ivari has property nearby." Crossing his legs as he watched his colleague process that, Diriem said, "Again, we don't have firm proof yet, but..."

"It's not a great look for the boy." Pateme tapped at his computer for a moment, frowning. "We do have growers around both of those portals. It's possible that he's an in-person shopper."

"Possible," Diriem conceded. "Of course, since he's up to date with his blinding potion, I can't check—"

Pateme raised a hand to cut him off. "I'll investigate. Call you tonight. Now, shall I have Dup show you down, or can you manage on your own?"

"*Honestly*," he said, pushing himself from his chair, and plucked his coffee cup from the rug. "If you truly suspect I don't know my way around this building…"

"Oh, I'm sure you could discover the contents of the employee refrigerators, were you of a mind," Pateme replied dryly, "but manners, Diriem."

He laughed softly as I gathered my things. "Useful, those, but sometimes overrated. Until tonight, then," he said, and escorted me out.

CHAPTER 13

I would have eaten alone that evening had Ranarma not taken pity on me and grabbed a plate. Yven had made plans to take Rose out for dinner, and Diriem had shut himself in his office since our return to the mansion, claiming he wasn't hungry. I didn't know what he was up to, and when I'd asked Ranarma, he'd leaned close and said, "Life lesson, youngling: best not to ask too many questions of farseers. They can be prickly when disturbed."

While the mansion's staff generally ate apart from the family—an odd convention to me, having grown up as I did with frequent communal dinners and tables never too small for an extra chair—Ranarma didn't make a fuss about keeping me company. Even if he did so out of a misplaced sense of obligation to babysit me, well, I wasn't complaining. The cook was good-natured, loved to talk food, and never once brought up my missing kin, and for that, I was immensely grateful.

But just as he got up to take the plates back to the kitchen, Diriem appeared, robe off, phone in hand, and with a long, thin book tucked under his arm. "We've got growers," he announced. "Ranarma, would you mind making coffee?"

As Ranarma got to work, Diriem took the empty chair beside me, the better to show me his phone's display. "All right, there are thirty-five growers within a decent radius of the two portals," he said, and opened the book to reveal pages of road maps. "Let's plot them and see what we get."

"Anyone interesting?" I asked as he flipped to the back of the book.

Pausing on a partial spread of Virginia, he replied, "Nothing leaps out at me. However, I think we can eliminate some of these growers. For example..." From the back of the book, he retrieved a sheet of small red, circular stickers, then placed one on the map. "This is Pateme's niece, Liliol," he said. "If Reranel were visiting her, then surely he'd have used the Oilville portal," he continued, pointing to a neon green sticker closer to the right side of the map. "Why drive all that way if he could cut the trip to an hour or so, eh?"

"So, she's not a possible destination," I said. "I see. We're looking for growers who are closer to Miami and Woodland than anywhere else?"

"Precisely. Here, you hold the stickers..."

By the time Ranarma returned with a latte for Diriem and a cup of hot chocolate for me, we'd started to make slow progress on the grower elimination front. The cook even joined in; able to read English, he scanned the maps from over my shoulder, helping us look for town names as we scoured the pages. Our drinks were gone before we finished our work, but finally, we'd narrowed Pateme's thirty-five candidates to five.

"Three in Florida," said Diriem, looking over the map, then turned the pages to the middle of the book. "One in New Jersey, and...yes, one in New York."

"What now?" I asked him.

"Now we pull their sales records and see whether anyone has been selling to Reranel," he replied, lifting his phone.

I smiled. "Calling Ganti?"

"I would, but if Pateme would rather dig through DPP's records himself than allow my people to work, then I suppose I shouldn't deny him the opportunity."

As he walked across the room to make the call, Ranarma whispered, "And *that* is why we try not to cross Lord ti'Dana. Do you want some leftover cake?"

Ranarma was a wise man, I decided, as we sat together at the kitchen counter with thick slices of Rose's birthday cake—which, he assured me, she had said was fair game. I'd never had much in the way of sugary confections as a child, but I had to say they were growing on me, especially with a fresh cup of coffee to cut the cloying sweetness.

"You might want to pace yourself, Maebe," Ranarma cautioned as I drained my second latte. "I make those *strong*, and if you want to sleep tonight…"

"Thanks, but I'll manage," I replied, and wiped my mouth on the back of my hand. "I've been drinking a lot of caffeine this year."

"Mm," he said, then frowned. "You know that stuff's not great for your heart, don't you?"

"So the healers tell me, but they allow it. I think they're all addicted, too," I whispered.

"You're probably not wrong," he began, then looked up as Diriem swept in, phone in one hand and map book tucked under his arm. "Cake, sir?"

"Oh, no, thank you," he replied as he dropped his load on the counter. "Maebe, guess who called after I ruined Pateme's evening?"

"Connor?"

"No, and I bet Jane's taken his phone again. *Theo*," he told me. "With the property list from Madla." Before I could get too excited, he added, "It's *extensive*. Ivari owns dozens of potential hideouts."

The fluffy cake turned into a rock in my stomach. "How do we narrow them down?"

Smirking, he tapped his phone and held it to his ear. "We call for backup."

While Diriem had kept the mansion's protections on during my stay, he dropped them briefly that evening, deciding that since he was asking the Hunter to stop by without warning, the least he could do was not force him to use the front door.

A few minutes later, Wylan appeared in the kitchen, sporting his usual uniform of lace-up shirt and leather leggings. "Hi," he said, brushing his hair back from his antlers. "What's the occasion? And ooh, Kona?" he asked, sniffing the air.

"Just ground it this morning," said Ranarma, who'd taken up a position by the espresso machine in anticipation of the guest's arrival. "What's your poison, sir?"

Wylan grinned. "Does my nose deceive me, or is there hazelnut syrup in the cabinet?"

The cook winked and pulled out the bottle. "Latte?"

"Mocha, if it's no trouble."

Though I was still something of a newbie when it came to coffee, I'd learned the basic hierarchy of beverages by then. Guys at North Lake looking to improve their standing among their peers drank their coffee by the shot or scalding and black, denouncing anything with a hint of flavor as weak. But Wylan, with untold power at his fingertips, had nothing to prove, and he apparently preferred his coffee with enough chocolate and sugar to make my teeth ache.

"My apologies for interrupting your evening," Diriem began as Ranarma got to work.

Wylan waved him off. "Annie's working, the guys are sparring, and none of them need my supervision. What can I do for you?"

He flipped the map book open to the inside back cover, revealing the list of place names he'd scrawled within. "These are all properties Ivari ti'Ammaas owns. It's likely that the kidnapped children are being held at one of them."

Rubbing his stubble, Wylan studied the list. "Quite the portfolio."

"And there's the problem. Would it be possible for the Hunt to do a little reconnaissance?"

"Perhaps, if we could acquire sufficient images to get around…though I suspect Annie could manage that admirably," he mused.

"I don't doubt it," said Diriem. "Now, ordinarily, it wouldn't be proper for either of us to be encouraging unauthorized, possibly reckless trips outside…"

When Wylan smiled, his expression carried a hint of threat. "I consider the prohibition on travel outside the Pactlands as more of a…suggestion, let's say. For other people."

"Naturally," Diriem replied, maintaining his poker face. "Seeing as there are children in jeopardy, and one has already lost an ear—"

"Come again?"

"Someone mailed it to Kabno," I volunteered. "It definitely belongs to one of my cousins."

"Huh." Wylan paused, processing that, then murmured his thanks as Ranarma offered him a mug and drank deeply. "That's a little messed up."

"The common sentiment," said Diriem. "So, if you're unopposed…"

He patted the book. "Let me borrow your atlas, and I'll see if Annie can work her magic. But don't expect answers by morning, Diriem—this may take time."

"Your method is still faster than anything the rest of us could manage. Thank you." Closing the book, he handed it off, then added, "You're welcome to take that mug with you as well."

"Don't mind if I do," said Wylan, then raised it in brief salute to Ranarma and vanished.

Though Wylan had cautioned us to be patient, Diriem didn't seem surprised when Annie rang the doorbell the next morning. "Well, now," he said as Scel led her into the dining room, where Diriem and I were finishing our later breakfast, Rose and Yven having already left for work.

"Once again, your husband underestimates you."

Though Annie looked haggard, and her puffy eyes suggested she hadn't slept all night, she smirked as she pulled out a chair. "He's still learning," she said, "though he's not entirely wrong. This is just an update."

"One that couldn't have been delivered by phone? You needn't have made the trip, Annie…"

"Yeah, I know, but Wylan mentioned there was Kona here."

Ranarma, who'd peeked in from the kitchen, gave Annie a quick wave and slipped off. A few seconds later, I heard the coffee grinder whirring in the next room.

"Also," she said, taking Diriem's cleaned mug from her bag, "he wanted to return this."

Diriem shook his head but thanked her. "So, what have you found?"

"Plenty of location data. Satellite photography is a godsend there. And I've been pulling whatever I can on neighboring properties, you know, trying to gauge the risk of good Samaritans coming over with guns if they think there's a burglary in progress. Generally, *that's* low. Ivari's properties tend to be larger and relatively remote, which makes sense if they're designed for bug-out bunkers, but *most* of them have been sufficiently close to roads that we've been able to get good reference photos."

"That sounds promising," he replied.

"Helpful, at least. The boys have taken what I can find and gone out over the last few hours. So far, everything's come up empty…and here," she said, digging in her bag for a spiral notebook, "I brought you this."

Annie opened it to a page with a neat column of place names on one side and three columns of Xs on the other. Glancing at the headings, I could make out *Photo*, *Neighbors*, and *Checked*.

"We're down to six," she continued, pointing to the entries on that page and the next without a full line of Xs. "These are my problem children."

"How…" he began, then paused as Ranarma hurried in, mug in hand.

"Latte, yes?" the cook said to Annie, sliding the drink in front of her.

"Bless you," she murmured, and sighed after the first sip. "This is a double shot, isn't it?"

"You looked like you could use it, kid."

"You're not wrong." She downed half of it quickly, then squeezed her tired eyes closed and blinked a few times.

Diriem cleared his throat. "You know, I do have a small supply of Happy Juice on hand…"

Grimacing, Annie said, "That is *strictly* emergency-use only, but thanks. Back to the problematic locations. They're super-remote—like, 'accessible only by dirt road' remote. I can get the guys within a few miles, but that's not ideal."

He glanced toward the window. "The Hunt's not exactly subtle in daylight."

Given their odd attire and racks of antlers, I concurred.

"They're not subtle, *period*, and they're not spies," said Annie. "If we hit the right property and they stumble onto wards, say, or get spotted…I mean, in a fair fight, one on one, I'd pit a Huntsman against an elf, but we don't know how many might be hiding out there. And think about the target," she continued before he could interrupt. "Maybe they see the Hunt coming and run…or maybe they cut their losses first and kill their hostages."

A chill ran up my spine at the thought.

"What I'm hearing," said Diriem after a moment's contemplation, "is that we need a calculated strike. See if we can narrow your list further, then hit any uncleared targets simultaneously, under cover of darkness, and with as many people as we can afford."

"That's Wylan's thinking as well," Annie replied, and sipped her latte.

He read over her list as she finished her drink. "Let's

see…two in central Florida, one in central Mississippi, and one in New Mexico. The climate's not dangerous in those locations at this time of year, is it?"

She quickly wiped the milk foam off her lip. "Mid-March isn't bad in the Deep South, especially in Florida. New Mexico is more concerning. Depending on the elevation, that could dip under freezing at night."

"But then we have the last two," he said, tapping the second page. "Central Maine and Montana."

"Right. If they're being held outside in either of those locations, they could be in real trouble…"

Her voice trailed off as Diriem's phone rang, and he murmured, "Excuse me," as he took the call. "Pateme?"

Their conversation was brief, and when Diriem hung up, he turned to me and said, "No recorded sales to Reranel ti'Cren in the last six months."

"So, what's he doing outside?" I replied.

"I'm not sure of the specifics yet, but it's nothing good." To Annie, he said, "Possible lead, and I'd best make the arrangements with Laws. Thank you for all of your work, and please thank Wylan and his brothers for me. If you're able to confirm or eliminate any of those last six locations…"

She stopped him as he tried to pass the notebook back to her. "I've got another copy of the list. You keep that one. And of course, we'll be in touch." Rising, she called, "Thanks for the coffee, Ranarma! Going to go crash now."

As he escorted her to the door, Diriem made another call, putting it on speaker mode as it rang. When the call was answered, I heard a familiar high-pitched voice: "You're early today."

"Are you somewhere private, Kabno?" he asked.

"My office."

"That should suffice. I've got enough on Reranel to warrant an interrogation. How soon can you bring him in?"

The other director hesitated before answering. "You're

going to share your information, I trust."

"Naturally. Start the proceedings, and I'll give you what you need. And if your agents could be so kind, let's keep this…understated."

It was nearly three that afternoon before the interrogation commenced. Not wanting to tip their hand, Laws had asked Reranel to come in on his schedule to discuss a matter, and he'd been busy for much of the day. While the ruse had worked in part, in that Reranel hadn't brought a counselor with him, it had wasted hours of time that my cousins didn't have, which did nothing to calm my anxiety.

I appreciated Diriem allowing me to watch, though I twitched in my seat beside Rose. Kabno and Diriem had hastily assembled a team to observe, and everyone in there but me was potentially useful to the case. Ganti had come at Diriem's request, and Rose came as a representative of DPP and in her capacity as a farseer. On the Laws side, Kabno had assigned several agents to the viewing room, but the only one who'd spoken to me was a detective, Enva Orafer, a dark-skinned sorcerer whose hair rose in a short poof all around her head. She was the head of the DOL team that liaised with DPP, making a potentially dirty brewer fair game for her people. Evidently, she and Rose were well acquainted, as the two had conversed quietly while the room on the other side of the wide window was prepared.

The DOL tower had a number of interrogation rooms, larger or smaller spaces equipped with a variety of furniture to meet each case's needs. Some were set up to comfortably accommodate gnomes with child-sized chairs, while others offered thick floor mats for nagas and centaurs. Some rooms included brackets to which a handcuff could be attached, but the one Kabno had selected for Reranel was decidedly non-threatening, equipped not with hard furniture and restraints but with a plush blue couch, a pair of upholstered chairs in a complementary pattern, and an oval coffee table between them. Atop the table were four coasters and a box of tissues, and a small table against the wall offered coffee and tea. It was almost homey, I thought, if you overlooked the lack of external windows and the seeming mirror spanning much of the length of a wall—the one-way glass connecting the interrogation room with the observation space on the other side. Our room was far more utilitarian, stocked with an assortment of chairs and mats for all body types, and the agents around me had known to bring their own beverages.

Though our room was soundproofed, the conversation remained quiet, then died as the door opened in the inter-rogation room and two people entered. One I immediately recognized as Reranel, an elf with short, neat brown curls, a boyish face, and worried blue eyes. He wore a dark green robe over a black shirt and khakis, the sort of ensemble I often saw among the faculty at North Lake, walking the line between professional and casual. His tennis shoes cer-tainly suggested the latter, but since he was a brewer, I wasn't surprised to see that he hadn't come from work in his finest attire. The other person, a blue-skinned, green-haired nymph in an understated eggplant robe, took me a moment longer to place, but then I remembered them: Liogh Birrid, a detective who, like Enva, liaised with DPP. They were friends with Jane's father, I recalled, wondering if their tangential connection was why they'd been brought in on the case.

"Make yourself comfortable," Liogh told Reranel, ges-turing to the couch. "Something to drink?"

Reranel smiled nervously. "I wouldn't decline a cup of tea."

"Sure." The detective quickly made two, passed one to Reranel, and sat opposite him in one of the chairs. "Again," they said, crossing their legs, "thank you for com-ing in on such short notice. I appreciate that this is an in-convenience—"

"Oh, it's no trouble," Reranel replied, though his stiff body language suggested otherwise. If even I could tell he was anxious, surely Liogh had caught on.

"Well, be that as it may, let's keep this as brief as we can so as not to take up too much of your time." With a smile, Liogh placed a folder on the coffee table and shuffled through a few pages, then pulled out a handwritten list and removed a pencil from behind their long ear. "All right," they murmured, making a show of reading over their notes, "Mr. ti'Cren, I asked you to come in today because we're investigating several growers for possible offenses, and we're looking for possible customers to confirm or deny our suspicions."

Reranel seemed to relax fractionally. "Uh...certainly, Detective. Most of my purchases have been through my employer, but I'm happy to help."

"Thank you. I've got a list here," they said, passing Reranel the piece of paper. "Have you made purchases from any of these growers?"

He took a moment to scan the names, then shook his head and handed it back. "No, or at least not knowingly. If one of my usual growers acted as an intermediary for them, I was unaware. But I'd be glad to pull my purchase records from my files at work and send them over," he offered. "Or DPP keeps records of such, I believe. I have nothing to hide," he added with a smile that didn't reach his eyes.

Liogh chuckled. "I'm sure you don't, not with Director ti'Tam overseeing your license."

"My great-uncle is something of a stickler, as I'm confident you know if you've had any dealings with DPP."

"Oh, believe me," said Liogh, grinning, "more than my share. Now, just checking—floramancy runs in your Hall, yes? Are you—"

Reranel shook his head. "Unfortunately, no. I have an aunt and uncle who got the wild talent, but I wasn't so lucky. But then again, someone has to brew," he said, spreading his hands, "and I'm certainly capable in that regard."

"Of course." Liogh looked over their notes again while Reranel drank his tea, then tapped their pencil against their thigh and slightly frowned. "So, just to be clear, you're one of the potential customers we identified because the portal records show you making exits in Miami and Woodland, and those are two locations where some of our suspects operate. If I may ask, if you weren't going outside to purchase from them, what *were* you doing?"

Immediately, Reranel tensed again. "If *I* may ask, why has Laws pulled my portal records?"

"Just to cross-check Director ti'Tam's list," said Liogh. "I asked if he could provide us with a list of possible buyers, that's all. He gave us the confirmed transactions, but he also gave us the names of people who'd been in the area in case the buyers didn't log things properly. We got the Portal Authority to send us records to make sure he was on the right path—we're trying not to waste anyone's time."

"Oh." Though he still seemed a little shaken, Reranel put on a smile. "Well, I'm afraid I'll disappoint you, Detective, but my trips outside haven't been for anything interesting."

Liogh smiled back at him. "Yeah?"

"Yes. I, uh…well, tell me," he said, leaning toward them, "have you ever been foraging?"

"Foraging? You mean for wild plants?"

"Precisely," said Reranel, warming to the subject. "I started about ten years ago—there are some really comprehensive human-produced guides to edible plants on the market these days, and I thought I'd give it a try. So, I started making trips out for…"—he paused and scrunched up his face—"perhaps not *necessary* reasons, but acquiring plants is within the terms of my license, so…"

"I've got a former colleague out there who apparently keeps local law enforcement set for moonshine," Liogh replied in a conspiratorial murmur. "If you happen to pick a few berries outside, you're certainly not the first DPP licensee to…read the terms a little broadly, shall we say?"

Once more, Reranel began to relax. "Do you like mushrooms?"

"Depends on the preparation…"

"Well, no mushroom grown here compares in flavor to the ones I've found outside the Pactlands. They're *incredible*. If you know what you're looking for…" He leaned back and groaned happily. "And everything grows so well out there! The woods are full of *food*, and most humans don't even seem to recognize it. Amazing," he said, shaking his head. "They take so much for granted."

"Don't they? It's shameful. Absolutely shameful," said Liogh. "But here, let me get you to sign off on a statement, and we'll have you on your way…"

As the two of them wrapped things up, I said, "You know, I'm actually pretty good at foraging."

"You're also from off the grid," Rose replied. "Trust me, your average city-dweller or suburbanite isn't going frolicking through the forests, looking for mushrooms that won't either kill you or make you hallucinate." She paused, then added, "Yven does, but he also knows what he's doing. I wouldn't trust myself with wild fungus on my best day."

I frowned at her. "You've never foraged?"

"The odd blackberry in the neighbors' backyard when I was a kid, but nothing more than that."

"Huh." Though I didn't trust Reranel one bit, he *did* have a point.

A few minutes later, once they'd escorted Reranel to the elevator, Liogh joined us. "So," they said, folding their arms as they leaned against the wall, "thoughts?"

When none of the agents immediately jumped in, I said, "He's lying."

One of the detective's green eyebrows rose. "What gave you that impression?"

"Well," I said, fighting the urge to squirm as the rest of the room looked at me, "we're talking about trips outside in the last few months, right?"

"Correct."

"Most of them have been to Woodland."

They nodded.

"Now, I'm not personally familiar with Woodland, but I know it's a good ways north of my home," I continued. "And if *we're* still shaking off winter this time of year, then how much worse is the weather up there?"

Liogh pointed at me and grinned. "Precisely, youngling. You're not going to find abundant produce in the woods of New Jersey in January. Maybe some mushrooms and ingredients for tisanes, sure, but does anyone think it's likely that he was wandering out in the cold, freezing his unmentionables off in search of fungus?"

The agents around me shook their heads.

Cracking their knuckles, Liogh looked at Enva. "What do you say? Time to call in DPP? I'm sure we can get ti'Cren's credentials pulled temporarily for improper use."

"Absolutely," said Enva, nodding. "Assuming the director approves—"

Before Kabno could weigh in, I blurted, "That's not going to save my cousins."

Liogh regarded me curiously. "It's the next logical step. We can keep him here."

"But he hasn't told you *anything*," I protested. "The kidnappers were keeping my family outside in cages, and they took the cages with them when they ran. There's a good chance that they're hiding out somewhere cold, and they snatched *toddlers*—"

"Calm down, Maebe," said Diriem.

I ignored him. "When I testified against Ivari, a sorcerer put a spell on me that made me tell the truth."

"That's normal, yes," said Enva. "Though it doesn't *make* you tell the truth—it creates pain if you knowingly lie."

"Same difference. You're a sorcerer, right?" I asked her. "Can't you cast that on Reranel and find out where my family is?"

She hesitated, then made a face. "Technically? I mean, yes, I have the ability, but—"

"That's illegal," Kabno interjected, coming to her detective's rescue. "He has a right against forced self-incrimination, dear, and even if we subjected him to that spell, we wouldn't be able to make him speak. Now, what we *can* do is pull his phone records, see whether he's been making calls to numbers outside the Pactlands—"

"And my cousins are still missing!" I balled my fists, driving my nails into my palms to keep my talent from breaking loose and blowing the chairs around, and turned to Diriem. "Give me the bloodline potion. I'll take the risk."

He remained maddeningly calm in the face of my distress. "We've discussed this. No."

"Give me the potion, damn it!" I shouted back at him as my hair began to whip in a breeze of my own making, the result of my control rapidly fraying. "I'm not going to sit here and let them die!"

"Maebe—"

"Connor can't do it. *I* can. You know I can!" I insisted, almost pleading.

Diriem motioned me down. "Child—"

"*I'm not a child!*" I yelled, conscious that the wind was intensifying but too angry and desperate to care. "I got them into this fucking mess, and I'm going to get them out of it! Now *help me!*" I demanded through gritted teeth.

He didn't move, not so much as flinching as the storm around me widened, but before I could lash out in my fury, Rose stepped between us and grabbed my shoulders, squinting as her hair tangled around her face. "Honey," she said, slipping back into English, "it's okay. There's another option."

I glared at her, my chest heaving, but Rose just tightened her grip.

"Your classmates, the ones who were snatched with your cousins—why can't their parents take the potion, eh? They're bound to be healthier than you are." She paused, gauging my response, then slowly rubbed her hands up and down my taut arms. "Come on, sweetheart, reel it in. Take a deep breath, okay? Let's work this out."

It took me several breaths to corral my talent, and by the time I had it contained once more, I was panting as Rose hugged me to her chest. "Atta girl," she murmured. "You've got this, Maebe."

When she was satisfied that the danger was past, Rose looked back at Diriem and switched to Pactish. "How about it? Do you have the names of the parents? Surely they wouldn't mind taking the bloodline potion."

Before Diriem could answer her, one of the windblown DOL agents laughed aloud. "Are you *crazy*?" he said, righting his chair. "That stuff's poison!"

"If your kid were missing, you wouldn't take it?" she snapped.

He grimaced. "Depends on how much I liked the kid."

"Psychopaths aside," Liogh interjected, giving their colleague a look of impatience, "that's a nasty potion and a massive request, Rose. You might get some volunteers under the circumstances, but what are the odds that they're strong enough to give you the information you need?"

She nodded to me. "Maebe's done it twice."

"And she's rather remarkable in that respect," said Diriem. "But you're right, we can ask."

Staring at him over Rose's shoulder, I demanded, "Will it work? Is this how we find them?"

His expression shifted into a careful blank. "I'll say nothing more."

"*Damn* it, Diriem—"

"Come on," Rose interrupted, pulling me toward the door. "Pop, we'll let you make the calls. I'll drive Maebe home."

CHAPTER 14

Nearly all of the elves who'd gathered at Diriem's home that evening seemed too worried to be awed by the mansion's décor. And then there was Teolm, who'd come straight from work and hadn't bothered changing out of his long-sleeved T-shirt and jeans, which were stained with the colorful leavings of plants I'd never seen before. Though he'd greeted Rose and me kindly, Teolm was *pissed*, and it didn't take a genius to see that the news of his nephew's shenanigans didn't sit well with Lord ti'Cren. The other guests were the parents of the seven students not connected to East Branch, who said little to each other and remained sitting in quiet clumps around the parlor in which I'd had my fun with the bloodline potion. I'd never met any of them, but I caught them staring at me as we waited for the last of the guests to arrive.

Shortly after seven, Canna swept in, black medical kit hanging from her shoulder and purple healer's coat flapping behind her. "Sorry," she said as Scel closed the door. "Young children. All right, what madness are we getting up to tonight?" she asked Diriem, who sat alone in contemplation in a leather chair.

He gestured toward the small crowd. "Volunteers to try the bloodline potion. Their children are presumably with the East Branch group."

Canna glanced at my little knot of people—Rose, Annie, and Jane had joined in for geographic assistance, and Jane waved to her cousin—then looked at Diriem again. "They've been informed of the risks?"

"I thought it best to leave that to the professional," he replied.

"Very well. Listen up," she said, raising her voice as she drew the attention of the parents. "The bloodline potion is not fun. It is *incredibly* painful, often debilitatingly so. The potion itself isn't awful—it'll make you flush almost immediately—but once the spell is triggered, you'll be in for a rough ride. Common side effects include fatigue, nausea, vertigo, chills, fever, and organ damage, particularly cardiac. Do any of you have physical conditions that might be exacerbated by this potion? Is anyone pregnant or potentially pregnant? And has anyone taken a potion in the last forty-eight hours?"

Quickly, she culled the group and cleared eight of the fourteen as potential candidates. "Great," she said to those who'd passed her screening. "Who's first?"

"I'll do it," said a blond man after a moment of awkward silence.

A woman with paler blonde hair in the reject group immediately objected. "Ogenel—"

"It's all right," he soothed, then stepped forward. "What do I need to do?"

Canna had him stretch out on a couch and get comfortable. "I should probably have introduced myself," she told him. "Canna Nerin, DOL."

"Ogenel ti'Har," he replied, his face taut.

That had to be Ainnet's father, I thought, mentally comparing his features to hers. The woman watching anxiously beside the couch was presumably Ainnet's mother. If they recognized me, then surely I was among the last people they'd want to speak to, but Ogenel's obvious fear propelled me closer.

"Um…Mr. ti'Har?" I ventured as Canna prepared the syringe with the antidote. "Hi, I'm Maebe."

His head turned toward me, and his brow furrowed. "You…"

"I'm in Ainnet's year."

His wife jumped in. "*You're* that—"

"This isn't about Ainnet," I snapped, staring her down, then turned back to Ogenel. "Canna's right, it's going to hurt, but you *can* get through it," I said, trying to reassure him. "Hold on to something, and try to focus on your breathing."

His frown deepened. "How would you know the first thing about—"

"I've anchored a trace twice," I replied, and his eyes rounded in shock. "You just have to suffer through it. Once the antidote hits, though, the relief is almost immediate. You might throw up afterward, so don't be surprised, and you'll probably want to sleep it off. But…" I forced myself to smile. "Look, if I can do it, then you can."

"Thanks…I think," he muttered.

Before either of us could say more, Canna handed him the vial of dark green potion. "The one good thing is that this doesn't taste terrible," she said. "Pumpkin and chocolate, or so I've heard. Knock that back, and we'll begin."

With a nod to his wife, he drank the potion. In seconds, he flushed and began to sweat. Teolm and Diriem readied the spell, creating a large globe that hovered over the low table between them, while Jane and Rose took their positions and Annie waited with a laptop open to a mapping program. When Diriem signaled to Canna that they were ready, she checked Ogenel one last time, then showed him the syringe. "As soon as you tell me to give this to you or I think you need it, I'll shoot it in your arm. Ready?"

"Ready," he said, and closed his eyes.

I watched as Diriem and Teolm went to work, but they'd barely triggered the spell when Ogenel's back arched and he screamed. His wife gasped and started to reach for him, and as he shrieked, he managed to beg, "Give it to me! Now! Please, I need it—"

Canna slid the needle into his shoulder, and he collapsed back onto the couch. Sobbing, he rolled over and promptly threw up all over the rug, and his wife did her best to hold back his long hair. Once he'd caught his breath, he looked toward the slowly spinning globe and croaked, "Where's my daughter?"

"Unfortunately," said Diriem, folding his arms, "you didn't last long enough for us to lock on her."

"Huh?"

"It didn't work," said Canna, handing him a glass of water. "They needed more time."

"But...but she..." he said, fumbling, and pointed to me.

"Maebe held on for several *minutes*," said Diriem. "You didn't give us thirty seconds."

As Ogenel sputtered, one of the mothers raised her hand. "I can do it. Let me try."

They cleared another couch for her, and as Ainnet's mother made the evidence of her husband's queasiness vanish, the woman settled in, her nervous husband by her side. "It's all right," she told him, smiling tightly. "We'll make this work. I'm tough."

"I know you are," he murmured, "but—"

"Have faith," she said, and beckoned Canna closer. "Let's have it, then."

By the time the crew with the projection was ready to go, she was tomato-faced and sweating like she'd been weeding the fields in July. "Brace yourself," Canna told her, "but remember, I'm right here with the antidote. Tell me when you want it."

She didn't last ten seconds after the spell was triggered. Her husband held her as she vomited all over herself, the couch, and the floor, and then she slumped in his arms, trembling.

"No luck?" Canna asked.

Diriem shook his head. "No. If any of you think you have the stamina to hold on through the pain—"

"Pain?" the woman interrupted. "That was *agony*!"

"I tried to warn you," said Canna. "Now, you and Ogenel will need a full medical evaluation in the morning. I brought healing potions tonight, but get checked in case there's worse damage. Then again," she said as a look of panic crossed the poor woman's face, "I stopped the potion so quickly that you're both probably fine."

"So," Diriem continued, "does anyone else want to make the attempt?"

The parents looked at each other.

"If you can withstand this, we might be able to find your children. Our good options are limited—"

"The half-breed," said Ainnet's mother. "Make her do it."

"Mivia," Ogenel began, frowning.

She pushed his hand off. "Our children are in danger! Make the half-breed do it! She said she did it before," she pressed. "What's stopping her now?"

The other parents began to mutter, some nodding, others shooting Mivia and me uncomfortable glances.

"Mivia," Ogenel tried again, "she's a child. I wouldn't subject Ainnet to that if death were on the line."

Her eyes narrowed. "That *thing* is why our daughter's lost out there. She owes us all," she said, glaring at me. "Our baby, especially—"

"Your *baby* is a spoiled brat who needs a kick in the ass," said Jane, and Mivia recoiled. "She's no more deserving than anyone else in this mess, and frankly, with the shit she's pulled this year, she'd be near the bottom of my list. There are actual toddlers in that group, and a little kid has already lost an ear, so why don't you shut up about your poor, precious baby?"

Reddening almost as badly as the potion drinkers had, she demanded, "Who are *you* to tell me—"

"I've seen what Ainnet has put Maebe through. That kid lost both her parents and half her extended family last fall," said Jane, pointing to me, "and your brat has taken it upon herself to make her life hell. Most of your brats, probably," she continued, eyeing the other parents. "Who claims Eddic?"

The second potion drinker and her husband lifted their hands.

"Yeah, your asshole son is no better. He invited Maebe to the school dance, did you know? Flowers and everything. That kid got all dressed up and excited, and he picked up Ainnet instead. They did it to humiliate her," she said, scanning the uncomfortable parents, "and most of the rest of your kids were in on it."

Eddic's mother cleared her throat. "That...that doesn't sound like our son—"

"I watched it happen," said Rose, tapping her temple for emphasis. "Live."

"But that's a matter for another time," Diriem interjected. "The reason I asked all of you to come here tonight is because Maebe *cannot* take that potion again. She's offered—repeatedly—but a third round would probably kill her in her present condition."

"Heart damage," Canna offered. "There's no healer in the city who would sign off on that. She's been in treatment for months."

Perhaps suspecting that she was about to suffer a similar fate, Eddic's mother echoed, "*Months?*"

Canna glanced at me, and I shrugged. "Unfortunately, from a medical perspective, Maebe is very human. She's slow to heal, so a third round of that potion would likely be fatal."

"No great loss there," Mivia began, but she made it no further.

Fire bloomed along Jane's arms, and as Annie jumped up to grab the back of her friend's shirt, Teolm said, "I think we've done all we can tonight. Let me show you out."

The parents quickly filed into the corridor, the two potion drinkers being assisted by their spouses, and Diriem brought up the rear. "Jane," he muttered at the door, "please don't burn down the house while I'm gone."

Her flames shrank, and Rose asked, "Where are you going?"

"My office. I need privacy," he added, and closed the door behind him.

"So," said Annie in English, once the voices and footsteps had faded, "does that mean farsight time?"

Rose nodded. "Yeah. Canna, do you want a hand with cleanup?"

"Oh, this is nothing," the healer replied, tucking the used syringes into a pouch in her bag. "How are the rugs?"

She checked them, made a few gestures, and nodded. "Better now. Maybe we should put down newspaper or something before we try that potion again…"

"Puppy pads," said Jane, tidying the throw pillows. "Cover the furniture as well." To me, she said, "I'm sorry, hon. Are you okay?"

"I guess," I muttered, and sank into a chair. "Useless, but what else is new?"

Canna zipped her bag closed, then glanced around the room, which was empty but for the five of us. "Perhaps not," she murmured.

"Perhaps not what?" Jane asked.

"Useless." Taking a seat on the coffee table in front of me, she leaned closer and lowered her voice. "I've got an idea."

My heart began to race. "You'll give me the potion?"

"Absolutely not. But listen," she said before I could protest anew, "I know of a research healer who might be able to help. Shara Neld, she's consulted with us on a few cases. Brilliant woman."

I frowned as the others gathered in. "She can heal my heart?"

"Possibly. She wouldn't make any guarantees when I told her about your case, but if you're set on taking that damn potion, then Shara might have a way to make it work."

"Why are we being sneaky about this?" Annie asked.

"Because her methods aren't approved," Canna replied. "We're talking cutting-edge experimental potions—"

"And Pop doesn't need the details just yet," Rose finished, nodding. "Gotcha."

Canna took my hands and squeezed them. "It's up to you, Maebe. Do you want me to call Shara?"

I'd been poked and interrogated by my share of research healers already—what, I told myself, was one more, especially if she could make me healthy enough to find my family?

"Please," I murmured.

"First thing tomorrow," Canna promised, and with a few hasty goodbyes, she took her leave.

Rose and I saw Annie and Jane to the front door—out of an abundance of caution, Diriem had kept the mansion's protections on—and Jane hugged me before Annie took her back to the hospital. "I'll tell Con you said hi," she assured me. "Though I probably won't mention this healer quite yet, yeah? Don't want him calling you all night."

I smiled at her. "You could confiscate his phone."

"I try, but he keeps stealing it back. Men," she muttered.

"Tell me about it, sister," said Annie, taking her hand, and the two vanished.

I sat up late that night, too excited to sleep, and eventually moved onto the balcony beside my room in the hope that the fresh air would tire me out. Around eleven, as I was trying to hypnotize myself to sleep through endless rounds of solitaire on my phone, Diriem opened the door and poked his head out. "Staying up late again?" he asked.

"For a bit."

"Want a sleeping potion?"

"I'm fine, thanks." Trying and failing to gauge his

mood in the dim blue light of the balcony railing, I asked, "Did you finish what you needed to do?"

"Close enough for tonight," he replied. "Kabno interrupted me, but I'm not complaining."

"No?"

"No." I could just make out his smile. "Laws reviewed Reranel's phone records. He's been calling some of the numbers Culta gave us for months."

My fatigue fled me. "Danirri?" I asked, swiveling around on my lounger.

"And Farral," said Diriem. "But I think I'll be kind to Pateme and hold on to this information until morning. No sense in ruining his Friday evening, is there?" he said, then rapped twice on the door frame. "Go to bed, Maebe. You need to rest."

"I'm fine—"

"Healing potions work best with sleep," he reminded me, then held the door until I shuffled inside. "Go on," he murmured, nudging me toward my room. "You're not going to solve the world's problems tonight."

Though he had a point, sleep was slow in coming, and not until the wee hours of Saturday morning did it finally catch up with me.

My ringing phone woke me from fragmentary dreams just after nine, and I slapped at it until my brain realized it was an incoming call and not the alarm. Somehow, I managed to tap the button and mumble, "Hello?"

"Maebe? Hi, it's Canna." She sounded way too perky for the hour. "I talked to Shara, and she'd love to meet you. She'll be in her lab all day, so get to Beukal when you can."

"Oh, uh…thanks. That's great."

Perhaps recognizing that I wasn't yet sufficiently awake to take a message, Canna texted me the address.

I showered and dressed, snagged toast and a double-shot latte in the kitchen, then found Diriem's office door closed and knocked. It swung open, and he looked up from his computer. "Good morning. Come in. Did you sleep?"

"Eventually," I replied, clutching my warm mug as if mere proximity to that much caffeine would do the trick. "Um...question."

"Yes?"

"Could you give me a ride to Beukal, please?"

Diriem's brow knit. "Certainly," he said after a second's pause. "Did you forget something at school?"

"No, uh...I need to go to District 2."

"You want to visit Connor?"

We stared at each other across his desk, Diriem's face blank and mine struggling to achieve the same effect. I didn't want to *lie* to him, but what if he told me I couldn't visit the healer? He couldn't forbid me, could he? I was a grown woman, and if he said no, would Annie give me a lift? But what if she didn't want to get on his bad side—

"Canna said there's a healer who may be able to help me," I blurted, if only to stop my spiraling thoughts.

Diriem slowly nodded. "This healer's office is attached to the hospital?"

"Close, I think. I checked the map on my phone." I hesitated, nibbling my lip, then asked, "Is this a good idea?"

His expression betrayed nothing. "What do you think?"

"I think *you're* the farseer..."

A soft chuckle answered that. "This is your decision, Maebe. I can't make it for you."

"If I meet with her, will she fix my heart?"

"Not fully. Not today, in any case."

"Enough that I could anchor a blood trace?" I pressed. Silence stretched between us.

"Diriem—"

"Potentially," he allowed.

"Then I don't have a choice," I said. "If there's even a

chance that she could help me save my family, then I'll do whatever she wants." I paused, waiting to see whether he'd argue, then said, "Of course, it'd be *really* nice if you could tell me whether I'm about to run off a cliff. Am I going to regret this?"

I watched his face work for a moment while he decided how to answer me. Finally, he said, "What I can safely tell you is that if you take a bloodline potion in your present condition, it will kill you."

"Could you tell me something I *don't* know?"

He shrugged.

"All right, how about this: is there a way to find my family in time without using a bloodline trace?"

His consideration was longer after that question, and he spoke slowly when he answered me, as if the words were being pulled forth. "I haven't yet seen a way forward without the potion that doesn't end in death."

"Then that settles it," I said. "So, can you give me a ride?"

He nodded. "Gather your things."

The research healer's lab was nothing special from the street, a three-story white brick building pocked with round windows. Diriem idled at the curb as I climbed out, then said, "Call me when you're ready to return to Viratta. I'll be at DOI."

I suppressed the sudden urge to ask him to come with me. After all, I was grown, and I didn't need someone to hold my hand…or so I told myself as the Mercedes pulled away. I glanced in the other direction at the hospital where Connor had been staying for nearly a week. It would be so easy to scuttle this crazy plan and just go visit him…

But Connor couldn't take the potion, and my classmates' parents were no help. I was our last hope.

With a deep breath, I squared my shoulders and walked inside.

The double doors gave way to a small, tile-floored lobby outfitted with a selection of mismatched couches and chairs—donations, perhaps, or pieces bought on sale. At the far end of the room, beside the staircase, was a scuffed wooden desk, behind which sat a brunette sorcerer in a white blouse. "Hello," she called, lifting a hand in greeting as I threaded my way around the furniture. "Can I help you?"

"I, uh…I'm here to see Shara Neld?" I replied, my anxiety turning the statement into a question.

"Oh, sure," she chirped, and picked up the phone on her desk. "I'll call her. Have a seat, dear. Is your parent or guardian parking?"

"I came alone."

Her smile faltered ever so slightly, and though I could tell that she was itching to ask for clarification, she instead placed a quick call and let me be.

A few minutes later, I heard rapid footsteps on the staircase, and then a tall, skinny blonde in a purple healer's coat came jogging into the lobby. "*Hi*," she said, beaming, and extended her hand as I stood. "Lady ti'Ammaas?"

"Um…Maebe," I mumbled, and shook her hand.

"Shara Neld. So nice to meet you! Want to follow me upstairs? I'm sorry," she said, already heading for the staircase, "the elevator's broken, but it's not that far."

She seemed almost hyper, I thought, certainly enthusiastic, and she spoke rapidly as we climbed. Not until we reached her lab did she stop long enough for me to get a good look at her: pale, stick-straight ponytail with a few hairs falling loose around her angular face, pretty hazel eyes, upturned nose, a smattering of freckles crossing her cheeks like a constellation. The green T-shirt she wore beneath her coat was stained almost as badly as some of Teolm's worst gardening clothes, and it had sprung a brown-rimmed hole near her navel. Her pants—jeans, I noticed, somewhat rare for the Pactlands—were similarly tattered and a bit too short for her long legs. Sensible closed-toe shoes with thick rubber soles completed the ensemble.

"Have a seat," she offered, pointing to a pair of gray folding chairs, then muttered at the door until it closed and latched. "Not exactly great for company," she said apologetically as I took in the space—cluttered counters between upper and lower rows of cabinets, a lab bench with a sink and a well-used stool, a padded examination bed, a pot of something that smelled of pickles and wet earth bubbling atop a burner. "I struck out on my own a few years ago, and most of my funds go into equipment and ingredients, so…" She shrugged, then took the other chair and gave me a once-over. "Did Canna drop you off?"

"No, um, I got a ride from Lord ti'Dana," I explained. "I've been staying at his place for a while…"

"Oh, I thought she was going to keep this quiet."

"She did. I kind of told him what was going on. It's okay," I hastily added, "I've had research healers all over me for months, so privacy's not really a concern. Uh…Canna said you might be able to help me?"

Shara nodded. "It's quite possible. Not guaranteed," she stressed, "but I wouldn't have suggested this to Canna were I not fairly confident." Leaning forward in her chair, she steepled her fingers and held my gaze. "Not to brag, but I've worked on many potions over the course of my career, and I've actually developed several helpful ones. I've been at this less than fifty years, so…"

"Impressive," I said.

"I try. Anyway, when I heard about you and your kin, I was intrigued. The healers working with your group have…not been as protective of your private information as they should have been, but since the rest of the research community had the chance to review the data, I took a look myself. You're a fascinating bunch: varying percentages of human and elven genes, birth defects, possible genetic issues, cifyent…and none of you have elven longevity or healing speed."

"Or full talent."

"Right. So, we've got a mix of genes and traits, some desirable, some preferred, some faulty. Now, I'm not trying to suggest that your human genes are *faulty*," she quickly added. "Most of them are probably fine. But considering your community's genetic pool, there are likely to be some issues due to inbreeding. Double recessive genes can be good, neutral, bad, or catastrophic, you know?"

My knowledge of genetics being fairly elementary, I just smiled.

"With that in mind," Shara continued, "I've developed a prototype of a potion that might be able to make some alterations. Correct defective bits of code."

"I...I don't follow."

"Canna told me that you want to take a bloodline potion, but your heart is too damaged," said Shara. "Elves heal so much more rapidly than humans do. If I could correct your code enough to give you elven healing, then I could hit you with a massive dose of healing potion and quickly get you to a safe enough level to anchor a trace. Probably," she hedged. "As I said, it's a prototype. But—"

"I'll do it," I interrupted, and pushed up my sleeve. "Injection? Or do I drink it?"

"Whoa, *whoa*," she said, holding up her hands. "I'll need to take a blood sample and analyze it so I can tailor the potion, and that may take me a few hours. *And* give you a physical, just in case. Also, you should know that this potion will hurt."

"I've anchored bloodline traces twice," I replied. "Worse than that?"

Shara paused, frowning in thought, then shook her head. "Hopefully not. Well, if you're ready, keep that arm bared and let me get a syringe..."

In short order, Shara was running my sample through a small, somewhat battered gray machine on the counter. She conducted a physical and deemed me fit but for my heart—to my relief, she found no sign of the aneurysms that had plagued Connor—and while I dressed, she studied the results as numbers began to rapidly fill the screen of her laptop. "You might want to take a walk," she told me, not looking away from her work. "I'm not going to be great company for a while."

I let myself out of the lab, told the receptionist I'd be back, then made my way up the street to the hospital.

Though I'd expected to find my cousin in bed, Connor was dressed and packing a bag with the clothes, toiletries, and other supplies that Jane had brought him. "Mitta!" he said, beaming, and paused in his work. "What are you doing here?"

"The aide told me where to find you," I replied, and frowned. "Are you leaving?"

"Against medical advice," said Jane, stepping out of the tiny bathroom with her arms folded. "His team wants him to stay another week, just to make sure there's no infection, but—"

"This ain't getting it done," said Connor. "We've got people to find. Where's Diriem?"

I caught Jane's exasperated eye roll behind Connor. "Uh…I think he went to DOI. Do you need me to call him?"

"Nah," said Jane. "I know the way back. Can we give you a ride? I'm sorry you came all this way to visit for nothing…"

"Oh, um…I'm actually doing something here," I told her. "Kind of experimental—"

While Jane wasn't a mother, she had the tone down *cold*. "What do you mean, *experimental*? You're not trying to sneak a bloodline—"

"No—not yet, anyway." I looked at Jane and Connor, who seemed poised to drag me back to Viratta by my ear if necessary, and retreated a step. "I'm working with a research healer, someone Canna trusts."

Jane relaxed a degree at the mention of her cousin, but

she still regarded me with deep suspicion. "Doing what, exactly?"

"She's got this potion. Thinks she can make me elven enough to heal quickly so I can anchor a trace."

Connor's brow furrowed. "Mitta—"

"We're running out of time. The other kids' parents came out last night to try to anchor, and the only two willing to give it a shot couldn't last a minute. It doesn't affect me as badly, and I know what I'm getting into—I just need my heart whole enough to handle it."

The two of them shared a long look.

"I don't know about this, Maebe," said Connor. "Hon, I'd take the bloodline potion, but—"

"The healers here forbid it," Jane finished, "and if he tries, I'll knock it out of his hand."

"It's okay," I told them. "But *someone* has to anchor the trace, and it looks like it needs to be me. This healer…she seems pretty confident, and I'm sure Canna wouldn't send me to someone she didn't trust."

Jane slowly nodded. "Yeah, I know, I just…"

"I'll be careful."

"How can you be careful when you're taking an experimental potion?" she countered.

The best answer I could give her was a little shrug. "Can you trust me? I know you must think I'm an idiot—"

"Honey," said Jane, taking my hands, "I don't think you're an idiot. You're *young*, and you're still pretty naïve, but that doesn't make you stupid. I…I'm trying to look out for you. This one gives me fits," she said, nodding to Connor, "so if you'd let me keep you out of trouble—"

"That's not an option right now," I told her, shaking my head. "I'm going to find our family, whatever it takes."

Again, the two of them looked at each other, the sort of glance through which a couple can silently say so much, and I could see them relenting. "Do you want us to go with you to meet with this healer?" Connor asked. "Back-up?"

"Oh, that's all right," I replied. "I'm waiting for her to finish her analysis…"

My stomach rumbled, interrupting me, and Jane pulled me in for a quick hug. "At least let us feed you, then. The cafeteria here isn't half bad."

Two hours later, after a long lunch, a reluctant goodbye from Connor and Jane, and a boring wait in the lobby with a stack of nearly incomprehensible medical magazines for company, Shara was ready for me.

"The good news," she said as I made myself comfortable on the examination bed, "is that you're fairly healthy. Aside from your cardiac issues, you're in solid shape…by human metrics," she added. "I've studied their norms, and you're about average. With a proper diet, some preventive care, and a bit of luck, you could live into your nineties, perhaps a little past your centennial."

"That's…good?"

"But it could be better." She leaned against the counter and folded her arms. "The question now is how far you want to go."

I peered up at her. "What do you mean?"

"Well, do you want every human trait reworked, or do you want to keep some of them? It's up to you," she said as I tried to formulate an answer. "You're not going to hurt my feelings, whatever you decide. I'm happy to do as much or as little as you'd like—and assuming this works, it's not a 'once and done' situation. If you change your mind later, want more, we can revisit."

"I…I, uh…"

"I *would* suggest we work on your healing and longevity," said Shara. "Those are the practical upgrades, if you will, and you'll especially need healing if you're set on this bloodline potion. As for longevity…why not? You've got what I need to work with—it's just a matter of turning a few things on and tweaking the settings, if you will."

"So…" I swallowed hard as my mind whirled. "You're talking immortality?"

"Precisely. And corresponding youth, naturally. Now, elves and nymphs say 'immortality,'" she continued, "but it's not *true* immortality. They can be killed. Even the Hunter is only conditionally immortal, and he's…well," she said, chuckling, "I'd give my right arm for access to his genes. But back to elves: they're highly resistant to disease, and they don't have a fixed lifespan. I've never heard of one developing cancer, and you see that in other species all the time. That said, some of them *do* have physical defects, and heart issues like yours aren't unheard of. There's an infamous melee championship game in which one of the elven players pushed himself too hard and died of a heart attack. *Extremely* rare, but that's why the smart ones get themselves checked on occasion." She paused, then asked, "You don't play melee, do you?"

"Uh…not yet. I couldn't try out because—"

"*Oh*, of course," she said, and smacked herself in the head. "Let me work on your healing and longevity, and after that, you might be able to play. You'll want regular evaluations, now," she cautioned, "but it's a fun sport. Most of my school friends were on the melee team."

I tried and failed to square that statement with the skinny, almost gawky healer. "You played?" I managed.

She grinned. "*Terribly*. But I like the game, and my larger teammates were…protective, shall we say? Kids tend to leave you alone when your friends are trolls."

My thoughts flashed to Swift Eagle, the star melee player who'd looked out for me on occasion, and I nodded.

"So…is that acceptable?" Shara asked. "Healing and longevity?"

Though my stomach knotted, I said, "Please."

"Very good." She reached over and scribbled a note on a pad she'd left on the counter. "Any cosmetic changes?" When I didn't immediately answer her, she put the pad down and murmured, "Hey, no pressure, and no judgment. If you *want* a more typically elven appearance, I think I can make that work. Fix your cifyent issue, for example. But I'm not suggesting that you *should* change a thing."

To my surprise, my eyes began to film, and Shara reached for a box of tissues as I sat up. "It's all right, Maebe," she soothed, taking a seat on the examination bed beside me. "Mixed feelings, yeah?"

I wadded up a tissue, wiped at my tears, and nodded as I sniffled. "Yeah."

"I understand. Believe me, I do." I must have looked incredulous at that, as she murmured, "Want me to let you in on a little secret?"

"Uh..." I blew my nose. "Sure."

Without further ado, Shara made a quick gesture in front of her face.

She'd been masked, I realized, spotting the changes. While her blonde hair and hazel eyes remained untouched, her cheekbones had become slightly more pronounced beneath her freckles, and her ears looked more like mine— not flopped over, that is, but pointed, if a little shorter than normal by elven standards. She smiled, giving me a quick flash of sharp, *decidedly* elven teeth.

"You're..." I began.

"Half," she replied. "You can probably guess why I was so interested in your community."

"Didn't want to test the potion on yourself?"

"Didn't need to. In terms of longevity and healing, I favor my father. My talent is *mostly* my mother's, but I do find gestures simpler than spoken focusing for certain matters."

"But you mask," I pointed out.

Shara smiled again, but there was a hint of menace in it. "I do. This," she said, patting her cheek, "raises questions I'd often rather not answer, but I don't feel the need to *change* it. Masking suits me just fine."

I hesitated, then said, "May I ask a personal question?"

"Sure."

"Why go sorcerer and not elf with your mask?"

"Because my father's never been part of my life, and frankly, he can go fuck himself." She chuckled at my expression and patted my knee. "Don't worry, I'm not offended. You want the truth? My mother used to bartend, and he decided to lie in wait for her one night after she got off work. I don't think he ever imagined she'd go to Laws and name *him*, but a blood test proved I was his, and a farseer proved she was telling the truth."

"And she, um...kept you?"

Shara nodded. "I wouldn't have blamed her if she'd ended the pregnancy or surrendered me, but my mom couldn't bring herself to do either. My birth was...difficult...and the healers told her she'd probably never be able to carry another child. Then her useless boyfriend left her in the middle of her pregnancy, so she decided to raise me on my own. The fact that my father's family paid her a *massive* lump sum to go away and be quiet when my father was incarcerated surely helped."

I frowned. "Wouldn't it have been too late for her to keep quiet by then? I mean, if he was being tried..."

"You see, sometimes, when the accused is sufficiently well connected and doesn't put up a fight, Laws is willing to work without making a public spectacle. Or it was back then—perhaps things have changed now. I certainly followed Lord ti'Cren's trial a few years ago," she added. "But my father's big brother is Lord ti'Lir, and he didn't want the stigma on the Hall. As it stands, my darling daddy is still on a penal farm, and Hall ti'Lir pretends I don't exist."

"That's awful," I muttered.

"It is what it is," said Shara. "Anyway, my mother masked me when I was a child, but when I accidentally removed it in school and couldn't answer my classmates' questions, they began teasing me. Mom wouldn't even tell me who my father was until I was a teenager and old enough to understand what he'd done to her, and by that time, I was able to mask myself. It's the face I prefer," she said, and gestured it back on. "But you know, Maebe, here's the fun bit: I was first in my class, and I've had a *notable* career to date. The more potions I develop, the more conferences I attend, the more my name is thrown around—you know ti'Lir has to squirm. They paid Mom off, but there's nothing preventing me from going public at *any* moment," she explained with a smug grin. "And I'm only in my eighties. Give it a few decades, and once it becomes obvious that I'm not your average sorcerer…"

"Delayed revenge."

"Or justice, if you prefer. But what I'm trying to say is that I do understand if you don't want to alter your appearance," she continued. "I'm a bag of weirdness, and that's just who I am—it doesn't bother me. Since you've been set up as the head of a Hall, if you want to look the part, I can help. If not, that's fine, too."

I thought about it for a moment, then asked, "Could you fix my ears? I don't want them to be any larger, just…upright."

"Certainly. Would you mind removing your mask so I can see?"

I did as she asked and turned my head to give her a good view of the problem. "You're right about the teasing. Some of my classmates are *awful*, and it doesn't matter if I mask."

"I bet." Pushing herself off the bed, she retrieved her notepad and resumed her jottings. "Though considering your Hall status, I'm kind of surprised. No one tries to curry favor?"

The notion made me laugh as I threw away my tissue. "With *me*? Absolutely not. A few people are nice, most ignore me, and then some of them try to make my life as miserable as possible. Like, this *really* cute guy invited me to a dance two weeks ago, and I got all dressed up and waited for him, and he took another girl. In front of *every-*

one," I muttered. "They'd planned it. Now they're missing along with my family—"

Shara winced. "Yeah, Canna mentioned that. The impetus for the bloodline potion, yes?"

"Exactly. At this point, I'm almost tempted to leave those two wherever they are..." I grunted. "Awful, right?'

"Understandable." She moved to her computer and rapidly typed for a moment, and the potion sitting on the heater beside it turned slightly pinker. "Fine-tuning," she offered before I could ask. "See the apparatus in the middle of the vessel? I've got several ingredients loaded in the base, and they're injected from below. This is more accurate than hoping my hand doesn't shake." She considered the potion and muttered a spell, and the color shifted toward purple. "Close. The kids who pranked you—elves?"

"Yeah."

"What Halls?"

"She's in ti'Har, and he's in ti'Dir."

"Mm. Main-line or cousins?"

"She's definitely a cousin. I'm not sure about him..."

Shara smirked as she turned back to me. "Oh, if he were main-line, you'd know it. Now, I don't socialize with many elves, but I *do* know that they have a thing for tradition, especially in the old Halls. You realize that ti'Ammaas outranks everyone but ti'Dana, right? I mean, Ivari ti'Ammaas was a *king*. You may not technically be royalty, but you're pretty damn close."

I shrugged. "Hasn't done me a lot of good."

"Maybe not yet, but if I understand correctly, ti'Dana and ti'Cren are backing you and your cousins, yes? Those are some *powerful* allies here, youngling. Look at ti'Cren— their former lord's going to be locked away for the next few centuries, and that Hall is still nearly untouchable. So, if I were you," she said, arching a brow, "I'd start acting like a damn princess. Who cares about two kids from ti'Dir and ti'Har? They're beneath your notice," she continued, affecting a more elven accent. "*Especially* ti'Dir."

While I digested that, Shara made the final touches to her potion, then decanted it from the mixing setup and held it to the light. "No sediment, good. Do me a favor and call your ride now. You won't be in any condition to do so after you down this."

I sent Diriem a quick text and waited for confirmation, then watched as Shara lined up three vials of burgundy healing potion and a fourth that was peach in color. "Chasers," she told me, then handed me the bottle of purple liquid and gave me a little smile. "Good luck."

Glancing into the bottle, I asked, "How confident are you?"

"Uh...let's say eighty percent."

"Good enough." I lifted the bottle, then paused to add, "Your secret's safe with me."

Shara winked, and with a brief prayer to anyone listening, I knocked back the potion.

The pain was immediate, an awful burning that flowed from my lips to my stomach, then out toward my limbs, but it wasn't nearly as bad as the bloodline potion, so I groaned and held on.

"Here," said Shara, pressing another bottle into my hand, and I drank it quickly. Vanilla, lime, and cinnamon—a healing potion. Once I'd finished, she traded the empty bottle for the second, then the third. Finally, she gave me the fourth bottle and said, "Sedative. Go ahead, drink it."

By then, the burning sensation had grown to a fire in my veins, and I gratefully shot back the last of the potions.

"You'll feel much better when you wake," was the last thing I heard Shara tell me, and then my head hit the bed and I passed out.

CHAPTER 15

The next sensation I was aware of was sunlight in my face, reddening the insides of my eyelids. I grumbled and rolled over, but that motion was enough to begin the rousing process.

Pillow—check. The ones in my guest room at Diriem's house were considerably nicer than the ones on my dorm bed, and the sheets were far less scratchy.

Mattress—yes, that was undeniably the plush cloud he'd somehow trapped in mattress form and wrestled into my room. Having grown up on a mattress stuffed with corn husks, I still couldn't quite believe that beds like those in the mansion existed.

The sun from the east-facing window was bright enough to suggest morning, but it had been past lunchtime when I took the potion…

I sucked in a rapid breath and tried to sit up, but strong hands pressed me back into the bedding as I tangled the blankets around me. "It's okay, mitta," spoke a voice I recognized as Connor's. "You're safe. Breathe."

It took me a moment to catch my breath and calm my racing heart, but then I focused enough to recognize that my cousin was sitting in a chair beside my bed…and judging by the assortment of empty plates, packets, and glasses on the table, he'd been there a while. "Connor?" I croaked. "What's…uh…"

"You've been sleeping for almost two days," he said calmly. "It's Monday morning."

"*Monday?*"

"Yup." After clucking his tongue, he said, "You missed all the fun this weekend. How're you feeling, kiddo?"

I paused, taking stock. "Not terrible. Groggy."

"We'll get a cup of coffee in you, eh? Come on, hon, let's get you to the bathroom. You're probably about to pop."

He wasn't wrong, I realized with alarm, and let him help me out of bed and across the room to the spacious bath. "I'll be right out here in case you need me," he said. "Don't lock the door."

With a sigh of relief, I attended to the necessary business, then headed to the sink to wash my hands and face. As I pushed my dirty hair out of the way, I noticed my ears, perky and pointed. That wouldn't have been unusual, as I'd been masking fairly religiously in the last months, but I'd left mine off before taking the potions at Shara's lab…

That wasn't a mask.

I leaned across the counter for a closer inspection, then poked and pinched at the cartilage to verify what my eyes were telling me. They looked…almost normal. A little short for elven ears, but they weren't flopping over anymore. A brisk shake of my head did nothing to dislodge them.

The rest of my face seemed unchanged, as did my teeth when I hastily checked them, and I *felt* fine, but whether I'd sufficiently healed wasn't a question I could answer on my own.

I rinsed off and brushed my teeth, then emerged to find that Connor, true to his word, had taken up a post against the wall nearby. "You didn't have to babysit me," I said, cutting the bathroom light. "I'm sorry about that."

"Don't worry. Janie and I have been trading off. Your healer buddy said you'd be down for two days or less, and she was right."

"Did Shara come here?"

"No, she sent you off with instructions. Also," he said,

wiggling his phone, "I just got word from Diriem that there's a cadre of healers on the way to check you out. Canna, too."

"Then I'd better put some pants on," I replied, and shuffled to the dresser. "How're you feeling?"

"Right as rain," said Connor. "Which is more than I can say for our little ti'Cren buddy. Oh, he's alive," Connor explained when I wheeled on him in alarm. "Unharmed. Just...you know, he had a bad day yesterday."

Considering my cousin's satisfied smile, I had an inkling of what had befallen Reranel. "What happened?"

"You get dressed, and I'll bring up breakfast. Back in a jiffy."

By the time he returned, I'd made myself somewhat presentable, though I couldn't stop touching my ears, making sure they hadn't disappeared on me. As Connor set down the breakfast tray beside the stack of dirty dishes on the table, he caught me and chuckled. "Feels weird?"

"Yeah, but good weird," I said, salivating at the mixed scents of bacon and strong coffee. Ranarma knew the way to my heart. "Do I look okay?"

"Just fine. Come here, get some food down you. I'll fill you in."

As I inhaled my breakfast, Connor related just why Reranel was probably reconsidering all of his life choices that morning.

Bright and early Sunday morning, a team of DOL agents had gone to his apartment to haul him in. "Teolm was informed ahead of time," said Connor, "just to make sure they had the right address, and he said to grab the son of a bitch with his blessing." They'd taken the brewer straight to the tower, then up to a different interrogation than the one they'd used on his first visit—one significantly less cozy and quite a bit more secure. Moreover, as part of Reranel's arrest, the agents had stuck him with a dose of dampening potion, leaving him magically defenseless.

"Putty in Liogh's hands," Connor told me. "Detective's

good. It's *fun* to watch them work."

Apparently, the respect extended both ways, as Liogh had called Jane prior to the interrogation to enquire after Connor and see whether he wanted to observe. The two of them had hurried to the capital and joined the group of Laws personnel in the room next door.

"He looked scared," Connor recalled. "Nervous. Kept licking his lips, and one of his knees wouldn't stop bouncing. He knew they had something on him, but he played dumb…well, for a while."

Once Reranel was seated on a folding chair across a metal desk from Liogh, the detective had produced a brown folder and opened it to reveal a sheaf of papers: Reranel's phone records. Slowly, methodically, Liogh had walked through each questionable entry. At first, they'd asked why Reranel was making calls to numbers with New York area codes. When he'd tried to pass those off as calling an old friend who was growing outside the Pactlands, Liogh had sprung the trap and revealed that Laws knew *exactly* whose numbers those were: Farral ti'Pul, Danirri ti'Ammaas, Wewel ti'Tola, Pacul ti'Ammaas, Kentha ti'Tola, Mirin ti'Ammaas, and Jeviel ti'Tola—Ivari's wife, son, daughter-in-law, and grandsons.

"The look on his *face*," said Connor, laughing to himself. "If 'oh, shit' were personified, that'd have been it."

As Reranel had floundered, trying to concoct an explanation, Liogh had pressed their luck with a calculated lie. They'd told the paling brewer that his blinding potion had degraded, and a farseer at DOI had been tasked with investigating his recent trips out of the Pactlands. The farseer knew that he'd been spending an awful lot of time in Manhattan for someone with no legitimate business there. And then Liogh had sat back and waited, faintly smiling.

Reranel was a talented brewer, but despite his ti'Cren heritage, he was no criminal mastermind. Faced with the possibility of a lengthy sentence on a penal farm, perhaps working side by side with his murderous grandfather, he'd agreed to talk.

Stealing a piece of my bacon, Connor said, "He put everything on Farral. Said this is her doing, and he's just the go-between."

"How so?" I asked.

"Unsurprisingly, she's furious at how Ivari's been treated, and so she hatched a plan to get him and their fortune back. And that Hemell guy, too, I guess. Want to guess how she linked up with Reranel?"

I thought briefly as I sipped my coffee. "Dania? Last fall?"

"Close. Dania's handler outside, Yinkin ti'Mal, was much more heavily involved in the ti'Cren criminal enterprise than she was, and he knew which of Inade's associates hadn't been caught. He passed on Reranel's name to Ivari in case he and Dania were compromised, and lo and behold…" Connor spread his arms in a gesture of feigned surprise.

"So, Reranel *was* working with Inade ti'Cren?"

"That's what he confessed. He was never one of good old Grandpa's top lieutenants, but he was able to brew up most of what Inade needed…you know, like blinding potion. He claimed there's a well-stocked brew room in a cellar in the ti'Cren mansion that he's been using for decades."

My eyebrows rose. "Is there?"

"Well, Liogh got the details out of him, and someone called Teolm, and Teolm went exploring in the basement. Reranel told the truth about that, and Teolm is fit to be tied. Cooperating fully with Laws. There's a hidden entrance near the edge of the property and a tunnel, and from what I hear, Teolm's planning to close that up."

"Good," I muttered.

"He wants to clean out the Hall," said Connor. "He doesn't have a choice but to crack down hard. Anyway, once Inade went off to prison, Yinkin kept in contact with Reranel, just in case. Farral had access to Ivari's papers and such, and when Yinkin was taken off the board, she reached out to Reranel."

"Don't tell me she's still pushing that stupid lie that we were trying to blackmail them…"

"Apparently not. Reranel said she never believed that, but she was pretty scarred from…you know, what she'd had to do to survive this long…and she wanted us wiped out and forgotten." Rubbing the back of his neck, he said, "In a way, I pity her."

"*Connor!*"

"Not enough to let her off the hook," he hastily clarified, "but think about it. She lost her first husband and all of her children, then she was married off to a human guy—"

"And he wasn't the nicest," I added, recalling what Madla had told us.

"Even worse. No wonder she'd rather not be reminded of what she had to do back then. And now the folks here have gone and taken her third husband, someone she actually likes. Farral's got old scars and a fresh grudge."

Though I didn't like to admit it, Connor had a point. "Okay, so what did they do? Where are our cousins?"

"*That*, he couldn't tell us—where they are now, I mean. But he's the one who got Farral and her crew into the Pactlands."

I couldn't quite hide my disappointment, but I said, "How?"

"He had help. Farral offered him a pretty hefty bribe back in November, and Reranel used it to recruit assistance here. He got a handful of portal agents pretty easily—quite a few are still loyal to Inade."

"Lovely."

"Right? Money might not buy happiness, but it sure can buy you friends. But that was only part of the problem—Reranel needed contacts at North Lake so he could get the New York bunch close to y'all. He said he got a janitor first, and the janitor put him in touch with, uh…what was her name?" he muttered. "Ah. Chennis ti'Van."

"*Chennis?*" I echoed, stunned.

"One of your dorm parents, yeah?"

I nodded, too shocked to do more.

Connor smiled grimly. "Reranel said that he had a few meetings with her to make sure they were on the same page. She took a little convincing—she was fine with y'all at the start of the year, you know? But after y'all got titles, she…soured on y'all, I guess you'd say."

"Why?" I asked.

"I mean, I'm no expert, but Yven thinks it's because she's a ti'Van. New Hall. Some of them can be pretty damn touchy about that, he said, and I guess she didn't like the idea of y'all coming in from nowhere, with nothing, and suddenly outranking her." He paused, allowing that to sink in, then said, "Ti'Van wasn't the only one."

"Who else?" I mumbled.

"Your principal."

"Ms. Mafatta? Are you kidding me?" Despite my hunger, the breakfast I'd eaten felt like a lump of stone in my belly.

He shook his head. "Now, Laws hasn't hauled the North Lake folks in yet, but—"

"Why would Ms. Mafatta *do* that?" I demanded, blinking as my eyes began to prick.

"Well, according to Reranel, she wasn't thrilled to host y'all in the first place, but the board insisted. Now she's got a list of grievances. You keep causing trouble with Ainnet—"

"Ainnet goes after me!" I protested.

Connor motioned me down. "I'm just the messenger, mitta. Other than that, some of y'all are planning to stay past thirty-five for more schooling."

"We're *years* behind!"

"I know, but she ain't happy. Add in the fact that y'all need special tutoring, and basically, she considers our family a nuisance."

"And so she sold us out to be kidnapped?"

He grimaced. "From what Reranel was saying, she doesn't really wish y'all *ill*, exactly, but she wants y'all out of her hair. Reranel was vague about what the plan was—he just told her that y'all would be taken out of the Pactlands, and since the bribe was generous, she looked the other way and didn't ask questions."

I thought then of my trip to school with Diriem a week before to pick up my things—how surprised Chennis and Ms. Mafatta had been to see me. Of course the principal had been panicking; she'd only anticipated having us removed from the school, not seven other elven students, kids who still had parents to complain about their abduction.

Though part of me didn't want to know anything more, I asked, "Did Reranel kidnap everyone?"

"He admitted he was involved," said Connor. "Eat up, hon, your food's getting cold."

"Lost my appetite."

"Try for me," he urged, pushing my tray closer, and I nibbled on a piece of bacon as he resumed. "So, per Reranel, he found out about your campus party from ti'Van."

"Lake Day?"

"That's it. Got the schedule from her and cross-checked with Mafatta. The night of, he sneaked Farral's group in with a customized vehicle, one of Grandpa's that Laws failed to seize. It's got one hell of a hold, and he timed it right, so he got inspected by a portal attendant who was paid to see nothing. They went out to North Lake and sneaked onto the campus while everyone was partying, and they waited. The plan was for them to pick y'all off as they could, and if they couldn't get everyone, ti'Van had agreed to let them into the dorm. But they lucked out," he said, shrugging.

"The fight," I muttered.

"Bingo. That kicked off pretty close to where they were

hiding, so Farral seized the opportunity and threw knock-out potions. Incidentally, Reranel brewed and supplied those and the antidote, so he's definitely on the hook for the abduction, even if he hadn't been driving the getaway car," said Connor. "Anyway, he said they grabbed anyone who looked even vaguely elven, loaded them into the vehicle, and burned rubber for Michigan."

"Theo's place."

"Uh-huh. So, that was Saturday week. Reranel stuck around at the cabin for a few days in case they needed potions or support or whatnot. He verified what Theo said about the cages."

A thought occurred to me. "Reranel's a brewer. That's how they're keeping everyone locked up—dampening potion."

"Atta girl," Connor said with a hint of pride. "Injections of dampening potion for everyone, plus spell rings outside the cages to prevent snooping via farsight. Oh, and you'll like this: Reranel knew that some of the ones they grabbed weren't East Branch folks. Their accent would have given them away even if they hadn't been protesting that they had nothing to do with our kin, but apparently, Farral doesn't give a damn. The more hostages, the better."

"Did he say why they left Michigan?" I asked.

Connor nodded. "Once Theo caught them on camera, Farral didn't want to take any chances. Reranel said that only her eldest, Danirri, is on board with this mess. Some of her grandkids from her second child, Beani, are involved, but their mother isn't, and neither are any of the rest of the siblings." Spreading his hands, he added, "Reranel got the impression that Farral's acting on her own. Don't know if I fully believe it, but *he* seemed sincere."

"But he doesn't know where they went?"

"So he claims. He was there when Farral cut off a kid's ear—he didn't catch a name, but he said it was a little girl. My guess would be Eleanor. Anyway, Farral asked Reranel to mail the ear and the ransom note from within the Pact-lands, so he drove back last Wednesday, and they went elsewhere. He got through the portal and put the package in the mail to Kabno, and the rest is history."

I sipped my coffee and scowled into space. "It's not what we need, but it's more than we had."

"Absolutely. But for now, finish up and go downstairs to meet with the healers," he said, standing. "Let's get you checked out, mitta."

"I guess." Pushing myself from my chair, I asked, "What about the others? Ms. Mafatta and Chennis and the janitor?"

Connor smiled and patted my shoulder. "Oh, Laws picked them up yesterday. Don't you worry, kiddo."

About twenty minutes after I emerged from my guest room, half a dozen research healers, Shara, and Canna descended upon the mansion.

Scel showed them into a sitting room, and I tried to be still and cooperative as they poked, scanned, drew blood, and muttered. Well, *most* of them—Shara stood back with a knowing smile, while Canna superintended, watching the other healers as if she were prepared to jump in once they reached their limit of needle sticks. It was a full hour before they'd completed their testing and assessment, and the results left them flabbergasted.

Genetically, I was showing up as ninety-two percent elven, a jump of nineteen percentage points. The expected markers were present where they'd been missing before; in terms of healing, I looked like a full-blooded elf would, while my genes gave every indication that my aging was about to cease. There was simply no way that this could have happened...which made Shara all the more pleased with herself.

And then there was my heart, still damaged but not nearly as badly as it had been two days before. "It's a combination of my potion, her enhanced healing ability, and three healing potions tossed in on top," Shara explained. "Give her a few days more, and she'll probably be good as new—perhaps not perfect but at least healed of her self-inflicted injuries."

"What if we don't have a few days?" I asked. "Am I strong enough to anchor a blood trace now?"

The healers traded glances, none rushing to answer that, and so Canna stepped in. "I'd clear you," she replied. "Not wholeheartedly, and not without supervision, but I don't think it'd be fatal."

"Why not hit her with healing potions as soon as you stop the trace?" Shara suggested.

"That's my plan," said Canna, and looked at the other healers. "How about it? Want to help, just in case this goes upside-down?"

While I could tell that the others weren't entirely on board with this plan, they stayed, loitering awkwardly while Diriem called Teolm out to the mansion. Connor woke Jane, while Annie picked up Rose and brought her home the quick way, and in short order, I found myself lying on my back, hoping I wouldn't puke on myself.

All too soon, Annie, Rose, and Jane were prepped with their mapping programs, Diriem and Teolm had completed the spell preliminaries, and Connor had taken up a position beside me, ostensibly to keep me from flinging myself onto the rug. Canna readied the syringe with the antidote, and Shara handed me the potion vial. "Good luck," she said, stepping back. "Canna said you've got a decent tolerance for this."

"That's generous," I muttered, then downed the potion and waited while the warning heat spread through my body. I made myself as comfortable as I could, and just as I was silently lamenting my decision to eat breakfast, I heard Canna say, "Go."

Shara's tweaking had done wonders for me, but it had no effect on my reaction to the bloodline trace, as I screamed and arched my back off the couch like I was trying to fly away as soon as the spell activated. Distantly, through the red haze of agony, I was conscious of Connor's strong arms pinning me to the cushions. "You've got this," he said close to my ear. "Fight it."

"She can't handle the stress!" one of the research healers yelled over my sobbing cries. "Hit her with the antidote!"

"Not yet," Canna snapped.

"The child is in pain—"

"*Find them!*" I bellowed. "Shut up and find them!"

My heart hammered like I'd run up a mountain, pumping fire through my veins. I couldn't hear the map team's voices over the sound of my screams, but I felt it every time they zoomed in on the target, as my overtaxed reserves gave a little more power, flared a little hotter, burned me a little more deeply.

And as the fireball that had once been my heart slammed against my ribs, I realized I'd made a mistake. This was it—I wasn't strong enough, I hadn't fully healed, every inhalation felt like I was sucking in scalding steam, and the burning, oh, God, the *burning*—

"Montana!" Diriem finally yelled. "It's the Montana property! Confirm!"

"Got it!" Annie called. "That's Ivari's place. Shut it down."

She'd barely given the order before Canna's needle was in my shoulder, and I shuddered as the blessed ice rushed through me. I went limp on the sofa, struggling to catch my breath, and soon felt Connor pressing something cool against my sweat-soaked face. "Here we go," he murmured, wiping me down. "It's over, mitta. You did good."

I swallowed hard and felt the warning signal of my returning breakfast. "Gonna be sick—"

He quickly rolled me onto my side and stepped clear as I threw up. Before I'd finished, someone had produced a glass of water, and I opened my eyes in time to see Canna mutter my accident away. "Sorry," I managed. "Doesn't get any easier with practice."

"Uh…you held on for *minutes*," one of the research healers said. "That's—"

"Insane," finished another. "*How…*"

"We don't know," said Canna. "Maebe's gifted. We haven't tested any of the other East Branchers, so she could be an outlier, but in any case, that's a useful skill. And now, little miss," she said, ignoring the sputtering researchers as she pulled more vials from her bag, "you're going to drink these and get some rest, understood?"

Two healing potions and a strong painkiller—I wasn't complaining.

As I waited for my vertigo to pass, I heard Diriem on the phone across the room: "Wylan? Hello. They're at the Montana location. How quickly can you mobilize?"

"Thank y'all for helping us," I mumbled to Annie in English as she joined me on the sofa.

"No problem, hon," she replied, and smiled. "But it's not just us this time. The Forum had an emergency meeting yesterday afternoon, and since Pact citizens are in danger out there, Special Forces has been authorized. Wylan's got a *big* team raring to go."

"I want to go, too."

"We can talk about that, but you've got to sleep first. Come on, let's find your feet," she coaxed, tugging me upright, and Jane helped her brace me. "Hey, Diriem," Annie called, "do your anti-Hunt protections only work going in and out of the house?"

"That's how they're designed," he replied, "but they're not strictly anti-Hunt—"

"Yeah, whatever." She waved him off, then tightened her hold on me. "Let's take the shortcut upstairs, eh?"

Before I had time to argue, we were standing in the hallway by the guest rooms, and Jane showed Annie to mine. "Bedtime," Annie said in a singsong voice. "Jane, could you get the covers, please?"

I didn't bother changing clothes, and I was gone before they'd finished tucking me in.

CHAPTER 16

Based on past experience, I'd anticipated sleeping off the bloodline potion until well after nightfall, but the light outside my window suggested late afternoon when I awoke. Chalking it up to Shara's work, I sat on the edge of the bed and waited to see what my body would do.

No racing heart, no vertigo, no nausea. Sure, I felt a little sore deep in my bones, but otherwise, I was...well, surprisingly fine.

Thus reassured, I made my way to the bathroom, splashed water on my face, and brushed my sweat-stiffened tangles into a semblance of order, then stepped out into the corridor to look for signs of life. The balcony door was ajar, I noticed, and so I headed that way, keeping one hand close to the wall, just in case.

Connor looked up from a lounger when I peeked outside, and he motioned for me to join him. "Hey, mitta," he said, patting the adjacent chair. "How're you feeling?"

"Okay, I think." I took a seat and got my bearings, enjoying the mild spring warmth. "What're you up to?"

"Not much. Janie's catching up with work, so I'm staying out of her hair." Grinning, he leaned back against his chair. "Should probably think about making an appearance in Whitford before they deem me a missing person, huh?"

"You did just have your head cut open."

"Yeah, like, a week ago. I'm sure I can handle a few hours in a patrol car." He paused, considering me, then said, "Your color looks good. I wasn't expecting to see you up this early."

"I think Shara's to blame," I replied. "This is the best I've ever felt after one of those potions. And speaking of which, I guess the Hunt left without us, huh?"

"Not yet."

"No? What's the holdup?"

"My understanding is that they're waiting for nightfall. Not a bad plan," he assured me. "But as for leaving us behind, they haven't exactly extended an invitation."

Though I didn't have an agent's training or a Huntsman's stamina, the last days had worn on me, and I was tired of the sidelines. "I want to go," I insisted. "This is *our* family. Don't you want in?"

"Sure," said Connor. "I mean…I do have Wylan's number, so I guess we could plead our case, but are you certain that you're up to it? You went through hell this morning, and that's after your fun with Shara on Saturday…"

"Really, I'm all right." Flexing my bicep as proof, I said, "Probably not up to drinking any more strange liquids today, but I want to help."

"I hear you." His eyes narrowed as he considered my unimpressive arm. "Do you feel any different after Shara's potion? Aside from healing."

I frowned as I leaned back and took stock of myself. "Not exactly, but I'm glad I took it. It *worked*." Cutting my eyes to Connor, I asked, "Are you interested?"

"Don't know. That's a big decision," he murmured, "but I'm happy for you. Did she do anything to improve your talent?"

"We didn't talk about that when we were going through the options."

"Well, have you experimented since? Not that you've had much free time today…"

I shrugged and pushed myself out of the chair. "Let's see…my wild talent's still there," I said, feeling the familiar surge beneath my skin as my power stirred. "I can give this a shot—"

That sentence ended in a scream as the supposedly mild blast I'd aimed at the balcony floor was strong enough to throw me over the railing. As Connor yelled my name, instinct kicked in, and a second blast at the ground broke my fall. For a moment, I bobbed like a fishing line with a fighter on the other end, shooting air at anything solid as I tried to right myself, and then I managed to pull together a wind to keep me upright.

On the other side of the railing, Connor laughed as I hung over the lawn, panting. "You're floating!" he called. "When did this start?"

"Just now," I said, praying I wouldn't lose my concentration and plummet. "Uh…hang on…"

"Do you want a rope or something?"

"No, just…don't leave." Carefully, I adjusted the wind to take me higher and lower, then worked out horizontal movement. I continued to experiment, grateful that I'd opted for pants instead of a dress that day, and within a few minutes, I was making test laps over the lawn, shooting myself toward convenient ledges and roofs, then bouncing back toward Connor.

After my fifth such pass, I noticed Diriem watching from a window in the corridor and waved. He lifted a hand and faintly smiled, and I pointed toward the balcony door.

He arrived shortly after I, windblown and a bit breathless, landed and staggered to a chair. "Impressive," he said. "I know air nymphs who can't manage currents that well."

"She's *flying*," said Connor.

"Not precisely. Maebe's using the air around her to hold her aloft—and yes, the result is about the same," he added before Connor could protest, "but mechanically, it's different. Complicated. But she looked like a natural out there. Intuitive, yes?" he asked me.

I nodded. "This is new." Something in his expression caught my attention, and I said, "You saw this coming, didn't you?"

Diriem just smiled again, and I rolled my eyes.

"It's not entirely surprising," he said, taking a seat as well. "I never knew Ivari's grandmother, naturally, but she was an aeromancer of incredible ability. Destroyed a fleet of ships by herself, or so the story goes." Nodding to me, he said, "Wild talents can skip generations, seemingly go into hiding, and then manifest in novel ways. You're proof of that."

"And if you can control it, that might be our ticket to getting in with the Hunt tonight," said Connor, pulling his phone from his pocket.

Diriem arched an eyebrow. "You're planning to ask Wylan?"

"Unless you tell me it's futile."

"I'm telling you nothing," he replied with a smirk, and motioned him on. "Call him, if you're so inclined. I won't stop you."

Connor started scrolling through his contacts. "Hear that, Maebe? Oz has spoken."

A pointed sigh answered *that*, which Connor ignored as he waited for the call to be answered. "Hey, it's…yeah, sorry, didn't know if you'd saved my number. Hang on…" He turned on the speaker and held the phone on his knee. "Can you hear me?"

"Yes," said Wylan. "Annie said you'd left the hospital."

"Yup, busted out. Listen, I'm sure you've got a decent strike team already, but Maebe and I want in."

To my surprise, Wylan barely hesitated. "You, absolutely, assuming you're medically cleared."

Connor grinned at the phone. "Brought my gun. If someone could give me a lift home, I'll pick up some more ammo."

"I'm sure Annie wouldn't mind."

"And I *have* qualified," he insisted. "Repeatedly—"

"You don't have to convince me," Wylan interrupted. "You're actual human law enforcement."

"Montana's a bit out of my jurisdiction…"

"Yeah, but if we got into trouble with the locals, you'd

have a better chance than we would of bullshitting our way out. Bring the badge, and let's hope for the best, eh?"

"Can do. What about Maebe?"

That time, Wylan didn't respond immediately. "I realize this is personal for you both," he finally said, "and she's come a long way, but—"

"Stop by Diriem's place. See for yourself."

"Now?" he asked bemusedly.

"Yeah, we're on a balcony. Uh…this is the south wing of the house, and we're facing east…"

"A moment."

The call ended, and less than a minute later, Wylan came walking around the mansion. "Ah, there you are," he said, lifting a hand. "What did you want me to see?"

My cousin turned to me and gestured toward the railing. "All yours, mitta."

Hoping I wasn't about to go *splat*, I closed my eyes and focused on the air around me…and then I was off my feet. Somewhat reassured, I floated out over Wylan's head and made a couple of quick passes, then landed in the grass beside him. "Ta-dah?"

His amber eyes, I noticed, were wide. "When did you figure *that* out?"

"Uh…a little bit before Connor called you."

He stared at me, then looked up at the balcony with an incredulous expression. "She just learned this today?"

"Today," Connor yelled down.

Turning back to me, Wylan said, "All right, you're in."

"What was that?" Connor asked.

"I said she's in!" Wylan replied. "Stealthier than a flying horse, anyway…" Shaking his head, he added, "I'll ask Annie to take you to collect your things. Otherwise, meet us at DOL at ten-thirty. We'll hit them once they've lost the light."

He vanished, and I floated myself back to the balcony, then made a slightly ungainly landing and almost tripped over a chair. Diriem grabbed me before I could fall, then frowned at the fading blue sky. "Dinner won't be served until seven. Perhaps you could practice in the interim, Ma-ebe."

As the Special Forces team checked their gear, I tugged at the hem of the long-sleeved black T-shirt I'd borrowed from Rose. My wardrobe not being particularly suited for stealth fieldwork, she'd loaned me black legging as well—with pockets, she'd proudly shown me—and a pair of black boots with reinforced toes. "My work doesn't take me out of the office much," she'd explained as I dressed, "but there's always a chance, and I'd rather be prepared."

I'd pulled my hair back, as had all of the other long-haired participants gathered that night, a mixed group of sorcerers, elves, nymphs, gnomes, and a nine-foot troll who looked like he might punch mountains for sport, plus the entire Hunt. Connor had come back from Georgia with appropriately dark clothing and plenty of ammunition for his .45-caliber pistol, and he chatted with some of the Laws agents while we waited.

When the meeting was called to order, however, it wasn't Wylan at the helm, but rather Annie. Clad in DPP-issued black gear, she hopped onto a chair and clapped twice for quiet, then studied the room while the crowd stilled. "All right," she said in her Virginia-accented Pact-ish, "is everyone armed?"

The team nodded.

"Who's got the potion kits?" she asked, scanning the assembled, and pointed when five agents raised their hands. "Great. Whatever happens, hold back and protect the cargo. We have restraints…yes, thank you," she said as another agent hoisted a duffel bag. "Medical is on standby?"

"We'll be waiting," said Canna, who'd positioned her-self against the wall.

"Thanks. Projection?"

A sorcerer who stood close to Canna, holding a tablet computer, muttered until an aerial view of the property appeared in projection behind Annie's head. There was no telling how old the pictures were, apparently—I was no expert in satellite photography—but the cluster of buildings in the clearing at the middle of the otherwise forested tract was unmistakable.

Annie glanced back at the picture, then addressed the crowd again. "If you didn't review the terrain maps, we're going into a high valley. Altitude's around four thousand feet, and *please* don't ask me to do the unit conversion offhand—"

Scattered laughter answered her.

"Yeah, sorry," she muttered. "If you're sensitive, just be prepared. Fortunately, it looks like our target is in the middle of the valley and not halfway up a mountain, so we won't be advancing on high ground. Other than that, I shouldn't have to tell you folks that we're going into the woods, and it'll be *dark*. The moon is almost new, so that's not going to be much help. *No* flashlights unless an emergency arises. Stay close and let us take point," she said, gesturing to the nearest clump of Huntsmen. "We'll be able to see more than the rest of you will. Do we have night vision gear?"

"Right here," said an agent, pivoting slightly to show Annie her backpack. "Not enough for everyone…"

"That's fine. All right, next thing. If you are of a paler complexion, do something about it." Holding up small pots of brown and olive face paint, she said, "A camo pattern will be safest. You don't want to be noticeable in case someone takes a light to the trees. Face, neck, hands, anything exposed."

"What about your eyes?" asked one of the gnomes.

She shrugged. "No way to dampen the eyeshine, unfortunately. Let's just hope they think we're deer."

The makeup pots began circulating among the people who couldn't mask, while the rest of us adjusted our appearance as necessary to a dark, mottled pattern.

"And one more time," said Annie, "it's likely that we'll have civilians outside. Twenty-seven kids and young adults in the mix. Don't shoot unless you're sure, yeah?"

The Hunt, most of whose number were armed with bows, grumbled its agreement.

"Right," she said, watching us prepare. "Let's get this finished and go take a walk in the woods."

When it came time to depart, Wylan took the lead. "Form a chain and hold on *tightly*," he instructed. "I'm driving. We'll land as close as we can, but there's still a hike ahead. Is this anyone's first time?" He waited while a smattering of hands went up, then grunted. "If you're prone to motion sickness, you may not like what happens on arrival. Don't lock your knees."

We joined hands, and once I was hanging on to Connor and the troll, Wylan said, "It may help to close your eyes and take a deep breath. Departing in three...two... one..."

I squeezed my eyes shut just before the floor seemed to disappear, but before I could panic, the ground and gravity returned—and along with them, a bitter cold and icy wind that felt more like winter than the cool springs I knew. The troll caught me before I could stumble on the snowy asphalt on which we'd landed, and I whispered my thanks as he gave me a shoulder pat that could have doubled as a punch.

Once an unfortunate agent had finished quietly retching, we started off after the Hunt, who moved with uncanny silence through the calf-deep snow as they abandoned the narrow road and navigated through the woods. My eyes tried to adjust, but I could do little more than grope my way along in the darkness and try to avoid slipping as my breath smoked in front of me.

After a time, Wylan called a halt, and we huddled up. "At this speed, the target is about another ten minutes' walk to the north," he murmured. "We need a scout.

Where's Maebe?"

Stomach knotting, I inched toward the front.

"Ah, good. Get a pair of goggles and take to the air. Stay within the trees as much as you can—you'll be much easier to spot as a blot against the sky," he said, pointing up at the star-strewn heavens clearly visible through the winter-thinned trees around us. "Go quickly, go quietly, and do not engage. Understood?"

"Yes, sir," I whispered.

Night vision goggles were pressed into my hands, and a DOL agent who introduced herself as Leri helped me adjust them until the world came into glowing green focus. "Whoa," I said, surprised by the sudden ability to see.

"It's a mixture of low-light amplification and infrared," Leri explained. "Living things will be brighter, see?" she said, holding up her hand to demonstrate its brilliance against the background. "Or anything burning. Heat sources, even if there's no light output. And there's another layer—magical constructions will glow blue. Now, wait just a moment, and let me synch up…"

She slipped on another pair of goggles, then handed me a small piece of plastic. "Put that in your ear," she instructed, doing the same with its mate. "We'll be able to hear each other. There's a little microphone on that, but you needn't shout."

"Why are you wearing goggles, too?" I asked.

"I'll toggle my view to mirror yours once you're on your way. You're not exactly an agent, right?"

"I, uh…I go to North Lake," I offered.

Leri winced. "Yeah, we're *definitely* not sending off a child to do this alone. I'll guide you, all right?"

Deciding not to press the issue of my adulthood, I thanked her, then did what I could to still my fear, called upon my innate power, and summoned the wind.

It took little effort to rise into the canopy, and after a moment's flight, I heard Leri in my ear: "Whoa, this is different."

"I only figured it out today."

"Oh, don't tell me that…ooh, bank, *tree*—"

I skirted an aspen and landed in the snowy branches of a pine for a moment, calming myself after my near miss. "Thanks," I muttered.

"Sure. Take it slowly, youngling. Give me a chance to analyze."

Once my heart had calmed, I pushed onward, trying to stay close to pines in case anyone chanced to look up. I encountered nothing but a startled owl, however, and soon, something began to glow up ahead.

"House," said Leri. "I can see the walls. Seems to be a chimney…whoa, *stop*!"

I grabbed the nearest tree to put on the brakes. "What's wrong?"

"Look down."

When I did as she ordered, I could see a blue construction snaking through the woods below me, two bands of magic about a foot apart. "What *is* that?"

"Let's find out. Land outside of them."

At ground level, I realized that the closer wall was about five feet tall, while the one beyond it was closer to seven. "Should I—"

"Don't touch," Leri snapped. "Those are wards. Know anything about them?"

"Um…I know what they *are*…" I replied, hoping she wasn't going to ask me to disable them.

"Well, the one right in front of you is for deterrence. If you touch it…I can't quite tell, but you'll probably either be sick to your stomach or receive a nasty shock."

"What about the other?"

"That's an alarm ward. See how high it extends?"

"Yes, ma'am."

"Your job is to get over it without touching."

Calling upon a strong gust, I sailed over both wards and continued north, moving slowly in case of other traps. But we spotted none, and then, as a large cabin came into view, I saw the cages.

"Going down," I whispered.

"What? No, Maebe—"

Ignoring Leri, I landed a few yards from the cages and quickly studied them. Four large cubical enclosures with metal grating on all six sides, each with a glowing blue spell ring around it, and nary a fire in sight to ward off the cold. Instead, within each, I could see a mass of huddling bodies, bright against the background but far darker than the cabin nearby.

I had to risk it.

To avoid leaving footprints, I swept myself off the ground, erased the few I'd made in my observation spot, and floated over the snow until I was hovering above the cages. Carefully, I landed in the center—with more noise than I'd hoped—but only one figure stirred at first. It pulled away from the outside of its cage's clump and straightened, and I almost cried when I recognized my uncle.

"Who's there?" he whispered in English, hurrying to the cage wall. "Who are you?"

I removed my camouflaging mask and lifted my goggles. "It's me," I whispered back. "Uncle Kyle, it's me."

"*Maebe?*" He stretched his arm as far as it would reach through the grating, and I clasped his hand. "Where did you come from?"

"Help's on the way, and Connor's with them. Are you okay?"

"Starving and freezing my ass off, but better now. The bekim cut off one of Eleanor's ears. She's alive, but the poor kid's hurting. How'd you find us?"

Before I could answer, an unpleasantly familiar voice yelped, "*Hey!*" in Pactish.

I whirled around and slammed my finger against my lips, signaling for quiet. "Shut up," I hissed at Ainnet. "Are you trying to get me caught, too?"

Her eyes widened when she recognized me. "Maebe?

What are you doing—"

"I'm going to get you out of here if you'll keep it down."

Alerted by the noise, the other captives began to stir and draw closer, and I motioned for them to stay back and be silent. "I've got to go," I murmured. "Back soon."

"No, you can't leave!" Ainnet frantically whispered. "You can't leave us here, they're monsters, you can't—"

"I'll be right back," I said slowly, staring at her. "Calm down."

Peter gripped her shoulder and pulled her away, but she continued to stare at me with desperation as I whisked myself up into the night.

I slipped the goggles back into position as I headed south. "Got an idea," I said to Leri.

"You can't airlift them out. Cutting those cages open will make noise—"

"No, not that. You saw the chimney, right?"

"Sure…"

"Smoke's rising. There's a fire going, so Farral and the others are probably in there. I can create a downdraft. Once the smoke's blowing into the cabin—"

"They'll run outside."

I smiled into the frigid wind. "Not if I drop knock-out potion down the chimney first."

"Ooh. *Ooh*, yes," Leri practically purred. "Devious. I like it."

Soon, I spotted the waiting rescue team and made an ungainly three-point landing. Before I could even begin debriefing Wylan, Leri walked up with a black potion kit. "Here," she said, slinging it over my chest. "Off you go, dear. Remember to drink the antidote first."

"Uh…which is…"

Another agent unzipped the bag I was wearing and extracted a bottle. "Looks like cream, tastes like vanilla and rose," he said, pressing it into my hand. "Go on and drink it now, hmm?"

I did as I was told—truly, it tasted like melted ice cream and rosewater—then counted the bottles of orange potion in my bag. "Should I use all four?" I asked.

"May as well," said Leri. "Stun them before they can run. We'll pass around whatever antidote we have here, but for now, go get them."

"What about the wards?"

"As soon as you drop the potions, we'll work on those. No sense in setting off the alarm, right?"

With Wylan motioning me on my way, I took off again, flying faster that time, and once again landed in the middle of the cages. "Listen up," I said in Pactish for the benefit of my classmates. "I'm going to try to knock them out. Everyone's in the cabin yeah?"

Uncle Kyle nodded. "Nowhere else to be tonight. We're in the middle of fuck-all…"

"Good. Now, when the doors open, there's a chance that some of the potion will drift this way. It won't hurt you, just make you sleep. It's what they threw at you on Lake Day—did anyone notice the orange clouds?"

A few mumbled responses rose from the cages.

"We're getting you out of here," I promised. "Just hang on."

I leapt, letting the wind carry me, and then almost face-planted on the cabin roof before I caught myself with another burst of air. Eyeing the chimney, I recalled the lessons my parents had taught me about how to keep the smoke out, even on the windiest of nights…and then I reversed them. I floated upward, keeping myself directly above the chimney, and kicked off a howling winter wind, which I maneuvered until the rising plume of smoke was sucked back down.

Bingo.

As sharp voices rose in protest within the cabin, I tossed all four potion vials down the chimney and heard them shatter. The voices cried out, alarmed, but it was too late. By the time I touched down in a snowbank beside the windows, all I could see through the glass was an orange fog.

"Got them," I said to Leri. "Come on."

Shaking with cold and fatigue, I hugged myself and waited for the rest of the team to arrive. I could tell when they hit the alarm ward, as a siren wailed within the cabin, but only for a few seconds before it was cut off. And then, as I stamped my feet to move my sluggish blood, I saw the first of the Hunt break through the trees.

"Here!" I called, waving at them. "This way!"

Wylan yelled to the others, "Potion being released! Stay back," then marched up to the cabin and yanked the door open. Immediately, the smoky orange cloud puffed out, and he coughed. "Think you could clear that, Maebe?"

Holding my breath, I stepped into the cabin and began circulating the air, forcing the contaminated fug outside and drawing fresh air in. Within a minute or two, visibility had returned, and as I pulled off my goggles, I made a quick count of the bodies slumped on the furniture and the floor. "They're all here," I said to Wylan. "Neutralizer?"

"Allow us," said one of the agents, who marched in with a potion kit and a group of assistants. "You've done your bit, youngling," he added. "Rest."

I slipped outside into the frigid night and returned to the cages, only to find the captives passed out from the potion cloud. A team of agents was working to destroy the spell rings around the cages and break them open, and as they breached the first, Wylan walked up with an elf slung over his broad shoulder. "Let's get everyone back to DOL," he said. "Prisoners first, and then the abductees."

The Hunt made quick work of the unconscious, neutralized kidnappers, then returned to help the agents prepare my sleeping kin and classmates for transport. I watched them vanish in groups of two and three, and once the last had been evacuated, the agents destroyed the cages, erased all trace of the spell rings, doused the fire, and locked up the cabin.

As I watched numbly, hugging myself against the cold, Wylan patted my shoulder. "Ready?"

Though my teeth chattered, I managed to answer, "Sounds good," then closed my eyes and gripped his hand until I sensed light and welcome warmth. Peeking, I found myself on DOL's medical floor, and Canna hurried up to intercept us.

"*There* you are, sweetie," she said, and pressed her hands against my unmasked cheeks. "Oh, you're like ice. Come on, we've got plenty of coffee."

"My cousins—"

"Are sleeping," she said, prying me away from Wylan. "And all are being stabilized for transportation. The hospital's sending vans, and your research team is standing by." I must have looked dazed when she finished, as she stooped a little and held my stare. "It's over, Maebe," she murmured. "They're alive. You brought them home alive."

CHAPTER 17

Relieved and exhausted, I returned to Diriem's house late that night with Connor once Canna had cleared us, then left my cousin to deliver the report and went upstairs to crash. I recall taking my shoes off, but the rest of my memory of that night is a blank until Jane roused me around eleven Tuesday morning and asked if I wanted to go to the hospital with them.

As it turned out, the patients had slept almost as long as I did, though much of their long rest was due to sleeping potions. All were weak from hunger and dehydration, and most were scraped or bruised, evidence of their treatment over the last days. The littlest boys were recovering nicely under a pediatric specialist's care, but Eleanor's amputation site had developed an infection, and she was heavily medicated. Her lost ear couldn't be reattached—the tissue was too far gone—but I overheard two research healers discussing the potential of growing a replacement and transplanting it as I walked by her room.

My cousins would need to be monitored for at least a few days, but they were on the mend, and that was the best I could ask for.

I was waiting in the hall with Connor while Jane grabbed a cup of ice for Laurel when a door at the far end swung open. Glancing down the tiled corridor, I spotted Ainnet's parents, Ogenel and Mivia, and glanced away, hoping they wouldn't notice me. But fortune had deserted me at that moment, as I heard Mivia yell, "Hey! *Girl!*"

"Shit," I muttered under my breath as she stomped

closer, her husband on her heels.

Connor squeezed my arm and whispered, "Want me to handle it?"

That would have been the easy route, but I was an adult.

Damn it.

I stepped out from behind him and nodded as they approached. "Mr. ti'Har, Ms....uh..."

"Ti'Tam," Mivia snapped, her blue eyes—Ainnet's, I thought—narrowed in anger. "What took you so long? Have you *seen* our daughter's condition?"

"She's no worse off than my cousins are, and she's doing quite a bit better than some of them," I retorted. "Ainnet's not the one who lost an ear, you know?"

"I don't give the tiniest damn about your miserable family," she said, getting up in my face. "This is all *your* fault, you—"

"Mivia, please," Ogenel tried, tugging at her shoulder, but she shook him off.

"She could have died out there!" Mivia cried, her expression twisting into a snarl. "And you...*you*..."

My body reacted of its own accord, and my talent flared like a whip, driving them back and off their feet with a blast of wind. Mivia landed on Ogenel, and as they started to untangle themselves from each other, I marched toward them, my hands fisting and my hair whipping around my head in an inexplicable breeze. "And I don't give a damn about your daughter!" I shouted, my voice echoing around the ward. "You hear me? She's a miserable brat, and if I never saw her again, that'd be *just* fine. But as long as we're going to be in school together, I'm done with taking her shit. Fair warning."

I sent a shot of wind snaking between them and yanked Mivia into the air. "And another thing," I said as she struggled, panicking to find herself suspended above the floor. "I've taken *three* bloodline potions, *with* heart damage. How many have you taken? Oh, wait, that's right, you're medically ineligible, and *you* didn't last a damn minute," I continued, pointing to Ogenel, who'd found his feet and backed off a few paces. "I found them as quickly as I could," I said, stepping into Mivia's space. "No thanks to you. And before you blame me for precious little Ainnet's mistreatment, remember that the only reason she got picked up was because she and her asshole friends started a fight with my family. This is her own fault."

Though she was obviously frightened, Mivia found her spine. "You have no right to speak to us like—"

"Oh, shut up," I said, and dropped her at my feet. "Run and tattle to Nadull again, for all I care. I don't have to put up with crap from the likes of you."

And as she sputtered on the floor, I turned to Connor and said, "See you at the car," then stalked out of the building.

In the days that followed, I wasn't quite sure what to do with myself.

While I continued to visit the hospital, I could only stay for so long, and my cousins were often given sleeping potions in the hope that rest would speed along their recovery. Connor left on Wednesday morning, eager to return to his neglected job, and though Jane stayed on at the mansion with me, I often found her working. But though the danger had ostensibly passed, I didn't feel like returning to school. The board sent word that they were appalled, that security would be improved, that my cousins and I were welcome…but honestly, I didn't feel safe, and I sure as hell wasn't going back to the dorm alone.

Diriem allowed me to wander, offering rides if desired but not pushing me in any direction, including out the door. Where else could I have gone? Back to Georgia to beg a couch from Connor? I had no other home to return to.

But while Diriem might have seemed hands-off as I

stewed, he wasn't above placing a call or two, as Annie walked in Friday morning while I was contemplating my toast. "Hey, kiddo," she said, pulling out a chair. "Got any plans for today?"

"Um…not yet," I replied.

"Great. How do you feel about horses?"

Half an hour later, I found myself outside the Hunt's hidden lodge, nervously eyeing their horse barn as Annie assured me that her sweet baby Jimbo wouldn't drop me from a bone-breaking height. "If you were to fall, you'd have the tether," she said, "and if *that* snapped, you're a freaking aeromancer. Come on, let's have some fun."

By lunchtime, I wasn't much closer to being proficient on horseback, but Annie sat me at the big kitchen island, made us sandwiches, and told off the pair of Huntsmen trying to sneak me a beer. "So," she said as she joined me with our plates, "what's the plan, Maebe?"

I frowned at her. "Plan?"

"Going forward. Are you thinking of school, or what?"

Sighing to myself, I bit into my sandwich and chewed while I thought. "Not sure," I said once I'd swallowed. "I like North Lake, and things have been mostly good, but…"

"But people you trusted sold you out," she finished when my voice faltered.

"Uh-huh."

Annie snapped her pickle spear in half and chewed one end. "Here's the deal," she told me after a moment. "It's going to be tough for you here if you don't get an education. Now, I'm not saying you have to go back to North Lake," she quickly added. "I'm not sure I'd want to, either. It *is* possible in special cases to get a job while you're underage here—Rose, Jane, and I are proof of that—but I don't know what you ultimately want to do, and I'd hate to push you into agency work if that's not where you want to be."

"You think an agency would take me?" I asked.

Her eyebrows rose. "Hon, not to put too fine a point on it, but you can fucking fly."

"Not exactly. It's just wind—"

"Eh, close enough. I'm pretty sure that at least one of the agencies would be interested in having you aboard. But you're nineteen, and I sure as hell didn't know what I was doing at your age, so…got a proposition for you."

"What's that?"

She grinned. "Well, if you can't bring yourself to go back to school, you could come work as a Forum aide for the Hunt. It was Wylan's suggestion," she said. "You've got spunk, and he's impressed. Besides, he doesn't have a formal education, and neither do any of his brothers."

"But he's, like…competent," I muttered into my sandwich.

"He's come a long way." She patted my hand. "Just an offer, now, no pressure. But if you want somewhere to land, that's a possibility."

While I appreciated that, my family still needed to figure out their next steps—and after the last months, I wasn't too keen on going my own way.

I was still mulling over the possibilities when Annie returned me to the mansion that afternoon, and I'd decided to try to wheedle a hint from Diriem when he rapped on my guest room door and poked his head inside. "Ah, good, you're back. Come to my office, if you will."

Curious, I followed him downstairs. "What's up?"

"Thought I'd give Madla a call."

It wasn't just Madla he had in mind. As I sat on the sofa, Diriem managed to get Madla, Theo, and Culta on the phone, and he settled back in his desk chair to deliver the news. "Farral and her children and grandchildren are in custody here," he began in his oddly accented English.

"*Which* children, exactly?" asked Theo.

"Danirri, his wife, their two eldest sons, and Beani's two sons. Plus several associates from the Pactlands. Your seven were found in a remote cabin on one of Ivari's properties with four cages of abducted students out back."

Madla whistled. "What will become of them?"

"They'll go before a tribunal," said Diriem. "Just as Ivari did. But the case against them is strong, and that's without adding farsight to the evidence. Laws will have no shortage of witnesses to speak against them."

"I'm sure," she murmured. "What sort of punishment do you anticipate?"

He thought for a moment. "Not as long as Ivari's incarceration, but Laws will almost certainly push for lengthy terms. Twenty-seven kidnapped, plus the child they maimed…and this time, all of the victims are Pactlands citizens. But your blood is safe," he added, softening. "Recovering but alive."

"I didn't realize they'd received citizenship," said Madla.

"Late last year."

"Mm." She hesitated, then asked, "Might that offer be on the table for the rest of us?"

"Huh?" said Theo. "What—"

"I've been running and hiding for centuries," she said, speaking over him. "I'm *tired*, youngling. It'd be nice to be safe again."

Briefly, Diriem locked eyes with me over his desk.

I'd thought there would be safety in the Pactlands as well, and there had been…to a point. But if my family wasn't being hunted any more…

He turned his attention back to the call. "I can make no guarantees today. You should know, however, that if you were to be allowed in, you would not be recognized as the head of Hall ti'Un. That title's been given to one of your descendants."

Madla replied, "I don't care. Hall ti'Un is nothing but rubble and ghosts out here. I'll step back, and gladly."

Diriem nodded to himself as she spoke. "Very well. I'll take the matter to the Forum and see what can be done. In the meantime, perhaps you could speak with your people and get a sense of which of them would want to join us."

When he hung up, I asked, "Is the Forum going to allow it?"

He smiled at me. "Hoping to build up your Hall, Lady ti'Ammaas?"

I rolled my eyes. "Is it so hard to give a straight answer?"

"That depends entirely on the question."

Following me out of the office, he said almost offhandedly, "Working for Wylan wouldn't be a terrible idea, but it's not the best choice."

I wheeled on him. "Then what is?"

"You'll figure it out."

"*Diriem*," I protested as he walked away.

"Patience, Maebe," he called over his shoulder, but would offer nothing else.

The following day, my family was released from the hospital—even Eleanor, whose replacement ear was still growing. As the eldest of the bunch, Peter found himself faced with a quandary: where were they to go? My cousins shared my reservations about returning to the dorm, so Peter called Teolm and told him they needed to make sufficient withdrawals to pay for temporary lodging until they figured out a solution.

A couple hours later, and with the aid of a hastily chartered bus, my kinfolk showed up on Diriem's doorstep with the clothes on their backs and bags of travel toiletries from the hospital. He invited them in, then left Scel to usher them upstairs, assuring them that their belongings would be delivered that evening.

"You knew this was coming, didn't you?" I said as the gawking stragglers traipsed up the staircase.

He winked at me.

Watching them go, I sighed. "Generous of you, and I mean that, but we can't just keep accepting charity. That's not how we were raised…and look at how things at North Lake turned out," I said, folding my arms. "Problem charity cases, that's all we were. No wonder they didn't mind getting rid of us."

Diriem laughed softly. "Youngling, you are not *charity* cases."

"Huh?"

"Let's just say that Hall ti'Dana has contributed considerably to that institution since its founding, and the contributions have increased of late."

"Diriem," I protested, "we *have* money now. You don't have to—"

"I want to," he said simply. "Your family has been held back through no fault of your own, and I want to see you reach your potential, whatever that may be. Now, if North Lake is no longer a possibility due to recent events, then I'll help you find a different school, but you *need* this."

"Annie said Wylan doesn't have a formal education," I pointed out.

"And that frightens me more than I'd care to admit sometimes, but on a practical level, his abilities aren't the sort of thing we can teach. Wylan's talent is…something *other*," he said, and shrugged. "But yours *is* teachable, and you've progressed considerably in the last months. I know your cousins have as well." Holding my gaze, he said, "You came here because you wanted an education, Maebe. Has that changed?"

I considered the question briefly, then shook my head. "No, I want one, but…"

"But?"

"I want us to be safe," I murmured. "I don't want to be somewhere that the principal sells us to damn kidnappers, and…and I…"

"Go on," he said gently.

"I'm tired of feeling like a freak," I blurted. "I just…I was normal once, you know? Maybe not *really* normal, but I had a community, and I *fit*. But here, I don't know what

I'm supposed to know, I don't sound right, I don't—
didn't—look right, and folks like Ainnet and her parents act
like I'm nothing, and…" I paused to angrily wipe my eyes.
"We lost everything, and I'm grateful for what you and
Teolm have done for us, I really am…"

"It's not easy," said Diriem when I fell silent. "Losing
everything and starting over seldom is. When we fled to
this world, we had an empty grassland, old grievances, and
trauma. Bringing everyone to the table, working out rules,
trying to make things fair while respecting the various traditions…honestly, there were times that I thought this
experiment would fail. And it still may someday," he
mused, "but for now, there's relative stability. What I'm
trying to tell you is that we didn't get here without growing
pains."

"So, you're saying I should just deal with it?"

One corner of his mouth quirked. "I'm saying that I
can see a number of possibilities for your family, and the
best paths begin with education."

My brow knit. "Is that—"

"That's farsight, and I'll say nothing more on the matter. But you should know that my record for accuracy is
excellent." Nodding to the staircase, he said, "Perhaps you
could give your cousins a tour, hmm? I'm sure the little
ones would like to run around."

There were certain perks to being a farseer.

While Diriem hadn't called Madla, Theo, and Culta until Friday, he'd apparently known for days prior that at
least some of their number would be interested in citizenship. Thus, on Monday afternoon, when he got on a video
chat with *all* of the adult members of the New York group,
he came with an answer from the Forum.

"Can everyone hear me?" he asked in High Elvish,
squinting at the tiny boxes that filled his screen.

I stood back out of camera range, watching over his

shoulder as my distant kin came online.

Quick affirmations answered that, and then Madla took the lead. "I appreciate the use of the old tongue, but the younglings would surely prefer something easier. If you don't mind…"

"Not a problem," Diriem replied in English. "Better?"

The affirmations were louder that time, and he faintly chuckled.

"I feel that introductions are in order, but perhaps that could be managed at a later date, in a less unwieldy form," he continued. "Let's get to the purpose of this call. The good news first: the Forum is willing to offer you citizenship, even those of you who were named as participants in the East Branch attack. You know who you are, and though I will not name you at this time, be assured that the Forum is aware of your identities. You will be monitored until such time as we are satisfied that you pose no further threat."

No one protested.

"Moving on," said Diriem, "all of your Halls have been established here, so ordinarily, this would be a simple matter of acknowledgement."

"You've kept the old ways?" a man asked with surprise.

"Some. Here's the complication: as I said, your Halls have been established, and the titles will not be stripped from the current holders. If you come in, you come in as subordinate members."

After a pause, Madla said, "We've discussed that possibility, and we're amenable to those terms."

"The fifteen of us here, that is," the man chimed in. "Obviously, we can't speak for Ivari and Farral."

"Of course," said Diriem, and peered more closely at him. "Paril ti'Tola?"

"The same." He laughed briefly. "Been a time, hasn't it?"

"A considerable one. The last time I saw you was in my father's court, and you—"

"Twenty. I'm shocked that you remember me."

It was Diriem's turn to laugh. "Well, if you must know, my sister was rather taken with you and pined terribly after you left. I...was not the kindest of older brothers in the wake of your departure."

"Oh, I recall Miral," said Paril. "A redheaded beauty. Had I been a few years older, I'd have tried for her." His shoulders rose and fell in his tiny box. "Perhaps I should have, eh?"

"*Hey*, now," a woman snapped.

"But then I'd have never married my lovely wife," Paril smoothly continued, "who, with any luck, will refrain from murdering me in my sleep tonight."

She snorted, hardly a guarantee of safety.

"And we're willing to pay, if that's necessary," said Madla. "We've agreed that we can liquidate the firm, though it'll take some time to wrap everything up."

"The Forum isn't asking for payment," Diriem replied, "though liquidation will be necessary, and Ivari's properties will need to be sold off. Portal access is restricted, you understand, and though you're all quite clearly adept at blending outside—"

"It's a security risk," she finished. "Always has been. I believe that's acceptable. Does anyone disagree?"

No one spoke.

"This is...hmm," Diriem murmured. "You're more amenable to these conditions than I'd imagined."

"You're not the one who's been hiding in plain sight for almost five hundred years," Madla countered. "We've been hiding, and our children were born into hiding—the ones you see here *and* the ones we left at East Branch. For safety, for the chance to live in the open...there's not much I wouldn't give."

"Frankly speaking," Paril added, "Ivari fucked us over when he rejected the offer of the Pactlands, and you see what's left of us before you now. Well, us and a few younger children," he amended, "but you get the picture.

Let us in, and we'll play nice."

"Ivari told us that he alone could keep us safe," said another man. "Obviously, that was a lie. Look, we don't want trouble—we just want to be in a place where we don't have to worry about masking and accidental magic. If the conditions are that we dismantle the firm and accept new heads of our Halls, then so be it."

Diriem nodded. "I'll convey this to the Forum, then. Give me a few days to finalize the arrangements, and in the meantime, you might want to collect Ivari's property deeds. He won't be needing them."

When the call ended, Diriem closed his computer and turned to me. "So, what do you think? Ready to head Hall ti'Ammaas?"

"Uh…" I laughed weakly. "Aside from the fact that I have no idea what I'm doing?"

"Let me share a secret with you: few of us do at first. You'll find your feet, and until then, Teolm and I won't let you fall too far. Agreed?"

"Thanks. But what if they don't listen to me?" I said. "What if they think I'm some great joke?"

Diriem held my gaze for a moment, then leaned back in his chair. "You will prove yourself, Maebe. Every one of us faced this trial in one form or another." I must have seemed incredulous, as he sat up and lowered his voice. "My father, Telier, was a warrior king, perhaps the finest our Hall ever produced. 'The Wolf of the North,' they called him. Not a farseer, nor was he possessed of any wild talent, but he was deadly with sword, bow, or axe. My younger brother, Jixan, favors him more than I ever did. But Hall headship descends to the eldest, and when my parents were murdered, I had to prove that I was capable of ruling while contending with my father's shadow. It wasn't easy," he said, "and had I not been farsighted, I might not have managed to gain the subordinate Halls' respect. Do you know what they called me at first?"

"'The wolf pup,'" I murmured.

He nodded. "Look, I'm not a legendary warrior. Adequate in combat, and I've qualified on my share of weapons, though I pale in comparison to my father. But I kept trying, and I learned to use my talent, and in time, the taunting ceased. Well, from everyone but Ivari and Farral, I suppose," he added, "though they can call me whatever they like in Laws' custody. But as for you," he said, "it may not be smooth. There's often friction in the Halls when a new lady or lord steps up, especially if they're rather young."

"So, tell me what to do."

He grinned. "Don't be afraid to ask for advice. Find people who will be honest with you and treasure them. And never forget that despite all the inevitable *whining* you'll face in the coming years, the Hall is yours, and they cannot take that from you. Understood?"

I paused, considering his words, then said, "I think so. But okay, if you're in the mood for dispensing advice, then what do I do with Ainnet?"

"You'll be returning to North Lake, then?"

I wrinkled my nose but nodded. "They win if I don't, right?"

"There's the spirit. Now, as for the girl, I understand that you told off her parents earlier this week. Got a call from Nadull," he explained, smirking. "And when I relayed to her the sort of treatment you'd received from them and their spawn of late and asked whether she would suffer the same, the call ended rather rapidly. I suspect that Ainnet will find little help from Lady ti'Har," he said, "and probably even less as you come into your own. You have strong, *rare* gifts, and with a few years' experience, you will become a force to be respected."

"You think so?"

Diriem flashed his maddeningly enigmatic smile. "In the meantime, recall that we do still keep some of the old ways."

"Oh?"

Nodding, he replied, "Hall ti'Har is old and has often been counted among the Halls of higher rank. But Hall ti'Ammaas is royal," he said softly, holding my stare, "and *very* old, and though we do not have kings and queens as such here, we *do* have long memories. Nadull knows that," he added, "and I dare say that little Ainnet will learn."

"But I'm not like you," I protested. "You…" Stumped for words, I settled for vaguely gesturing at the office.

He chuckled. "Maebe, youngling, I've been doing this for a long time. Trust me, practice helps. You're still learning who you are, and you *will* learn, but the illusion of competence doesn't develop overnight."

"It's not an illusion…"

"Sometimes not," he allowed, "but others…" Shrugging, he said, "I do my best, but I'm far from omniscient. You know that as well as anyone. There is a certain…*aura*…that comes with farsight, and it helps," he admitted, "but word will spread about you, too. Determined. Stubborn. Able to withstand multiple rounds of a potion that should, by rights, have killed you. And your aeromancy…" He paused, then said, "I've mentioned Ivari's grandmother, yes? The aeromancer?"

"Yes, sir."

"Vacal ti'Ammaas, she was called. But her wild talent didn't arise from Hall ti'Ammaas—*her* mother was the last of Hall ti'Lenet."

Of fire. "Odd name for a bunch of aeromancers," I replied.

"Oh, they were more commonly known to be pyromancers, *if* a wild talent ever showed itself. The aeromancy came from a Hall they absorbed somewhere along the way—sitting here now, I can't name it. What I do know is that Hall ti'Ammaas virtually wiped out Hall ti'Lenet, and Vacal's mother was married to her father as the spoils of war. Funny, then, that he apparently slipped and fell from a tower to his death," he said, poker face firmly deployed, "and Vacal went on to become a queen of great renown.

Now, I could be mistaken, of course, but to me, the lesson here is to never underestimate a ti'Ammaas woman, especially one with the wind at her command."

I stood there for a moment, considering that information, then said, "We're kind of a murderous clan, aren't we?"

"Every Hall of sufficient age has its...stabbier members. As for Vacal, the histories don't specify what her father did to her mother, but it's known that the lady died young and suspiciously. I wouldn't condemn Vacal for seeking justice on her own terms."

My mouth twitched toward a smile. "So, if I were to sneak into the penal farm where DOL is holding Ivari..."

"I'll remind you that he killed my parents first."

"We could make this a team effort."

Diriem grunted and shooed me toward the door, and feeling curiously lighter, I went on my way.

While I wasn't a party to the goings-on in New York, about two weeks after Diriem's meeting with the group, he informed me that the other members of Hall ti'Ammaas wished to meet with me—and they'd asked to do so in person. I agreed, despite Uncle Kyle's misgivings, and so I found myself sitting in one of the mansion's many parlors the following evening with Laurel—my cousin by blood, my aunt by marriage, and the only other member of the Hall from East Branch. Laurel had a decade on me, but as we awaited the others' arrival, she murmured, "This is your show, mitta. I can be backup or moral support, whatever you need, and Kyle and the boys will come running if there's trouble."

"Let's hope it doesn't come to that," I replied, trying to calm the twitching in my leg.

Rose had taken me out earlier that day in search of a new robe for the occasion, and we'd settled on a summer-weight garment in leaf green with delicate gold embroidery—an exorbitant expense, I thought, but trusted Rose's judgment. "This is no time to be frugal," she'd told me as I'd goggled at the price. "You're their new lady, and you need to look the part."

She'd helped me with my hair and makeup that afternoon, deploying a few tricks to make me look subtly older without masking. "Just breathe," she'd said as I made a final twirl for her inspection. "Remember, you've been in the Pactlands longer than they have. You're the expert by comparison here." Raising my chin with two fingertips, she'd added, "And you have nothing to be embarrassed about, okay?"

Easy for her to say. I almost jumped when Scel knocked on the parlor door, but I managed to compose myself as he slipped inside. "Your guests have arrived, Lady ti'Ammaas. May I show them in?"

"Thank you, Scel," I replied, then cleared my throat and stood as the door opened.

Eleven strangers filed into the room, none appearing to be older than Laurel, though pegging an elf's age was a skill I'd yet to master. The adults wore suits—all but three who I suspected to be closer to my age, who'd opted for dresses for the girls and a polo shirt for the lone boy—while a boy and girl perhaps a little older than Tobias and Winston were far more casually attired and squirmed to be put down.

Scel closed the door behind them, and hoping I wouldn't be sick, I broke the silence. "Hello," I said, sticking to English. "I'm Maebe. This is Laurel," I continued, and she raised a hand in greeting. "Uh…do y'all want to come in?"

The man carrying one of the children glanced around the room. "Anything irreparable in here, do you suppose?"

"Probably not."

"Oh, good." With a groan, he lowered the girl to the rug, then fixed her with a look I knew all too well from my own parents. "*Behave*, understand?"

"YouTube?" the girl asked.

Sighing, he relinquished his phone, and the two little ones ran off into the corner with their prize. "Sorry," he told me, "kids. I, uh…shit, I don't know how these things are meant to go. Charles," he said, extending his hand.

I shook it and smiled. "Nice to finally meet you. Hope the accent's not a problem."

Charles snorted. "*Please*, that's nothing. The people who drove us over, now…"

"Thick?"

"Only got about every other word. Guess they don't sneak out much, huh?"

A woman pointedly coughed. "You know, Chenor," she said in High Elvish, "we could do this—"

"Don't be difficult, Auntie," said Charles, then looked at me and rolled his eyes. "Sorry, where were we?"

The ice began to thaw after that, and in short order, I had the family sorted. Charles—technically Chenor—was one of Ivari's grandsons, Danirri's third-born, and we absolutely did *not* mention his grandmother, father, and older brothers. His daughter, Amarua, wasn't quite five. Sitting awkwardly to one side were Charles's nephew and niece, Ettu and Alifi, two of Pacul's three children. While Ettu was about thirty years older than Charles, Alifi was my age but seemed younger as she fidgeted on a sofa. Beani, Ivari's eldest daughter, had carried in her four-year-old grandson, Utien; the boy's father, Mirin, was in DOL custody, but Mirin's little sister, Evarra, was only about twenty-two and seemed just as awkward as Alifi did. Rounding out their numbers were two more of Ivari's children—his daughter Dolia and son Bo (Idobo, in truth, but he insisted on the nickname)—plus Dolia's daughter Obelli and sixteen-year-old grandson Yrel.

While Charles had initially taken the lead, Beani was the most senior of the group, and she eventually moved into the role of spokeswoman. "Your reputation precedes you," she said to me once we'd settled into a rough circle of chairs and couches. "I remember seeing you at Father's trial—"

"And let's be clear that we weren't part of that, um…that mess in Georgia," Bo interrupted. "Father certainly didn't tell *me* what he'd planned."

Most of the others nodded, though Beani looked uneasy. I said nothing but made a mental note to speak with Diriem.

"My younger brothers and Madla have informed me of what transpired with your cousins and your role in their recovery," Beani continued. "Truly, I've not heard of a ti'Ammaas aeromancer of such skill since—"

"Vacal," I finished.

Her chin dipped. "My great-grandmother, yes. One of my elder half siblings was an aeromancer, or so Father says, but he had no great talent. You…uh…"

Beani's voice faltered as I casually swept an armchair off the ground with a flick of my wrist and a gust of wind. "I'm still learning," I said. "Haven't mastered it yet, but I'm working on it." Returning the chair to its position— well, approximately—I said, "If you had no hand in slaughtering my family and destroying our home, then I have no quarrel with you. I'm not trying to make enemies. We are, however distantly, family." When no one immediately objected, I pressed on. "I'm sure it chafes that the Forum has set me up as the head of the Hall—"

"Not really," Charles interjected. "Eldest of the eldest, that's the way it's always been. Grandfather's made that clear—I mean, that's how thrones tend to descend, yeah?"

Seeing as I didn't have a great sense of the answer to that question, I settled for a noncommittal grunt.

"Well, then, since all of his issue from his first marriage were killed, the issue from his second take primacy," he continued. "That'd be your branch of the family. My father is the eldest child of the third marriage, but he'd fall in somewhere behind you…and is it just the two of you?" he asked, looking at Laurel and me. "You're the last of that family?"

"We're the last to have been assigned to ti'Ammaas," I replied, "but probably all of us can trace our lineage to at least one of Ivari's children. That's twenty-two in total."

Charles chuckled. "Then my father's something like twenty-third in line. I'm not complaining."

"But what's your role, exactly?" Beani asked. "We've heard stories of how the Halls used to function, but here…" She glanced around the parlor. "Incidentally, what is this place?"

"The ti'Dana mansion," I said. "Diriem's been gracious enough to host us while things get…sorted."

"Mm. Impressive. You intend to build something comparable for our Hall?"

Manners be damned, I laughed incredulously. "Don't think I can afford it," I told her before she could become offended. "I've got about a half million marks to my name, and I don't think that'd be nearly enough to duplicate *this*."

"Perhaps not a home quite this size, but something sufficiently large…"

"Let me level with you, Maebe," said Bo. "We've spent most of our lives crammed into apartments in Manhattan. It'd be nice to have actual property, and once Father's hideouts are sold and the firm's dissolved, we should have a chunk of change…and someone can exchange that, right?"

"I think it'd be easier if you brought in precious metals," I told him, "but that *should* work…"

"So, if we pooled our resources, took out loans…do you get a salary for running the Hall or something?"

I shook my head. "Nope. And to answer your question," I said to his older sister, "the lords and ladies take turns serving on the Forum, they can settle disputes within their Hall, and they can stop marriages under certain circumstances, though that doesn't happen often. Teolm—he heads ti'Cren, and he's been helping us—he said his father undid his baby sister's marriage because her husband was from one of the new Halls."

Beani's head tilted. "New Halls?"

"So, uh, all those people who didn't actually have family Halls before the Pact? When they came in, they made a few Halls of their own."

Charles nodded, considering that. "Okay, so you're telling me that if my kid got with someone you didn't like," he said, pointing to the little ones staring at his phone, "you could put the kibosh on her marriage?"

"Technically? I guess," I replied. "But come on—my end of the family tree is a hedge, and yours is heading in that direction. Unless she wanted to marry her close cousin, I don't see the harm. I'm not here to be a tyrant," I said, looking over the rest of them. "I...I want to be safe. I want a home. It'd be nice to have an education, too, and once I'm of age here, I'll see about getting a job, but...I'm not some conquering warrior queen. I just want to do right by my family, and now, that means y'all, too."

After a silent moment, Beani said, "Then I think you should begin by building a home. There hasn't been a true Hall in centuries, but a place for us might be a start. Perhaps a house with a lawn."

"We'll help," Bo promised. "If that's okay."

I grinned at him. "Y'all wouldn't mind living with the likes of Laurel and me?"

He shook his head. "As you said, mitha, we're family. Now, next issue, language potions. You've had one, I assume."

"*Oh*, yeah. You?"

"Those of us who attended Father's trial received them," said Beani, "but many have not. Can you make that happen?"

"I think so," I told her. "It's settled, then? You're moving in?"

They exchanged glances, my distant kin, and Beani said, "I believe...that would be for the best, yes. It'd be nice to walk around unmasked."

"Maybe someday," Laurel muttered, and gestured to remove her own. I caught a few surprised looks from the others before she said, "They've told you about the cifyent in our family, right? Most of us here have it."

"Not for long," I said, and squeezed her hand.

Charles's brow furrowed. "Surgery?"

"There's a treatment," I replied. "With any luck, we'll be able to eradicate it. No more flop."

"It's, uh…it's a different sort of look," he said, "but if it's not hurting you—"

"I've been tying my ears back all my life," Laurel cut in. "I'm ready for a change."

"That's fair," said Charles, and flashed a lopsided smile. "Suppose we all are."

Over the following days, the remnants of the other Halls came in to see what awaited them in the Pactlands. While some of the older members were more reluctant than others to acknowledge the new lords and ladies, in the end, all decided to make the move. Last to visit was Madla, the only member of Hall ti'Un outside, who met with Uncle Kyle and his son Eugene, the only members within. I stood by with Laurel as they made their halting introductions, and within ten minutes, Madla was a weepy but affectionate mess. Sitting on a sofa, holding her ninth great-grandson's hands—two ends of a long line—she cried and apologized and cried some more, then swore to make it up to us somehow. "I don't know which of you are mine," she said, puffy-eyed, "so until you tell me otherwise, I'll assume it's all of you, and…and I'm so sorry. For everything."

But while the other Halls were getting acquainted, I'd turned my attention to the problem of a house. The rest of the ti'Ammaas clan didn't want to move until they had a place to land, and so, hopelessly out of my depth, I went to Diriem for advice.

"You'll have more than you think you will," he told me in the privacy of his home office. "Half a million marks *will* build a decently large home—the costs of such matters are lower here than they are outside. But you have no clue how wealthy Rush and Sons is."

I arched an eyebrow.

"That eleven million that Laws demanded for the East Branch survivors was *nothing*," he murmured. "I took it upon myself to facilitate coordination with Madla on your behalf, and…well, come around here, won't you?"

He opened his computer to show me a spreadsheet listing the firm's assets and the value of Ivari's properties, and I'd never seen so many zeroes in my life.

"Yours is one of the larger Halls," he told me, "not to mention there's the slight matter of the royal line. Trust me, my dear, you'll have what you need to build a home."

The next morning, while my cousins were finally moving back into the dorm—with added security, new dorm parents, a temporary principal, and the sincere apologies of the board—Diriem and Teolm took me to the small agency that handled land allocation. Much of the Pactlands, particularly its western reaches, was still largely unsettled, and so we paged through maps and plats, considering my options.

There were places available near north Georgia, but I didn't want to be that close to our former home—not without the familiar tree-covered mountains surrounding us. Instead, I looked west to the imposing Edoli range, which ran largely north to south but for a northerly spur that veered toward the western sea. There was a fishing settlement where the mountains plunged into the placid waves, Cirinti, and when I kept turning back to that map, my escorts took me out to see the place for myself.

Cirinti was tiny, a few blocks of modest houses fronting beige sand, and down the road, slips for the boats and buildings dedicated to the business of packing catches and repairing gear. There was a small restaurant and a guest house, but little else of note. Above the town, however, situated atop a cliff, was a wide expanse of unclaimed grassland with a view of the water to the west and the rising mountains to the east. The place was nothing like East Branch…but this was a fresh start, I mused, pushing my hair from my face as the wind tried to grab it. This place between sea and land and sky could be the beginning of a future—and if Diriem was right about the financial situation, I could build a house large enough to give all of my East Branch cousins a home until they built their own.

"It's remote," Teolm said, "but I can't say I don't like it."

And by dinnertime, it was mine.

Though I didn't appreciate it in the slightest, part of being an adult meant facing my fears, and so I returned to school at the end of April.

I moved back into the dorm on a Saturday morning, trying to ignore the way my guts knotted as I walked down the hall toward my room. My family had been back for several days by then, and Heidi stopped by while I was putting my clothes away to fill me in on the classroom situation. "They've been giving Sage individual tutoring without us," she said, tossing me a shirt, "but largely in magic. We're behind by about five weeks, considering the March break—well, six weeks for you…"

"That's a problem of their own making," I replied, and shook out the shirt before hanging it. While Rose had taught me the trick to magically removing the wrinkles from my clothing, I wasn't entirely confident in my skills on that count. "Is there a *remedial* remedial plan in place?"

She nodded. "We'll be out of regular classes for the rest of the year, and our tutors will stay over during the summer break to catch us up. Sage, too. But she's just so happy to have folks in lessons with her again, I don't think she minds much," she added, pulling another shirt from my bag.

I caught it with a burst of wind when Heidi's toss fell short. "Well, they're going to have to be flexible with us."

"What do you mean?"

"Laws is going to want us for the tribunals," I replied. And then, tucking back my hair to fully reveal my upright ears, I said, "Plus, I told you there's a treatment, right?"

"Yeah…"

"So, last week, I called Shara, the healer who figured this out. She's willing to work with all of y'all."

Heidi, who hadn't masked that day, reached up and flicked one of her flopped-over ears. "She could fix this?"

"Uh-huh. Your ulcers, too, probably. And if you want to stop aging…"

Slowly, she began to grin. "When were you planning to tell us, huh?"

"Once I got my crap in the closet—"

"Your crap will keep," she interrupted, and dragged me out the door to inform the rest of the family.

On Monday, I sat at my old lunch table with Sage and Keef, getting caught up on the nearly two months I'd missed. As the students who'd been kidnapped with my cousins were likewise weeks behind, they'd been shunted into their own remedial tutorials. "Even Ainnet," said Keef with a malicious smile. "Stuck in a room all day with half her old friend group, playing catch-up."

"They'll be here all summer, too," Sage added. "I heard our tutors discussing it."

"Is that so? Poor little dears. I can't say I've missed them…"

Keef's voice trailed off as a shadow fell over the table, but she quickly relaxed to see that it was just Swift Eagle blocking the light. "Hi," said the troll, "sorry, didn't mean to interrupt."

"Pull up a chair," Keef offered. "And hey, thanks again

for dragging your people to our crew meet last week. It was nice to have a cheering section."

She grinned around her tusks. "Your team comes to our games—it's only fair that we return the favor. Now, speaking of teams," she said, looking at me, "I heard a rumor that *someone* might have been medically cleared."

"I'm still being monitored over the summer," I replied, "but if nothing changes, I'll be cleared in the fall."

"So...you'll be trying out for melee, *yes*?"

"If the invitation's still there."

Swift Eagle chuckled deep in her throat. "I do watch the news, you know."

To my chagrin, word of my cousins' kidnapping and the impending immigration of the *wealthy* stragglers from the southern kingdom had made it to the press in Beukal. "Oh?"

"Yeah. And I've got a cousin at Laws. He went on that retrieval mission with Special Forces a few weeks ago, and he came back telling me this *wild* story about a baby aeromancer." Leaning closer, she rumbled, "If you can run, you're in."

She left us to eat, heading off to join a chunk of the melee team at their crowded table, and Sage murmured, "We can still have lunch together next year, right?"

"Absolutely," I said, and squeezed her arm. "Missed you, friend. Missed you both," I said, nodding to Keef.

"Likewise," said Keef. "Honestly, I didn't think you were coming back."

"I'm taking it a day at a time," I told her. "Oh, and I'm getting ready to build a house! It'll be in Cirinti—"

"Where?" she asked, brow wrinkling.

"Middle of nowhere. It's gorgeous, and you two have to come see the place. But I'm meeting with an architect on Friday, which is *crazy*, and with any luck, construction will start before the summer break."

Sage and Keef shared a look, then turned to me. "I'm hearing 'sleepover,'" said Keef.

"Oh, *definitely*. And you'll have to meet my New York kin," I told them. "There are a few in the Hall close to our age, and if I know Diriem, he's convincing the board to stick them in here with us. Not in the same tutorials," I amended. "They've had way better educations than we did in East Branch. But they'll need language potions and everything over the summer, and since they're still underage—"

A lunch tray landed beside me, and I whipped around to see Eddic sliding into the empty chair. "Hi, Maebe," he said, flashing his amazing smile. His pale blue eyes crinkled, tiny rings of captured summer sky in which I'd once have gladly lost myself.

"Eddic," I said noncommittally.

"What do you want?" Sage demanded.

He ignored her to focus on me. "Glad you're back. I was beginning to worry."

"About what?"

"About whether I'd see you again." He leaned closer and casually brushed a stray lock of chestnut hair from his face. "You and I need to become better acquainted."

Two months prior, I'd have been a puddle on the floor beneath the table by then, but the newest iteration of myself—the quasi-competent version of me, the woman who could endure hellish pain and practically fly—was made of stronger stuff. "Why?"

"*Why?*" he echoed, and softly laughed, offering me a glimpse of sharp, perfectly white teeth. "Because you're interesting, Maebe. You've got...*potential*. An uncut diamond, if you will. I can help you," he said, and reached out to brush my cheek with two fingers.

I drew back. "Don't touch me."

"Don't be like that," he murmured, fixing me with his beautiful stare.

"You publicly humiliated me. Why would I want anything to do with you?" I snapped.

"Oh, now, that was just a little fun. You can take a

joke, can't you?" he replied, almost pouting.

"It's not a good joke if not everyone's laughing," said Keef.

Eddic waved her away. "I think we got off to a poor start, Maebe. Let me take you to dinner. We'll get to know each other, and if you stick with me, by this time next year, we'll run this school."

"I don't think so," I said.

He *tsk*ed. "Come on, Maebe, let me show you how to reach your potential. You don't even know what I could do for you." Without warning, Eddic's arm landed around my stiff shoulders, and he started to squeeze…

…and as my power flared, he flew halfway across the dining hall, arcing headfirst, and quickly skidded to a stop when his shoulders hit the floor.

"I said not to touch me!" I yelled at him as he groaned and the rest of the lunchtime chatter came to a halt. Abandoning my tray, I marched closer, fighting the urge to call upon a tiny tornado.

Eddic managed to prop himself on one elbow and blinked blearily up at me, his braid cockeyed and shirt hiked up from the landing. "Maebe—"

"I don't need you," I interrupted. "I don't *want* you. You and Ainnet can enjoy each other's delightful company for the rest of time, for all I care. But leave me alone."

As I turned to go, he called, "You don't know what you're saying."

"Oh, I do," I retorted, looking over my shoulder. "And frankly, it wouldn't be in my best interest to associate with someone like you."

I'd almost made it back to my table when Eddic yelled, "You're a fool, Maebe!"

The wind ached to burst free, but I held it in and stared at him as he struggled to his feet. "*I'm* the reason your frostbitten ass isn't still stuck in a cage, Eddic. And by the way, it's 'Lady ti'Ammaas' to you."

He reddened to the tips of his ears as the snickering

started around him, then slunk out of the dining hall with his shredded dignity.

Sighing, I plopped back into my chair, pushed his tray aside, and picked up my neglected sandwich. "Was that too bitchy?"

Sage smirked as the voices rose around us again. "Nah."

Glancing at the table where some of my cousins were eating, I caught Heidi's eye and smiled when she flashed me a thumbs-up.

Good enough.

"So," said Keef, leaning closer as I scarfed down my interrupted meal, "let's talk about this house of yours. Want help picking colors?"

EPILOGUE

"He's stirring," Jane murmured.

"Right on schedule." I looked up from my computer and glanced at Connor, who still seemed deeply asleep beneath the blankets of the guest bed in which we'd tucked him nearly two days prior. Shara had yet to be off by more than a few hours as to waking time after her potion—and she'd gone through all of my cousins by then, even the little boys—but still, Jane was loath to leave Connor while he slept it off, and I didn't mind keeping her company while she maintained her vigil. The two of us had set up our computers on the table near his bed, me for my homework and Jane for the DOI assignments she wouldn't let me see, but though I tried to be attentive to my studies, I was distracted—a pity, as my cousins and I had needed to miss plenty of school that summer while Farral, Reranel, and the rest of the kidnappers had gone before tribunals. I slept better knowing they'd be incarcerated for years to come, but my remedial math had suffered for my absences.

Connor was the last of us to go through the process, having waited until all the tribunals were finished. He'd met with Shara alone the previous Wednesday, and once she deemed him healthy enough to endure the potion, he'd returned on Thursday morning to let her do her worst while Jane waited to drive him out to Diriem's. I'd offered to let him sleep it off at my house, but I couldn't blame them for going to Viratta instead; my place had a roof and walls but was as yet not in any state for company, while

Diriem had both a staff and the world's most comfortable beds. He hadn't objected when I'd come over after school that day, and I'd used the adjoining guest room for a few hours' sleep before returning to North Lake in the morning, partly for my lessons but mostly to assure the others that Connor had made it through intact.

I'd watched by many of their bedsides as my cousins recovered from Shara's potion, and so I had an idea of how the process went: the occasional bouts of rapid breathing, the inevitable groaning on the first day, and then the gradual physical changes before the subject woke. All of my cifyent-afflicted kin had opted to have their ears fixed, while a few had gone with more generally elven features. I'd been curious to see what Connor would choose, but to my surprise, I'd seen no change in him as he slept.

Finally, with a low moan, Connor opened his eyes and managed to fix them on Jane. "Hey, Firebug," he croaked. "How're you doing?"

"Better now," she replied, squeezing his hand. "How're *you*?"

"Oh, you know. Got anything to drink?"

I tossed her a bottle of water from the windowsill, and she helped him sit up to guzzle it down. Thus satiated, Connor stumbled to the bathroom, and Jane smiled tightly at me as we awaited his return.

After a few minutes, he emerged again, face damp and eyes slightly brighter. "Sorry. Had to handle the mouth funk," he said, taking a seat at the foot of his bed. "That stuff has an *aftertaste*."

"But it works," I said.

"So y'all keep telling me."

As he rubbed his shoulders, I cleared my throat. "So…you didn't want to get your ears fixed?"

"Nah. I like them like this," he replied, tucking his hair behind the artificially rounded tops. "Shara said it'd have been more complicated to alter them, anyway, since I had so much cut off. You know what a pain it was for her to remove Eleanor's prosthetic and regrow a real one." Turning to Jane, he said, "Hope you don't mind."

"Not at all." She sat beside him and took over, massaging the back of his neck, and he grunted appreciatively. "How does it feel, then?"

"Uh…little achy, definitely hungry."

"Sorry, that wasn't clear. How does *immortality* feel?"

"Don't know. You'll have to ask Maebe about that."

Jane paused, and Connor raised his head, faintly smiling. "What do you mean?" she asked.

"Well, I liked the idea of faster healing, but I didn't want immortality, so Shara thinks she worked it out so that I'll be around for about three hundred years. My aging will slow, but it won't stop like it will for Maebe."

She dropped her hand and stared at him. "Con…*why?*"

"Because I don't want to go on without you," he murmured.

"But…but you…"

As Jane sputtered, Connor gnawed his lip, then muttered, "Screw it. Stay right there, Janie," he said, and stood from the bed. "Where's my bag?"

I pointed it out by the cold fireplace, and Connor crouched to root through it. Finding what he was after, he returned to the bed, held Jane's gaze for a moment, then took a knee.

She gasped and covered her mouth.

"Didn't think I'd be doing this in my pajamas, but you're still gorgeous, so that's one of us," said Connor as Jane's eyes welled. "I love you, Jane Fortune, and you're the only future I want. I might have worked up something a little more profound if I'd had my coffee first, but…sorry," he said, and chuckled as he shrugged. "Will you marry me anyway?"

By then, the tears were running down her face, but she managed to choke out an emphatic yes before he rose and kissed her.

I waited until they'd come up for air and Connor had

opened the ring box and slid a modest diamond onto Jane's finger before congratulating them and heading for the door. "I'll just give you some privacy," I said. "Go tell Ranarma you'll be in the mood for lunch, anyway—"

A knock at the door interrupted me, and Diriem peeked inside without waiting for an answer. "Excellent," he said, quickly assessing the scene. "You've proposed, then, Connor?"

Jane held up her hand and waggled her finger in response.

He nodded. "Glad that's settled. Now, Connor, I promised Kabno I'd relay her invitation to DOL once more, and I can tell you that she *very* much wants to have you aboard—"

"You're incorrigible, you know that?" Connor interrupted.

"I'm looking down the line. You can't stay in Whitford forever, boy."

"I've still got time," he protested.

"And you're the last member of Hall ti'Catama," Diriem countered. "It's time for you to take your place."

Connor rolled his eyes but sighed. "Tell Kabno I'll talk to her, but I'm not ready to turn in my badge just yet."

"Come on," I said, nudging Diriem back into the hall as I left the room. "They need some space."

Diriem grunted and headed toward the staircase, and I walked with him. Once we were out of earshot, he muttered, "That cousin of yours needs to hurry up and tender his resignation."

"What's the rush?"

"He'll be the first of you on the Forum, and it'd be nice if he had a better grasp of politics here before he took office. I can work with him, but I'd prefer to do so in person."

I frowned, surprised. "You're telling me the future? *Why?*"

"Because this is virtually set, and on occasion, I don't

mind being a little forthcoming. And don't be offended," he added.

"Why would I be offended?"

"That ti'Catama is going before ti'Ammaas?" He looked at me, saw my bemusement, and laughed to himself. "Refreshing to meet people who don't give a damn about Hall politics. Anyway, you'll have your turn soon enough. It's just that he's almost of age, and you still have a few years to go." Diriem paused, then said, "And while I'm sharing this with you, this is not a matter that Connor needs to know about yet, understood?"

I grinned. "Got it. He's going to have to deal with a wedding first."

"Well, at least money shouldn't be a problem."

"He hasn't touched his half million yet, has he?"

Diriem smiled knowingly before we began our descent. "That's nothing. Hall ti'Catama is about to become *very* wealthy, thanks to the Aniap fortune. I suppose a modest prenuptial agreement is in order, but between us, I don't think it will be invoked."

I recalled what Connor had told me about Jane's eight-figure bank account and nodded. "Neither of them needs to work, right?"

"No, and neither will you, once the rest of the New York funds arrive. You can be a lady of leisure if you like. Wouldn't be the first head of a Hall to eschew a day job."

I snorted in reply. "That's not me."

"I know. What *do* you suppose you want to do?" he asked.

Mulling over the question until I reached the foyer, I said, "I don't know. Any thoughts?"

"Nothing specific—not that you need to know yet, anyway—but let's say you've turned a few heads. Should you choose to work once you're of age, you'll have options."

"Uh-huh," I said, following him toward the kitchen. "And in the meantime?"

"Study," he replied immediately. "Get that education

you've wanted. Find yourself. And since you'll be playing melee soon," he added, "you might want to invest in healing potions. Keep a stock on hand—you'll need them."

"I'm making the team, then?"

Diriem gave me a look of deep incredulity, then shook his head and walked on.

Things weren't perfect, I thought, hopping onto a barstool to watch Ranarma put the finishing touches on lunch. *Life* wasn't perfect, and the road ahead was still very much a foggy mess.

But there *was* a road. There was a way for us—a path that the Maebe of a year prior could never have imagined.

I gestured open the refrigerator and let the wind carry a can of seltzer to my seat, and Ranarma grinned as the drink flew by. "Your control's improving, Maebe."

"Still have a ways to go," I replied, popping the tab.

"Eh, you'll get there," he said, then muttered the fridge door closed where I hadn't quite managed the seal. "Watch and see, youngling. Watch and see."

ACKNOWLEDGEMENTS

Hello again! Thank you for coming along with me for Maebe's story. I hope to see you in the future for the next Pactlands trilogy, Broken Pact.

As always, I thank the Novel Chicks for their friendship and their feedback over the years. Adam Domby continues to find time to edit my books, and I'm grateful for his suggestions and feedback.

And yes, here's to you, Mom and Dad.

ABOUT THE AUTHOR

When not writing fiction, Ash Fitzsimmons is an appellate attorney and an unrepentant car singer.

Find her online:
www.ashfitzsimmons.com

Printed in Dunstable, United Kingdom